As a teenager, Ralf aspired to work on animated Disney movies (that was before they made them with a computer) and create the next Batman. Instead, he got into studying economics, aiming to solve the world hunger problem. He ended up as a corporate storyteller for a global IT firm, dealing with the benefits of information technology, ubiquitous access and artificial intelligence can bring to people in his day job and contemplating about the risks that come with it in his spare time.

The Big One is Ralf's debut in commercial fiction.

For Felix, Alex, Max, Lukas, Johanna and Jan.

For Debbie, Jack, Meg, Corey, Johanna and Iris

Ralf T. Gruenendahl

THE BIG ONE

AUSTIN MACAULEY PUBLISHERS™

LONDON * CAMBRIDGE * NEW YORK * SHARJAH

A CIP catalogue record for this title is available from the British Library.

ISBN 9781035826971 (Paperback)
ISBN 9781035826988 (Hardback)
ISBN 9781035826995 (ePub e-book)

www.austinmacauley.com

First Published 2024
Austin Macauley Publishers Ltd®
1 Canada Square
Canary Wharf
London
E14 5AA

A big thank you goes out to Wolfie Christl and the team of Cracked Labs, Max Schrems and his team at NOYB, the people at institutions such as Citizen Lab, ACLU, the Electronic Frontier Foundation (EFF), the pioneers of the Chaos Computer Club (CCC) and others for their in-depth investigations and relentless fight for transparency on personal data.

A very special thank you goes to my dear friend, Sandra, who was the first to introduce me to the Silicon Valley (and to Cinnabon at Valley Fair, unfortunately, hooking me on to it for the rest of my life).

Preface

This book is a bit premature. We initially wanted it to be published right on the day when the big data dump is actually announced. To explain why it was inevitable. What it means. To help you prepare. Adjust. And, of course, to sell the first four re-prints right off the bat.

So, we prepared everything, cleaned it up, polished it, loaded it onto trucks and eBook servers and waited for the announcement to come out.

It didn't.

At some point we figured, what the heck? With the big moment happening any day now, since the book is sitting there ready to roll, we may as well start selling a few copies already. So that you, as an early reader, get a bit of lead time to prepare. Maybe even change a few things to make your own exposure less severe.

Even if that means not selling reprints one to four within just a few days. Undoubtedly, it will pick up quickly once the announcement breaks and the party starts.

Day of the Big One, Monday

Those special days changing the fate of nations forever usually start just like any other ordinary day. It is much later that people recognise spilled morning coffee, burned toast or open shoe laces on the way to work as early warning signs of events to come.

When people woke up on Black Monday, it was just one more hangover morning after another roaring party weekend in that era of optimism.

Folks in Pearl Harbour were just minding their own business and expected the rest of the world to do the same.

The citizens of Dallas were preparing for a youth- and hopeful president to tell them what they can do for their country on a glorious morning.

Different then in movies, in real life, it hardly ever rains on days like that. The weather app promises ten hours of sunshine from coast to coast for today.

Early morning traffic jams in Silicon Valley are perhaps a little more aggressive than usual. Yet, with life moving pretty fast, how can people be expected to handle doom on a day like this?

Folks hustling in the streets of New York are perhaps a bit ruder than they usually are, anyway. New Yorkers have seen it all, so how could this day trip them up?

What goes down, though, on the very top of one of the latest and tallest additions to the city's skyline, even the most hard-boiled New Yorkers have not seen yet. Should they look up for once, while rushing through their lives or having a break and a bagel at one of a thousand food trucks across the city, they might spot a teenager on a tiny platform in thirteen hundred feet, unshielded from the chilly breeze blowing around the top edge of the skyscraper, leaning way out over the end of the grate, no railing holding her back from a fall, musing at tourists on the observation deck ten stories below her feeling brave for posing on a glass floor.

From her crow's nest, the city looks full of ants swarming about, trying to hide from the big drop coming up soon. Tenth Street is pulling on her like a rubber band. She feels dizzy. Succumbing to the magnetic attraction of the abyss seems just as beguiling as when she made out with her boyfriend's best buddy on a binge – despite the consequences.

The next moment, she feels like she can fly. She could dive south, past the sky deck, straight into the minuscule looking fifteen-story honeycomb maze of staircases they call the Vessel. From up here, it seems funny to her they closed the Vessel because quite a few folks jumped to death off of that tiny structure.

She could glide east, all the way into the glass-roofed atrium at Penn Station two blocks away.

She takes a few selfies, first towards Brooklyn, against the bright sun high over Empire State right at the centre of the midtown skyline; then up Hudson River bank toward One World Trade Center, towering over downtown in the distance.

One of the visitors on the sky deck shrieks terrified, as she spots the extreme selfie. The sudden scream in her back startles the danger seeker, who almost loses her secure footing. She turns to the excited crowd gathering at the back end of the protruding triangle to get the best view of what might be going down high above their heads.

"Come back here right now!" a security guard shouts from the end of the stairs leading up to the Apex. "How the fuck did you get up here?"

Sky girl gives the guard the finger, picks up a cardboard sign and presents it to the audience below. The crowd starts clapping and hooting with delight.

"Get the fuck back down!" the security guard yells, hesitant to move any closer. Quite a few helicopters from various broadcasters buzz the tower like bees.

"Really?" she shouts, smirking, against the noise of the choppers while peering down on parading ants on 10th.

Sky girl turns her attention to the TV cameras. "If they dump, we will jump!" she chants five times, poking her fist out.

She leans out backwards even further, extends the selfie stick to the max to capture the cheering audience on the observation deck and the distant downtown skyline in one shot, sticks out her tongue and flashes the sign saying,

#StopTheDrop.

***

Eight days earlier…

Big One Minus 8, Sunday

Siliconettes

"The world as we know it may come to an end on a Monday! Monday next week, to be exact.

"Why, you ask? Listen to this:

"'TO THE PEOPLE OF THE WORLD:
IN EXACTLY EIGHT DAYS WE WILL EXPOSE ALL DATA EVER COLLECTED ON ANY OF YOU.'

"Today, exactly at noon US Eastern time, this brief yet momentous message was delivered simultaneously to major news media around the globe. This is CNN Breaking News, Sunday edition, bringing you the latest updates on this troubling story.

"The message was sent to the head offices of hundreds of media corporations on all five continents, totally old-school via fax. The statement is signed with 'by order of The Horrible Siliconettes'. Neither government officials nor representatives of major corporations CNN approached were available for immediate comment.

"For an initial assessment, I am connected to our tech stock correspondent, Jim Wheeler, over in New York. Jim, what do you make of this? Must this be taken seriously? Or is it just a premature hoax for April Fool's Day?"

"You would expect this to be a hoax, wouldn't you, Tom? Something like this seems impossible. Yet, the fact that authorities and corporate America decline to comment shows me they take this very seriously."

"Tell us, Jim, why could the content of this announcement be a major concern for the markets, in your view? What could this mean to corporations?"

"Exclusive knowledge of their customers is a critical element of the business models of major tech companies, particularly the likes of Amazon, Google or Meta. The dominant position of these firms in their respective markets is very much driven by the fact these corporations simply have much more data on

consumers than others. Far more data over a longer period than any of their competitors. Their market dominance relies very much on the fact this information is only available to them and no one else. The statement says a lot of such data, in fact all of it, will be made available to everybody. A massive exposure and the political fallout resulting from it could have a substantial impact on the business models of these corporations."

"The message reached us, and it seems everyone else, news media around the entire globe, at the exact same time, noon, US Eastern; just a few hours ago. Stock markets are closed on a Sunday. Do you have any indications yet, Jim, what we will have to expect when markets open up tomorrow?"

"Some major tech stocks trade lower off market already, Tom. I would expect a fair bit of uncertainty on Wall Street tomorrow morning. We will see what transpires when Tokyo opens up this evening at seven o'clock eastern time, which is already Monday over there. Tokyo does not have pre-market trading, so we will have to wait for markets to come online."

"Even though it's Sunday, you managed to speak to traders and analysts already off the records, didn't you, Jim? What was your perception? Is the primary concern about the purport of the announcement, the consequences of that? Or is the lack of guidance from officials the biggest concern at this stage?"

"Well, Tom, I guess it is both. I hope we will get official statements later today, before Tokyo wakes up, or at least before opening bell in London and New York tomorrow."

"Did you get any intelligence on the peculiar name of the signatories? 'The Horrible Siliconettes'? Do we know anything about this group? It doesn't sound like a terribly serious name. Could this indicate it is just a hoax, after all?"

"The signatories' name, you said it, Tom, is a little peculiar. None of us here at the CNN newsroom could make any sense of it. Only when I talked to a senior trader for a Swiss bank, he said it reminded him of the name of a musical band at the CERN research institute in Switzerland, which existed there many years ago. CERN is where the concepts of the internet and the World Wide Web were conceived in the late eighties. They had a ladies-only show band of staff calling themselves Les Horribles Cernettes on stage. He told me the ensemble existed for quite a long time, in changing line-ups, yet ultimately dissolved over ten years ago."

"What makes you think this could be more than a coincidental resemblance?"

"The snapshot of these ladies on stage, which you see here, was the first picture ever posted on a website in the internet's history. The internet's first social media content, if you will. Your guess is as good as mine, what this should tell us. Other than this resemblance, we could not find any traces of such an organisation or grouping ever appearing on anyone's radar until today."

"Thanks, Jim, for this first assessment. You heard it here first, on CNN Breaking News. Next up is the weather on this beautiful Sunday."

***

Pied Piper

The type of patrons and the background playlist change for a third time since he had set up shop for the day in this popular downtown Palo Alto café. First, nineties hits set the pace for the kids' Sunday-sports chauffeur fleet, hurrying in for a soy latte between drop off and pick up to show off their tiger-mum must-haves; next, contemporary Spotify best-ofs catered to the brand-conscious shopping crowd flocking in to take stock of their purchases; just now, fashion-agnostic college students are treated with chill out epics for late breakfast.

Surrounded by furnishings Jony Ives might have imagined in a collab with Charles Eames, the more serene soundtrack should help him focus on a paper he kept procrastinating on for weeks already; he is a well-versed procrastinator; not the lazy kind, rather a believer that ingenuity has a lot to gain from the artful patience to let your subconscious do its job and give birth to great ideas when they are ready.

For the last two hours, he had allowed himself to be distracted by conjecturing on the lives' stories of the people coming and going. Watching people is his Candy Crush. He enjoys being alone, and for him, being alone works best among people.

"Ahoy Andy!" a familiar voice interrupts, what could otherwise have been the rise of a decent thought. "Didn't expect to meet you here?"

"Mic? What's up?" He gives his old friend a lasting hug. "You told me this was the best café in town, remember?"

"Best latte, I said. Did I caution you about the tacky music, though?" Mic's wide smile is barely visible underneath his decidedly non-hipster, fuzzy, orthodox-style beard. Just without the side curls and the orthodoxy. The sole thing Micah is fundamentalist about is good code.

"Have you settled in yet?" he asks.

"Making initial progress to pick up the ways of the natives."

"I see you've put on quite an effort to fit in," Mic smirks at his friend's Pied Piper tee.

"Come join me. I wasn't getting anywhere, anyway."

"Sorry, can't. Pizza session with my squad; important show-and-tell with senior management coming up."

"So sad to see you allowing the evil forces to exploit your genius so shamelessly."

"So sad to see you hang on to those conspiracy theories so despairingly," Mic prods his friend.

"While you touch on it, any idea why I got a tail since this morning?"

"A tail?" Mic asks.

"There is a Nissan parked outside with two cliché John le Carré characters in it. Have been tracking me all day; sat in the car kerbside for hours. Every once in a while, one of them drops in for two lattes to go; eyeballs me; makes daft efforts to be inconspicuous in his suit and tie in a hipster joint. Is that the customary welcome package for Big Tech critics here in the Valley?"

"Can't be us," Mic grins. "We'd send drones, not Nissans. Self-driving Nissans, minimum." Mic scans the lurkers through the café's large shop window. "Seriously, any idea who that could be?"

"Nope. Guess I'll just ask the Monks on my way out what they're up to."

"There is my squad." Mic hails his teammates over. "Let me introduce you real quick. Especially to the most stunning gazelle eyes ever!" He winks.

"Leeza, meet Andy!"

"Folks call me Flake these days," he says, nudging his friend. *Mic is right about the intense, bent, brown eyes smiling at him,* Flake thinks, *which are really quite big for an Asian girl.*

"My bad." Mic senses some up-thumbing in the way the two goggle at each other. "I have known Andy...Flake...since pre-school. Wanna tell Leeza why they call you Flake?"

"When I got into Harvard, in the first week it started to snow. I had never seen snow before in my life. Where Mic and I come from, winter is the wet season; so, I got all excited. The natives felt that was cute, so they called me Snowflake. Flake was what stuck."

15

"In his blogs about social media and artificial intelligence, he still calls himself Awkward Andy, though. Pretty provocative stuff. I'll send you a link."

"So, you're awkward?" Leeza's intrigued almond eyes break the teasing gaze merely for slow motion blinks.

"Very much so!" Flake beams back from behind cheeky curls bopping across his face.

"I'd be curious about your awkward views on these Siliconettes, then?"

"Don't get him started," Mic intervenes. "We'll miss our deadline for sure. Flake will be here all summer. He's research assistant to Professor Timberley, who lectures over at Stanford this quarter."

Leeza peeks over to Mic in surprise, then hastily turns her focus back to Flake. "You work for Benjamin Timberley?"

"You know the man?" Mic asks.

"That's like working for Noam Chomsky in my line of studies."

"Must be a linguist or an anarchist then," Flake teases. "Which one is it?"

"Don't listen to him!" Mic says. "Told you my friend likes provocations. He is a very nice guy, really. A data-dystopian, I'm afraid. But a nice one."

"Who is that Chomsky character?" their colleague chips in from the side.

"Apologies. How rude of me," Mic says. "Andy, meet Tim."

The sporty looking squad leader sizes up his counterpart with an inquisitive stare and a mean handshake that feels more like a test of strength.

"Chomsky is the most quoted intellectual alive today," Leeza says, regretting her sniffy tone right away. "The man is an icon ever since he debunked the propaganda perpetuating the Vietnam war."

"Should ask my grandparents about him then," Tim says, a little moody, like any alpha aspirant when the proper pecking order needs yet to be established.

"Even Zack de la Rocha did an interview with Chomsky," Mic says to Tim. "It's on YouTube. Cool to watch how this radical Rage tough guy turns geeky class president in the face of his idol."

"And what is this professor's claim for fame again?" Tim asks.

"Professor Timberley is one of the geniuses behind the World Wide Web," Leeza tries hard to come off less lecturing this time. "He worked at CERN back in the days."

"His inaugural is tomorrow," Flake beams at her. "Wanna come? I'm sure I can sneak you in."

"I'd love to. But we have to work on our pitch. Sorry!"

"Mic told me that's why you put on the weekend shift. I leave you to it then. Happy to talk about the Siliconettes some other time, since we were so rudely cut off by my old buddy."

Mic gestures a Vulcan farewell, smirking as he watches Leeza hover backwards until ultimately, she has to turn her eyes off of Flake in order not to trip.

The group huddles in a secluded corner for privacy, since many of the other patrons could be competition, presumably working for some startups, fantasising about being the next unicorn.

"What do you guys make of these Siliconettes?" Leeza asks while they struggle to fit the still life of all their tech gear on the tiny table.

"Not sure," Mic says. "They call them terrorists. Extortionists, maybe?"

"Have demanded no ransom yet, as far as I know."

"If it's not for cash, what are they trying to achieve?" Tim asks. "What is this good for?"

"Maybe a political statement?" Leeza says.

"Saying what, exactly?" Tim asks.

"Don't know. Just sounds to me like that kind of message."

"Which kind of radicals would they be, then?" Mic asks. "Leftist or fascists?"

"Good question," Leeza says. "Could be either, I guess."

"Do you think it's even realistic?" Mic asks. "What they say they will do? Publishing all data ever collected on any of us. Is it even possible?"

"You're the overpaid big data guy, aren't you?" Tim pinches Mic on the chest. "You tell us."

"At first, I thought it wasn't. The more I think about it…"

"Honestly?" Mic's dark tone alarms Leeza. "That's scary. I'd die should all my stuff be out there for anyone to rummage through. Let's hope it's just a joke."

"I will not lose any sleep over it," Tim says.

"You hardly sleep anyway," Leeza replies. "You work day and night."

"Good lead," Tim sits up straight, "should get on with our prep work. Need to nail it when we present to Zach. If he doesn't sign off budgets for an additional squad in the next PI, we won't fly in time."

"Waitress!" The Abercrombie poster boy and his entourage of Kim and Khloé lookalike contestants had been obnoxious ever since they had occupied a table right in the centre of the café. As much as Flake wanted to get some traction on his paper, the entertainment provided by pharma-fostered muscle-Ken and his surgeon-spawn mega-Barbies kept him distracted. Mostly because the six-foot-four showboat ballooning out of his tight moose polo perfectly exemplifies the type of big shot ego Flake found to be quite prevalent in Silicon Valley during his people studies since he arrived. It's the in-your-face ego of a guy who tries to hide that he, in fact, has a small dick. It contrasts quite strongly with the dominant type he knows from the east coast, who shows the smug confidence of a guy with a big member joyfully expecting to flaunt it soon enough. Metaphorically, of course, not actually suggesting scientific correlations of egos and excitable extremities.

The attention craving threesome makes quite a fuss even though they talk little, being busy taking selfies or typing relentlessly into their smartphones. Ken pops a muscle on every pic and the Barbies make sure their silky long hair neatly frames their perfect angles at all times.

"With the advances of the modern age in the last century," Flake dictates to himself, "people in many traditional cultures around the world held on to the superstition that taking a picture with a photographic device steals the object's soul. Generation Z, on the contrary, seems afraid to lose their souls, should not their every move get captured in a snapshot."

"Waitress!" Ken Z hails impatiently.

"Coming right up!" heralds the servant over her shoulder, skilfully balancing a tray of highballs a few tables away.

"What can I get you?" she asks impeccably politely as she approaches the heckler's table.

"You must be new here. What is your name again?" The pesterer gawks at the girl's bust. "Paula," he reads from her tag. "Look, Paula," he leans back, still talking to her cleavage, "the caramel double shot macchiato you served us was awful. Got here cold; I'm sure the milk wasn't skimmed and the cream was watery. Didn't want to mention it; be nice to the new girl. Give you a chance, right?" Sleazy Ken looks up at her face, finally, tilts his head a little and puts on a devious smile.

Since he obviously demands a sign of subservience, Paula delivers as ruefully a look as she can.

"You know who I am, don't you?" the heckler asks.

"Of course. You are the captain of the college soccer team."

"Ha!" shrieks the Kim clone to his left. "He's the quarterback, bitch!"

"It's football," the quarterback grumbles, undecided whether to shoot Kim first or Paula. "Soccer is for pansies. I am the quarterback of the Stanford Cardinals. This means I'm king around here. Not used to be kept waiting!"

"I'm so sorry. Won't happen again."

"Sure as hell it won't. Your boss is a big fan of mine. He'll send you packing on the snap of my fingers."

The king enjoys what he considers shock on Paula's face. Actually, it is the struggle between the angel of retreat and the devil of retaliation.

"I said, I'm sorry. Need the job to pay for tuition," wails the angel.

"Where do you study?"

"Foothills."

"Falls under my jurisdiction."

The big man sneers like a devious teenager, then pushes his coffee cup across the tiny table all the way to the edge. Paula subdues a reflex to grab it while the chuckling mental minor gradually tilts the royal china. She jumps back as the cup bursts into pieces.

"Oops. Now you dropped it," the quarterback says, prompting dirty laughs from the beach babes.

Paula's cheeks turn red, her fists white; she inhales deeply and counts to ten. From the look on her face, Flake expects her to go for a head-on attack. The dish boy beats him to action as he comes running with the cleaning gear.

"Let me get that," the youngster says.

"Paula doesn't need any help," the king rules.

The kid hands her the equipment and whispers: "the dude will get you fired. Trust me. You wouldn't be the first."

Paula vigorously wipes up the pieces, hustling cranky queens to pull up their stilettos high in the air to come clear of the mulish mob. The king seems to enjoy the nauseated faces of his entourage just as much as the fighting spirit of his victim.

He says: "I will show you I am a gracious king. Will let you off the hook this time. Better make sure I don't regret it."

"Thank you!" Paula sighs in a brilliantly soft voice, the quarterback takes for the desired servility and Flake understands as irony. He decides to stage a rescue mission for decency. With Mic's help.

When Flake arrives at his buddy's table, Leeza is about to set off. "What a major jerk!" she clamours. "Someone should bust his balls!"

19

Tim feels an impulse to act on Leeza's call, sizing up the odds against this pretty big bully. His temper got him into quite a lot of trouble in his youth, not always with pleasant results.

"If you ask me, Aberclumsy & Bitch are begging to get punk'd," Flake grins like Ashton Kutcher prepping a celebrity prank. Tim drops back to his seat.

"Remember what we talked about the other day?" Flake asks Mic. "Let's try that on Biff."

"You want to hack the king's messenger?"

"Exactly!" Flake glows with anticipation.

"How will you get to his phone for the sync request? He never puts it away for even a blink."

Flake turns to the counter. "Paula, could you come over here for a second, please?"

"You really shouldn't…" Leeza says.

"The guy shouldn't treat people like this," Flake replies. "That's a white hack. Social self-defence."

Leeza surrenders her case to his Ashton-smile.

"What else do you like?" the waitress asks.

"How about a frozen retaliation latte," he says, "with skimmed wickedness and some gluten-free contentment on top? We would like to play a little prank on your new friend."

"I'm in!" Paula trills.

"Nice. You need to take a picture of the QR code on Mic's screen, please. Can you get the king to scan that pic, you reckon?"

"There is one thing that will get his attention off the small screen: him on the big screen. I'll put up a rerun of a Cardinals game on the TV."

When the game gets on, the king can't help but brag to his entourage about his heroic contributions to the win. He can also not resist a massive VIP discount offer eloquently presented by a vengeful waitress.

"Tada! We're in!" Flake jubilates. "I'll only have a quick peek. Just enough to dig up something entertaining."

"I don't feel good about this," Leeza offers some half-hearted resistance. "We are infringing on his privacy."

"Just a second ago, you wanted to infringe on the man's private parts," Flake quips, while he swipes through thumbnails. "I agree, though, we'll educate him on privacy issues the hard way."

While Leeza ponders whether she would actually have wanted to castrate the man or make do with verbally chastening him, it doesn't take Flake long to find what he needs.

"Copied the evidence, ready to go. Mic, if you wouldn't mind recording this, please. Got a feeling my subscribers may like it."

"Your buddy is on YouTube?" Leeza asks, while Flake gets on his way.

"With quite a lot of subs, actually," Mic replies. "On one of his channels, he does pranks. Just watch. We got front row."

"Hi ladies," Flake greets at his charming best. The messy shags, a mischievous glow in his green eyes and a boyish smile seem to be very much to the liking of the salacious sisters, switching on their rutting gaze for the phat prey. *No wonder,* Flake thinks, *Cupid paired these door knobs with an alpha impersonator like the king.* It's clearly a match.

"I don't know too much about it," he says, "but my British professor told me, soccer is a gentlemen's sport, sadly mostly played by barbarians. While the rugby, they call it the rugby in England, you know," Flake tries his best British accent on this, "the rugby, the true man-to-man struggle, is a barbarian sport played by gentlemen. Contrary to common belief, I guess that means football stems from soccer."

The quarterback and his pack evidently struggle to process the input.

"Or rugby has come a long way of decay," Flake continues, "to end up with barbarians hiding in heavily armoured mock superhero costumes behind hot cheerleaders, like you, ladies, to compensate for the lack of action in a game you guys call football."

"Boy, your pal knows how to make friends," Leeza whispers to Mic, who struggles to keep the camera steady while chuckling away.

The luscious ladies smile somewhat proudly as they got nothing other than the hot chicks comment. The king got the gist of the offence, yet was dumbfounded by the audacity of the uninvited gadfly.

He concludes he couldn't be bothered and remains in the role of gracious king. "I don't know who you think you are, dickhead, but should you not vanish within five seconds, I will give you some action you will remember forever through the scars on your face."

"Was talking to the ladies," Flake replies, "but since you mention dicks, look at what I found." He turns back to the queens. "Are you aware your king here sends both of you pictures of his royal sceptre?" Flake swipes through a series of R-rated close-ups. "You recognise this dick?"

"By the way," he turns to the baffled athlete, "you actually named your phone 'GOAT'? Seriously?"

On the final pic of the pecker parade, the chicks look up from the screen, eyeball each other and shoot spaying gazes at the king.

"Let me get this straight," Flake says. "You, Candy, are the king's official queen? Not for very long yet, it seems. Likely not for very much longer, if I look at the history…"

Candy gazes at the king for help.

"You, Sheela, are Candy's BFF? It is good to be in an open relationship with your BFF, I suppose."

"Hey dumbass!" The king swipes at the vexatious insect. "You are one word away from a flogging. Don't mess with me, you hear? Lose it, Loser."

"If I went out to the parking lot now," Flake grins, "would I find a silly muscle car with GOAT on the licence plate? Please tell me you are not that shitty?"

The big man puffs himself up; the buttons of his shirt are about to pop. Just like his top.

"Oh, ladies," the gadfly buzzes on, "you may want to know the king here sent the same dick pics, plus a few more, to a guy called Marvin."

The king, just about to get up and take action, freezes in shock.

"They met on Grindr," Flake tells the girls. "Not seeking genuine commitment, I suppose. Probably just a phase? Side effect of the roids, maybe?"

Flake turns to an ailing king, who looks like he is about to puke. "Marvin? Really?" he asks. "What kind of guy is called Marvin?"

He raises a brow and turns back to the slush puppies. "Doesn't sound like classy competition for top catches like yourselves, ladies."

A brief, flattered smile on the deceived's faces gets immediately usurped by an emasculating stare fired at the cheater.

"I'd love to show you what he looks like," Flake continues, "but Marvin's profile pic is Wolverine…" He taunts the big man with a Logan look. The king growls.

Flake zooms in on one pic and mumbles, more to himself, "That thing looks a bit like a tiny baseball bat…wrong sport, I guess…well…not my problem…more Marvin's…"; as if reality snaps him back, Flake smiles at the girls to add, "…and yours, of course!"

The quarterback grunts ever louder, slowly pumping himself up from his seat.

"Would love to continue chatting, ladies," Flake takes a bow, "late for a date, though…sorry. See ya!" He rushes towards the exit.

The charging bull almost knocks Sheela out as he rambles past her to go after the fleeing prankster. Flake may have gotten the horns before he even made it to the door, if it wasn't for the brave dish boy casually crossing the path of the one-man stampede, toppling the big bull with his mobbing gear, giving Flake a little edge.

While Flake slaloms his way through a crowd of strolling couples and rushed shoppers cramming the arcade in front of the café, his furious follower catches up quickly, tackling aside everyone not stepping out of his path fast enough.

Just as the athlete goes for the neck, his bait crouches abruptly. The king's massive body crashes into the obstacle full force, topples and bowls down half a dozen bystanders. Flake shakes off the pain from the impact and rushes back in the opposite direction while the angry crowd flocks in on the quarterback.

The huddle doesn't hold the athlete down for long, though. He muscles his way out of the commotion and picks up the chase.

Flake zigzags between cars like a hare on the run with a coyote on its tail. Each time the hare gains a slight advantage by turning a surprise corner, causing the coyote to bounce into passing shoppers, the hunter quickly catches up again. After they circled the entire parking lot for about four rounds, it becomes apparent it is only a matter of time before the predator catches his bait. And that time measures in seconds.

Running out of steam and ideas, Flake seeks shelter behind an excessively pimped Dodge pickup. While he gasps for air, he realises the licence plate. It says 'G.O.A.T.'

"Come on, Kong. Let's call it a truce," Flake pants.

"I will kill you. Right here, right now," puffs back the royal primate. The two combatants circle the muscle car a few times, first clockwise, then counterclockwise.

"This is pointless, man! You shouldn't keep the girls waiting for so long. Can we not talk this over some other time?"

"You won't talk ever again with your teeth smashed in your brain."

The two men circle the obstacle some more.

"You notice I am trying really hard here, don't you?" Flake wheezes. "Didn't even make another joke about your licence plate. It's a peace offer. Come on, take it."

The quarterback climbs onto the loading bed of the Dodge. Flake hides behind the driver's cabin, hoping that the battery of oversized searchlights mounted to the roof would slow Kong down.

Unswervingly, though, the athlete leaps over the hurdle and glides down the windshield. Flake squeezes between two sedans and takes advantage of an elderly lady pushing by a shopping cart; even the roid-raged rowdy doesn't want to run over the shaky senior and waits out her passing. Flake uses his lead to hop onto the bumper of a Silverado just exiting the car park, turning into the main street. He waves back at his haunter, grinning broadly as his ride picks up speed.

The quarterback puffs and blows, unloading his frustration in a forceful round-kick, hitting a sign post. As the athlete adjusts his stance to go for a second shot, the cheerfully waving Flake notices his ride slowing down and his hunter's face lighting up. He anxiously turns to see the traffic light ahead change to red.

The panicking prankster jumps off the bumper to dash on. One block down, his hunter is only a few yards behind; Flake turns the corner into a small street with plenty of outside seating on the broad walkway. He pulls every empty chair he passes in his pursuer's path, yet barely slows down an athlete trained to hurdle race through fierce defence lines. He is glad not to lose any more ground.

Flake has not been in this part of town before. He doesn't know where best to head, where best to hide. Maybe, he wonders while dashing down the boulevard, he should have thought this through beforehand? Did he actually believe he could outrun a professional athlete?

The distressingly steady wheezing and snorting in his back, purring like the knock of an old diesel engine coming ever closer, sends power surges through his spine and vivid fantasies of suffering through his brain. Luckily, his panic-stricken subconscious redirects all energy to running the engine, throttling the supply to his synapses, so he can't keep pondering the many ways this could end badly.

The racers head towards El Camino, when another traffic light ups the ante, turning a green light on the interstate. Eight lanes of accelerating traffic block the hare's path. In his despair, he sees no other option than to try his luck and head straight onto the road, greeted by a cacophony of honking horns. The hounded quarry makes it to lane three before ever faster speed merchants stop his momentum.

Flake heads along the median for about a block, trailed by his hunter on the sideline. The smug grimace on the predator shows he expects the prey to die in open traffic or come rushing right back into his fangs. At the first slightly wider gap in traffic, Flake jumps on the fast lane.

A virtuous circle of squeaking brakes barely avoided crashes, more alarmed drivers and more squeaking brakes opens up a high-risk path for the desperate fugitive. Flake slides over hoods, bumps into doors and bounces off of trunks to twist and turn his way across. Yet, slowing traffic also allows his hunter to get back in pursuit. Multiple near-death experiences later, both men reach the other side of the interstate with no decisive edge for either runner.

The chase continues along El Camino for a few blocks and into the next avenue, with the quarterback continually gaining on his prey.

The weakening evader turns into Whole Foods, desperate to find a hiding spot in the endless aisles to catch his breath. No matter how many turns he takes between the shelves, though, no matter how often he topples a pallet of boxes, pushes carts in the hunter's path or throws cans at the predator, he never manages to get enough of a lead. As the quarterback nimbly dodges every attempt to get him off balance, second by second Flake's spirit tanks and his panic level rises.

As he passes the fresh fruits section for the third time, Flake snatches his last hope: a canary melon. He knows it's a longshot when he tosses the egg-shaped object over his head. Yet, the athlete's reflexes, drummed in by ruthless coaches in endless repetitions, kick in unfailingly; he launches off for the amber pigskin and secures it in a flying catch before he hits down hard on the concrete floor.

Flake rushes into the next aisle, glimpsing back at the receiver, who rolls off, seemingly unfazed by the painful drop, and picks up pace way quicker than expected. The athlete reaches back wide and releases the ball in full swing for a well-targeted shot. Over his shoulder, Flake watches the approach of the smoothly rotating missile; right before impact, he turns another corner and just avoids crashing into a three-hundred-pound defensive tackle crossing his path. The projectile dives straight onto the defender's wobbling paunch. The giant winces from the hard hit, yet his paddling hands manage to get hold of the mysterious missile.

The fridge peers back and forth between the fruit in his paw and the originator of the assault, the upcoming quarterback. He smashes the melon and assumes position. The king goes for a trick move to evade the roadblock ahead, yet his feet lose grip on the pulp covered concrete; he stumbles, just evades the massive arms reaching for him and topples over, right behind enemy lines. Frantically picking himself up before the one-man defence can nail him; the quarterback spots his prey already on his way out.

Back on the street, Flake has a decent lead but still not a lot of options. He had hoped carrying a two-hundred-pound frame would take a toll on the punk'd powerhouse at some point; that his rage would cool off. Neither is evidently the case. Only Flake's outrageous adrenalin levels kept the muscled menace at bay for now. Yet, not even the turbocharger fuel will keep his dead engine running for much longer.

At the next junction, the hunting party's path crosses El Camino again, this time with traffic waiting; the pointlessness of this chase overwhelms Flake as he recognises they will reach back at the café soon. Maybe, his sapped body lures his crestfallen mind, maybe he should give up on this hopeless escape. Maybe he has worn out the aggressor just enough to limit the harm he can do?

Just as he is about to give into the inevitable, he spots a Waymo a few yards ahead, releasing one last energy reserve. Flake bounces between the parked cars onto the driveway, going for the unmanned vehicle. His tail follows barely ten yards behind. He ignores the upcoming traffic, runs up to the front of the driverless car and rams his shoulder against the door as hard as he can. The Waymo's algorithmic brain does the math as predicted and initiates an emergency stop; within just a few feet, the Waymo comes to a halt; too fast for the charging bull in pursuit to swerve the obstacle. His massive body thuds full force into the trunk, knocking his wind out; dizzy, he goes down.

Flake stops to catch his breath and consider his options to make the best use of his opponent's momentary weakness: continue the flight or take the chance to pick a fight. The decision is made for him when the tumbling terminator rises from behind the hazard flashing vehicle. Flake rolls his eyes in despair and bolts as the deranged T-model stumbles back in pursuit, much less dynamic yet just as determined.

What was a speed race just a few miles ago, now looks like a zombie run. Flake's circuits are about to force-hibernate should the Zombinator not even catch up on him before that. Like a battery warning, the thought pops into his mind, whether he carries his organ donor card.

In this moment of complete despair, he recognises the Nissan with the suit squad still parked kerbside one block down. Flake barely makes it to the compact before collapsing. He frantically fiddles with the back door handle while, from the corner of his eye, he watches the undead mad muscle monster hobble on resolutely. The door won't give. "Come on guys, open up," he cajoles, while the guy in the driver's seat lowers his window and grins provokingly. He can almost smell the approaching AberZombie's foul odour already. In the very last second, the jolly driver releases the door and Flake breaks down onto the back seat; yet, with a strong finish, the T-model gets to grab a piece of his pants and tries to pull him back out. Flake kicks about wildly, desperate, panicking, breaks loose, slams the door and secures the lock.

"Get outta there, pussy," shouts a fretting and fuming attacker, slamming the roof of the sedan.

"Hold it, buddy," orders the suit in the driver's seat.

"Get outta that tin can, you bastard!" the zombie king yells at Flake.

"I don't know what your problem is," the suit rebuffs, "but you better calm down, buddy."

"Not talking to you!" the king hisses, huffing and puffing. "Stay outta this, asshole!"

"Watch your language, son, and beat it before I lose my temper." The agent flashes a badge.

"Okay, Okay, I'm cool." The wheezing king takes a few steps back. He points at Flake, his hand forming a pistol. "I will get you for this."

"Beat it, buddy!" the agent repeats.

The king fires a series of shots from both hands and then heads off, seriously struggling to strut royal ruler style.

Flake puffs and pants on the back seat.

"Get out of the car now!" the agent commands.

As his heart rate gradually comes down to non-hazardous levels, Flake's system suspends survival mode and restarts non-vital functions. "You can drop me off near Hoover Tower. Thank you!" he says.

"I said: get out!"

"You are not my Uber?"

"Quite funny," the agent on the passenger seat says in an emotionless tone and hands Flake a business card. "Come to our offices tomorrow, Mr Thomas. My colleagues have a few questions."

"NSA? Wow! Boy, am I glad you guys could squeeze this rescue mission into your busy schedule."

"Couldn't wait for you to wake from a coma. Should you not stop by tomorrow, we will bring you in. Goodbye Mr Thomas."

Half way to the bus station, Flake's phone buzzes.

"Ahoy. Are you alright?"

"Check. Was close, though."

"That was wicked. Should have seen the birds when he steamed out. Just sent you the video."

"Holy cow! Vexed vixens bitching big time."

"Click on the next one to see the king come back."

Flake almost trips over his own feet laughing when he realises Pink's Revenge playing in the background, snuck into the café's playlist either by the mischievous goddess of shopping mall music, an ingenious iTunes algorithm or a sassy waitress.

"What's in those gigantic bowls?" he asks.

"Paula said the ladies asked for the largest drinks on the menu."

"I have an idea where this is going. Here comes the king."

"He was bragging so hard about how he crushed you to pieces. Nobody messes with the king and shit. I got really worried about you."

"That's sweet."

"Leeza was worried, too!"

"Oh, was she?"

"Watch out for attentive dish boy, Luis, to sneak in from the side."

"Whoops. The ladies puke the drinks right in the king's face. What a splash. The look on the tool's face is dope."

"Grand exit of the cheerleading squad. In comes Luis with his handy Swiffer."

"The boy's got guts, tripping the big guy again."

"You can see in the king's face that he considers squashing tiny Luis for it."

"Grand appearance, Leeza!"

"She was so cool. Pretentiously offered the poser help to get up. How embarrassing. Brilliant move. Not so grand exit: moulted cardinal."

"That worked out fine, don't you think? Thanks for your superb camera work, buddy."

"You will not upload this, though, will you? He is a doofus, alright, but to expose him like that…?"

"Don't worry. Might have gotten carried away a bit. Pricks like this press a lot of my buttons. Text me the contacts of lovely Leeza, will you?"

"Check!"

Big One Minus 7, Monday

Taking Stock

"This is CNN Breaking News. Yesterday, we reported on an announcement issued by a group calling itself The Horrible Siliconettes, in which this group threatens to disclose all information ever collected on you, on me, on anyone out there."

"After failing to comment on this yesterday, a spokesperson of the Attorney General said this morning, I quote, 'The United States government considers this a terrorist threat. The AG's office, collectively with the FBI and the National Security Agency, will conduct a full investigation into this matter'. However, the spokesperson continued, so far, no security breach had been accounted for at any government facility, be it on national, state or local level. 'We therefore,' the spokesperson concluded, 'regard this threat not to have material impact on national security for now'."

"Also, this morning, the Federal Trade Commission published a statement to say that it had issued an inquiry to all corporations registered at US stock markets to learn whether any breach of corporate security at any of these companies has been encountered. The statement continued that, so far, no such incidents have been accounted for and that, for the time being, the Commission does not expect any material impact on the markets."

"I am connected to our correspondent, Jennifer Conolly, in Washington. Jennifer: what does DC make of the note?"

"Good morning, Tom. In all our conversations, government officials were quick to point out there is no indication that any infringement of security of any considerable severity has transpired. However, they also reiterated the note constitutes an act of terrorism and will face drastic repercussions. You don't joke around on matters of national security, one official told us."

"Jennifer, tell me, what is the consensus on what this means, making all that information available? What data are we talking about?"

"Good question, Tom. It could be any data; limited to personal data, though, it seems, because the note refers to data gathered on individuals. There are tens

of thousands of databases in government and corporate organisations. If we look at government databases, we talk about tax data, medical records or criminal records, just to name a few."

"Should they disclose these documents, all my neighbours could see how much tax I pay? Which income I declare?"

"Yes, Tom. Exactly. Our viewers might be interested to hear that in countries like Sweden, for example, all tax records of all citizens are public. Everybody can look at what the prime minister declares, your neighbour, your boss. Your news anchor."

"Interesting point, Jennifer. If we consider criminal records, we already publish at least some of that information today as well. Sex crimes, for example; child molesters and the like; we make certain, once these people get released and live in a particular neighbourhood...we make certain that their neighbours know about the criminal biography of this individual; know that a, let's say at least former, to be careful here, a former child molester moved in next door. We believe communities are entitled to know about the potential threat. I suppose most people would agree, should you commit a felony, especially such a severe offence, this information belongs in the public domain."

"What I would say, Tom, is that it is tough to strike the right balance between the person's legitimate claim to be given a second chance to lead a decent life and the aim of protecting our communities from potentially dangerous individuals."

"Absolutely, Jennifer. What about medical files? Let's look at that."

"As you know, Tom, health care is a split system. On the one hand, you have the state-run providers for Medicaid and Medicare. Organised on the state level. And then you have private health insurance. To get a complete picture, all those databases, and we are talking hundreds, would need to be hacked. Plus, hospitals, doctors...thousands of sources."

"I am also connected to our Wall Street correspondent, Jim Wheeler. Jim: What's the latest from corporate America? Are executives worried? What information do these companies have on all of us?"

"Good morning, Tom. Let's start with the dominant ones: of course, Meta has an abundance of information on its users. Your entire timeline and posts on Facebook, your chats and posts on Instagram, communication on WhatsApp and the Facebook messenger, plus many additional services that may hold specific user information."

"That sounds like a severe issue, in case all that information should get published, Jim? Even though a lot of it is visible already, to your friends, at least."

"Meta issued a statement today to say its information was absolutely safe, no security incidents were recently detected and that security and protection of user privacy was their most pressing concern."

"Good to know, Jim. What about the others?"

"Another big player is Google, or better, the holding company, Alphabet. First off, all your inquiries with their search engine. They also run YouTube. Then there is Google Maps. All of your searches with any of these platforms might be stored. And, of course, everything they do with Android, which runs on billions of phones globally. Such an operating system also collects information on the device's user."

"That is also a lot of data. Do people have good reason to be worried?"

"Not all the information these big players gather is in one central data centre. Any hacker who wanted to get to all this information would have to hack a multitude of data centres."

"That is an excellent point, Jim. Should someone be able to hack into all these companies, who each spend a fortune on security controls, where would they store all that data? If these corporations cannot fit it all in one place? Am I being naïve here, Jim?"

"No, you're not, Tom. This is a very valid question. I have asked the experts at Amazon, who run some of the largest data centres in the world, and who we have not yet spoken about, but also have a lot of user related information. I have asked those guys what it would mean. Here is what they told me: The world's largest data centres are the size of the Pentagon, which, as many of our viewers are certainly aware, is one of the largest structures in the world. We are talking millions of square feet of space, Tom. Over 100 football fields. You would need a few dozen facilities the size of the Pentagon to store all the data we are looking at here. Seems unlikely that such structures could have been built without anyone noticing, don't you think, Tom? Each of these Pentagon-sized data centres would consume the energy of a complete city, by the way."

"Fair point, Jim. Speaking of Amazon, who have even built data centres for the Pentagon, to refer to your analogy, they also run the world's largest cloud service, AWS, and provide data centre services for thousands of businesses all over the world. Netflix is on AWS, Twitch is, Uber, Airbnb, also Meta uses their

services, LinkedIn, over 100 of the Fortune 500 list use AWS. Could we gain access to all their data just by hacking into their cloud?"

"Good idea, Tom. But I am afraid not. AWS run many data centres for all their clients. There is not just one entrance door to boot in and there you go."

"Let's talk about the markets next, Jim. When the announcement broke yesterday, there was a lot of irritation at first. How did that evolve?"

"We initially saw a lot of stocks tank, especially tech stocks. With a lot of bad momentum from Tokyo, Frankfurt and London, some stocks were down ten percent and more. After statements from government officials and large corporates, though, this has stabilised. We saw markets recover quickly, almost having claimed back all the early losses already, Tom."

"Would it be fair to say, Jennifer, Jim, if we look at the full picture, that, after some initial irritation, in the political sphere as well as in the corporate arena yesterday's announcement by this group, The Horrible Siliconettes, does not cause too many people a headache at this stage? Would you agree with that summary? Jim?"

"For the markets, that certainly seems to be the case, Tom. I am sure corporate America will have another thorough look at their security systems, but in general, the consensus seems to be that security is on an excellent level, with corporations investing billions of dollars to protect their data. It seems implausible that such an incident, a huge incident, as presented in the statement, is in any way perceivable."

"Jennifer?"

"Political America seems to agree to that judgment as well, Jim. Yet, security agencies are not at all amused that the announcement, and if only for a short period, has caused such instability in the markets and widespread irritation among the public. They will not rest until whoever is behind this group, The Horrible Siliconettes, is detained and prosecuted with all the rigour of the law. Should this be just a hoax, whoever did this got themselves into very serious trouble."

***

Valley Fair

An unassuming, delicate gentleman in his sixties, dressed in a three-piece tweed suit and bow tie, observes the chattering crowd from his position in front of an oversized chalk board.

The ascending rows of the auditorium are occupied by way more people than there are seats; the expectant assembly of students and faculty members even fill the stairs of the vast amphitheatre left and right.

At the full hour, the professor ostentatiously clears his throat and takes a few steps towards the settling crowd.

"Ladies and gentlemen. Thank you all for coming here this morning. My name is Benjamin Timberley. It is my honour to be invited for a visiting quarter with you here at Stanford University." The only sounds in the vast space are creaking wood and the slight coughs inevitably imposing themselves on people who try really hard not to crush a moment of silence.

"I regularly teach at MIT over on the east coast," the professor says in a comforting, low voice. "That means I am not smitten with whatever it is you have here in your water or in the air, or maybe it is the sunshine…whatever it is, that makes you dwellers of the Valley so amazingly optimistic and future happy. When you live in the Boston area, where it basically rains every other day, where it gets freezing cold in the winter with snow storms and all that…well, more often than not, you seem to come out with a different perspective."

As he wanders up and down, the professor makes eye contact with students across the auditorium as if he is talking to each of them individually.

"To make it even worse, I originate from England. Some of you may appreciate what this means concerning the weather. I ask you to remember that and be patient with me, okay?" An amused chatter waves through the crowd.

"Today, I want to tell you a little story…" the professor continues, scanning the attentive congregation, "…from the perfectly normal life of…" he narrows his focus, "…this young lady over here," and eventually points at a pretty redhead in the second row with a personable appeal.

"May I ask for your name, my dearest?"

"Ashley," utters a slightly intimidated student, who quickly assures herself of the support from the girl to her left.

"Ashley. Thank you. May I inquire: Is this young lady next to you a friend of yours?"

"Kyla? Yes, sure."

34

"If you don't mind, the two of you will be the lead characters in this story. Are you okay with that, ladies?" The girls nod warily.

"Imagine you, Ashley, and your friend, Kyla, go to the Valley Fair mall on a Saturday. That is the biggest mall around here, isn't it?" The girls nod in unison, much more at ease already.

"You don't really look for anything specific. Just browse the shops, try things on, have fun."

Since the young women seem comfortable with where this is going for now, the professor takes a few steps back and addresses the whole auditorium again. "Let's say you start at Macy's in the formal dress section. You and Kyla try on a few rather expensive gowns. You take snapshots of each other in the dresses, looking flirty, sexy, maybe even doing duck faces for fun."

The professor zooms in on the friends again. "Is this a realistic story so far?" The girls seem comfortable with their place in the spotlight and rush to take a selfie with the professor in the back, who puts on a sunny smile for the occasion.

"Every once in a while, a guy carrying a sandwich board passes by. You know, one of these things with a board in front and one in the back, covered with marketing messages. You know what I'm talking about, don't you?" The professor scans the nodding auditorium.

"On those boards, sandwich guy presents you snapshots of more evening dresses. Some with a big discount tag. Some from Macy's and some from different stores in Valley Fair. And some indeed from other malls. Many of the costumes look familiar; you realise you have tried on similar ones, a few weeks ago on your last spending spree."

The professor looks into quite a few irritated faces. His leading ladies, though, seem at ease.

"Next you go to Nordstrom. Again, the same sandwich guy passes by. This time he shows you shoes, which would look great with an outfit you bought a few weeks back.

"You find sandwich guy odd, yet forget about him right away. After a while, though, you notice sandwich guy follows you all the time. Even when he doesn't carry his poster boards. He constantly roams somewhere in the back, between the shelves and cloth stands, and seems to take a lot of notes. If he doesn't take notes, he is on the phone. Girls like you are, of course, used to getting a lot of attention. So, you make no big fuss about it."

Ashley and Kyla smile at each other complacently.

35

"What you then realise is that the guy, when he is not following you, seems to know already where you are headed next. Because when you get there, he already fiddles with the merchandise; rearranges the items. You wonder what he does that for? Well, he checks his notes to see which items you might have already considered in the past. Which ones you went for. And he is on the phone again. Takes a lot of calls. You want to know why?"

The professor takes the girl's puzzled faces as a yes to his rhetorical question. "He constantly phones all outlets in Valley Fair to inform them what you show an interest in. Asks them what they can tell him about your preferences. He also calls up a few stores around town. And Nordstrom's store manager, of course. From all of them, he gathers additional information on you; and he collects bids; bids for what to show to you on his billboards and how to arrange the merchandise. The highest bidder gets presented on the billboard or gets the best placement in the racks and on the hangers."

The leading ladies lean back and fold their arms in perfect sync.

"He also overwrites the price tags. He changes them according to what his notes say you might be prepared to pay."

The professor approaches the bench. "Can I have a look at your phone, please, Ashley?" The young woman proudly waves her handheld.

"Well, I'm not too much of an expert in these things, but I would believe sandwich guy is marking the prices up for you," the professor says, "because his notes tell him you are susceptible to luxury branding and prestige items." The crowd giggles and the friends beam at each other, seemingly not offended at all by that profiling.

"By now, you are truly annoyed by this guy popping up everywhere you go. You appreciate, though, that the guy had a few helpful pointers on his boards. You even buy a pair of sneakers at Bloomingdales that you had learned about on his boards when he crossed your path at Nordstrom."

The professor waits out a brief chatter wave.

"Wherever you go that day in Valley Fair, the guy follows you around. And takes notes. A lot of notes. And phone calls. Even as you go for a salad at the food court, after a strenuous shopping experience, your guardian lurks around and notes down your diet." Meanwhile, Ashley and Kyla are obviously miffed by their tail.

"You are too exhausted to go confront the guy. You could tell the security guard at the entrance of the food court about the harassment. She is a woman;

she would surely understand and tell the guy to beat it. Then again, you ladies have had many undergraduate geeks stalk you around campus over the years, so you kind of gotten used to ignoring it. It was a great day, regardless; both of you secured fantastic additions to your wardrobe, many at bargain prices. Happy and content, you head home."

Ashley and Kyla giggle like teenagers, delighted with the results of their mall marathon; they even look like they already consider for which occasion to wear the new gear first.

"On the drive home, the two of you recap the highlight items in your shopping bags and the cutest boys you encountered during the day. Maybe there was one of these model types at Hollister that caught your attention? Maybe you reminisce about some Jake Gyllenhaal type guy that was dragged through Victoria's Secret by this humdrum chick that cannot possibly be his girlfriend and who he would surely dump right away once he sees you in this new gown you just snatched out of Ann Tailors?" The girls seem to have a vivid picture of such encounters in mind, chuckle and exchange conspiratorial looks.

"Whatever it is you are talking about, you don't want the fun to be spoiled when you catch your shadow just two cars behind at every traffic light. He follows you all the way home; when you pull up the driveway at your house, he also pulls over, lines up his car at the opposite kerb and waits." The ladies seem ready to go confront the guy, finally.

"Since you now have realised your tail, you recognise he follows you everywhere. Every day, wherever you go, every shop, every café, every bar or restaurant, the guy shows up and takes notes. It bugs you gravely. You decide to get to the bottom of this."

The girls nod in anxious expectation.

"On your next visit to Valley Fair, you don't have to wait too long for your shadow to appear. Between the shirt racks of Banana Republic, the two of you corner him. The guy says: '*Hi, Ashley. Hi Kyla*'."

"'*Why do you know our names?*' you inquire.

"'*I have to know your names. How would I connect my notes to your metadata otherwise?*' he responds. You want to ask him what the heck metadata is? Yet even more urgently, you want to know why on earth he draws up all these notes after all?"

The determined expression on the girl's faces confirms the professor's analysis of priorities.

"He says his name is Alex. And that his job is to make sure you always find the best bargains. That is why he notes down what you show an interest in, and yes, he even times you when you look at a certain dress; he also notes which things you ignore; that you occasionally go back and look at items again; all of that.

"He takes notes on many other girls all around the country as well, he explains. In fact, all around the world. By comparing all these notes, he determines what fits best with what you already own; what others have purchased that like similar things then you; based on that, he comes up with recommendations.

"'*You like my suggestions, don't you?*' he asks. '*You picked up a bunch of them*' he hurriedly adds, as he sees you ponder."

The professor allows the thought to sink in.

"Alex seems offended by your hesitance; challenged even by the bothered looks on your faces. From behind a dress rack, he produces one of those pilot-trolley-cases business travellers jam the overhead compartments of local flights with. He pulls a file folder from that pilot-trolley-case. The binder contains a collection of captures of items you recently purchased he presents to you with a triumphant look on his face.

"'*You see?*' he radiates, '*I recommended these!*' Among the pictures that drop from the folder is a photograph of your cousin."

The professor steps forward to address his leading woman. "You have a cousin, Ashley, don't you? What's her name, please?"

"Vicky."

"You detect the photograph of Vicky in Alex's collection and you ask Alex why he has that capture on his files."

"'*You liked Vicky's dress when she posted this picture a few months ago from a party she attended. Wait,*' he says, '*I have the comment here somewhere*' and searches his trolley-case. '*Usually,*' he continues, '*we do not use likes that are over 6 months old in fashion items. But since you are more of the mainstream type…*'."

The professor pauses and studies Ashley's reaction.

"…he doesn't complete the sentence because he notices your sudden frustration."

Ashley is, in fact, taken aback by Alex's commentary.

"'*I am what?*' you ask," the professor translates Ashley's gaze.

"'*Well,*' winces Alex while he evades direct eye contact, '*our profiling shows you lean strongly towards adaptor, not so much first mover. Not even early adopter, mostly*'." Absolutely outraged, Ashley looks at Kyla, who subdues a smile.

"Your initial reaction is to set the record straight on this appalling assessment of your fashionista preferences, yet you have something more crucial to address.

"'*How did you get this picture and how did you get my comments?*' you query the guy."

Ashley's eyes give away her most pressing urge would be to argue on the fashionista scoring. The professor continues his train of thought, regardless.

"'*I have many pictures of all your friends,*' Alex replies. '*I follow all your acquaintances, too. Remember, you told us who your friends are?*'"

"'*I told you about my friends?*'" you ask.

"'*You allowed me to copy your full address book,*' Alex responds, '*and you told me who you like best. I note down everything they do as well, what they like, where they go. I collect everything that helps to serve you better*'."

Ashley and Kyla look as grossed out as Daddy's darlings on sleepover night, watching a creepy lurker playing with himself from the kitchen window.

"Ashley, do you recall giving Alex your address book?" the professor asks.

"No way!" Ashley barks.

"Want to know what Alex says?

"'*You didn't exactly hand it to me,*' he concedes. '*But you allowed me to copy it. So, I found it on your phone and I copied it. It's in the terms and conditions*'."

Ashley seems ready to jump up and stamp her foot like a fourteen-year-old who fights for more Wi-Fi time not to miss any Huda Kattan beauty tips.

"You ask Alex to stop stalking you. Alex says he can't do that. You tell him you don't want him to follow you and take notes of everything you do. That you don't like it. At all! Alex is quite upset you neglect the value of his service. He reminds you that you owe many of the coolest items in your closet, events you attended, books you read to his diligent collection and extensive comparison of notes. Then he produces a picture of you in a lovely flower print frock."

The professor raised his voice to show the shopping assistant's frustration: "'*Do you remember*' Alex inquires testily, '*how many times I had to show you this gown before you finally turned the corner and snatched it? At a bargain price I arranged for you? Do you remember?*'"

The professor looks at Ashley and Kyla as if he actually expects an answer on behalf of Alex.

"'*Today,*' Alex continues, '*it is one of your favourite pieces. I have plenty of pics of you wearing it. You should consider yourself extremely fortunate,*' your shadow gripes, '*that your forbearing servant Alex and Ann Taylor had never given up on you. Their flagship store bid at least in 20 auctions to present you the dress'.*" Ashley and Kyla mental-scan Ashley's closet for a flower print Ann Taylor dress.

"'*I don't even expect a big thank you. I just want to serve you humbly in the shadows'.*" The professor's impersonation of Alex now sounds a bit like an emotional RuPaul.

"'*What do you get out of it?*'" you confront your piqued servant.

"'*I'm happy when you are happy!*'" he boasts.

"'*No!*' you insist, Ashley, '*I mean, how much did you make on these 20 auctions?*'"

"Instead of answering the question, Alex acts up a bit. He neatly sorts his papers with a huffy look on his face and puts them back into his pilot trolley. When he is done, he asks you, in a grave voice, if you really want him to stand down his invaluable assistance for you."

Ashley's desperate eyes seek moral support from Kyla.

"When Alex understands he can't change your mind," the professor confirms a choice he knows very well Ashley is not yet ready to make, "he says: '*But you signed up for this service!*'"

"'*No, I didn't,*'" you insist, Ashley.

"'*Yes, you did,*' repeats an affronted Alex. '*When you entered the parking lot of our mall for the first time some years ago, you accepted the terms and conditions of this facility,*'."

"'*I signed nothing,*' you seek to correct, Ashley.

"'*You didn't have to,*' jubilates Alex. '*We have made it much more convenient for you. We didn't want to bother you with lots of fine print; keep you from enjoying yourselves. Our terms just state that by entering our facility, you approve. Isn't that great?*'" A determined look on Kyla's face encourages Ashley to stand her ground.

"'*Just by entering the mall?*' you ask, surprised."

"'*Yes,*' Alex says with disarming content, '*very convenient for our shoppers, isn't it?*'."

"'*Why do you follow me around everywhere I go? When did I approve of that?*' you inquire."

"'*Well,*' Alex says patiently, '*since we want to know as much as we can about you, we contracted with the maker of your car to tell us where you go with it; for how long? If you came out with a lot of bags? You undoubtedly must have noticed our sign on the inside of your trunk, right underneath the spare? This helps us immensely to come up with even better recommendations for you*'."

The professor beams at Ashley like Alex would, completely content with his achievements, while the leading lady looks devastated, like if the two hottest boys in high school had both asked her out for prom night, but her dad had grounded her.

"Since you do not seem appeased by this explanation," the professor picks up the storyline. "Alex elaborates: '*We have those agreements with many partners,*' he says. '*Many shops, bars, restaurants. Many businesses. They all report to us what you look at, what you buy and all that, whenever you pay them a visit. This way you let us know what you like automatically, and do not have to explain it to one of our shop clerks when you come here next. This is just so much more convenient, isn't it?*' Alex smiles content."

The swelling murmur in the audience conveys empathy and encouragement for a highly irate Ashley.

"'*When a shop clerk asks me how he can help, I don't have to tell him anything,*' you argue, Ashley. '*I can say, I'm fine, just browsing around*'."

"'*Well,*' Alex says, visibly shaken, '*you can, of course, not come to our mall again*'."

That suggestion seems to have come as a shock to Ashley, so the professor gives her a second to come to terms with it before he continues.

"'*Will you delete all your notes, then? Should I not come anymore?*' you ask, Ashley, because you feel a little sorry for the poor guy, whose best intentions you are inclined to concede.

"'*Oh no,*' says Alex. '*Don't worry. We will keep the notes. Other stores may use them to recommend items to you*'."

"'*Should I quit coming to your mall, will you stop following me around?*', you ask next, Ashley."

"'*You don't have to worry about that either,*' rejoices Alex. '*I will still support you wherever you go, and take notes of what you like, to make sure you get the best possible service in all the other shops*'."

Now Ashley looks more as if her boyfriend dumped her just before prom night. A fellow student a few seats down comes to her aid. "Is that even legal?" he asks. "That shops, or other places, tell anyone what I do when I visit them?"

"Well, that is a tricky question. I am not a lawyer, but, you see, in the past the US government held the position that your telephone data, as one example, the information who you called, and when and for how long and how often and all of that, that this information does not belong to you but to the phone company. Therefore, the phone company does not have to ask you for permission when they give this information away. In line with that position, one could argue, to note down what you look at in a shop, for how long, if you try things on, if you buy them, all of this the shop owner can do, or, for that matter, allow anybody else to do on his behalf."

"That is creepy," the student says.

The professor turns back to Ashley and Kyla. "Being stalked by such a creepy lurker in the Valley Fair mall, you would probably have called the cops at some point. You certainly have noticed by now that the story is more of a metaphor. This same thing is happening online. Yet online, you probably did not realise all of sandwich guy's activities yet. But he is there. Him and many colleagues of his. Always!"

A student in the first row looks up from his iPad and raises his hand. "You see, professor," he says, "I don't really mind. I have nothing to hide. Should anybody want to fill up valuable storage with details of my boring life...well, what the heck?"

The wave of laughs in the auditorium only partly stems from pity for the slowpoke, but just as much from relief that someone called out, it is all just half as bad.

"You have every right to feel that way," the professor replies. "My point is, it should be completely voluntary what you allow the Alex's of this world to know, track or store. Why is it, I ask, that I shall have to explain myself when I do not want certain information on me to be noted down, analysed, stored and shared with god knows whom? Why is it, I ask, that it is not Alex and his mates who have to explain to us what they do and why they do it? I argue that most, sometimes even all, of Alex's notes are not pertinent to the service I want to use."

The professor lets the murmur die down before he continues.

"Should they want to provide me with services that benefit from Alex taking more notes, I say, let them explain what I get out of it. Then, I can freely opt in. Or not, if I so choose. Wouldn't you agree that makes sense?"

Most heads in the rumbling auditorium seem to nod apprehensively.

"Is it not true, Professor," the student asks, "that all of Alex's notes, as you call them in your story, are needed to create innovation? The next generation of services?"

"This is, of course, what Alex and Alex's boss and the bosses of all the other Alex's out there will tell you. Alex will tell you there is an excellent reason he gathers all his notes and stores them forever in gigantic pilot trolley data centres. Even though he may not be able to explain to you just yet what he may need it all for in the future. How you will benefit tomorrow from allowing him to stalk you already today. He will call it innovation. Alex will say, we don't know what we don't know. Of course, that is correct. He will argue we need all his notes on all these individuals to play around, experiment, research, have all his great artificial intelligence do its magic on these notes. Eventually, they will come up with something great that you will, once they brought the light into this dark world, not want to live without ever again. Like the cave dwellers and the fire."

"What exactly is wrong with that, Professor?" another student asks.

Flake picks himself up from the stairs. "You mean, apart from the fact this rather generic reason serves as a justification for the broadest surveillance in the history of mankind?" he says. "Like the fact that the average app has about six trackers to follow you around. Trackers that send data about you home to their makers to do with it whatever they please. Sensitive data, like your location every minute of the day. Give it away to others at their discretion. When all you wanted to do was to play a game. Or use a weather app. Likely one of the worst spy apps on your phone. The average app shares everything they learn about you with ten different third parties. Just to be clear what it means when you give access to information on your phone: The average phone holds about thirty thousand pages of personal information on its owner. On you! Should you print this out, the pile would be over 7 feet tall! Your personal data!"

This time around, the chatter wave is more like a tsunami. Flake raises his voice to counter the buzz. "The average website shares your personal information with over one hundred third parties. All of which pass all that information, personal info like gender, preferences, all of that, on to another few dozen parties…your personal details spread through the internet exponentially. None of this may have anything to do with the service you thought you used."

"You are jumping ahead, Flake," the professor says. "Ladies and gentlemen, this outspoken fellow is my assistant, Flake Thomas. For those of you who will attend my seminar, you will get to see much more of him."

Flake walks up to the professor and faces the audience. Persistent pockets of murmur in the otherwise calming crowd tell him some folks have noticed his tee displaying the SKYNET logo and the caption '*If you are listening to this, you are the resistance*'.

"Apart from the fact," the professor continues, "that this data collection is rather all-encompassing, it has another downside. Which is the fact that Alex has set up his own sweatshops by now. Whenever his data shows that you and many other folks, he follows around on their shopping trips like a certain product particularly well, Alex has his own factories copy that product. Next thing he does is, he shows you and all the other potential buyers his own product with higher priority than the original. This way, he captures a significant share of every promising market. Sometimes he manages to take over the complete segment."

"If need be," Flake adds, "by selling his copy at bargain pricing until competition is dead."

"I only buy brands," the student in the first row says.

"Oh, don't be fooled," Flake replies. "Alex doesn't market his products as Alex Copycat Sweatshop. Or Rip-off Retail. He creates his own brands. He gets better at that all the time. Often enough you can't tell the difference, especially when looking for new and coming labels, not the old school classics, Levi, Ann Taylor, what have you."

"This is obviously not ideal to create innovation. Should you want useful innovation," the professor says, "should you want the best brains to come up with the best ideas on how to combine and use the data people volunteer for this research to provide them with life altering new things, some people argue, make the data available to the public. Put it open source. Do not let it sit in Alex's pilot trolley until Alex figures out what to do with it."

"Professor," another student asks, "are you suggesting these Horrible Siliconettes dudes do just that? Is that what they are all about?"

"Well, thank you for addressing the elephant in the room. Maybe that is why they do it? I don't know. As you are aware, they have not made themselves available to explain their motives so far. Yet, should this be what they seek to do, they approach it the wrong way. The data we put open source must be provided voluntarily by the individuals who this information is about. As I sought to spell out in my story, Ashley and Kyla and all of you have not given that consent freely yet. You were tricked, coerced, bribed, call it what you want."

"What do you mean by bribed or coerced?" a student from the very back of the room enquires.

"Let me give you an example." The professor approaches the benches. "Have you tried to use WhatsApp without granting it full access to all your contacts? Regardless of whether you intend to ever message most of the people listed in your address book? Ashley might advise you she has issues with Alex copying her full address book, I suppose. The conditions that apply if you do not approve are like your landlord saying: should you not allow us to put cameras in every room and record your life 24/7, you can only have a flat with a five-foot ceiling. Yes, you can live in it. It's a two bedroom with ample floor space, a state-of-the-art kitchen and two bathrooms. But you can merely move about with your back bend. Or on your knees. Very much less convenient than to agree to the cameras."

The reaction in the crowd shows it needs a less subtle approach. "Let me give you another, a little more drastic example," the professor therefore continues. "Do any of you know Monty Python?" Very few hands show up and only one guy looks like he's not confusing names.

"They were a British Comedy Group. For those of you who like British humour, I highly recommend watching some of their work. If not, in fact, all of their work. It's marvellous. Anyway, they have this clip where two mean looking fellows dressed all in white, looking like doctors, pay a surprise visit to a guy who signed an organ donor card. I'll spare you the hilarious details of the endeavour, which you should really go have a look at some time, but these shady characters tell the man they came to collect his liver, which he promised them by signing the donor card. The chap objects, of course. He reminds the gentlemen that the card says 'in the event of death'. The two intruders just smile at the man and proudly explain that nobody had ever survived their particular procedure of extracting a liver. The rest is a bloody mess."

"He definitely should have read the fine print," Flake says, trying on a John Cleese face. "The question is, which options do we have to stop the organ thieves? The abusive landlords? Does it need breaking up the monopolies to take away the leverage to bully us into anything they want? Is putting out everyone's data possibly a first step to make that happen?"

"I suggest we dive into that some more in our next session," the professor says into an upcoming murmur. "To prepare for that, I have a first assignment for all of you. The average person uses about 200 online services that require credentials. I ask you to prepare a list of all such services you use yourself and put against each of them the type of information these services collect on you. As far as you know, of course. We may fill in some interesting gaps in our next session."

"I would like to thank you again for coming here this morning." Into the tapping choir crescendo, the professor adds, "I would also like to extend a special thank you to Ashley and Kyla for volunteering to take us on their shopping trip. Enjoy your day, ladies and gentlemen."

Applause fades into a muddle of sounds and voices as people leave the auditorium. A couple of students grab a hold of Flake right away to quiz him on the way out about the upcoming seminar.

Two dark suits make their way against the tide towards the stage.

"Professor, would you have a minute?" The guy in the better fitted attire opens. "We would like to talk to you some more about these Horrible Siliconettes. Can you give us your take on that, please?"

"Sure, Gentlemen. I am flattered you made the long trip from Crypto City just to see me. You could have just tuned into NBC later today, though. I will be interviewed on this very topic."

"We are just field agents from the Frisco branch office, not from headquarters. My name is Willis. This is Special Agent Friends." He points at his grim looking partner.

While Special Agent Willis carries his tight fit couture like superhero armour, his partner conducts himself more like a farm boy dressed for Sunday service in an Agent Smith one-size-fits-none party costume.

"Oh, don't be too modest, gentlemen. I am fully aware of the relevance of the Valley branch of the NSA. I suppose you wouldn't be here; would you not expect me to understand this quite well? Would you?" The professor intently observes his counterparts processing the double-twisted question. "If you don't mind," he says, "please follow me to my office." He places a hand on Special Agent Willis' shoulder and guides his guests towards the lecture hall's back door exit.

"What do you think, Professor?" Special Agent Willis asks. "Which organisation or state is capable of such a hack?"

"Assuming this leak is indeed real, of course?" the professor asks back.

"Do you have doubts about this?"

"Well, if I'm not mistaken, the chiefs of your agency and the rest of the intelligence community have previously declared it isn't! Isn't that correct?"

"We cannot allow panic to cloud people's judgment. Wouldn't you agree?"

"Should something like this announced data leak actually take place, I think the public would have all the right to be extremely concerned."

"Let's assume it would be possible…"

"…and you can't stop it?"

"…and we can't stop it, yes!" Special Agent Willis grumbles. "Who would be capable of pulling this off? Who would have the resources?"

"Well, for all I know," the professor stops and turns to the agents, "this would be you!"

"Seriously, Professor! Who could administer such an attack on the American people?"

"The Siliconettes did not limit the threat to the United States, did they?"

"Professor!"

"Okay. Let's look at the sources of all the information these guys have pledged to publicise."

The group strolls along an endless hallway with vast windows to the right, overlooking the campus lawn, and a lineup of massive office doors to the left.

"Some people argue," the professor says, "you need to hack into quite a lot of different companies. A lot, though, gets sold back and forth between various aggregators anyhow. A few dominant data brokerage firms amass information from quite a lot of public institutions and merge it with information from banks, insurers, media, hundreds of sources. Most websites and apps sell data to those brokers via various channels. I would argue if you combine the data of such big brokerage firms with what Meta, Google and Amazon keep exclusively to themselves, you already get a very comprehensive picture. So, we need to ask who would have the means at their disposal to hack into these organisations and lift all that data."

"That is the relevant question, exactly!" Willis nods.

"Foreign states? Leaving aside your friends? You trust the Five Eyes, I suppose?" Timberley smiles at the agents conspiratorially. "The Germans wouldn't be up for the task…"

"Let's focus on the not so friendly parts of the world, shall we?" Willis says.

"Clearly Russia, KGB, FSB, GRU. Russian players contribute seventy percent of the hacked content on the darknet, mind you; not necessarily government agencies, mostly not; there is abundant experience and a vast pool of expert hackers in the former Soviet states. The country would also have the funds for bribery where needed to open doors. Plus, a scrupulous security apparatus that would come in handy should other means of persuasion be called for."

"What about China? Do they play in that league as well, in your view?"

"I would think so. North Korea and Iran may have the predisposition for this kind of doomsday attack. Likely the skills. But not the funds and the reach."

"Could North Korea play a role in a China scenario?"

"Certainly. Since we mentioned China, this raises another interesting point. When I look at the scope alluded to in the announcement, all information globally, you would likewise have to get the data from the Chinese Big Tech giants, Jack Ma's former empire, Tencent, Alibaba, WeChat, and from the Chinese surveillance community. Who would have the ability and determination to go head-to-head with China? That does not really make the Russia theory most likely."

"In your view, Russia would not pick this kind of fight against China?"

"That is how I see it. There is nothing in it for them at this point."

"Any other candidates?"

"While we are on the point of having the funds and a scrupulous security apparatus…the former head of the Saudi Arabia's intelligence agency, Turki bin Faisal Al Saud, has invested in one of the largest data brokerage firms called SafeGraph which collects personal information on individuals around the globe. As you know, Saudi intelligence doesn't even shy away from killing critical journalists on foreign territory. SafeGraph is even a supplier of location data on potential targets for the US military."

"Are you suggesting Saudi Arabia could have an interest in this kind of attack?" Special Agent Friends asks from the back.

The professor turns to the windows and gazes out on the campus lawn. "I didn't tell you anything you didn't know already, did I? Even have a lot more detail about." He turns back to the agents. "What did you come here for, gentlemen?"

"I am sure you have a guess, Professor?" Willis replies.

The professor strolls on, palms folded behind his back.

"When you pitched in Saudi," Special Agent Willis enquires, "you said SafeGraph supplies data to the US military. Why did you mention that?"

"Well, they are one example of the million ways the US intelligence community gathers data. I would argue a lot of the information in question already resides in the sphere of influence of that community. From domestic and foreign sources. Potentially including…"

"You don't seriously suggest," Friends interrupts, "that the US intelligence community would plan and execute such a strike, are you?"

"I certainly do not believe it is in the interest of the US government to risk the turbulence and anarchy most certainly arising from such an act."

"What are you saying?"

"What I suggest considering is whether, instead of breaking into hundreds of organisations, the likely target might be downstream. Where most of this data ends up, anyway. Get it from one place instead of many."

"You are suggesting these terrorists have hacked the NSA?" Special Agent Friends looks as if Timberley had suggested the LA Chargers could actually win the Super Bowl this season.

"Should that be where the data is?" The professor seeks to subdue a smile.

"Of course, it is not!" Agent Friends quickly rebuffs, evading his partner's apprehensive look.

The group arrives at the professor's office.

"You will not speak of this to the American people, will you, Professor Timberley?"

"This is not actually a question, is it, Special Agent Willis?"

"We need to maintain the trust of the American public in the US authorities at all costs, Professor. At all costs."

"You do not mind me mentioning the Russians and the Chinese, I assume?"

Willis' long, hard stare fades into an ominous smile. "Thank you very much for your time, Professor Timberley. Good luck with the show."

"We'll make sure to watch. We will contact you should we have more questions," his partner says in a somewhat intimidating way.

Half way down the hallway, Timberley still brooding in front of his office, Special Agent Willis turns around. "One more question, Professor. This assistant of yours back in your class…"

"Flake? Flake Thomas?"

"…do you think he is a radical?"

"He is an immensely talented individual. With the typical inclinations of his age to creed and conviction. But a radical? No. And certainly not a terrorist, should this be your question?"

"I didn't think so. Good bye, Professor."

***

The Revolution Will Not Be Televised

An uncordially-looking police detective shows Flake into a narrow, scarcely furnished room. A large flat screen in the back presents the NBC news show; two suited silhouettes obstruct the view.

One of the shadows turns around half way and points at a chair. A derogatory eyebrow twitch suggests he notices Flake's tee with a print of 70s songwriter Gill Scott-Heron and a caption of his song title *The Revolution Will Not Be Televised.*

Timberley: "…we have heard the US government accusing Iraq of building huge underground multistorey factories to produce weapons of mass destruction already at the times of Saddam Hussein. We suspect North Korea to have enormous subterranean facilities used by their military. North Korea is one of the most aggressive nations in state-run hacking. The country finances a considerable percentage of its national budget via online fraud, theft and blackmail."

"But let me come back to hiding data centre infrastructure: Anything built way out in the Russian tundra or the north of China might be particularly hard to uncover as well. Mind you, until recently we did not know about the vast camps China has set up to detain Uighurs. These are entire cities housing half a million prisoners that went unnoticed. Despite continuous global satellite scanning."

Interviewer: "One last question, Professor. Why do you think the group is doing this? Is it a terrorist act, as government officials called it? Extortion? Give us your view."

Timberley: "That is indeed hard to call, Jenna. There has been no claim for a ransom or any other demand issued with this announcement. That doesn't mean it will not follow later. I guess the key question is: what could be accomplished with it? And who would benefit from such a leak?"

The agents switch off the TV and turn their attention to Flake.

"That is precisely what we would like to examine with you, Mr Thomas. My name is Special Agent Willis, and this is Special Agent Friends."

Willis drops in the chair opposite Flake.

"Willis & Friends?" Flake repeats with a broad smile on his face, "glorious name for a folk group, should you ask me. Willis & Friends opening for Benny and the Jets. Special guests: The Horrible Siliconettes. One night only."

"Mr Thomas," Special Agent Friends attempts to control his tone, "do you agree with what your professor just said? You did not seem to agree with him in the auditorium earlier. Did you?"

"I knew, I'd seen your faces before," Flake says. "So, it wasn't in Get Smart?"

"You're not a big fan of Big Tech," Willis asks, "are you?"

"These companies are run by sociopaths," Flake replies, "complete narcissists. These people are evil. There is no doubt about that."

"Oh. Good." Willis takes a note on a scribbling block. "Cutting through the case, are we? I like that. Are you a communist?"

"It wasn't me stating that. Well, I just said it, but merely as a matter of quoting a much smarter person. That was Steve Bannon in an interview with CNN's Oliver Darcy. Is he a communist?"

Agent Friends, who still wandered up and down the space, leans in on Flake: "You are a Steve Bannon fan-boy? How much so?"

"Whatchumean?"

"How much of Steve Bannon's political agenda do you agree with?"

"Do I consider myself an Alt-right? A white supremacist? Not exactly. I'm not one of those QAnon weirdos either. Although, I must say, I'm very much against paedophilia."

The agents exchange looks and readjust their negotiation tactics, since their opponent obviously enjoyed his time with the Harvard College Debating Union.

"…but I like pizza," Flake adds, "just as a preorder, in case this takes longer…"

The agents settle on frozen faces and minimalism.

"Any of you gentlemen from Arizona?" Flake asks while holding firm to his opponents' stare. Both agents continue to peer at him motionlessly.

"Didn't think so. I am. As you are certainly aware. Near a little town called Snowflake. In Arizona, where it never snows…well, that might explain some of me…at least it explains my nickname." The agents don't even blink.

"Where was I?" Flake merrily sucks up his counterparts' grumpiness. "…Ah, yeah, speaking about white supremacy. Are you aware they founded Arizona after the defeat by the Unionists in the civil war? With the purpose of being the ultimate fortress for those Confederates determined to pursue the fight for survival of the white race. To withstand the assimilation with the negro tribes. Did you know they originally meant to call it Aryzone? A sanctuary for the Aryan race to uphold its integrity?"

Flake enjoys observing the agents' attempt to hide the turning cogwheels. It works amazingly well, he has to admit. Even interrogation bots could hardly display less emotion.

"They tricked Lincoln into signing this off by masking it a bit. Called it Arizona. Led Abe and his crew to believe this was some kind of native Indian term, supposed to mean something like little spring…were you aware of that?"

Special Agent Willis checks on his partner's rising unrest and reaches for a document folder from the top of an impressive pile on the table.

"You didn't know that, did you?" Flake smirks. "Most people don't. We…with that I mean us Arizonians…until today mostly vote for republican presidential nominees. Does that make me a white supremacist, gentlemen?"

"There is absolutely nothing wrong with voting for a republican candidate," Special Agent Friends follows an impulse to comment.

"I'd argue there was a lot wrong with a bunch of recent republican candidates," Flake says, crediting himself for getting one agent to blink after all, "but that's another matter." Special Agent Friends' eyes also tell him at least he had bought into the Aryzone story. Not a poor start, as this tough talk is only prepping the duellists for the actual shoot-out.

"Should start giving us some answers," Special Agent Friends says, "otherwise, we will have to resort to more serious measures than this nice little chit chat."

"You have not actually asked me a lot of questions yet, have you?" Flake balances his tone somewhere between provocation and concession. "Guess you wish to talk about this other boy band? THS? The Horrible Siliconettes?"

Agent Willis looks up from the file.

"You asked me if I am a white supremacist," Flake says. "The authors of the announcement do not seem to discriminate against any race or colour. I understood they plan to disclose all data ever collected." Flake can feel the temperature rising in Agent Friends' boiler. "It's not a Black Data Matters type of thing, is it?" he smirks.

"Better stop bullshitting us right now, snowflake!" the interrogator explodes in a disturbingly determined tone of voice that leaves Flake wondering about the plausible retribution options in case he wasn't complying.

"Mr Thomas, if you don't mind," he says.

"That's because you have not answered our initial question so far, Mr Thomas?" Special Agent Willis says calmly, while his partner looks like he will jump all over Flake any second. "The question, whether you are a communist? You quoted Steve Bannon. Bannon said he shares the same goal as Lenin. To destroy the state. Destroy the establishment. Do you also share this goal, Mr Thomas?"

"Got no fantasies decapitating the FBI director, as Mr Bannon once called for; if that's what you're asking."

"Earlier, in your professor's lecture, you seemed to agree with the goals of those terrorists, though."

"THS are terrorists?"

"What would you call them?"

"Don't know. Didn't have a chance to deliberate about their motivation with them yet. Might just as well be decent patriots, if you ask me."

Special Agent Friends closely leans in on Flake. "So, you admit you are in contact with them?"

"No, of course not. Nobody knows who they are."

"You just told us you didn't speak to them about their motives. That implies that you have spoken to them about other matters. You called them a boy band. So, you know they are males."

"That was pretty lame, detective."

Special Agent Friends sits himself on the tabletop, eye to eye with Flake. "You misread the situation you are in, snowflake. Terrorism is a severe criminal offence. An attack on US national security is a punishable act. You better start cooperating."

"Is this when I have to call for my legal counsel? After you have read me my rights?"

"This is not the Sopranos, buddy!"

"What is it then? What do you want from me?"

"Answers!" Friends shouts. "In Timberley's lecture, you said monopolists like Google, Meta or Amazon need to be broken up and that the terrorist's approach to publish all their data is a good start."

"Facebook harvests the data of 228 million Americans and uses this sensitive information in dangerous ways," Flake replies. "A few massive corporations have control over vast swaths of Americans' lives. They have endangered our democracy and enabled the spread of disinformation and hatred on their platforms. Amazon has amassed control over the e-commerce industry, capturing a full 50 percent of the market and using its power to drive down wages for workers and prices for suppliers…"

"This justifies extreme measures?" Special Agent Friends shouts even louder. "To break the law? Threaten national security?"

"I don't know. You tell me. You can also ask Bernie Sanders, senator for the lovely little state of Vermont and the longest sitting independent member of the house of representative. It was him who said this."

"This is not a game, son!" Special Agent Willis intervenes. "Do you support the extreme methods of these Siliconettes terrorists to act against what you called a serious evil?"

Flake straightens himself out. "To my knowledge," he says calmly, "we don't even know at this point what kind of information these activists are going to make public. If any. Let alone how they got this information. Who says it is not someone from inside Amazon or Google, who feels the public is entitled to know what information these firms collect on them? Is that an act of terror, then? Or wouldn't that be whistleblowing?"

"Do you concede," Special Agent Willis turns to a later page in the file in front of him, "to have written in your blog, that if people would truly understand the amount of data assembled on them and what corporations do with it, this would cause a rebellion?" He looks up from the folder, straight at Flake. "This is not a quote from some left-wing senator. This is you in your blog."

"Whistleblowing it is, then?" Flake replies. "I wasn't sure you guys ever embraced that concept, really."

"Something else was interesting," Special Agent Friends says. "We were wondering why an individual like you, who communicates a great deal on the internet, with a blog, a few YouTube channels and other stuff, why such an individual does not have a Facebook account. Seemed odd." Special Agent Friends shivers in anticipation. "We checked on existing accounts using the same Wi-Fi as you did, common locations, common IPs. Guess what we discovered? You have a Facebook account. As a matter of fact, you have more than one Facebook account. Using pseudonyms. The same with many other social media platforms. Don't you agree, this smells?"

"You'll send me on a trip to Rikers Island for violation of Facebook community guidelines?"

"Answer the question!"

"No, I don't think this is suspicious! It's an act of self-defence. Against the intrusive conduct of anti-social media. I simply don't want to make it too easy for them to stitch it all together." Flake leans back in his chair and folds his hands behind his head. "I'm pretty sure Facebook found me out a long time ago; correlates all my stuff, anyhow. It seems, though, they keep secrets from you? Maybe there is some decency in the Zuck clique after all."

Agent Friends assumes a combat position in Flake's back. "One of your profiles you registered under the name of Al Rosenberg. Albert Rosenberg was one mastermind behind Nazi ideologies. During the second world war he was the so called Reichsminister for the occupied eastern territories." Special Agent Friends puts both hands firmly on Flake's shoulders. "You idolise Nazis, Mr Snowflake!" he hisses in his ear. "With this profile, you follow an amazing number of right wings groups, protagonists of Alt-right and shady characters we associate with QAnon."

"These morons in the movement do not recognise it's obviously a fake profile. They don't even know who this guy was; confronted me more than once for being an alleged Jew with that kind of name. That tells you how little they know about the cult they serve."

"Are you suggesting you follow this scum just for fun?"

"Actually, yes. Tested out my Aryzone story on a few of those groups. Amazing reactions."

Special Agent Friends, on the verge of losing his temper, instead falls back on wondering about.

"Spread really fast," Flake says, "people developed many quite surreal additions to the myth. Can tell you some of them, if you like? Great fun. Nobody checked the facts. It's not hard to tell this lie. Wikipedia will do. Maybe my sense of humour is not for everyone, though. I give you that."

"You create misleading and fraudulent propaganda, which is chargeable as incendiarism by the way, and now you try to tell us it is just a joke," Special Agent Willis asks, while his partner still takes some time out to regain his composure.

"Oh, no! It's much more than that. I try to understand how the indoctrination works. Prepare to fight it. As you certainly have noticed, I have a similar profile to follow the extreme left."

"You want us to believe this crazy story?" Willis asks.

"Right there, you have shown why it's advisable to not associate the rest of my life with these profiles. Because people could think exactly what you are thinking."

In Flake's back, Special Agent Friends rises like a monster wave, ready to break and drown any bold surfer dude daring to ride it. "All bullshit!" he spews. "You just try to hide your true ambition. Do you concede to have spent hundreds, if not thousands, of hours in the darknet? Tell us. What was the purpose of that? If not to prepare the data dump?" The monster wave breaks and locks Flake in the green room, as boarders call the tiny space inside the translucent tunnel of water threatening to squash them.

"You can read a detailed report on this in my blog," he says. "The articles are called 'Andy goes underground'; on my experiment, whether life outside of the surveillance infrastructure is workable; what compromises it requires. The results were not very encouraging." Flake breaks out through the doggy door at the end of the tube. "It reassured me we have to claim back the internet as it was intended."

Willis drops the folder and eyeballs Flake. "You want us to believe you spend month over month on the darknet just to test out secure messaging protocols? Shall I tell you what we believe? We believe you went there to buy passwords, access codes, maybe find co-conspirators to prepare your big leak."

Flake folds his arms. "What evidence do you have to support this allegation?"

"Do you dispute to be connected to a significant number of individuals that conspire as so-called cypher punks?" Special Agent Friends enquires from the back. "Including one of these punks going by the name of XploitPimp? Wanted for hacking into state agencies. That you employ a vivacious exchange with Chris Shannon, who is a lobbyist in Washington for the Centre for Civil Liberties and agitates to break up Amazon, Meta and other large corporations?"

"Is any of this a chargeable offence?"

Special Agent Friends rises behind Flake again. "Among your recent book purchases are *The Age of Surveillance Capitalism* and *Network Propaganda*, he says. "Over the years, you have purchased the biographies of Mao Zedong, Ho Chi Minh, Chen Guevara and Fidel Castro, plus many more of that calibre."

"True," Flake says, still engaged in a staring match with Special Agent Willis, "and those of Nelson Mandela, Mikhail Gorbachev, Martin Luther King and others, including all respectable American presidents of the last one hundred years. Before you ask: No, I confess, I have not read a book about George Dimwit. But on his father."

"You have watched several hundreds of hours of footage online on subjects such as mass psychology and revolutionary movements in history. Documentaries criticising American foreign policy, especially in Latin America and Indochina. Including plenty of stuff from propagandists we consider extreme. Do I need to continue?"

"Don't forget, I hardly ever miss Steven Colbert. So what?"

"Do you dispute recently visiting Seattle, Redmond, Chicago, Atlanta and Bluffdale, Utah? Few days ago, you moved to the Valley. Are you telling us this is just a coincidence? You showing up in the places where the largest data centres in the US are and the corporations with the most data on private citizens have their headquarters? Do you dispute to have met with employees of many of these corporations? You'd better not, because here are all the names and dates." The agent reaches for a thick file folder on the very top of a second pile of papers and drops it with verve in front of Flake.

"Seriously? You made a printout of that list to put it in one of these filing cabinets I know from old black and white movies? Do you guys even use typewriters still? With carbon paper? They charged you boys with chasing cyber-crime…? Jesus…! Good luck then."

Special Agent Friends kneads his hands and obviously contemplates to jump ahead in interrogation protocol to the phase that involves advanced techniques.

57

"To answer your question," Flake says, "no, I don't dispute that. I met with these individuals because I work on a paper on implications of machine learning and the need for regulation of decision bots. These companies are the places where the experts are."

"Experts on big data?" Special Agent Willis enquires.

"Exactly, yes."

"What a convenient coincidence," Special Agent Friends says from halfway across the room. Flake wonders if the angry agent takes a run-up or still some time out?

"And I thought, I am paranoid," he says. "I suppose, with you boys, it is an accepted occupational illness, though?"

"What about all the dubious contacts my partner just read out?" Agent Willis asks.

"Does it actually surprise you," Flake replies, "that a guy with my background is in contact with other individuals who share the principle belief that fundamental change is needed to the present system of online commerce and social media?"

"Are you not the ones who always whine about echo chambers and filter bubbles?" Willis replies.

"Touché." Flake grins and leans back in his chair.

"This is all such bullshit!" Special Agent Friends feels inclined to spoil the ephemeral moment of consent from the room's far end. "I will not listen to this any longer!"

The agent makes himself uncomfortable on the table again, his probing eyes so close Flake can actually feel his hot temper. "Besides your radical views, something else we found quite revealing. As long as you just sit in your kitchen to write blogs that no one reads, it is all good…"

"Eighty thousand subs, actually…"

"…but you, Mr Snowflake, have an urge for activism. Let me show you…"

The agent fiddles with the remote until the flat screen comes to life and displays footage that looks like taken by a CCTV device, yet with quite good sound to go with it. You can overhear several conversations. A guy in a luminescent yellow vest over a motorcycle jacket with a black NYPD baseball cap makes his way through a tightly packed flock at a subway station.

The agent pauses the video to point at the screen. "This is you, isn't it?"

"The NSA subscribed to my YouTube channel? Wow, what an honour."

"You pose as a police officer. That's a public offence right here."

"The cap I got at a stand in front of Ground Zero, an emergency vest from a friend's car and a clip board...If that makes me impersonate a police officer...well..."

Friends pierces him and restarts the video.

The vested guy stops and the camera zooms in. With a commanding voice, officer Flake addresses a guy who has his back turned on him. "Sir...Sir! I'm afraid I will have to ask you to leave the platform asap."

The massive guy turns his head a little to check if he was the one spoken to.

"Sir, I repeat, you have to leave the platform right now."

"What?" The man swings his immense booty around, triggering concentric waves in the dense flock.

"According to the conditions of carriage of the New York transit authority that came into effect on January 1, access to platforms and trains at peak traffic times is restricted for significantly obese individuals," Flake lectures the giant.

"What are you talking about? What conditions?"

"The rules of the subway, Sir. These rules say that massively overweight people can't be using our services at peak times. You see how busy it is right now. Folks can hardly breathe. This rule aims to reduce the crush, the threat of people getting injured or even pushed onto the tracks by accident."

"I don't understand?"

A skinny Asian guy, who almost got folded by the big man's rotating butt earlier, looks up from his manga to offer translation services. "Let me paraphrase that for easier consumption," he says. "They banned fat guys like you from platforms and trains between 8 and 10."

"Are you crazy?" The offended looks back and forth between Flake and the translator.

"Come on, man. You must be 400 pounds, surely?" the Asian guy says while he peers at his manga a little anxiously.

"You see how crowded it is here, don't you? For every individual of your calibre, Sir," Flake explains calmly, "we can transport two or even three standard size people. We cannot have these people be late for work."

"Just because you cannot control yourself," manga boy adds.

"You are damn right I can't control myself. I will kick your stupid ass right now," oinks supersize guy, wavering whether he should go for Flake or manga boy first.

"You are on the platform illegally and now you threaten a New York state servant?" Flake asks.

"Damn sure I am. I have been riding the subway to work for the last ten years. This is the first I hear."

"These are the new rules. We publish them on huge signs at the entrance to the station. I can provide you a handout if that helps."

"If he is even literate…" manga boy chips in.

"Now I will kill you!" The big fellow jumps forward and in that shoves the entire population on the platform with him. Everyone has noticed the quarrel by now. Yet, in good New York ways, nobody wants to get involved.

"Sir, you urgently have to move now. Your presence obviously endangers others. A train is approaching."

The colossus turns back to Flake, which causes another swell in the crowd. He grabs his vest and pulls him close. Flake fetches a whistle from his pocket and blows it. "Officer down. Officer down" he shouts hysterically.

"Shut the fuck up, asshole," supersize guy swears.

A resolute lady intervenes. "Leave the man alone. He has every right to be here. This rule is ridiculous. This is a free country."

"Well, Ma'am," Flake says while the big man still clings on to his vest, "I recommend you do not engage yourself in this matter. Otherwise, I may have to reexamine that in your case, I was quite generous so far." The angry lady hits him with a folded newspaper.

"I will drop you in front of the train," the big guy threatens.

"Under no circumstances can I allow you to board this train, Sir. It is bad enough that you occupied so much space on this platform. But not on this train…I repeat: You must leave the platform at once. You can come back after 10. Understand?"

"You're so dead," supersize guy hisses through terrible teeth.

"Let the man go," mumbles a gentleman in a suit and tie two rows down in the crowd. "He is just doing his job."

"What's it to you? You stay outta this!"

"He has a point," the gentleman adds. "You take up a lot of space. And you are smelly."

Supersize guy drops Flake and wobbles over to the elegant offender. He shoves the slender man into the phalanx behind him, which bounces him back. Multiple members of the crowd finally feel inclined to engage. Quickly, the entire platform swells back and forth with people yelling things like:

"This is a free country,"

"Need to follow the rules,"

"I paid for the service like everyone else,"

"You should pay double when using twice the space" *plus many nasty personal insults, often inferring sexual preferences, while you see Flake making his way up the staircase.*

At this point, the video stops.

The leading man smirks at Special Agent Willis. "That was good fun, wasn't it?"

"We think this is very unmasking."

"Unmasking? Don't think that came up in the comments, yet."

Special Agent Friends walks up and down like a caged tiger again. "How did you hack the cameras on the platform?" he asks. "That requires some advanced hacking skills plus serious criminal energy."

"All it requires is a video editing tool," Flake replies. "Took the footage with a GoPro fixed right underneath the CCTV box; carried an extra mic. My video editing software has a rendering function for many cool effects, CCTV being just one of them."

"You confess to deep-faking evidence, snowflake?"

"Lame again. I hope you did not ask me over to discuss my oeuvre on YouTube, did you? What does this have to do with THS?"

"This video and other stuff on your channel, the stunt you pulled back in the café yesterday…you hacked this guy's phone…"

"Yeah?"

"Well, son," Willis says, "there is a pattern here. What you did at that subway station and in the café is to provoke a riot. You put something out there and you trick folks to get into a fight. And quickly, all hell breaks loose."

"Wow. That was a profound psychological analysis. I'll have to think about that. Until now, I felt I just had a little fun with some not so clever people."

"There is the next pattern. You think you are very clever. You got it all figured out. You need to lead the rest of us into the light. Don't you?"

"That makes me a terrorist? This gets bizarre. I suppose I should talk to a legal counsel."

"Why do you expect we will charge you? Because there is something you are hiding from us?"

Flake closes his eyes and starts a count to ten. On five he bursts. "All the decent patriots out there have nothing to fear, right? Is that it?

"I guess this implies only bad guys have to worry about the data dump either, then? The dump will doubtlessly uncover a bunch of bad guys and what they are up to. Fraud, collusion, conspiracies, many evil deeds will be brought to light. Does this mean the Siliconettes are doing your job? This is a tremendous opportunity for you boys."

Like a python ready to choke, Special Agent Friends squirms in from the back. "Think this is funny? Hacking corporate databases is not a joke. This will easily get you a life sentence. Plus, endangerment of national security. Plus, espionage. We are looking at three to four times life. Would you agree?" He turns to his partner.

"Minimum. Surely," Willis confirms.

"Now you are pressing charges?" Flake says. "Does it not irritate you Bernie Sanders and Steve Bannon both agree fundamental change has to happen? Our government must deal with monopolies by enforcing our antitrust laws. It doesn't because the politicians have been bought by those monopolistic corporations to keep them from being regulated."

"Let me guess," Special Agent Willis raises a brow, "that is another quote, isn't it?"

"Yep. From a man who certainly knows what money can buy. Billionaire hedge fund manager turned political fundraiser, Tom Steyer."

"Why don't you stop hiding behind other people, Mr Thomas? I am confident you have a point of view of your own to offer, don't you?"

"It's like climate change, actually," Flake says after a moment of contemplation. "An industry hooked on exploiting personal information, which they even call the new oil, has produced an abundance of toxic waste that threatens to wreck our civilisation. The carbon dioxides of this industry are 24/7 surveillance and intimate profiles of every single individual; prone to be misused to manipulate us; endangering our liberties, our freedom."

"Get a life!" Special Agent Friends shouts. "This alleged threat to society is just an invention of your twisted, alarmist mind. To deny people the advances of innovation, modern technology. Whatever weird way of living you aspire to go back to in your reclusive geek cave."

"Now, you are in the quotes business? This is pretty much what the establishment said to the scientist who published the first IPCC report on climate change in 1990, you see? Don't want to overdo the analogy, but besides the encroaching surveillance of individual's privacy, the way the industry works heats up the social debate pretty dramatically already."

"You see yourself following in the footsteps of a UN panel?" Special Agent Willis probes.

"I'm afraid I can't claim any credit for it. I suggest you have a little chat with Al Gore, since this climate change evangelist also claimed to have invented the internet. Maybe it is him behind all this. To show the inconvenient truth about corporate surveillance and division of society."

"I say we lock this snowflake up, until he is willing to cooperate," Special Agent Friends hisses. "That shouldn't take long."

"Not yet," his partner objects; his piercing gaze seeks to extract last insights from Flake's alert eyes.

"Don't leave town, Mr Thomas!" he says.

On his way to the door, Flake senses Special Agent Friends' violent fantasies in his spine. He flinches from a sudden loud noise caused by the frustrated agent violently kicking the table.

Right after he turned the corner, though, Flake takes a quick peek back into the room. "You surely have some advanced AI to look at all the stuff you gathered on me? Unless it is all fanfold? I would be very interested in the results. Keywords, patterns? Maybe you can share that next time? Open data, you know? I'll bring a floppy disk…Can you guys handle three and a half inches?" Having said this, Flake bails, roadrunner speed.

"Why did you let that snowflake run?" Friends confronts his partner. "It all figures perfectly. He thinks he knows the cure for the diseases of society. He's the saviour. The guy contacts extremist groups who want to overthrow our system. He establishes relations with people who can help him pull this off. He buys illegal material on the darknet. This is a classical radicalisation story."

"Don't buy that. He's cocky, all right. And clever. It's like my first partner used to say. To interrogate a guy like this is like eating crabs: it takes an enormous effort, you get very little out of it and it leaves you with a pile of garbage."

"He's so clever, he can even fool you? The guy shows all the signs of a psychopath. He's a poser, a wiseass, a gifted phony who manipulates people. He's a windbag who spins his stories the way his victims need to hear them. He doesn't take any responsibility for his actions…"

"OK Gideon, I get it. The guy may qualify as a narcissist, I give you that. Yet, I don't take him for an extremist. He thinks, though, he is invulnerable. I suppose we all did when we were his age, didn't we?"

From his partner's gaze, Willis can tell he doesn't recall that state of mind at all. "Anyway," he says, "I agree. We certainly need to keep a close eye on the man."

***

Beacons and Baby Care

"The Big One. That usually refers to the terrifying thought of a truly massive earthquake along the San Andreas Fault that threatens to flatten all of California. It is also what people here in the Valley started to call the exposure of very personal information on millions and millions of people announced for the coming Monday by a group with the name The Horrible Siliconettes."

"…You know, I honestly don't get what all the fuss is about. What's the point? These Horrible Siliconettes jokers will make some stuff on me public? So? Who gives a rat's ass? Who cares whether someone you don't know looks at your vacation pictures? The shopping history? I mean, honestly, Rachel! Who would wish to look at that, anyhow? Why would anyone want to see which shirts I bought recently? I mean, I wear them in public, right? People can see them anyway."

"But people do care, congressman Findley. People do not want strangers to look at snapshots with their friends. People do not want everybody else to know about everything they buy. There is a reason the fourth amendment declares the home to be a sacred place where we can feel completely protected. We need an equivalent of a home online as well. As an appointed representative of the American people, congressman, do you not think you have to defend this constitutional right?"

"Should you indeed get worked up about people you will never meet looking at your vacation snapshots, you should seek consultation, in my view. Should your credit card company know things your spouse is not aware of, like your tab in seedy table dance bars or monthly charges for subscriptions to dubious websites, you may need marriage counselling or other professional help. By the way: Should all husbands who cheat on their spouses get dragged out into the spotlight, that surely must be a side effect you would welcome, wouldn't you, Rachel? Anyway: Users have voluntarily signed up for this. Nobody gets forced to use any such service."

"You believe individuals have signed up for this, congressman?"

"Absolutely."

"You believe people understood what this meant?"

"Unlike you, obviously, I don't think people are stupid. I think people realise what they sign up to and they are fine with it. Because they value the benefits from using these brilliant platforms. Besides a few liberal, self-proclaimed freedom fighters, people simply do not mind."

"There was this company setting up a free Wi-Fi service in London some years ago. All you had to do was to accept the terms of use. Yet, these terms stipulated that the user would hand over their first-born child to the service provider. Everybody ticked the box and agreed. Do you think users were actually fine with handing over their babies to that provider? Or did they simply not read the fine print?"

"This is a ridiculous example. The platforms we are speaking about do not call for you to sign up to such nonsense."

"They may not ask for your first-born. Yet, they do ask for a lot. The point is, people are commonly not conscious of what they are agreeing to."

"Unlike you, Rachel, I have faith in people. I believe they are well capable of making rational choices."

"In a recent poll, three out of four Facebook users were not aware a database of their preferences, traits and interest existed."

"That's what I say: People do not care about these things the way the liberals want to make us believe."

"I think people do care, congressman: after they were shown what Facebook collected on them, more than half of users claimed they are uncomfortable this information gets assembled. Still, that was merely the surface; the aggregation Facebook presents its users. People didn't even get to see the detail behind it."

"I can just reiterate: People have signed up for the service freely. Nobody twisted their arm!"

"Is this actually the case these days? Do you have the choice to not be on social media, congressman?"

"Should you wish to enjoy the benefits of modern media, you have to be prepared to pay the price. I think it is an outstanding achievement all these great services are available today and they are accessible for everyone for free. Don't you agree, Rachel?"

"Dina Srinivasan, a fellow with the Thurman Arnold Project at Yale University, describes it like this: Consumers effectively face a singular choice – use Facebook and submit to the stipulations of Facebook or forgo all use of the only social network. Do you honestly consider this a voluntary decision?"

"Absolutely. Everything in life comes at a cost. Marrying the love of your life comes at the cost of giving up on sleeping around. Every coin has two sides."

"Is this price we pay not way too high? Srinivasan goes on to say 'accepting Facebook's policies means accepting broad scale commercial surveillance'."

"These platforms use the information to make sure they do not bother you with irrelevant advertisement. Don't you agree it is wonderful you merely see ads that mean something to you, that address an actual need you have? Don't you agree this is major a benefit?"

"Well, the point of how relevant ads for the same electric toothbrush are, which I already bought six weeks ago, is a whole different matter. In principle, though, I agree that making ads more relevant is a good thing. Yet, three out of four Americans say they consider most forms of personalisation at least somewhat creepy. If they were properly asked for consent, merely one in a thousand would actually approve."

"In my view, your example with the toothbrush shows the platforms do not even know that much. If they would have realised you already made the purchase, they would show you something else, something relevant again. Your surveillance theory doesn't stack up."

"Interesting point. As long as there are elements social media monopolies do not know about me yet, there is no problem? Is that your point, congressman?"

"My point is, the liberal elite is hysterical and wildly exaggerates the powers of these companies while they systematically downplay the tremendous benefits our society gains from connecting via social media. Did you ever wonder why

someone went through all the trouble to program a cool game, app or feature and then give it away for free? Because we all live off applause? Guess again. What they get is the data. That's the way it works. It works to the advance of all of us. We should stop inflating the drawbacks and focus on the marvellous opportunities with those new technologies."

"It is certainly true there is still a gap in the data compiled on all of us. Like in my example of the electric toothbrush. As a matter of fact, one in three Facebook users think the profile Facebook creates doesn't accurately reflect them. A different debate would be, if individuals are any good at knowing themselves; if not, most of the time, an external view represents you better than your own self-perception. Yet, that's philosophical."

"Damn right that's philosophical. You make your own life way too complicated, Rachel. Most people do not think like this. They shouldn't. I don't!"

"Let me ask you this, congressman: Do you think, when they subscribe to the services of these platforms, users were aware they consented to combining their data with dozens, if not hundreds of additional sources, like mortgage databases, information obtained from a multitude of data brokers, including government and public records. Even things like consumer contests, warranties and surveys, loyalty card purchase histories or magazine subscriptions. Do you believe users understand this when they sign up? Can even assess what this means? How complete a personality profile one can create with the combination of these sources."

"I think people value the continuous innovation that comes from all of this."

"Or did they simply click the yes-button to upload pictures of their re-decoration project, congressman? Only thirty percent of users think providing data results in better services! Whereas seventy percent think tracking online activities for the purpose of marketing is unethical. Honestly, what do you believe, congressman?"

"I simply don't get why this makes you liberals so hysterical. What's the big deal? Nobody gets hurt. When Facebook started to track the sites you visit, a technology they called beacon, they really hadn't figured out yet how to make this work. Remember the media coverage when they send a note to a wife giving away her husband had just bought a huge diamond ring? Big scandal. Lots of hate in the media. I am sure today this is one of the favourite stories of this couple. They will surely reminisce and laugh about the fact that at first, she

thought he had bought the ring for another woman. Until he gave it to her for their anniversary, if I recall this right."

"Interesting example…"

"Or look at the case when Walmart sent this family all the coupons on maternity clothing and baby care items. Because the purchases showed someone in that household was pregnant. The problem was it was the underage daughter. And the parents didn't know that yet. Don't you think this is a family laughing matter today? That baby must be in junior year now. Social media has come a long way since then. Such things do not happen anymore. It's a much more relevant and helpful experience because of all the work that has gone into understanding the users. I think this is wonderful. Don't you?"

"We will return to our conversation with congressman Findley right after a quick break…"

***

Gates of Hell

"The Gates of Hell?" Flake marvels at a colossal cast iron mock entrance portal mounted to a free-standing backdrop wall. Countless figurines emerge from the black surface of the twenty-five feet tall structure.

"Amazing, isn't it?" Leeza says, relieved to see her sculpture garden idea was spot on.

"Had no clue they had a Rodin collection here at Stanford."

"I promised I'll show you all the hidden gems, didn't I? Rodin worked on this piece for decades. Dante's *Inferno* inspired it."

"There must be a hundred of these small statues mushrooming all over the thing; look like snatched from a Mexican baroque church; turned into zombies, though." Flake enjoys watching Leeza immerse herself into the dark masterpiece even more than the startling work itself. To indulge in the details and not speak a single word for about five minutes doesn't feel awkward at all to either of the two.

"Rodin wanted an inscription on the top," Leeza says eventually. "'abandon all hope, ye who enter here'. A quote from the *Inferno*. His sponsors didn't like that very much."

Flake mischievously turns to her. "Any jokes about social media and gates of hell will get me in trouble, I suppose?"

When Flake had called her up last night after they had met in the café, the two had talked for hours about a myriad of different things before they got around scheduling this date. *Finally, here's a guy,* Leeza thought, *you can have a good fight and a good laugh with at the same time.* Leeza loves a good fight. Yet, for this first date, she prefers to avoid potential date crashers. So, she ignores the comment and focuses on the arts.

"I come here a lot," she says, "to look at all those intricacies again and again. I don't know…it clears my head. Not all figurines are doomsday characters, actually; despite the dark appeal. There are lovers, courtesans, a collection of quite unique characters."

"Up there on the top. That's the thinker, isn't it?" Flake asks.

"They have another larger-than-life copy inside the Arts Centre."

"Speaking of thinker. You said you love Chomsky?"

"Oh, totally! He revolutionised linguistics. My line of studies. And he took a stand on the most important political issues for decades. When I read 'Manufacturing Consent' in college, it changed the way I look at the world."

"How can you be a fan of Chomsky's yet work for the most powerful opinion manipulator ever? Much more powerful than classical media ever was?"

"On the contrary, actually, if you ask me," Leeza replies. "Social media takes opinion-making out of the hands of big news corporations and democratises it."

"Is that so?"

"Look at the New York Times. The world's leading liberal voice with two thousand journalists. They are owned by big capital firms…"

"Even Chomsky reads them and calls them the best of the bad."

"You see! Nowadays, they make their money via online subscriptions. Their online readers are a very engaged community; comment extensively on the site but also in social media. Those comments often affect how the Times operates. This public feedback loop has a controlling and correcting effect. People can influence what they get to read. What these excellent journalists focus on."

"You actually think the parallel universe of fakespeak, incitement and confrontation, called social media, should have more influence on news?"

"You seem to confuse social media with Fox News."

"Fox kind of invented it. But social media pulled peeping Tom off his couch and turned him into a wrecking hater. Way more effective to create a proper cancel culture; especially once combined with filter bubbles, effectively leading to thought prohibition. Tell me, how does this propel opinion making, exactly?"

As much as Leeza doesn't want this date to turn into a debate, she is not prepared to lie down her arms just yet.

"You don't have a lot of trust in the people, do you?" she says.

"People are schizophrenic," Flake points at the INGSOC logo on his tee. "They tell their Alexa to order a copy of Orwell's 1984; wouldn't even think that's odd."

Half of Leeza's brain was busy preparing the change to a more light-hearted subject, so she is caught off guard.

Flake puts on a disenchanted face.

After a quick recalibration of brain cells, Leeza's face lightens up. "Oh! Get it. Big Sister Alexa," she says. "You are a sinister man."

Flake smirks like a ten-year-old caught pilfering chocolates from grandma's drawer. "The NSA dudes said that as well. Are you in their camp?"

"I'd love to convince you we're not the bad guys. I honestly think these tools make people's lives better."

"As far as I can see, social media companies benefit from – and therefore promote – confrontation, hate, cancellationism and prohibitionism."

On that cue, the wrinkles on Leeza's forehead disappear and small dimples form in the corners of her smile. "Ism's, in my opinion, are not good!" she recites in the tone of a Miss America contestant quizzed on her values in life. "A person should not believe in an -ism, he should believe in himself!"

"Wow!" Flake drops to his knees. "Now I am in love! You just quoted Ferris Bueller!"

"Love this movie. Watched it at least two dozen times. Remember the scene at the Art Institute of Chicago? Ferris, Sloan and Cameron mimicking that statue, folding their arms, looking very sincere? It was on one of the movie posters. That statue was also a Rodin."

"How cool is that?" Flake says, mostly for having found a soul mate rather than the Rodin coincidence. "I strongly agree, though," he adds, "people should not believe in -isms. What do you think? Does this include journalism?"

"Totally!" Leeza smiles. "As a Chomsky disciple!"

The couple spends quite a while examining a group of three men in strangely bent postures with drooping heads, joining their sagging hands, like musketeers join their rapiers. On closer inspection, looking at it from left and right, back and front and all possible angles, they found it to be a line up of three gradually rotated and intertwined copies of the same sculpture, actually.

"What is it?" Leeza asks, trying to follow Flake's brooding gaze past the triplets to the other end of the square.

"Quarterback alert!" Flake says. "Plus, backup."

Leeza spots the king and his entourage carrying huge sports bags, taking a shortcut through a line of trimmed cedar trees about fifty yards away.

"May I suggest avoiding another wild chase?" she smirks.

"Now that the king and I seem to have a common interest in the arts?" Flake asks. "Maybe we can be really good friends, even."

Leeza grabs Flake's hand and hurries him along into the cover of the nearby trees; she moves ever faster to get some distance between them and the enemy; before you know it, the couple engages in a little catch me if you can, crisscrossing the wide lawn of Stanford Oval along picturesque s-shapes flowerbeds. Leeza comes out on top and conducts a Rocky Balboa victory dance against the backdrop of Hoover Tower.

When they arrive at a group of larger-than-life statues looking like zombies creeping across a chessboard, it dawns on Leeza that her script for this date is a bit heavy on depressing art. The sad story behind this group of despairing sufferers, called the Burghers of Calais, who had sacrificed themselves so that invaders would spare their hometown, will offer Flake more starting points for provocations at least.

"Coming back to Chomsky," Flake doesn't even need a new trigger just yet. "What about his point on distracting folks with bread and circuses from attending to the actual issues?"

Leeza tries to remember a more light-hearted piece they could go see next.

"The media preoccupy people with stupidities," Flake continues. "It used to be soaps and dull TV programs. Nowadays, it is six hours per day on Facebook and Insta."

"I agree not enough people engage in making a positive difference in this world. Yet, is that the fault of social media?"

"They are the ones keeping you focused on apolitical consumerism."

Leeza gently pokes him on the chest and gives him a sly look. "There is another -ism. You really like -isms, don't you?"

Flake gazes apologetically, yet like for a sin you are actually proud of.

"Honestly," she says, "it's all new, for all of us, still. We have to learn how to control this thing. Yet, I truly believe it can grow into a means to organise political decision making in truly democratic form."

"The platforms that screw up every civilised debate today will turn into a means to organise a democratic exchange tomorrow? How is that going to come about? These platforms are not the cosy community cocoon you want to see in them. They are businesses only interested in profits."

For this date to serve its originally intended romantic purpose, Leeza feels, it's high time they take an exit from Controversy Road to Philander Avenue. "You call it cosy community cocoon," she says. "I say it's people focusing on what is most meaningful in life: relationships with other humans. You can share so much more of the lives of your loved ones than ever before. How can you not find this fantastic?"

Flake has already fallen in love with Leeza's enthusiasm. Her sincerity. He genuinely hates to disagree with her. "You know the movie *Fight Club*?" he asks, though he has no idea why his intuition served this up as the best next talking point.

"Sure?" Leeza says, as curious as Flake where he may go with this.

"Like it?" his brain auto-chats to buy some time to figure it out.

"Yes. Is that the correct answer?" Leeza pulls a nagging face.

"That movie shows precisely what I mean. Even though it wasn't about social media at the time," he bargains for even more time to set up the details. "Don't you see?"

Leeza's eyes clearly say she doesn't. They also say she would love to change to lighter subjects. Yet, the latter is still lost on Flake. "Folks post pics of their IKEA cocoons," he tutors, "for their followers to look at, who they often don't even like very much; single serving friends, remember? They post pictures of their artfully arranged, politically correct, biodiverse vegan bowl dishes they just as often don't like very much either."

Leeza tries out some ironic, open-mouthed marvelling.

"Showing off to your so-called friends," Flake continues, "who are often only distant acquaintances, is not really heartwarming communicating with your loved ones. It's showboating."

Since Flake doesn't seem to get the signals, Leeza feels she needs to go for a less subtle approach. "What could be wrong with people communicating about trivial subjects? Not everyone wants to be substantial all the time."

Flake does well sense something is lost on him, but he doesn't yet get what it is. "Don't you see where this ends up…?" he takes another wrong turn, leaving Leeza no other choice but to go for the kill move.

"Not everybody wants to spend their first date on intellectual examination," she says as casually as possible.

Flake's dejected gaze meets Leeza's disarming smile.

"Oh, is that what this is? A date?" He smiles submissively.

"You tell me? Maybe to drag you to the Gates of Hell wasn't such a great idea?" She tries to look despondent.

"I'd love this to be a date," Flake rushes to say. "The gate is perfect. All those sculptures are brilliant. This is a phantastic spot. Thank you for bringing me here."

"Don't overdo it, okay!"

The two lovebirds beam at each other.

And keep beaming.

Yet, they miss the boat to Love Island; the ephemeral moment when making out would have been the next sensible thing to do.

So, they keep beaming.

Leeza eventually breaks the increasingly awkward silence. "Care for me to tell you what kind of movie I see when I watch *Fight Club*? Very different movie than the one you seem to see."

"Got my expectations up alright," Flake says.

Leeza wonders whether he referred to her movie review or the whole date thing just there. "Let me first sum up the flick you see, mister anarchist. Fincher wanted to make a movie criticising consumerism. The twisted hero realises that his life is shallow, a Potemkin's village to hide the emptiness, so he embarks on a quest to find authentic passion. The deepest emotion, maybe even deeper than love, is fear. Fear for your life. The most basic instinct in a man is to fight for survival. And pain; genuine pain; physical pain. Pain from being hit right on the jar, cutting your flesh open; manly pain. Boy's stuff like that."

Flake looks down, cap in hand, like a boy who claims it wasn't him setting fire to the cat's tail.

"Our hero organises these fight clubs," Leeza continues. "Of course, it escalates; he ultimately decides all of society needs to feel this pain. He turns into a terrorist. Blows up the city. Is this about right?"

Flake imitates the suffering posture of the Burghers of Calais. "The way you tell it makes it seem weird…but, yeah, sort of."

"Well, then. Here is the movie I see: Fincher wants to attract large box office crowds by shamelessly exploiting the beauty of Brad Pitt. It works. He got me, at least. Remember, Brad's first ever lasting impression in the movie business was a shirtless scene in Thelma & Louise of less than 30 seconds. This sufficed to make him famous. If 30 second of Brad shirtless can do that, what will 30 minutes do? To avoid audiences thinking, he just shot a soft porn flick, he hires some legit actors: Norton, Bonham-Carter."

Flake seriously questions his usually so reliable intuition on choice of subject. Yet he enjoys Leeza's excellent mood.

"Should you wish to show off Brad's impeccable pecs and abs covered in glistening sweat," Leeza revels on, "what do you do?" Since the question is just a means to make Flake suffer a bit, so she's happy with his sad gaze as a response. "Fincher's answer: have him fight for half the movie. Bare-chested, of course. Senselessly. Sweat covered. Sixth rule of fight club: no shirts! Remember? For no apparent reason. The fat guy even gets to keep the tee on. Well done."

Leeza almost feels sorry for Flake, looking at his really cute submissive gaze. Almost. "Brad is exceptionally sexy when hurting," she tightens the vice a little more still.

"Think so?" Flake asks meekly.

"Uuhhh yeah! The rest of the movie, Fincher dresses Brad up in the coolest of outfits. Outright ridiculous this should convey a criticism of consumerism. It's a Dolce & Gabbana fashion journal."

"Spot on. I was dying for his leather jacket."

"Yet, they lacked some sort of frame narrative. There is this lovelessly scripted conspiracy story, which they don't even properly explain. They don't really care. They rattle through all the great consumer critique in the first 20 minutes of the movie. Entertainingly delivered, I admit. From then on, it's Brad looking gorgeous. That is why I like the movie. My eyes were not opened. They were glued to Brad Pitt's abs. Drooling."

Flake knows it's time for unconditional surrender. "I get it," he says. "Life comes down to boy meets girl."

Leeza seems pleased.

"Trouble is," he adds, "there is no competing with young Brad Pitt."

"Didn't look the type who gets discouraged easily."

"I'm not. Just lost for words."

"Don't worry. Happens to the best."

The Love Island ferry returns ashore to take new passengers.

"I am Flake's pitiful performance," Flake quips. "I am Leeza's adorable duckface on a post from her date." Encouraged by Leeza breaking into a laugh while she tries to put on big lips, he asks, "Have you ever kissed a guy whose views on society you rejected?"

"If I wouldn't," she replies, "Friday nights in the Valley would be very lonely…"

***

Big One Minus 6, Tuesday

Rose

"Micah just joined the firm straight from Cambridge," Tim makes another attempt to get Zach's attention. The head of product marketing arrived ten minutes late to the show-and-tell session, extending only a very cursory no-look greeting, while his thumbs hammered away on his handheld; he dropped in the chair closest to the exit, his feet on the next one, and hadn't taken his eyes off the device all throughout Tim's introduction of the team.

"Cambridge University, that is," Tim says. "Not Cambridge Analytica." Even the poor joke doesn't do the trick.

"Shall we get started, chief?"

"Yeah, yeah, go ahead. Sorry, have to send these off real quick. Be right with you. Got to leave five minutes early, though. Meeting with the big guy, short notice." Zach says all of this while still typing away at maximum speed.

"Today, we present to you a prototype of a feature for our messenger software. We call her ROSE."

"In a chat with your friends, ROSE will make advanced suggestions for your next response…"

Since the chief still works his smartphone, Tim decides it is time for plan B. "Suppose it's best we show you straight on your device. Let me activate the feature."

He wrestles the handheld from Zach and quickly scans the QR code. "Here we go. We'll mirror your messages on the big screen."

Zach looks puzzled.

"Let's pick any random casual chat with a good friend of yours," Tim instructs, "nothing too personal."

Like any modern manager, Zach prides himself for promoting bias for action in his subordinates. He does as he is told, pointing at a suitable chat. "Is this like auto reply in email?" he asks. "Suggesting a response in complete phrases?"

"That would be like comparing the Z3 to TensorFlow," Mic chuckles.

"What Mic means is," Tim translates to fuzzie for his boss, "it is way smarter than that."

"We neither use ChatScript nor Mitsuku," Mic bubbles away off script, "but have used a new tool our big data team has developed. Way superior to anything used so far. For the first time, it can make use of brute force algorithms instead of patterns and make it work. Even better than TensorFlow. Because we could use so much more data than anyone ever before. This is ground breaking…"

"Mic can truly lose himself in this stuff," Tim tries to remind his colleague they had agreed to avoid tech speak.

Mic, however, takes the remark as encouragement to dive to the next level. "We clear the mangled language of a conversation by identifying the canonical terms, with spelling corrections applied and so on and so forth. We use the lemmatised version as well as the original version…"

Zach's helpless gaze prompts Tim to cut his colleague short. "Let's show you how it works in real life. Once ROSE gets activated, we display the suggestions in a separate box. In fully fleshed out sentences. The user simply clicks on any of them and we transfer it to the response box. Of course, you can still correct, change or amend before you send it off."

"Looks quite intuitive," Zach nods. "That's good."

"But the best part is we emulate the way the user usually communicates," Leeza says.

"Make it sound like me?" Zach asks.

"Exactly!" Tim says. "Short forms, acronyms you use, punctuation or not, it's all there, exactly the way you write. Absolutely amazing. You will think you wrote the stuff yourself."

"That's important!" Zach says. "This will only work if the other party doesn't recognise it is a tool they chat with."

"ROSE will pass the Turing test any day!" Mic radiates a proud father's graduation day smile.

"On top of the grammar," Leeza says, "we also emulate the best tone for a specific conversation. By looking at the sentiment in previous chats; relationship of the users, quality of interactions, likes, comments, responses. In all your communications channels…"

"This means," Zach interrupts, "the suggestions not only sound like how I would write them, but how I would write them to you specifically?"

"You got it."

"Wicked!"

"That's what we thought, too," Tim says. "We created a sophisticated scoring matrix, which Mic is happy to walk you through at the end in case you want to know the details."

It is obvious Zach takes this more as a threat than an offer, while Mic seems to already be sorting his talking points.

"In the interest of time," Tim says, "all I am going to say at this stage is: this will tell us, if our suggestions should be funny, serious, formal, provocative, maybe even sensual, lots of different categories. Should you usually prefer to be flirtatious with someone or even go for innuendos, ROSE will propose just that."

"Flirtatious, you say…" Zach murmurs. "Could we build a dating app with your ROSE?"

Leeza pierces Zach as if he just called ROSE a hoe.

"Is a dating app not supposed to connect real people?" she asks.

"A dating app," Zach lectures, "is supposed to keep real people engaged as much as possible. Doesn't matter how you do it."

"Like the idea!" Tim chips in, eager to make use of Zach's full attention. "We'll look into that. Might need to call her ROXANE, though."

Tim senses Zach didn't get the Cyrano reference, but he well got ROSE's potential.

"Sixty percent of men using dating apps would like to get more messages. Great potential there. How do you choose the content of the conversation?" Zach asks.

"We determine commonalities. Joint interests. Music, for example; a special song both parties like; literature; books both have thumbed or bought. Movies the user has referred to in other channels. Any subject, actually, both parties independently have revealed an interest in. Anywhere! Ever!"

Zach nods rhythmically; his milling mind seems almost ready to give birth to a major revelation.

"ROSE prepares between three and five ideas," Tim continues, "depending on the level of intimacy we have. For most users, there is an abundance of stuff to base proposals on, so we will present five."

"Rather go with three," Zach says. "Let's not confuse folks."

"To suggest content like books, movies or songs gives us great potential," Tim says.

Zach nods faster.

"Not only does it measurably increase the engagement time and user satisfaction…"

"…we can also promote products," Zach completes Tim's train of thought, "leading to purchases and, thus, to revenues. Splendid!"

"Exactly! The results in our internal trials were amazing. In about forty percent of the chats, we saw an opportunity to weave in a direct referral to a product; a book, a song, a movie, whatever. Need to do more research to decide whether we should use a clickable link or rather just call out the product. At least initially, we want to test the waters and be subtle."

"Brill. It shouldn't be invasive."

"Good point. Here is another warning. Test users loved the suggestions; used them a lot. Quite frequently, though, they forgot about ROSE's recommendations right away. Because it wasn't actually their idea. When their chat partner referred to it later, it caused confusion. Sometimes even harsh debates."

"We should be extremely prudent; only use obvious recommendations, strong commonalities. The AI can do much more; spark really interesting debates. Need to test this out carefully. Gain experience how much complexity users can handle. How advanced we can be."

"Gang!" Zach jumps from his seat. "This is brilliant. Love it. Excellent job."

"Next, we want to run external test groups," Tim says, "to get broader feedback; improve usability."

"Your girl, ROSE…could she also influence mood, sentiment, that kind of stuff?" Zach asks.

Leeza looks down on him like a big sister protecting her sibling from a creepy boyfriend. "We identify the mood of the user," she says, "emulate; not manipulate it."

"And this is great," Zach says. "Have another look at how we can apply this to alter moods, okay?"

"Will do, Zach," Tim says. "Good point."

"I'll run it past my boss," Zach tries to wrap things up, "and also engage our compliance folks, just to check. Political climate is a bid difficult these days."

On his way out, he adds, "May even want to pitch this to the big guy."

"Glad you like it," Tim says, blocking his path. He expects the next bit to be really tricky. He had taken his boss for a jog a couple of times. The guy would rather take a shortcut on the stadium lap than to just follow the track; even if that meant adding more shortcuts for the necessary mileage to meet the training goals set by his Apple watch.

"Since you mention compliance," Tim says in his best sweet-talking tone, "…we wanted to ask you about this THS announcement. Discussed this quite a lot in the team."

Cornered Zach would clearly bail instantly if squeezing past Tim wouldn't be unworthy of a manager of his calibre.

"Can you tell us anything about this?" Tim asks. "Is it possible these terrorists have our data? Did we get hacked?"

"Absolutely not!" Zach acts up as if Tim had suggested a top dog like him could still be a virgin. "The best security professionals work for us. We monitor our network 24/7. We spend shitloads of money on that stuff…" he rattles like tallying up his chick list to refute the virgin charge.

"How can we be sure, Zach?" Mic interrupts. "Did management not concede the leak of five hundred million sets of user data just a few months ago? I mean…did we investigate this new threat at least?"

"Should these THS guys have what they claim," Tim says, "it must include our data. Nobody has more data on people than us. They must have gotten to it somehow."

Zach's shutters close like a corner shop when a rally turns into a street riot. "We bring great services to people, guys, okay? Put great tools at their disposal; to communicate; share experience. Keep them connected to their loved ones."

"Absolutely, Zach!" Tim ponders for ways to get his manager off quoting marketing boilerplates from behind closed curtains. "No doubt about that. We were just wondering…"

"Don't get me started on that privacy shit, okay!" Zach rants away. "To invest in our platform, continually improve it, run it, costs a lot of money. You know we pay you dearly so that you can spend your time inventing fantastic features like your ROXANE. The firm found ways to pay for all of this…" The pep talk seems to have a calming effect on Zach. "Our users allow us to pick up what they like and we use it to provide them with better recommendations. Can't see anything wrong with that. Much of the cash we spend is to make sure the information our users entrust us with is safe. We're talking billions here." Zach looks around, expecting a cheer from the audience.

"From Snowden's files, we know the firm delivers data to the NSA, right?" Mic says. "What data do we hand them? Could this get hacked? Where do they keep it?"

"Gang!" Zach reloads to blast his way out of his corner. "You're crossing a line here. As good corporate citizens, we support our authorities in their efforts to maintain national security. There is nothing wrong with that either. Anyone have a different view?"

"We are truly worried," Leeza says in as soft a voice as possible. "For ROSE, we looked at a lot of stuff...people write about very intimate things on our platforms. Should that be exposed..."

"When we sought for subjects to propose in our prototype," Mic says, "we looked at all information we have on individuals. Our own channels, external sources...not even my best friend knows me as well as our algorithms do. This should not be public."

"Gang, what do you expect from me?" the manager asks.

"I have friends in Hong Kong," Leeza makes yet another attempt. "These folks fight for free speech; against the constraints imposed by the Chinese government. My friends organise their protests with the help of our platform; keep connected via our groups. Should all this get exposed to the government...forces in power could identify everybody connected to the resistance. Wouldn't it be terrible to be responsible for that?"

"I feel you, Leeza," Zach says. "Is this where your family is from? China?"

Tim notices Leeza's almond eyes turn pistachios. He remembers well how he made a similar mistake when they first met. To her, this was like asking a Swede if she was from Spain. She had given him an elaborate monologue on fat, jolly Chinese Buddhas versus slender, tranquil Siamese Buddhas; about way more Christians than Buddhists living in Korea; about cultural ignorance and all the rest of it. Before he can step in, though, Leeza gulps that monologue and softly replies: "My family is from Seoul."

Zach takes a moment to readjust his defence tactics.

"If you have something you don't want anyone to know, maybe you shouldn't be doing it!" he says. "Wasn't it Eric Schmidt who said that?"

"We provide services to billions of people," Leeza adds another layer of compassion to her tone. "In, I don't know, maybe 150 countries and 60 languages..."

"Which I think is great..." Zach interrupts.

"…in many of these countries," she continues, "it is the good guys who have to hide."

"Political opposition in Venezuela, Hong Kong, China, Russia," Tim adds. "Journalists that report on corruption or government crime. All these people connect via our platforms."

"Should our data get disclosed, all the pieces come together," Mic says. "The messages, the likes, the links, address book, timeline, all of it."

"That makes it really easy for any oppressor," Tim concludes, "to uncover the entire network of the opposition. All the details on every alleged enemy of the state."

"Authorities even get pictures of my friend's front lawn," Leeza says with a cracking voice, "to find their house with ease when they send in the squad team to arrest them." She clears her throat. "Or worse!"

Zach's face clearly shows that instead of listening, he still plots his escape.

"Don't you think this would be dreadful?" Leeza asks. "Because of us?"

"Maybe," Tim says, "we should take our platforms offline until we know what is behind all this?"

"Slim down our database at least," Mic says, "delete everything we don't really need."

"Gang, really!" Zach retorts, "you are being hysterical! Anyway, should these hackers have gotten hold of our data already, what good would it do to delete it or take it off the grid?"

"You just said we can't get hacked," Leeza says in a faint voice.

"How can we ever even know we are not hacked?" Tim asks. "Maybe it is an inside job? We can still find them? Wouldn't it be better to cut the risk?"

"Look," Zach lectures, "this is not a charity. It's a business. A highly successful one. The community appreciates our services a lot. You said it yourself. They need them. We can't just drop it."

Leeza looks at him as if he had suggested to run over a kitten for fun. "Don't you think the community would much rather do without updates to their timelines for a few weeks than to know people will get hurt?" she asks.

"Gang, appreciate your concern. Leave that to the pros, okay? They got this covered. Again: great product. Love it. Gotta run. Be in touch." Zach rushes past Tim, who forces a quick meditation exercise upon himself he learned in a violence prevention training.

Mic buries his head. "You were right about the guy, Tim. Attention span of a five-year-old short on his ADS prescription."

Leeza's hands tremble. "This is so ignorant!" she utters almost inaudibly.

"Our senior execs don't take this seriously," Tim says after finishing his meditation. "We need to do something about that."

***

Notorious

"Hello. Is there anybody out there? Just nod if you can hear me.

"This is Awkward Andy. Welcome back to the number one channel for paranoid data-dystopians.

"Today I want to talk about the data exposure announced by a group calling themselves The Horrible Siliconettes. The odd name shouldn't trick you into not taking this seriously. Mind you, we are talking about doxxing billions of people, you, me, all of us. Making all our private information public. For those of us who thought doxxing is just a problem for celebrities whose street address and phone number get published by some mean hater, making them a target for paparazzi and stalking fans, think again. This time, it may hit all of us. I'm pretty sure all of us have some part of our lives we do not want anyone to know about. At least, if you are not the Kardashians. Or have some other form of digital death wish.

"Don't tell me you have never done anything you wouldn't want your mum's bridge friends to read about on the front page of your church community's newsletter?

"Whatever your most treasured secret is…stuff your best friend must never learn about; your spouse…It will have left a trace online; or in an app…

"Everywhere you go is noted. Everyone you meet can be reconciled. Every message or comment you write, about politics, your friends, your family, your spouse…from taunt to treason…it's on file. Don't think for a second any of that stays anonymous when it all comes together in one big dump.

"Every item you ever searched for; everything you buy; or sell; every service you pay for. It's all captured somewhere.

"In case you have a secret that does not leave such a trace? Tell us about it in the comments.

"You all heard the placations from Big Tech they have it all under control? That we don't need to worry about a thing? You also heard from Big Tech's

friends in Washington that the intelligence community is not concerned. They just want to lock up the bad guys that created all the fuss and woke them from their lunch nap.

"Many people seem to buy into this happy-juice rhetoric. Eighty percent of people polled yesterday said they believe the announcement was a hoax. That it will not affect them.

"You must be joking! Come on! Big Tech are notorious liars when it comes to issues of data privacy and protection of civil rights. It is almost impossible to count how often Big Zuckster has lied to our faces without blushing. He is notorious for his deficits in empathy, mind you. Anyone remember when he sold out your privacy to these Cambridge Analytica jokers? Or when he lied to us about his intentions to, of course, join up our information on WhatsApp, Instagram, and Facebook? He claimed it would anyway not be technically feasible. Hilarious! Not even Butters from South Park would have believed in that if he ran the FTC. Yet, they did and Zuck got away with it.

"I quote courageous congress woman Maxine Waters, who said it straight to Zuck's face: 'Perhaps you believe you are above the law. It appears that you are willing to step on or over anyone, including your competitors, your own users, and even our democracy to get what you want'.

"Well said, Ma'am!

"That is the guy we shall now trust our private data is in excellent hands with him and there is nothing we need to worry about? Really?

"I will explore this some more with a buddy of mine, IT security expert Martin Levinsky, who worked for Shin Bet, the internal security unit of the Israeli government, Amazon Web Services and others. Martin, good to see you again."

"Thanks, Flake, good to see you, too."

"Martin, tell us a bit about Meta and security."

"When I think about this subject, I feel just like the guy on your t-shirt, Flake: I'm mad as hell and I can't take it anymore!"

"You even looked a bit like Peter Finch in Network with the crazy stare just there. What makes you so mad?"

"You pointed out the Cambridge Analytica scandal already, which was only uncovered two years after the actual incident. It exposed data of some 80 million Facebook users. Wasn't actually a hack but an exploit of a not so well protected service Facebook provides to app partners, which the Cambridge Analytica people took advantage of. Can't even say what I find more alarming: that these

potential leaks can exist for so long, two years, and did not get detected by Facebook but uncovered by external experts. Or the way Facebook senior management dealt with the problem. It needed tens of thousands of individuals to delete their Facebook accounts for Zuckerberg to speak out about it and apologise."

"I'm sure they learned their lessons from that, didn't they?"

"The lesson they learned was about managing public opinion, not about security and privacy. Because, in 2018, another striking incident happened. This time, 50 million user accounts were affected and this time these accounts included those of Mark Zuckerberg himself and that of Sheryl Sandberg, who was his co-CEO at the time. This hack did not just expose user data to the bad guys. The intruders could indeed control the accounts. Imagine that."

"A Taiwanese hacker announced publicly, he would delete Mark Zuckerberg's own account on his very own platform in a live stream, didn't he?"

"How embarrassing is that?"

"Again, folks: This is the guy who wants you to trust him that he's got it all under control. That your data is safe with him. He can't even protect his own user account! On his own platform!"

"Humiliating indeed. To make things even worse: once the attackers got into the profiles, they also had access to services like Spotify, Instagram and hundreds of others that allow to log on via Facebook."

"Yet most alarming is a recognisable pattern of misuse, cover up and ignorance for the law. Already in 2012, the FTC brought on charges against Facebook of misleading or, better yet, clearly lying to the American people about the use of their personal data. They made our friends-lists available to external app developers without even checking on these apps' security measures."

"The FTC was warned the thumb suckers don't play fair?"

"More than once. Right after he settled this allegation with the FTC, what does Zuck do? He does it again. Judge Timothy Kelley, who ruled about this in a District Court, denounced 'the unscrupulous way Facebook violated both the law and the administrative order' and called this 'stunning,' which in court lingo means: outrageously ignorant!"

"So much for Meta. What about the other Silicon Valley masterminds?"

"Where do I start? Let's, maybe, turn to another example of cover up and miscommunication. This one backfired big time. Ride-hailing app Uber had 57 million user accounts breached. But instead of reporting the incident to the

authorities and have it properly investigated, the company paid the attackers one hundred thousand bucks to keep it under wraps. Luckily for the public, this was not the end of it. Word got out and Uber ultimately got fined for this cover up with the biggest data breach fine in history. 148 million for violation of state data breach notification laws. Want to hear more?"

"Keep 'em coming, Martin. Already feel much safer."

"Twitter, as another example, left the passwords of its 330 million users unmasked in a log. For months. Now you may say, Uber and Twitter do not actually have any sensitive information on you and me..."

"Well, Uber at least knows my home address, payment information. Yet something tells me you have more severe cases than that."

"How about your bank? Is that serious enough?"

"It sure is."

"In 2019, Capital One bank suffered a breach that affected 100 million customers in the US and 6 million in Canada."

"Is that the one where the attacker was a former employee of Amazon Web Services? A colleague of yours, if you don't mind me putting it like that?"

"Well, I have never met the guy, but yes, a former AWS security expert conducted this."

"AWS, the guys that now tell us they got it all covered?"

"Exactly. The attacker had obtained personal information of the bank's customers and people who had applied for credit cards. The information stolen included names, addresses, zip codes, phone numbers, email addresses, dates of birth, self-reported income and credit scores, balances, payment history, even social security numbers."

"Did the bank get fined for that?"

"Sure did. Again, the authorities were not happy with the way the firm handled this. They had to pay 80 million dollars in fines."

"The same authorities, which in case of this latest announcement by the guys with the funny name, The Horrible Siliconettes, tell us they are not concerned about it. I want what they are drinking. Don't you?"

"Sure do. But only after we have sincerely looked at this threat and made sure it undoubtedly is under control."

"Fully agree. Why do you think it is the authorities do not seem to care too much?"

"If you ask me, I would say there is way more going on behind the scene than they tell us about. I can't believe the bureau and the NSA are not asking a bunch of questions right now. They just seem to handle this very secretively, not to irritate the public too much until they know more."

"Well, I can tell you firsthand, the agencies have no clue. Even invited yours truly over for a chat yesterday. Quite obviously have no good leads."

"To close it off: What was the biggest ever data loss you can tell us about?"

"How do 3 billion user accounts sound for you?"

"Yes, that will do. What was this all about?"

"This was Yahoo. The bait for the hackers included names, dates of birth, email addresses and passwords, plus security questions and answers. For all of Yahoo's account!"

"Wow. That is massive. Thanks a lot Martin, for these insights."

"You guys out there: As always, I leave you with the quote of the day, this time from Philip K. Dick in A Scanner Darkly: 'Strange how paranoia can link up with reality now and then'."

"Thanks for wasting some of your precious time on my channel. Please consider subscribing or press the like button as your chance to vote for more supervision over the world wide wack. I'm Awkward Andy, your favourite digital boy scout."

***

Unicorn

Zach pulls up his driveway in a frozen-Tulum-blue X7, swerving a rubber unicorn blown across the concrete by a sudden blast. After a shitty day, he feels tempted to run over the rainbow-coloured toy which his younger daughter keeps bringing to the front lawn despite joint parental efforts to restrict use to the pool. Or, even better, run over the guy bumming about in front of his garage, oddly looking like an Amish incarnation of Sheldon Cooper with a black base cap for a Mennonite Stetson.

"You're late," hollers Dutch-bearded Sheldon after Zach as he ignores him on his way to pick up the unicorn. "We said five."

"Get in, before anyone sees you," Zach hisses, entering the pin code at the front door. "It's a nosy neighbourhood."

Zach pulls the plug to wrestle the air out of the unicorn while scanning the area nervously.

"Was your idea to meet at your house," smiles the guest, enjoying the slapstick performance.

"Wasn't gonna drive across town with fifty grand in my trunk."

"Got the cash?"

"Get the fuck inside, damnit."

Zach squeezes the rubber toy through the frame sideways.

"Don't even try giving me shit," the pesterer says, "Benjamins with hidden colour marks, consecutive numbers, or any of that bull."

"There's not gonna be any pay up!" Zach states as firmly as possible, drops the half-collapsed unicorn and stems the fists in his side. He adjusts his stance a few times until the pose feels right.

The racketeer seems more intrigued than irritated.

"Oh," he says, "is that so? Why did I have to come here, then? Did you ask me over to watch you confessing to your wife? That you've been cheating on her for years?"

"Shut the fuck up." Zach adjusts his stance again and kicks the slumped, pitiful unicorn to the side.

"With girls you couldn't even pick up in a bar because of legal drinking age."

"I said shut the fuck up!" Zach takes a firm step forward, yet looks a bit like that determination caught himself by surprise.

"Some had barely two years on your oldest."

The unwelcome guest gives the memories time to blossom.

"By the way, how are the girls?" he grins.

"What kind of twisted freak are you?" Zach hovers two steps backwards.

"I meant your daughters," the intruder beams, "not your fun bunnies."

Zach kicks the unicorn down the hallway. "Last week, you show up here threatening to destroy my home and now you act like you are an old friend of the family? Stop the bullshit, alright! Extortion is off."

"Do I have to remind you what's at stake?"

"I told Karen everything. We will get through this together." Zach straightens himself out.

"That's cute," the intruder smiles.

"You won't have any luck breaking up my family. Wanted to say that straight to your fucking face. Now, get out of my fucking house before my family comes home. Don't want them to bump into you scumbag."

"Zach, buddy, what a bummer!" the intruder practices some dramatic overacting. "I need a drink on that piece of news. We should toast to your new, monogamous life, even?"

He walks past Zach down the hallway. "The other week, you posted something about an amazing tequila you snatched at BevMo?" He points at the doors to his left. "Keep it in the study, don't you?"

Without waiting for a response, the pesterer grabs the deflating toy at his feet by the horn and enters the room he knows from many of Zach's postings unboxing fine spirits. He places the unicorn on top of the massive mahogany desk, drops himself in the leather gamer chair and takes a long look around.

"That's the new painting, isn't it?" he asks. "A Gamez de Fransisco, if I remember rightly? You bragged a bit about it, I must say."

"Get out of my fucking house!" Zach shouts.

"Seems we could both use a drink. There was another post this morning. A little home story. Karen and the girls arriving at her mum's in Santa Barbara to inaugurate your mother-in-law's new pool? Huge pool. Lovely mansion."

Zach looks caught with his pants down. He pours himself a tequila.

"Brave Karen probably went to tell her mum about your infidelity. Am I right? That she is willing to forgive you? Hopes your mother-in-law can forgive you, too? How did the girls take it? Maddy and Emily?"

"One more word about my family and I will kick your teeth in. And get off my fucking chair!"

"Don't be so sensitive, man." The intruder gets up.

"Didn't worry too much about your family when you plugged those girls on your lunch break; or on a detour after work to that Marriot next to the interstate. Did you?"

The host drops himself in his gamer chair.

"Don't tell me you were late to our meeting," the pesterer leans in on him, smirking, "because of a stop-over blow job? Zach, man! Gimme five!"

Zach leaves him hanging. "Spare me your lecture in moral, o.k.! Coming from a guy who makes a living out of blackmailing people."

"Oh, that's just a hobby. My kind of charity. Exposing cheaters like you; teachers with a serious drug problem; medics; policemen. Dangers to society, in my view. Teaching bad people a lesson, basically. A bit like a superhero. Who knows, maybe I even changed a few lives for the better?" The avenger smiles complacently and pours himself a tequila. "Not all that different, if you ask me, from your presidency of the local Rotary club. Or your service in the New Apostolic Church."

"What kind of sick, twisted ethics is that?" Zach gets up. He can't stand his opponent looking down on him. "You fucked up bastard."

"Trying to make the world a better place is never completely selfless, is it?" the intruder continues the lecture. "Sometimes all you get for it is respect; good vibes; sometimes it ups your karma account, sometimes it ups your cash account. We all do it to make us feel better. Don't tell me any different. A guy like you?"

"You know nothing about me!" Zach shouts.

"I beg to differ. In many respects, I obviously know you better than your wife does. Not just your undercover sugar-daddy lifestyle, your love nests, the tacky gifts you buy for the chicks, your favourite candle light dinner spots. I know way more about you than just your screwing around. I know you're a hypocrite. Even worse, you're a phony."

"I won't be lectured by a sociopath. A loser feeding off the success of others. Get out of my house. Payday is off."

"Calm down, man. I get it. Freud said offenders want to get caught. The desire to be punished stems from the same oedipal complex as your wish to sleep around. You really got Mummy issues, my friend."

"Done with your analysis, psycho?" Zach shouts.

"I simply suggest you rethink the consequences. What will these Rotary babbitts say when they find you out? The Betty Whites you spend your church's charity weekends with? Your nosy neighbours? You are about to throw away your entire life. Just because you can't stand a little lecture? You big shot managers always have to be right about everything, can't take any criticism and shit…I get it. But is it really worth it?"

Zach gets so close his opponent's face becomes blurred. "You're not gonna get a penny out of me!" he hisses before slumping back down into the chair. "It's all gonna come out anyway, when that fucking data dump happens in a week's time."

"Ah! That's what your big shot brain worked out. Cut your losses? May need the cash when your life goes down the drain? Ha? Since this lovely house, your lifestyle, your trips to Europe, it is all paid for by your wife's family's money?"

"Get out of my fucking house."

"Your wife's house," his opponent grins. "Tell me: why do you even think there will be a dump? That it's not just a hoax?"

The doomsday-prophet-look on Zach's face irritates the intruder big time. He would love to probe what exactly Zach thinks he knows; yet decides to focus on the job at hand for now. "Okay," he says. "What makes you believe all my intel on you will be in the dump these Siliconettes buggers will release on the world?"

He wipes the unicorn off the desk and sits himself on the top. "Can I get a little respect here, please? I'm a professional data scientist. With an ivy league diploma. It needs sophisticated analytics to derive all that intelligence from the data. It even took a whizz like me quite a while to figure it out."

"What the fuck are you talking about? The data is the data."

"Hell, no. Tinder doesn't sell Zach's cum diary. All I get from them is a nameless profile of a guy sleeping around like there is no tomorrow. It is hard work to re-engineer backwards from that set to find out it is not a hormone overdosed adolescent in his exploratory phase but a married middle-age manager with ego issues. That it is you, Zach!"

"Re-engineer? You don't even have any proof?"

"What Tinder does tell me, is where exactly an unknown cumjunkie used the app. The trail of futility, if you will. You compare that to location histories of tens of thousands of people. Millions, if you have to. Until you find this one person who logged in at the exact same places at the exact same times as the serial Tinderista."

The data whizz gets up and strolls towards the tequila, watching a promiscuous life pass before Zach's cerebral eye.

"How do you..." Zach mumbles, maybe halfway through recapping his extramarital cum count.

"I guess about fifty of the apps on your phone sell your location stats. Candy Crush, Snapchat, Subway Surfer...and you own firm's apps, of course. Fun fact: instead of getting a warrant from a judge to trail a suspect, nowadays the police often just buy that information from a data broker." He unscrews the bottle.

"Put that back!" Zach urges. "Why me?"

The intruder carries the open bottle and two glasses over to the desk. "Not just you Zach. You Valley folks always think you are so special...you are not. Fifteen percent of women and twenty-five percent of men cheat on their partner.

91

A lot of them leave a trail of infidelity on Tinder or Grindr. My AI models can tell potential offenders from their mug shots. Point out all candidates with a tendency to moral indifference."

He pours two drinks.

"Fun fact," he adds, "the software identified ten percent of congress members as potential white-collar criminals…cool, isn't it?"

"You have a sick sense of humour!" Zach says, making a mental note to check this feature with the AI team.

"Look at it this way: your generous investment tonight will help fund my startup. This is the next big thing. Once I ironed out some kinks."

The intruder raises his glass and extends a toast towards the sad remains of the unicorn on the carpet before he turns his attention back to Zach. "All that was left to do was to verify whether a match was useful."

"Commercially exploitable, you mean?" Zach asks, half disgust, half impressed.

"Plus: something to lose. Yes," the whizz says. "When I looked at the happy family pictures, house in Atherton, your community service and all of that, I knew I had a winner."

"You stalked me?" Zach downs the drink.

"Virtually. Your firm's platform is the ideal source for that check. Couldn't be doing my job if it wasn't for you guys." He raises his glass.

This is the second time today someone tells Zach his company sucks, and it pisses him off, yet he forces himself to focus on his imminent problem. "Could all just be a coincidence, couldn't it?" he asks. "Me being in the same places as some other guy using Tinder?"

"Well, you didn't seem to close the app ever…the match was pretty telling. But you're right, it could just be a coincidence. There is no footage of you and luscious Lizzy in bed at the Marriot. I'm not a detective. I'm a data analyst."

"You mean a fucking hacker!"

"No need to hack anyone for this. All completely legit. Anyone can buy the sources."

"Any doofus with a bit of compute power can do this once the Big One is out?"

"If you want to take your chances on it, be my guest," the data scientist says, more than a little pricked for the lack of appreciation. "The others are all paying up."

Zach gets up, grabbing the half empty bottle.

"At best, they are buying some time, from what you are telling me. Only a few days, even."

"Is time not the most valuable asset in life?"

"Fifty grand is way too much." Zach pours himself another drink. "Anyway, how do I know you won't come back for more?"

"I actually think my ask was very moderate. Looking at your friends, your colleagues, your acquaintances…trust me, I have some experience in this…the things you have done will not go down well with them." The intruder begins wandering about. "What will they say about you banging that teen slut in a trailer park while you and your wife were on a weekend trip to Vegas? Well, you knew your way around the Strip from all those business trips. You were almost steady with that girl. All the money you spend on her, one would think, she could have moved out of that trailer."

The intruder strolls back towards Zach, giving the unicorn corps a little kick on the way. "Or my favourite: when you hooked up with those twins while spending a week with your family at a beach resort in Cancun. I hand it to you, leaving your wife arguing with the kids over a coke at the pool while you enjoyed happy hour in the twin's bungalow…that's audacity."

Zach appreciated the long-winded bill of indictment because he needed time to think this through. These pretentious ROXANE buggers cornered him this morning. It won't happen to him twice in one day.

"Okay, look," he says. "I give you ten grand and never see you again. Final offer. Turn away." Zach approaches the vault fixed in a bookshelf next to his desk.

"I'm not here to bargain," the intruder says. "Lousy ten grand I can get off your colleague Nate anytime. For telling him how to secure his promotion, tripping the competition. By the way, if you put ten grand on top…can do the same for you. Nate is a by-catch, really. Not enough to get him fired or ruin his life any other way, but enough for you to work with, if you play your cards right. You see, I have done my homework."

The racketeer seems happy with his extortion upsell pitch.

Instead of cash, Zach produces a handgun from the vault.

"Won't get any money," he says. "But you get to choose: Can turn you over to the police. Or you get out of my fucking house and my fucking life right now, you scumbag! Don't show up here ever again."

Zach enjoys a hint of panic in the intruder's eyes.

Just as his opponent seems to regain his composure, Zach presents his second surprise. "I've also done my homework, Elijah!" he says.

The intruder's face fades to a blueish shade of pale.

"Yes, that's right," Zach continues. "I know a lot about you as well, Elijah Miller. 28-year-old Harvard dropout; founded various startups over the years; all of them failures. Went bust even, a few years ago, right after the IPO with a firm trying to predict share prices via deep learning algorithms." Zach enjoys his opponent's empty gaze.

"Don't need deep learning skills to predict your share price would tank," he continues. "You're a loser, trying to rip off the winners. But you messed with the wrong guy, buddy."

Miller's baffled face shows him brooding about how his victim found him out.

"You'd be amazed," Zach triumphs, "at how well face recognition works. Despite the fake beard; that ridiculous wig. Our wizzes know a trick or two as well."

He points at an innocuous hole in the cupboard, the size of a penny. "Cams; all over the house. Was quite easy to find your timeline in our database."

"You won't shoot." Miller's organic neuronal network determined a ninety-five percent likelihood for this hypothesis. "Better put the gun down before anyone gets hurt by chance."

"Last call!" Zach readjusts his aim.

"You wondered," Miller says, "if I would come back for more."

"A pinscher like you will not let go."

"Well, now that you threatened me…How do I know you won't call the cops the second I'm out the door?"

Zach's forehead wrinkles; his left eyebrow starts twitching.

"Guess that means," Miller continues, "have to disappear completely. Start over. I'd say the price for your peace of mind just went up."

"Get the fuck out!" Zach shouts, pointing the weapon straight at the intruder's forehead.

"Had the first gun in my face in grade school over my lunch money." Miller puts on an arrogant smirk.

"Bullshit!"

"Take it from me," Miller lectures. "If you want to scare off a guy with your cute little girly gun, you have to make it sound like you'd love to shoot the man but graciously grant him a chance to get out." Miller tries to look straight outta Compton. "Yet you're shitting your pants, hoping I'd bail, so you don't have to make the tough choices."

A legit thug would probably jump at the gun at this point, as Zach's mind is trapped in an infinite loop for seconds as endless as silence on the radio.

Instead, Miller says: "There's a lot of cash in that vault of yours."

Zach unlocks the gun.

"Come on man," Miller grins, "you played tennis in your posh college. You're not going to shoot anyone. Don't make a fool of yourself."

"Try me."

"I do character scores on my business partners. You are Briggs-Myers Type ESFP, the performer," Miller says, as if this was the punchline to a joke.

"You will be aware then," Zach replies with no hint of a smile, "this means I am a protector of my family."

"How will you explain a corps of an unarmed man in your study to the cops? Killed with a weapon registered to you?"

"Oh, that's easy. Caught you breaking into my house. Smashed in a window in the back. How could I have known if you carry a gun or not?"

The opponents play a round of mental Mikado.

"You really believe I came unprepared?" Miller asks. "All my intel on you will go out in a bulk post to the police, your family, friends, and the entire neighbourhood if I don't return safely."

"Don't think so." Zach smiles. "The profiling I had our experts do on you tells me differently. You're a cocky bastard from Bakersfield who believes he's smarter than the rest and deserves to get what he wants; because you think you're special. You are the kind of guy who doesn't think he needs a backup."

"Takes one to know one, I guess."

You can virtually hear Charles Bronson play the harmonica while the opponents try to read each other's minds.

"You know what?" Miller asks. "I'm gonna get me a hundred grand from that vault of yours now. Don't even have to give it to me." He steps forward, staring hard into Zach's twitching eye.

"Sure as hell you won't!" Zach puts the gun on Miller's chest and tries pushing him backwards. Instead, Miller takes another step forward, forcing Zach to retreat. And another one. Neither man blinks.

"Put it down," Miller says. "You are a phony even when playing tough."

Cornered Zach hastily hovers two steps back to get away from Miller, trips over the rubber unicorn in his path, glimpses down at the flattened toy, keeps stumbling, looks back up, spots Miller going for the gun and tries to pull it out of his reach. A shot is fired.

Miller looks startled, disbelieving, peers down on the rapidly spreading stain on his chest, squints back up at Zach's horrified face, drops to his knees and falls over sideways.

The smoking gun slides out of Zach's trembling hand in slow motion; he stares blankly at Miller's motionless body framed by an ever-spreading poodle of blood.

The shooter slumps down as if his plug got pulled and all energy leaves his body.

***

Metropolis

"You actually know every line of dialogue, don't you?" Flake beams at Leeza as they step out of Stanford Theatre's neoclassical lobby into the gold-plated evening.

"Watched it for the first time during an 80s revival week on HBO," Leeza says with the same blissful gaze she displayed pretty much ever since she lip-synced Ferris' opening monologue to Sigue Sputnik. "Must have been like sixteen. Some friends and I have a sleepover once a year to watch it."

"Ah! Pyjama party. Great!" Flake winks.

He notices a well-known Nissan across the street; he resists the temptation to go chat up the passengers, not to risk his date's excellent mood.

"This Metropolis tee is my favourite night dress, you know?" he says, pulling Leeza into a backstreet alley.

"I just realise…" she says, "don't think I have ever watched this movie with a guy before. Me and my girls had a major crush on Mr Broderick."

"Oops. Pretty boy pitfall again? Like with Brad Pitt? I thought with Ferris it was more about the cool than the looks?"

"The girls and I thought he was really cute."

Flake drags his feet.

"No need to worry, though. I have outgrown that crush."

"That's encouraging."

"Besides, he outgrew his pretty phase quickly as well."

"Whatchumean?"

"A lot of boys are cute before twenty. Yet, most of the handsome heartthrobs in my high school…when you meet these guys a couple of years later, the boys that all girls had a crush on…once they turned thirty, most of them look average at best. Think Ryan Phillippe. Sexiest sociopath ever in Cruel Intentions. At thirty…? Or Val Kilmer."

"Or that colleague of yours? What's his name again?" Flake regrets the lame attempt to find out if there ever were any vibes between the two right after it came out in a very wrong way. For all he knows about girl's taste in guys, Tim is prime beef. In a smug way, though, like most dudes with a pop star level scoring record.

Leeza is courteous enough not to dwell on it. "Beauty is a bitch," she says. "Often turns to the next guy. Some guys who did not turn many heads in high school grow into foxes only in their late thirties."

"Case in point?"

"George Clooney. Didn't exactly jump out of his yearbook. With greying temples: badaboom. Sexiest man alive. Patrick Dempsey is another one."

"There is hope?"

"At least, you boys have hope. Us girls…it's only downhill from twenty…"

"Wow. Puts a lot of pressure on our relationship."

"Why is that?"

"You just said, chances are that your ravishing beauty will crackle and fade within the next few years, while this pupated caterpillar may turn into a colourful butterfly that sits on the withered rose, wondering where to flutter next."

"That's the kind of guy you are, eh?"

"A modern-day Walt Whitman?"

"More yesterday's Tiger Woods?"

"Well, you know…"

"What if you don't turn into a beautiful butterfly?" Leeza gives him the most adorable wink ever.

"Let's examine that over dinner. Why don't you show me the best Korean joint in town? My treat, of course."

"Not sure you are ready for authentic kimchi just yet," she smiles. "There is a decent Japanese place just a few blocks away. Up for sushi and a little walk?"

The couple strolls down a busy boulevard, the setting sun lighting the bustling scenery in a hundred hues of smouldering orange. It's a constant coming and going in bars and restaurants as the early dinner crowd hands the shift to the party people. A few late shoppers rush brand bags along.

"You got me thinking," Leeza breaks the serene silence.

"Is that a good or a bad thing?" Flake grins. "Look, if it's about the butterfly…"

"Did you ever read *Runaway Jury*?" Leeza asks in an oddly serious tone.

"Grisham. Sure did. He likes conspiracies, and so do I."

"Few weeks ago, when I looked for stuff to sell on the charity flea market, I came across my old copy of that book."

"Like a physical copy? From back when they still printed these things on tons of paper?"

"Yep. A hardcover paper copy."

"Do you know how to operate these things even? Which buttons to press?"

"Since we only read Mangas in Asia? Which we operate from back to front?" Leeza feigns a little indignation.

"How culturally insensitive of me," Flake smiles. "Hope you can forgive my micro-aggression. I'm well aware you call it Manhwa in Korea, though. Binged all volumes of Solo Levelling in one weekend. Left to right."

"I like paper copies," Leeza says with a wistful voice, as if she is mourning a runaway cat.

"Well, isn't that cultural appropriation on your part, then?"

"What do you mean?"

"Is it okay for you to adopt sentimental attachment to an element of the culture of the elderly? Like paper copy books? Are you not exploiting the attainments of senior citizens?"

"Can you never stop making fun of my convictions?" Leeza smiles ever so slightly. "Besides, that's not my point. When I recovered the book from the basement, I recalled how much it had bothered me. Couldn't really tell why, though. Started reading it again last night. And you know what?"

"Tell me."

"This time, it outright scared me. Remember when they pick the jury for the high-profile trial? The opposing sides seeking the soft spots of the candidates to single out those jurors they assume would follow their pleas?"

"The defence attorney plays dirty. Does all that spy work on potential jury members; studying their habits, investigating their past, keeping them under surveillance, secretly taking pictures…to pick the ones they can manipulate best during the trial."

"Totally blew my mind when I realised…we wouldn't need to do that anymore…"

"Mic and his gang just run a quick script on your files and it is all there? The perfect character scans for your case! How to play the jury. How to best manipulate to swing them your way. All of that?"

"Don't get me wrong. This is not what we do…"

"Know what you mean…Mic and the guys just want to play with their cool tools. Explore what tech can do. Like the two Steves in their garage assembling the Apple I. Just this time, the boys in their geeky Woz-mos don't realise evil forces use their gimmicks in nasty ways."

"I love what we create. The internet, what you can do with it, I believe, is the single greatest invention ever. Bigger than electricity. Bigger than the moonshot. It's just…I don't know…"

Flake would like nothing more right now than to reignite Leeza's infectious enthusiasm. "Did you know," he says, "that when they launched Apollo 11 to take Armstrong and his crew to the moon, they had no idea how to get them back to earth safely."

"You're kidding!"

"It's true. They were just sure they would figure it out somehow before they would need it."

"And they did."

"Many things on this trip were just luck. They were lucky nobody died. That we ended up a nation of great visionaries and not a bunch of Sci-Fi lunatics ridiculed by the rest of the world."

"That's amazing."

"The internet is just like that, in a sense. You were right the other day. It's still an experiment. A lot of it is a trial. We have no idea how we get out of this without casualties. How to put the trolls back into pandora's box. Hate, fakespeak, propaganda, manipulation...all of that negative energy...back into the box."

"Speaking of box: Bento Box, anyone?" Leeza points at the tiny restaurant across the street. "This is the place I was talking about."

Busy watching the brooding lines on Leeza's forehead fading as he chats away her worries, Flake fails to notice the Dodge with a batterie of searchlights second in line in waiting traffic as he and Leeza cross the street. The GOAT, however, doesn't notice the couple because he is busy texting with the Tinder match he's late to meet. As the stoplight turns to green, the quarterback continues his ride into the setting sun, unfazed by a missed chance for revenge.

***

Cheats and Addicts

"Welcome back to the show. I'm your host, my name is Jon Stewart, and my first guest tonight is the best-selling author of 'Fakebook – we are all cheats and addicts'. Please welcome...Wolf Krysztal."

Jon: "Good to see you, Wolf. Welcome to the show. Have a seat."

Wolf: "Great to be here. Thanks for having me."

Jon: "Wolf. You have an extremely busy schedule these days. Every program wants to have you on. Thanks for taking the time to stop by our little show."

Wolf: "Very kind of you to have me."

Jon: "No honestly. You are a hard man to get these days. Your book, 'Fakebook – we are all cheats and addicts,' sells like crazy and you seem to appear on all channels all the time."

Wolf: "Well, of course it is great when audiences want to hear what you have to say. That was not always the case. I'll enjoy it while it lasts."

Jon: "You don't think it's just the cover?"

Wolf: "The cover of the book? You like the cover?"

Jon: "I have a copy of it here. There is this icon on the cover that resembles the like button, but instead of a thumbs up, it gives you the finger. And then there is the title, that reminds of a rather popular social network."

Wolf: "I refer to them as anti-social networks. Anyway, I hope it is not just the cover."

Jon: "Don't get me wrong. I think it is very thought provoking. Tell me, could it be possible, though, part of the reason for the tremendous success of your book is that it launched right when these Horrible Siliconettes, THS as people call them now, announced they will disclose all data people have entrusted to social media platforms. I guess I don't have to sound a spoiler alert when I give away that your work is rather critical of social media."

Wolf: "You have a highly educated audience, Jon. They might have inferred that already."

Jon: "Would you agree the announcement of the Big One has boosted sales of you book significantly?"

Wolf: "Absolutely."

Jon: "This show is known for its investigative journalism…"

Wolf: "Oh, is it…?"

Jon: "It certainly is. We have a name for relentlessly digging up the dirt. Tell us, Wolf, is there a connection between you and THS?"

Wolf: "What do you mean by connection?"

Jon: "Don't you find it suspicious that your book's publishing date coincides with the announcement proving all the scepticisms and doomsday scenarios correct you outline in your book? We here, at this show, find this very suspicious."

Wolf: "As investigative reporters that you are?"

Jon: "Absolutely. Why don't you use this opportunity to come clean and tell the American people the truth?"

Wolf: "Okay, can't take the pressure any longer. I admit, I am the Siliconettes. I have issued this announcement to promote my book. And tell you what? It worked."

Jon: "Well done. That revelation should certainly boost our ratings as well now."

Wolf: "I'm sure it will."

Jon: "Instead of appearing on USA Today and The Tonight Show some interviews you will be invited to in the next few days might be hosted by the NSA or FBI, though, don't you think?"

Wolf: "Suppose they will just look at a rerun of your show. Since you will have dug up all the dirt already."

Jon: "You're right, you're right. Now that we got this settled…."

Wolf: "Always good to address the elephant in the room right away."

Jon: "…let's get started with our relentless interrogation. I already mentioned, you are extremely critical of social media. You go as far as to say, social media, and many other activities on the internet, should be classified as prescription drugs. What do you mean by that?"

Wolf: "These services are addictive. It is like gambling. You can't stop. They get created and configured to hook you on to them. Almost like a drug you need, otherwise you start to tremble, high blood pressure; same symptoms as with the prohibition of other addictive substances. Have you seen how teenagers react when you take their smartphone away from them?"

Jon: "Oh, yeah! When I grounded my son once and confiscated his smartphone, thus denying him the ability to react to every incoming message instantly…I know what you mean. That looked like turkey for sure. Major family crisis."

Wolf: "They create this sense of urgency for every update. This fear of missing out. It is truly addictive."

Jon: "Many people argue, though, that these services enrich people's lives. You don't seem to agree to that."

Wolf: "Angel dust makes you happy! The poison is in the dosage. You have to limit the exposure."

Jon: "You also state in your book, that social media makes us all less honest. You call us cheats, actually. Why do you say that?"

Wolf: "Have you ever taken a closer look at all these posts people put on social media? It is absurd theatrical exhibitionism. It is pretend. Instead of actually living their lives people spend their time curating their social media profiles; as if the purpose of life is to curate an exposition of entertaining encounters; of affection artifacts."

Jon: "What exactly do you mean by that?"

Wolf: "It is like Stepford Women on digital steroids. Everybody pretends to be perfect, all the time. People pretend to live perfect lives. High fashion Barbie-dolls, surrounded only by other beautiful people. Leading exciting lives in perfect homes with perfect families. Going on perfect holidays. Having a great time 24/7. It is all just a shallow, duck-faced facade."

Jon: "Don't you think this is an appropriate representation of the American society? It is the land of milk and honey, mind you. God's own country."

Wolf: "Psychologists say it is unhealthy if what you are, what you think you are and what others think about you divert too far apart. I think social media promotes this diversion way too much."

Jon: "People are lying on social media?"

Wolf: "Most people are not good at lying. They are not happy with it. Most people have a problem when they know they are lying."

Jon: "You still call us cheats?"

Wolf: "Well, we all need to create some attention. That's also true if you want to promote a book."

Jon: "So you don't really mean that?"

Wolf: "People are not comfortable lying. What they do is they start believing the image they have created. They create this perfect facade, they share it with the world, but they also look at it themselves and at some point, they take it for their actual life. That is why it is so dangerous."

Jon: "Should this be what people want to believe? Why is that dangerous in your view?"

Wolf: "You see, there is no such thing as an objective memory. This one initial file that is written to your hard drive when an event happens only exists temporarily."

Jon: "The brain does not work like a computer?"

Wolf: "It doesn't, no. On a computer, you can load the file as often as you like. It doesn't change just by looking at it."

Jon: "In your brain it does?"

Wolf: "Every time you pull up a file, you remember an event, you change it. The file you write back to the drive is different. And it overwrites the original file."

Jon: "So the next time you pull it up, it is already altered?"

Wolf: "Sometimes it just lost some detail. But you can just as well idealise your memories. You just write back a prettier version of your event to your hard drive."

Jon: "Especially with a prettier version of me in it, you mean?"

Wolf: "For example, yes! This is also how we block out a trauma, by the way. This mechanism is there for a good reason. We do not just delete complete files, like most people think. We also change files to overwrite the traumatising parts in it and keep the good bits. Or add some new good bits we just make up. We overcome a trauma by altering our memory."

Jon: "That is why my uncle Greg keeps telling the same old marlin fishing stories over and over?"

Wolf: "I bet you he became more heroic every time he told it, didn't he?"

Jon: "Spot on! By now he's somewhere between Santiago from Old man and the sea and Ahab in Moby Dick. You say this happens with social media as well?"

Wolf: "It seems to me this is what it was created for. Or at least why it is so popular. Because it helps us pretty up our memories."

Jon: "Why is that not a good thing?"

Wolf: "If I look at selfies people post on Instagram, I can see the insecurities behind the pose. The self-doubt of the ugly duckling behind the duck face. This diversion between image and reality grows in people. It is like a cancer."

Jon: "Where does this lead, you think?"

Wolf: "What remains, if you do away with all the clichés that people stage in their curated catalogue of their lives? Which is most often obviously wishful thinking rather than reality. Or, more benignly: ambition rather than virtuality? I will tell you what remains: sanctimony, hypocrisy, mendacity."

Jon: "That is a pretty harsh description, don't you think?"

Wolf: "Well, might be. You know what is best about it? It doesn't even make sense. We all know life is not a permanent streak of happiness and love. Don't we? So why would we ever believe this lie?"

Jon: "Because we want to believe it is possible?"

Wolf: "Yet it isn't! For most of us, at least."

Jon: "Know what you mean, though! Did you ever notice that most of the songs you play on a romantic night, the songs you slow dance to with your date to get to first base, did you notice these songs are mostly not about love? They're not. On the contrary. Most of them are about being left, bygone love, loss, that sort of thing."

Wolf: "It that true? Haven't noticed that."

Jon: "I bet everybody in this audience has scored at least once to *In The Air Tonight*. Did you listen to it? It is about letting a person die out of jealousy."

Wolf: "Wow. OK! You are right…It works, though!"

Jon: "It does, doesn't it? Becky Albright in ninth grade…sweet…Want another one?"

Wolf: "Sure."

Jon: *Tears in heaven* by Eric Clapton? It's about the loss of his four-year-old son! *Bright Eyes*, Art Garfunkel? The bright light that turns pale? R.E.M.? 'The one I love'? Should better be called 'The one I left'."

Wolf: "I get your point. My favourite smooching background song: *Everybody Hurts*. It is even in the title. Yet R.E.M. is always kind of depressive, right?"

Jon: "Springsteen. *The River*. Very sad story. *Total Eclipse of The Heart*, Bonnie Tyler? '*Once upon a time there was light in my life, now there is only loving in the dark'. Time After Time*, Cindy Lauper? A bit of a twisted love song. Not really a happy case. The Rose, Bette Midler. The list goes on and on."

Wolf: "I remember the tear running down Sinead O'Connor's face in the clip for *Nothing Compares 2U*. Obviously not a cheerful story. But one of the most romantic songs ever."

Jon: "Absolutely. Even arguably the greatest love song of all time, Whitney's *I Will Always Love You* is actually about losing someone."

Wolf: "The simple truth is: art does not flourish from happiness. It flourishes from pain."

Jon: "You might be right on this one. Even though I probably shouldn't say this in a comedy show."

Wolf: "This dominates people's lives: sorrows, enviousness, distress. Trying to hide this all away does not improve our lives. And why would we? It is pathetic."

Jon: "People should watch more comedy shows when they want to cheer themselves up? Not exercise online self-hypnosis?"

Wolf: "Can't overdose comedy. Yet to cheat yourself doesn't improve your life. That's why I talked about sanctimony. These other emotions are there. And I believe you can see it in the snapshots people post."

Jon: "You say you can actually see the gap between what a picture is supposed to show and the reality?"

Wolf: "Yes. Just that most of us have lost those senses. If you want to be poetic, you might say the eye is the mirror of the soul. I think it is more profane than that. I can see it. It is there. Even in photographs."

Jon: "You will have to explain that a little more."

Wolf: "You know the effect of red dots in people's eyes when the camera flash is reflected by the retina at the wrong split of a second, just as the shutter clicks?"

Jon: "My phone has a feature to make sure this doesn't happen."

Wolf: "Are you aware that certain eye deficiencies, such as the Coats disease, will cause a white reflection in the eye instead of a red one? Most people could not tell that there was something wrong with a Coats patient. Yet the affected eye is most likely almost blind. It is not easily detected. Children developing that disease often do not even notice it, since the second eye covers for most of the deficiency. But it is there. And you can see it in a photograph."

Jon: "Okay?"

Wolf: "We have just lost the senses to see it."

Jon: "Being the investigative journalists that we are…"

Wolf: "…who just made the scoop to uncover the true identity of THS!"

Jon: "Absolutely! As investigative journalists, we wanted to get to the bottom of this. Find out if it is true. We have designed a highly sophisticated test. What do you say?"

Wolf: "You want to test me?"

Jon: "We will show you a few randomly chosen pictures from social media accounts and find out if you can actually look behind the facade. That is what you claimed, right?"

Wolf: "Let's try this out."

Jon: "Ready for the first picture?"

Wolf: "Bring it on."

Jon: "Here is our first picture. Family of four. Mother, father, two boys, maybe age 10 and 15? Dressed for the occasion, perhaps the shoot for the official family Christmas greeting card. Very nice picture on first glance, wouldn't you agree?"

Wolf: "Very nice indeed."

Jon: "All smiling, not too broadly, just right for the occasion. Christmas has a serious background, mind you; might send the greeting card off to a rather extended list of acquaintances. Family looks happy, I'd say."

Wolf: "I see a father who desperately wants this shot to portrait the loving family he always aspired to, yet fails to achieve day after day. Because after a long day of work in a classically burn out prone line of business, he cannot muster up the needed patience. Patience for the imperative guidance to teenagers; even though he really tries."

Jon: "Can you be a little more specific? What in this picture tells you that?"

Wolf: "Look at his eyes. From the corner of his eyes, the guy checks if everybody smiles, looks happy, poses the right way. He desperately needs this picture to be perfect. So that he can look at it and pretend for another while that everything is fine. More importantly: that all their friends will think so. Yet you can see the desperation. Suppose this is attempt number ten or more to get this right. His own smile is well practiced but still feigned."

Jon: "Should you be watching this, Sir, this is just Wolf Krysztal's personal opinion."

Wolf: "I see a mother who hates to be photographed. Who never thought well of her own talents. Even though these talents of empathy and selfless caring are the ones that truly count yet usually go unrewarded, financially and emotionally. You can see the insecurity in her gaze. She hates to be photographed because she knows her way to compensate for the mental exhaustion of balancing out all those strong family egos is a lack of dietary discipline."

Jon: "That was more on the positive side. I hope this was okay, Ma'am?"

Wolf: "You can even see that she hates her own fake smile. She smiles, but she scorns to be putting it on. She knows she will see it on the final shot and she thinks everybody else will see it, too, and she feels bad about it already now."

Jon: "Wow. That is complicated. Are we also so complicated?"

Wolf: "The more self-reflected among us, yes!"

Jon: "What about the boys?"

Wolf: "The older kid hates the insincere family protocol and only plays along because the price for disobedience is just too high. He probably already crushed the first nine attempts to get the shot done, though. Just to have his opposition on file. Usually, he embraces every opportunity to document his staged life; he just wishes this could be arranged in a more presentable, much cooler fashion. The younger boy actually likes the ritual but detests his sibling for scorning it, yet keeping up the facade so shamelessly."

Jon: "That was picture number one. Here comes picture number two. A selfie of son and Dad frolicking about. Quality time, you think, don't you?"

Wolf: "Well, I see a ten-year-old who imitates social media genre poses because he learned nothing else. Even though he has not yet figured out how this all is actually supposed to make you feel more accepted in this world. Second, he plays along because he knows it will help him in the negotiations for more Wi-Fi time later, which he needs to continue above quest."

Jon: "That sounds familiar."

Wolf: "I see a father whose resigned smile poses as tranquillity, because he has learned to accept that the emotional energy in his batteries will always only suffice to contain the most important crisis of the day. That, for quite a long while, he will not be able to recharge enough to aim for anything more, even though his mind keeps offering him all the great options life could hold."

Jon: "Here comes picture number three. A selfie of two best friends posing in sexy dresses at a rooftop bar above a nightly skyline. The perfect setting for a perfect night for beautiful young people enjoying life and friendship. What do you see, Wolf?"

Wolf: "I see two girls who are never in the moment, but always only in the picture. Who spend more time to upload the evidence than to take in the smells and sounds, the tastes and touches, actually. When you take away their smartphones, they may not even remember the night. I see the girl holding the camera, who knows that every guy receiving this post will want to be there with her in that rooftop bar. And her BFF in the back, she knows it as well and hates her friend for it; and herself for feeling like this."

Jon: "You can see all this in these pictures?"

Wolf: "The internet is full of these documents of self-hate and self-delusion, genre clichés and bad acting."

Jon: "Maybe there should be something like the Golden Raspberry Award for the worst performance in social media self-exposure?"

Wolf: "Sounds like an excellent idea, Jon."

Jon: "How would you respond, Wolf, should I tell you our highly sophisticated set up works more like a Rorschach test?"

Wolf: "You mean the test where a psychiatrist shows his patients pictures of splodges and asks them what they see in them?"

Jon: "Exactly. The picture in a Rorschach test is irrelevant. What you see in it, though, tells the psychiatrist a lot about the patient's state of mind."

Wolf: "Well, interesting thought. I'd say we will find out in a few years whether I am right."

Jon: "And how is that?"

Wolf: "One day, in a not-so-distant future, neuronal networks in artificial intelligence will have perfected today's flawed face recognition. They will do psychological face diagnostics. Some machine will spit out all the proof points for all the mendacities in our posts."

Jon: "Sounds like another doomsday scenario."

Wolf: "Maybe more like a catharsis. An Israeli startup, Faception, already claims it can detect terrorists and paedophiles just by analysing your passport picture and scanning social media. From decades of timelines, this machine will confront us with all the snapshot posts of couples on which the seeds of doom for the relationship were visible way before their community witnessed the hate. The machine will pinpoint all the jolly selfies of BFFs on which envy, ill will, and jealousy are hidden. This machine will mill its way through the internet and stamp-mark all posts it finds that display any kind of deception."

Jon: "For every pic the machine finds, they'll subtract points from your social score? You really are sceptical about social media. Is there a silver lining on the horizon?"

Wolf: "Of course. But to know how this can all end well, I'm afraid, you will have to buy the book."

Jon: "Wolf Krysztal, folks, author of 'Fakebook – we are all cheats and addicts?' in books stores right now. When we come back, my guest will be Timothée Chalamet, leading man in Dorian Gray, premiering on Broadway this weekend, and another good reason to talk more about the Big One, if you catch my drift…"

***

Big One Minus 5, Wednesday

#DontDoxxMyDudes

"This is NOYB TV. Hardly anything has been talked about more in recent days than what we, here in the Valley, now call 'The Big One'. Many folks still believe it's a hoax, making fun of this in social media. Creativity runs wild. Under #HereComesTheBigOne people share alleged snapshots, mostly deep fakes, as far as we know, of male celebrities' private parts. Many of them not all that big. A rather blurred snapshot of a huge Johnson allegedly belonging to Timothée Chalamet leads the share-and-like lists, with millions and millions of clicks every day, closely trailed by a rather tiny specimen allegedly attributed to Justin Bieber. Both gentlemen had their management deny the authenticity of the photographs."

"Others take this matter very seriously. Recent polls suggest almost forty percent of people think the Big One will go ahead. A growing number of people also state they expect it to affect them personally. Fifty percent are concerned or very concerned about this whole matter."

"Someone who takes this extremely seriously is a 32-year-old senior product manager who works for one of the tech giants here in Silicon Valley. He kicked off a campaign yesterday that goes by the hashtag DontDoxxMyDudes and went viral within just a few hours."

"In this campaign, the product manager, his name is Tim Rozen, calls for his colleagues in the Big Tech firms and in the rest of corporate America to push their management to come clean regarding what they really know about a potential data exposure."

"I am connected now with Tim Rozen, live in Palo Alto. Tim, why do you do this and what are you trying to achieve?"

"First, let me say thank you for having me and for the opportunity to point out to your viewers why this is important. After the proclamation by THS, many of my colleagues have approached our senior management for answers. We expected a thorough analysis of potential breaches to be conducted; investigations. Yet, nothing happened. Our management evaded the questions. I

talked to the community. To friends who work for other companies here in the Valley. Guess what? It was the same all over. All we got was placations like we hear them from the government as well. That is just not good enough."

"You don't trust in the official version? It seems like you are very concerned about this Big One and what it could reveal?"

"You know, those of us who work here in the Valley, we all believe we make great products. All of us are proud of what we do. We feel we have a positive impact on people's lives. We love what we do. People put a lot of faith in us, entrust us with a lot of very private information about them. They open a door to their lives on our platforms. That gives us great responsibility in my view."

"What, in particular, are you concerned about?"

"First and foremost, we do not perceive right now that our senior management takes this responsibility seriously enough. Is transparent enough about it. Only with transparency we will sustain people's trust. You know, I work on our messaging products. Of course, I have an idea what we do in the rest of the company, with posts and timelines and all that. Yet, even I do not know all the pieces we assemble across our platforms. How complete a picture of an individual we can compile?"

"You think people should know?"

"The critics say we trick or even force people into allowing us to use their data. And that we exploit it in some mean way. I don't think this is what we try to do. It's certainly not what I try to do! And all the people around me who work extremely hard to create value for the community every day. I would go as far as to say this is not what we do as a company. And I believe we have to be straightforward with our community. Otherwise, users will stop trusting us."

"What specifically is it you seek to accomplish with your campaign, Tim? It goes by #DontDoxxMyDudes. Tell us what that means."

"I want people to go to their management and demand answers to the hard questions. How can we be sure the information our companies have on people is safe? What is it we collect? What is it we do with what we collect? Who do we give it to? And how do we know those we give it to keep it safe as well? I want people to ask management these questions and share what they find out."

"A very valid concern, I would say."

"We should not fear these challenges. We should be prepared to sit with our users and spell out to them exactly what is happening. If our services are as

valuable as we claim, and I honestly think they are, the community will appreciate what we do and trust us."

"You want to push firms in the Valley for higher transparency in this matter?"

"Not just the Valley. All of corporate America needs to think about this. But we, and I explicitly include our brothers and sisters in the northern outpost around Seattle, the sector usually labelled Big Tech, have been particularly in the public eye regarding our treatment of personal data. When something like the Big One happens, people are looking at us. We need to set the example."

"You are a brave man, Tim, and I wish to thank you on behalf of us, the users. I could imagine, though, your bosses will not be happy you associated the Big One and Big Tech in the same sentence just there."

"To be precise, it was two sentences. People are doing it, anyway. Let's not kid ourselves. Just duck and cover will not be good enough here."

"Duck and cover? People used that phrase in the 50s to educate folks on what to do in case of an attack with a nuclear bomb. Very naïve propaganda videos. Did you use this analogy to point out the naïvety of the industry? Or is this supposed to associate the Big One with a drop of an atomic bomb? Do you feel it is that serious?"

"I don't wanna to make inappropriate comparisons; that is not what I meant. I was referring to a crisis response. We must be conscious there may even be lives at stake. Maybe not here. But you may recall the Arab Spring a few years back. People in the Arabic region had risen against their oppressors. These activists used our platforms to organise rallies and distribute information. Or look at what is going on in Hong Kong today. The opposition there. To expose these people, their communication, their network of contacts, all of that. This could, no, this would most certainly endanger their lives. This is what we need to acknowledge; what our crisis response must consider. If we fail these people, we may lose the trust of our users. Losing that trust could, over time, mean the end of our industry as we know it. And let me repeat: As we love it today!"

***

Icarus

The crooked old trees behind the central campus library seem a bit tired from many years of service, providing much needed shade in the eternal Californian summer to the patrons of the busy campus café pavilion. The student crowd is all the livelier, though; a dizzying sound cloud of chatter and Spotified tunes makes it merely hopeless to focus on any studies unless shielded in isolation by a set of headphones.

After reading in Mao Zedong's biography that the Great Chairman had practiced his ability to focus his mind by doing his studies in busiest traffic on the largest crossing in all of Beijing, Flake had tried that for a few weeks on Massachusetts Avenue during rush hour. Yet he had failed miserably. Listening to his special Trent Reznor instrumental playlist with a pilot-sized headset, however, will get him productive even in a stampede.

Leeza makes her way through hundreds of anarchically dropped bicycles, jamming the campus walkways, and flocks of students scattered between the tables and chairs as she looks to pay her friend a surprise visit.

She waves right in front of Flake's eyes as if to trigger a motion sensor switching on his social interaction module. Leeza loves the way Flake's face comes to life when he turns his attention to someone. When his mind rolls up the blinds like an ice cream shop opening for business, pushing the wing doors open on a sunny morning; his curious eyes lure in thoughts and ideas like flashy-coloured umbrellas lure ice creme-craving kids. *For a guy who claims he loves best to be alone, this is quite remarkable,* she thinks.

Flake drops the Sennheisers.

"Feel free to finish this up," Leeza says. "Seemed to be in quite a flow. What are you working on?"

"That article for Wired." He pulls his backpack from the second chair.

"The one that's gonna save the world?" she smiles.

"Wanna have a peek?"

Leeza leans over his shoulder and reads, whispering in his ear with a dramatic voice: "*...They call it the kill zone on Wall Street. If you get too close to the business of the internet monopolies, your wings will melt like those of Icarus. They will squeeze you out or buy you out. Whatever works best...*" She raises a brow at Flake, takes a seat and continues in a more businesslike tone. "*...and the reason they make all that money is they have all that data. It is a virtuous circle,* *a natural monopoly, as the economists call it. I would call it a vicious circle. Vicious for our privacy rights...*"

Leeza continues reading silently for a couple of paragraphs, wrinkling her forehead. Flake loves the amazingly cute wrinkles on Leeza's forehead. Yet, he doesn't like to be the reason for them.

"Ah, here comes the hopeful part," she says. "*We can fix this. If internet service were just set up the right way...make them delete all information collected on us latest every three months...send Big Tech on a data diet to avoid data diabetes...*" She looks up from the screen. "Data diabetes? What's next? Data Diarrhoea?"

"I knew you make a great muse!" Flake radiates. "Mind if I use that?"

"*...collect only what they actually need,*" Leeza mumbles on, "*...require explicit consent...store only as long as it is needed...Use and store anonymised...*" Leeza throws Flake a cursing look. "This aims at us again, doesn't it? *The very fact I can only exchanges messages with other users on the same platform creates natural market dominance.*"

"Folks on Yahoo can send email to folks on Gmail, right?" Flake says. "Sprint subscribers can call T-Mobile subscribers, can't they? Why can a Signal customer not send a message to someone on WhatsApp? Or iMessage?"

"I see. People stay with the service their friends use."

"It's set up to avoid competition. While regulators look the other way."

"Last time you agreed we have created some fantastic services, didn't you?"

"Surely," Flake smiles, "yet, so did these guys." He points at the logo on his polo: CYBERDYNE Systems Corporation.

"I'm serious," Leeza says. "I think we have created amazing possibilities to connect and communicate."

"Actually, you rather bought out new players than create new things yourself. The kill zone? Your firm alone has sucked up over one hundred competitors before they could start eating into your lunch. Google even bought out two hundred fifty."

Leeza gives Flake another set of adorable wrinkles.

"Okay," Flake says, "let agree, for argument's sake, that all the stuff you assemble can actually help create wonderful new things. And people are actually fine with some strangers looking at it and using it to invent these wonderful new things. In that case, you shouldn't keep it to yourselves. Even without your wealth of data, these one hundred competitors had invented cooler things than your own folks. Which is why you needed to buy them out. Imaging what the geek squads out there could do if they had access to your treasures."

Leeza looks right through her friend, lost in thought. Flake loves how she takes things to heart. With Leeza, he doesn't even want to be right.

"Spoke to Chomsky about your theory," he interrupts her inner dialogue.

"You did what?"

"I spoke to Chomsky," he repeats casually while looking at his screen as if he reads her the campus canteen's daily special. "Wanted to hear what he had to say about your position on social media democratising public opinion making."

"You're kidding me? You know Noam Chomsky?"

"Met him a few of times. He is professor emeritus at MIT, you know? He sometimes comes to events on campus. He and Timberley are quite close."

"Why didn't you tell me earlier?"

"You didn't seem like the groupie type," Flake winks, even though right now Leeza's blissful smile looks like she is waiting backstage for Lenny Kravitz.

"You called up Chomsky and said: Hey Noam, old chap, what's the beef?" she asks.

"The words are kind of correct. Just it was Timberley saying them. I discussed your point with him this morning. So, he picks up the phone and says pretty much exactly these words before he puts the man on loudspeaker."

"Wow. How cool is that?"

"Timberley handling a Bluetooth box?"

"Yeah, right? What did good ol' Noam have to say?"

"In summary, he agreed with both of us."

"He's an idiot," Leeza puts on a grumpy face, "never liked him; senile old fart."

"He agrees social media platforms could go a long way to provide a means to allow facts and opinions to be shared more easily and less controlled by corporate powers."

"Great guy," Leeza triumphs, "the best; smartest man ever; always knew that."

"He also agrees, though, the way currently dominant social media companies work is actually more of a threat to democracy than a benefit. They manipulate opinion to serve profit interests. Access to information is very much controlled and gated. Not very much different from corporate media in the past. The 'propaganda model,' as he calls it, is still very much applicable, he said."

115

Leeza looks straight through him again. "That's not what we do," she mumbles. "We don't control and manipulate. I think…"

"Too much power in too few hands. They control what you see. They block nothing out completely, of course. Don't have to. Just rank it down. Who, ever, makes it to page 4 of the google results list?"

Leeza decides to continue the quest to save the world another day. "So, good ol' Noam agrees with both of us, eh," she smiles, "…where does this leave us?"

"Should join forces in the battle to improve the system? Claim back the ideals of the internet?"

"I meant: where does this leave us right here? Right now?"

"Whatchumean?"

"I'm confident you will get there, eventually."

"Wanna write a joint essay on privacy rights in social media for my blog?"

"Wow, you can be focused."

Flake drops the lid of his notebook. "Permission requested to invade your privacy…"

"You know damn well us social media addicts do not care about permissions. Or privacy. Kiss me, smart boy."

"Yeah!" a distinctive voice booms in their back, "kiss her, smartass! Draw your last breath from the lips of a sweet girl, so you can end your expendable existence with a pleasant memory." When the two turn their heads, the king towers over them, smiling complacently.

"Give you five seconds to kiss your girl and your life goodbye." The athlete strikes a pose. "In case she still wants to kiss you in the sight of these." He flexes his impressive biceps in turn.

Leeza gets up to stand chin to chest with the giant. "Geez, you're swole," she grins, poking his ballooning pectorals.

The quarterback examines her extensively while making his pecs twitch and bounce underneath his pink polo.

"The king will attend to you momentarily, lovely little lotus." He gently picks up Leeza like a coat stand and puts her to the side. "First, I have to check with that uptight limpet if he's okay with me shagging his widow."

Flake and the king size each other up from about three feet apart.

"Behold that sweet taste," the king hisses. "It will soon blend with the leaded taste of blood."

"Shouldn't bet on me doing mouth-to-mouth on you after you go down," Flake replies.

An appearance of the Cardinal's quarterback always gets some attention, but since this could get particularly interesting, the entire crowd takes notice.

"This is exactly what I have to talk to you about!" Leeza tells the big guy off from the back. "I wasn't done with you yet."

"Hold it right there," the king points his finger at Flake, "ain't done with you yet, either," and turns around to Leeza with a smug smile.

"I don't get it," Leeza rants away. "You got a lot going for you: Chris Hemsworth's body. Liam's good looks! A mighty hammer, I take it?" She turns to the crowd anxiously looking on. "Most girls would kill to date you…"

"Can't blame 'em," the king strikes another pose.

"…and most guys would kill to be you." Leeza's quick scan of the audience meets many faces in agreement. "I really don't get why you have to treat people like shit?"

"Didn't I behave like a perfect gentleman just there?" The quarterback smiles graciously, folding his arms. "Offered to help you through the pain after I'm done breaking this little fag's spine. Once that's taken care of, happy to show you what the fuss is all about. You'll see it's very well justified."

"You have no idea what a girl needs, do you? Maybe that social media superstar in your jockstraps, the best documented dick on campus, is actually noteworthy," Leeza turns to the crowd, "do we have any eye-witnesses in the audience?"

Leeza feels quite a few hands stay down just to stay out of trouble.

"It still fills only about ten to fifteen minutes every other day," she continues. "If we assume you do a good job on that and it is not just another posing routine."

On that cue, the athlete hits a few for the many smartphone cameras capturing the event. "This body is a machine," he smiles, "ready to shoot 24/7."

"So sad. I sincerely hope someday you will get your emotional issues sorted; may even figure out why you never felt loved in the first place?"

Leeza watches the king finish his posing and straighten out his shirt. He leans down to her. "Listen, little lotus…" he begins with a smug smile.

"Maybe," Leeza interrupts, "it would help if you could get your mum to tell you about your real dad?"

The audience sucks up their breath in emphatic phantom pain like a ring side crowd waiting to see the effect of an unexpected uppercut right on the chin. The king's stare turns truly intimidating and his tensed-up physique seems ready to retaliate any second. Folks in row one take a step back for good measure.

Flake hastily swallows his chuckles as the Hulk turns to him.

"You pipsqueaks really piss me off," he spits from only inches away. "Listen carefully, little man: I will smash your face now, but as long as you can still utter sound, you better tell your pretty bitch to stop if you don't want me to stomp her, too."

"Or maybe," Leeza continues in his back, "it is because you know your glory days will be over soon enough? Because less than two percent of college stars make the pros? Its preemptive revenge? Because you know damned well that, eventually, the nerds will win? Preemptive revenge on all those who will surpass you in life, when fame and looks fade and you fall back on poor education and even poorer social skills. When athletic gifts don't help much in keeping up with the robots in Amazon's high-bay warehouse?"

The king's eyes shoot laser beams at Leeza, marking the aim of a major missile strike. While the quarterback still struggles with his plan of attack, a student steps forward: "Want me to tell Timberley, you won't be making it to the seminar today, Professor?"

After a brief pause, he adds, "Or the next few weeks?" looking really worried.

"Thanks for the vote of confidence," Flake hollers back. "Just tell class I might be a few minutes late."

"This clown is a professor?" the king scrutinises the unsettled student.

"Assistant professor," Flake corrects, desperately trying to get into that special state of mind the sensei talked about in a self-defence course last summer; the state where everything flows, all is just cause and effect. Move like water; be still like a mirror; respond like an echo. Something along those lines.

The king raises his fist, hesitates, looking confused.

The mighty oak tree will be felled by the wind because it tries to resist the elements, Flake thinks; *the bamboo bends with the wind, and by bending, survives.*

"Maybe you shouldn't level the guy, Miles?" the brave student puts forward timidly. "Could mean trouble. He is with this famous MIT prof. The dean may be pissed; have the coach kick you out."

"Your fellow is right," Leeza seizes the opening, squeezing in between the combatants, "we can't have the Stanford tree fall victim to a beaver in the middle of season prep."

She firmly pushes Flake backwards, while the boys keep eye-fencing.

"You can't run forever!" the quarterback shouts after them, pointing his hand like a gun. "I will come for you. Ain't done with you yet."

The brave arbitrator hurries off to class before the king will start looking for an object to vent his frustrations on.

"You knew I got this, didn't you?" Flake winks as the couple drifts off with the crowd flocking back to their seminars.

"Absolutely!" Leeza smiles. "Didn't want you to steal my thunder."

"It sure was quite a performance! Where were we, though, when the king invaded our privacy? Ah, yeah!" Flake takes Leeza by the hand, pulls her out of the stream of people into a corner and they start kissing.

***

The Big Stick

"...Heated arguments have stirred up all parts of our society over the last few days about an announcement of a group called The Horrible Siliconettes. THS, for short. The so far unknown group had announced last weekend to publicise a lot of information on all of us. Here at CNN Breaking News, we were among the first to cover this."

"The controversy in the markets, in the political sphere and among the American people was about whether this is a menace to individuals' ways of life, a risk to stock markets and business models, a genuine threat to national security or all of the above. The Harris Administration, the Attorney General, and the NSA have all called the announcement a terrorist attack. Regardless of that terminology, the security agencies were quick to highlight they regard this announcement as unsubstantiated. The American people seem to disagree with this judgment more and more, Jennifer?"

"That is right, Tom. Ever fewer people seem to trust something like this could never happen, even though that's what the authorities are telling us. The sentiment voiced in social media varies. We hear calls to break up Big Tech; and we hear defeatists saying 'we all knew this was coming'. An increasing number

of people become suspicious about the motives for data collection and the ability of corporations and government bodies to keep their information safe."

"Policy makers on both sides of the aisle are falling in line with this public judgment. Congresswomen Fairchild, for example, told the media today that, I quote, 'it is about time we looked into Big Tech's practices of collecting and using the data of the American people for their own financial benefit'. A spokesperson of Margarethe Vestager, commissioner of the European Union for the Digital Age, reminded corporations doing business with European citizens, including, of course, all major American corporations, that regulation in the EU foresees penalties of up to four percent of global annual turnover for security breach incidents."

"The spokesperson pointed out that the EU authorities must be notified of any breach to the integrity or privacy of personal information as soon as it becomes known. In response to questions from the media, the spokesperson indicated such notifications have occurred in the aftermath of the recent announcement but declined to provide any details or give any comments if these notices are perceived as in fact related to the announcement."

"That is a pretty big stick. With over 1 trillion dollars of annual revenue at the big five GAMAM corporations alone, Google, Amazon, Meta, Apple and Microsoft, this would mean a hefty fine of 40 billion dollars. Worst case. That's about the military budget of the UK per annum. Did markets factor this in already?"

"I don't think so. Think about it. In case all the S&P 500 corporations are hacked, we end up with fines in the trillions. Just in the European Union."

"Let's look at the rest of the world. How are other countries reacting to all of this?"

"The originators distributed the message around the globe. It went out to news media in virtually every region in the world. For the first few days, however, nothing had been reported in China on this subject. It was not present in official media at all. Of course, you can never completely block something like this out, not even the all-powerful Chinese government, but for most people in China, it was as if this had never happened. However, over time, word spread through unofficial channels. Yesterday, finally, the Chinese government issued a note stating data of corporations and government institutions in China was safe, this was merely a problem of capitalist societies, and that the announcement was

a western conspiracy of either private or state actors seeking to trigger unrest in the public."

"Well, I suppose that was to be expected, wasn't it? What can you tell us about security incidents in China?"

"Very little, since corporations and governments in states like China or Russia are historically very secretive about this subject. However, we know that Sina Weibo, for example, suffered a serious security incident in the past. With over 500 million users, this is China's equivalent to X/Twitter. A few years back, it was revealed that real names, usernames, gender, location, and, for 172 million users, phone numbers had been placed on the dark net for sale. That was one of the rare occasions such information became public."

"Do we know what ordinary people in China think about this?"

"Good question, Tom. It is extremely delicate to get people to talk openly to western media. We can't carry out proper polling or scientific research. What we can get, however, are anecdotal opinions of individuals who are prepared to talk; under the shield of anonymity, mostly. The Chinese government promotes the implementation of a social scoring system for many years already. In this system, a lot of information about citizens, their behaviour, their activities, their conduct is reflected in a social score."

"This score will determine many of your privileges in the future. Access to university, granting a newlywed couple a lease on a flat, many privileges can, in such a system, depend on a flawless record. It can depend on your participation in community groups, for example, or in any other activity the communist party desires. And, even more importantly, not taking part in any activities the government does not approve of. Constant official propaganda was fairly successful in convincing the public such a system is beneficial to society. You can imagine people therefore are not overly concerned when information on them gets made public. In a way, it is already, in the eyes of many people."

"It needs to be said, though, Jennifer, we do not want to compare the Chinese state-run system which aims to discipline individuals by amassing surveillance data on them to the criminal exposure of personal data originally collected for legitimate purposes by service providers in a market economy."

"You are absolutely right, Tom."

"Another interesting question is, Jennifer, whether the dump will also include the information that Chinese and Russian actors have collected on US citizens?"

"Viewers may remember the scandal with FaceApp, Tom, when this platform based in Russia was accused of sending all mug shots uploaded to this app to servers located somewhere in Vladimir Putin's empire. 150 million people had downloaded the app. I am sure Russian intelligence would love to have hundreds of millions of face shots of people around the world linked to personal information collected from the app user's phone, like places you went or which other apps you use."

"Face recognition experts could do great things with that. God knows which other apps and web sites have collected information about us for the Russian or Chinese intelligence communities."

"Another example would be TikTok, a Chinese app that has seen over 2 billion downloads globally and has over one hundred million regular users in the US Most probably your own kids. They have also been accused of sending data back home. Both companies have always declined any links to state institutions in their home countries, though."

"When we come back, we will shift focus back home and talk more about the reactions of both politicians and their constituents here in America. This is CNN Breaking News…"

***

641A

"Hello. Is there anybody out there? Just nod if you can hear me.

"This is Awkward Andy. Welcome back to the number one channel for paranoid data-dystopians.

"Hope you like the new outfit? The first five of you who can tell me down in the comments section what 'chain up in your rubberhose in room 641A' on here could mean will get a free copy of this shirt. Should you be thinking Fifty Shades of Grey now, I suggest you have another look at my earlier videos.

"Let's get down to business, shall we? Are you concerned information about you, which you'd like to keep close to your heart, could get exposed? I'm sure you've all heard these THS boys announced they will publish all personal info ever compiled? On any of you? And they will do so coming Monday?

"Government and Big Tech tell us they've got us covered. There is no need to worry. I tell you: You'd better be worried! And I'll tell you why.

"Where do I even start? There are excellent reasons you don't have to tell your firm when you are seeing a doctor; what you are treated for. Imagine your boss would know when you are seeing a shrink. Know when you are treated for high blood pressure or an ulcer. How does this affect your chances in the next wave of layoffs?

"Has it happened? Have medical insurance companies, doctors, or hospitals been hacked? Certainly, they must put a lot of focus on making sure that sensitive information is very secure, don't they? Turns out this sector is among the worst in protecting data. 21st Century Oncology: over 2 million records stolen. Advocate Medical Group: over 4 million records exposed. Anthem Inc.: 80 million. Community Health Systems: 4,5 million. LifeLabs: 15 million. Quest Diagnostics, a clinical lab: 12 million. The list goes on and on. So, should you not have told your spouse about your herpes, your tripper, think again. Should you not want a health warning to be added to your Tinder profile...Well...

"Speaking of your Tinder profile and your spouse: are you concerned your spouse could see your Tinder selections? Adult friend finder, the provider that runs penthouse.com, had over 400 million user accounts exposed with name, email address and password.

"In case you are old-fashioned and do not want your colleagues, neighbours or your wife to know about your porn consumption, you may also find this case interesting: the website Luscious.net exposed 1 million of their users by allowing access to user names, locations, genders, personal email addresses and even some full names. Also available were activity logs detailing what users had liked, uploaded, commented on, and shared. Cam4.com lost 7 terabytes of data, including first and last names of users, login credentials, country of origin, gender preference, sexual orientation plus payments logs, including the amount paid.

"These are just a few examples. To get a more general understanding of the state of security, I invited a guest today. You were probably wondering already if they have put your favourite youtuber under nanny supervision for all the controversial stuff I keep talking about here on my channel. Fear not! This shady gentlemen to my left, even though he looks like Agent Smith disguised in geek wear to trick us, is one of the good guys. His name is Jacob Lysiky, and he works as a senior advisor at WhiteKnight, a company specialised in cybersecurity. Hi Jacob!"

"Good to be here. Glad you like my outfit."

"Jacob, is what I just described a rare exception? What's your experience in finding, stopping, and remediating attacks on your clients?"

"I suppose it is fair to say every major company has been targeted or is targeted by a cyberattack as we speak. More and more often, these strikes are successful. Not just the number of incidents goes up. So does the severity. By the way, ninety-five percent of data breaches have their root cause in human error. You can make systems as secure as you want; as long as there are people involved, you will never get to a hundred percent."

"Why do these attacks happen? Are these blackmailers? Is it espionage? What is it?"

"Only ten percent of data breaches are motivated by espionage. The vast majority are directly financially driven. A significant segment is selling the bait on the dark net."

"The hackers do not ask for a ransom? Instead, they sell the data they have stolen to other fraudsters? Like a villain chain instead of a value chain?"

"Good one! Correct. On the dark net and via other means, you can basically buy anything. Look at Russia, to name an extreme case. Corruption in all parts of society, government organisations or private corporations alike, is so severe that you can basically buy every single piece of information you want. You go to the right forums on the dark net, advertise what you need and someone will either hack it or buy it for you. Or use other means we do not want to get into now."

"You mean it works like placing a search ad for a house in a real estate portal?"

"Pretty much. For anything you can think of. Someone's bank details, medical records, tax records, full payment history, social media data, anything really."

"This is very uncomforting."

"That is a nice way to put it, I'd say. But it is not only Russia. Experts assume you can buy the data stolen in one hundred thousand different hacks across the world. 100 thousand incidents where an organisation was hacked! In the US alone, 6 billion personal records were hacked, lost or leaked only last year. That is 19 records per person living in this country! In one year!"

"I can go out there and pick up your password for your social media profile? Should that be of value to me? Or your bank account?"

"Yes, quite possibly. A simple login credential would cost you 15 bucks a piece. If it is for a more valuable account, price goes up, of course. For an

account at a financial institution, bank, insurance, you pay 70 bucks on average. It goes up to a couple of thousand dollars for admin rights."

"What you are saying is almost like: These THS boys are offering us an all you can eat dark net data mart subscription. Flat fee. For free. Is that it?"

"Well, so far, for all we know, we can't be sure it's all there in one go. But it is quite close, I'd say."

"For a lot of this, though, you don't even need to go to illegal channels. Anyone who can spare twenty bucks can get a comprehensive profile of you out there. Completely legit."

"You are talking about data brokerage firms now, aren't you?"

"Exactly. In recent years, some of these information brokers have collected strikingly comprehensive profiles of most individuals on the planet. Certainly, every citizen of the United States. The US based firm Kochava, for example, claims to have data on 1,3 billion people, collected from 6 billion devices and ten thousand different apps."

"And they are not even the biggest of these types of corporations, correct?"

"Correct. Axiom even has twice that number, profiles of 2,6 billion individuals. That is almost seventy percent of all people online in the world. With one company. They can give you ten thousand attributes to sort and identify users. They have twenty-three thousand servers constantly gathering data. Fifty trillion unique data transactions per year using tracking cookies, browser fingerprints, beacons, IP addresses to match it all. These are massive figures. Some people call them the biggest company you have never heard of."

"Yet you should have! From what you are telling us. Tech lobbyists often argue that this is not a problem, because a lot of it gets anonymised. What do you say to that?"

"That is correct. Yet, other service providers offer de-anonymisation services. To link it all back. There are patents pending to match people's real names to all their online pseudonyms."

"This data comes mostly from apps and websites?"

"It includes a fair bit of offline data as well. The US firm IRI claims to have access to information from eighty-five thousand shops, from groceries to pet stores. Oracle, another giant in this game, claims to collect data from 1500 leading retailers. Nielsen from nine hundred thousand shops worldwide."

"It is safe to assume all these companies can also be hacked. Did Facebook not even stop the partnership with a few of them because of disputes on privacy and security?"

"That is correct. It remains in question, though, whether they just wanted to defend their turf."

"And yes, of course, these firms can be hacked. Actually, in 2019, 1,2 billion personal records were discovered online. 4 terabytes of personal information."

"What do you mean by 'discovered' online?"

"This massive dump was freely available on publicly accessible servers. Nobody knows how the file got there. And by whom."

"You must be joking?"

"I wish I was."

"Sounds almost like a test run for the Big One?"

"Scary, isn't it? We could trace back, though, where the data came from. No Horrible Siliconettes. The information largely originated from a brokerage firm called People Data Labs. Among the profiles this company offers for sale…"

"…you mean if they are not floating it online for free?"

"What they sell are detailed profiles on 260 million US citizens."

"Before I get a heart condition, let me sum this up. It seems like it is perfectly perceivable that an immense volume of data, a substantial percentage of all the personal information individuals might worry about, could indeed get disclosed. Is this a fair statement?"

"I would think so."

"Shall my subscribers change all their passwords now?"

"We don't know whether the hackers previously got all the data they intend to expose. Or whether they have to do that yet. In a worst-case scenario, bad guys have just recently infected your PC with a keylogger. Should we all, troubled by the announcement, log into all our two hundred odd password protected accounts to change them…this would hand the attackers all accounts in one go."

"Which could be just what they want? Why they made the announcement?"

"Exactly."

"Ok, maybe you should rather run a daily security scan on your PC. Thank you, Jacob, for being with us today. If you guys out there want to know more about the big dump and how the Siliconettes might store all your data, tune back in tomorrow for the second part of my little chat with Jacob. For now, I leave

you with your daily dose of paranoia. Tom Clancy said: 'I know, I'm par
Question is, am I paranoid enough?"

"Thanks for wasting some of your precious time on my channel. Pl
subscribe or like as your chance to vote for more supervision over the privacy
pirates. I'm Awkward Andy, your favourite digital dystopian."

***

Red or Blue Pill

"Want to hear my pitch for the hackathon?" Mic breaks the awkwardness of Leeza and him staring silently at their notebooks, waiting for Tim. "Put it up this morning," he points at the wall of ideas right behind the café lounge. He takes Leeza's smile as an invitation to elaborate. "I'd like to set up an AI tool to generate a novel. The cool thing is, though, this novel would be patched together from lyrics of pop songs."

"Let me get that…" Leeza looks up from her screen, "the storyline of an entire novel, maybe two hundred pages, pieced together from pop song quotes? Automatically? By some software?"

"That is the idea! There are 75 million songs on iTunes. The tool will search for lyrics and find matching quotes for the storyline made up of keywords the user defines."

"All you may want to write about has been covered in one of those songs?"

"Maybe not all possible twists of every subject. Yet, there are songs about so many things…enough to put together a novel, I suppose."

"Isn't quite a lot of that preposterous gibberish like the Killers?"

"I always wondered whether I'm dancer," Mic smirks. "Didn't you?"

"Oh, certainly. On my knees, mostly. Digging real deep to find another rhyme to answer," Leeza pantomimes scanning the floor with binoculars.

"Dylan won the Nobel prize for literature, didn't he? Kendrick Lamar won a Pulitzer."

"Okay, let me test that." Leeza puts her notebook down on the coffee table. "Not the easy ones, love songs and stuff. Give me lyrics on…let's see…coming of age, for example."

Mic freezes for about thirty seconds with his eyes rolled up like an unplugged robot. When his face comes to life again, he starts typing away on his notebook. "One of my favourites: LCD Soundsystem, *Loosing my Edge*. A

127

guy dissing the youngsters claiming his fame, who haven't earned their scars yet. Beautiful art school kids from Brooklyn, Berlin and Tokyo shamelessly feeding off of past classics." He turns his screen to Leeza.

"Wow!" Leeza applauds. "To the point critique of cultural appropriation already twenty years ago. Impressive."

"You can fill a complete chapter with just that one song. So many brilliant lines."

"Want another one? *Time*, Pink Floyd?"

"I know that song," Leeza says, starting to chant, quite off tune and too fast.

Mic makes an attempt to balance his expression between appreciation of her efforts and timid signals to please stop the earbleed. He fails. "A guy hustling to catch up with life," he chips in, "after wasting it when he was young; failing in even planning out a better tomorrow while his time ticks away, day after day, in a relative way."

"Not a dull day in my life, thankfully," Leeza winks.

"I love Floyd," Mic says while typing again. "How about *Dogs*? A song on how to make it in live by making friends only to scam them. Put a knife in their backs even. Picking the easy targets, luring folks with a club tie and some sophistication. Here you go. Not really a sing-along-song, I'm afraid." He smirks.

"Salinger couldn't have said it any better. Will be a very sad novel, though," Leeza laughs. "Let's pick another typical sad subject: Father-son-issues."

"Rufus Wainwright, *Dinner at Eight*," Mic is quick to shoot. "Let me check."

Leeza reads the lyrics out loud.

"It's all there," Mic says, "the old wounds; the doubts; the buttons you press; hating yourself for always falling into the same trap; hating your dad for leaving you so vulnerable."

"Ready for print. Amazing. Got even sadder, though. You really should see your shrink about the melancholia," she smiles.

"Just tells you how miserable teenage life was back home in the land of copper and cactuses. Andy and I either binge-watched movies or listen to music all night. When we were not coding, that is."

"He didn't tell me that. He quotes a lot of movies, though."

"I plan for a collaboration tool with a voting function to decide on suggested plots and twists."

"Sounds really cool."

"Could use your help; being a linguist and stuff. You could teach me how the structure of a novel works. Create a strawman. Maybe even a basic plot, keywords for a beta of the first story?"

"Like in these Bollywood movies?" Leeza smiles. "They all tell the same story, right? Boy meets girl, they fall in love, they split by some unfortunate incident; he is about to marry another girl; they meet again; it looks like it all turns out well; yet it is not the happy ending, just the point where the next drama happens; before, eventually, they get married and live happily ever after. That sort of thing?"

"Pretty much! Maybe a little more profound? And no dancing, please."

"That will be fun. I'm in."

The two get back to peering at their displays.

"Are you aware," Mic asks after a while, "there is even a song that represents the Fibonacci sequence?"

"These numbers we use for story point estimates in agile sprints? You're kidding?"

"No, really. It's a song by Tool. Syllables in the first verse follow the first six Fibonacci numbers in the pattern, 1, 1, 2, 3, 5, 8, ascending and descending. The chord progression also follows that scheme."

Despite intense pondering, neither of the two can think of anything meaningful to say to follow up on this subject. Just before the silence becomes really awkward, Tim finally shows up, an hour late.

"Sorry guys!" he greets. "Had to get some fresh air. Felt like running the gauntlet all around the office after the interview aired this morning. Seems we have violated the cult's code and get excommunicated."

Leeza eyes Tim's soaked sports gear. "Ravenswood Trail, full circle?"

Tim holds up two fingers.

"Sure you don't want to take a quick shower first?" Mic says a little pricked.

"Will head home after this." Tim collapses into a comfy chair. "Before I get into a fight with these schmucks."

"A lot of colleagues think we have a point," Leeza says, "yet do not dare to speak their minds."

"Most of the guys in IT are behind us all the way," Mic says. "The guys had put up two huge glass bowls. One with red M&Ms and one with blue. It was like a vote. Guess what? The red ones are all gone!" He grins, content like a boy who just ate that candy all by himself.

"So?" Tim asks, a little aggressively.

"Don't tell me you have never seen *Matrix*?"

"Our campaign works," Leeza says. "I overheard some folks in market research. We are the highest-ranking hashtag out there. Same with X, they said. Anyone from senior management talk to you yet, Tim?"

"Not a word. From no one. Looks like they keep ignoring the problem," Tim jumps back up, "keep ignoring us!"

"What if there really is nothing?" Mic asks. "What happens then?"

Tim looks puzzled and still a little aggressive. "That would be fantastic. That is what we all hope for."

"I mean, with us?" Mic clarifies. "What happens to us?"

Leeza puts a hand on his shoulder. "Until we know there is nothing, I am concerned about the people who might get hurt by this."

"We could get hurt by this," he says.

"Do you want out?" Tim asks in a huff. "You didn't go public. Didn't put yourself out there. You can go back into stealth mode if that's what you want." When he realises Mic is genuinely upset, he adds, a little more mildly, "I mean it. You don't need to keep doing this with us."

"It is still us, isn't it?" Tim turns to Leeza.

"There must be something more we can do," she says. "We can't just wait for the campaign to work. We need to do what we asked folks out there to do: keep digging in our own backyard."

"Maybe I already found something." Tim pulls his notebook from his backpack. "We still had this connection to Zach's messenger, remember?"

"You read his messages?" Mic gets worked up. "We said we'd disconnect it."

"We did. And I didn't. Sue me. Zach's got other problems right now, anyway. Didn't you hear he shot a burglar in his house?"

"It was all over the news," Leeza says. "They said it might be connected to those Siliconettes?"

"I heard a second guy got away," Mic says, "with a hundred grand in cash."

"Next time," Leeza says, "we should collectively decide something like this, Tim!"

"Was hoping to find some pointers on what senior management is doing about it. Zach's level would certainly be engaged somehow, I reckon, should they seriously consider the options. Yet, I found nothing."

"Bummer!" Mic's timidly slammed fist bounces off the well-padded armrest of his lounge chair. It makes him feel a little embarrassed.

"Ask me what I did find."

"Tim!" Leeza's eyes fire bolts of reproach.

"What I found was a lot of chats, all the way to the very top, debating tweaking the algorithms to make sure people stay calm; explore how best to rank up positive news; messages stating there's no problem, your friends are all not bothered. That kind of stuff."

"Spinning up a cosy community cocoon!" Leeza sighs.

"How poetic. Yes, you could call it that. We need to look into it some more; compare the usual bias of the network to what they have configured it to now; need to show to the community what these buggers are up to. Mic, your job." He scuffs his colleague.

"Once we got that figured out," Leeza says, "maybe we can publish it on Flake's blog."

Tim pulls a face as if Leeza had suggested to give him a head start in a bike race. "We don't need that guy…"

"Folks, please!" Mic intervenes, "this is cute, okay, but it must wait. I agree with Tim, though, Leeza. We do not need Andy. We need his Professor."

***

The Dish

The radio telescope's majestic hundred fifty feet iron grid bowl on top of a gentle hill poses serenely against the backdrop of a setting sun. It looks oddly fallen out of time. Not as much, though, as the professor's knickerbockers, worn with knee-high Burlingtons ending in old school leather boots.

"I hope you don't mind joining me on my evening stroll?" Timberley asks.

"Not at all. Thanks for taking the time to see us, Professor," Tim responds while he struggles to keep up, since the old man's hiking speed is too slow for his companions to jog, yet too fast to walk.

"Are you aware," Timberley asks, "that they built this dish at the climax of the cold war, right after the Bay of Pigs and shortly before the missile crisis in Cuba? It was used to learn about Soviet radar installations pretty much right on the opposite side of the globe. Of course, radar signal from the Russian tundra do not travel around the earth's curvature. They constructed the dish to pick up the signals that bounced off the moon. Isn't that phenomenal?"

"It certainly is!" Leeza says while she switches again from running to walking.

"The dish was later used to communicate with spacecrafts, like the Voyager, all the way to the outer reaches of our solar system. An amazing testament of human ingenuity, if you ask me."

Flake notices two runners headed towards the group; the older man seems an eager beaver conducting his exercises with the same utmost diligence as all his other duties in life, while he tries hard not to show any weakness before the eyes of his younger companion, most likely his son; the son is clearly more focused on a running style that looks cool rather than being efficient or easy on the joints. Flake can't help but smirk at how both men adjust their posture as they spot Leeza and only breath again after they passed by. None of the others seem to have noticed, especially not Leeza, who is generally not aware of the attention she gets from guys, even if she is not as concerned and focused as she is right now.

"We need to talk to you about some very irritating observations," Tim says, having a quarrel with himself for not coming up with some clever transition from the moon bounce into their cause. "Take it away, Mic!"

"Suppose I don't have to explain how social networks operate?" Mic asks timidly.

Flake pulls a face as if his friend had asked for permission to fart. "As in the socio-economic consequences of social media?" he asks. "The professor's most recent paper published on that was last year. Or as in implications of machine learning algorithms in social media on the necessity for regulatory oversight on automated selections and decision engines? The paper will come out later this year."

"Sorry, Andy," Mic says, already a little short of breath, "just need to know where to start, okay?"

"I will not be shy to ask stupid questions, young man, trust me," Timberley turns his hiking speed back up a notch.

"Generally, what our platform and most of the other social media and news platforms do is to create as strong an emotion as possible. Because strong emotions lead to more intense reactions; lead to more time with the service. In simplified terms. Negative emotions have proven to be stronger in this sense. The more negative the emotion, the more time people spend on debating. Again, very simplified."

"The reason there is so much hate and rage in social media is that it plays right into our hands," Tim adds. "We love trolls."

"You make me wanna quit right away," Leeza says.

"It's not all black and white," Tim says. "Of course, certain things better get promoted in the warm and tender spirit of a loving home. We make sure this exists in our community as well."

"The point is," Mic says, "usually, the algorithms are tuned to escalate! However, the last few days, the platform has completely reversed that."

"Everybody confronted with the subject of the Big One," Leeza says, "or our #DontDoxxMyDudes campaign will be overwhelmed with soothing messages systematically; news reports that explain it is impossible to happen; would not have any consequences, regardless; that kind of coverage."

"This, of course, is not black and white either," Mic says. "The platform does not cut off other news altogether. Yet it is a particularly strong bias. Much stronger than the negativity bias we usually employ. Does this make sense, Professor?"

"It perfectly does, I'm afraid."

"We spoke to friends at this thing that used to be Twitter and all the others," Tim says. "They checked at their end and noticed something similar in their data. The platforms are all colluding."

Timberley takes three puffs from his asthma inhaler without even slowing down. "What do you suggest doing with this?" he asks.

"There is more," Tim replies. "Mic!"

"We discovered a countermovement as well," Mic explains. "Herds of accounts which promote, retweet or share doomsday stories. Many of these are on the firm's watch list of suspected fake or troll accounts. You know, accounts that are solely set up to play the system, trick the algorithms and elevate certain messages the coordinators of these accounts want to push."

"Like when certain forces sought to manipulate public opinion or even elections in the past?" Timberley asks.

"I'm afraid, yes!" Tim replies.

"Do you have any leads regarding the association of these accounts? Who coordinates them?"

"You guessed it already," Mic sighs. "Many of them were involved in the attempts to influence the elections."

"That sounds bad!" Timberley says. "What can I do?"

"We were counting on you, Professor," Leeza replies, "to help us let the public know what's going on."

Timberley stops, takes another puff from his vaporizer and gazes broodingly at the sinister silhouette about to fade into a dramatic night sky.

The two runners pass by once again, this time having an even harder time to hold the pose and look energetic. The younger guy's shirt slips up briefly as he jumps over a fallen tree trunk, revealing what looks to Flake like a belly band holding a gun in his back.

"Thank you for coming to me," Timberley says, pulling Flake out of his paranoid thoughts as he watches the runners disappear into the gloom.

"Let me make a few phone calls."

***

Big One Minus 4, Thursday

Troll Wars

Interviewer: "It is half time today, between the announcement of the Big One four days ago and the day it is scheduled to happen, coming Monday, another four days from now. NBC's latest polls show people are more and more concerned. A striking sixty percent believe that the Big One will happen and forty percent say the Big One will have severe or very severe consequences. Thirty percent also believe it will have severe consequences on them personally. With me here today is Benjamin Timberley, institute professor at MIT and advisor to several administrations. Good morning, Professor Timberley.

"Professor, of those who expect the Big One will go ahead, some seventy percent think it must be attributed to a foreign power, with a majority suspecting Russia to be behind all this, with China and Iran being distant second and third. What do you say to that?"

Timberley: *"Good morning, Jenna. Thanks for having me. I have seen no compelling evidence to suggest Russia or any other foreign power is involved in the announced data dump. What I can say, though, is that Russia has a vested interest in making sure people are worried about it. As a matter of fact, there is compelling evidence showing Russia as a major contributor to the concern and irritation of the American people."*

Interviewer: "Of what nature is this contribution by Russia you refer to, Professor?"

Timberley: *"Massive campaigns happen on various social media platforms to promote fear and anxiety in the public. To foster the belief, the Big One will happen. To push content aimed to underline the negative, if not catastrophic, consequences of it. Others promote the narrative of a surveillance system installed by devious corporations, yet often combined with the usual stereotypes of conspiracy theorists like Jewish world domination, aliens or the Illuminati."*

"Many of these campaigns use the same mechanisms and often the same distribution agents as previous campaigns organised out of Russia. For example,

when they, quite successfully, influenced the presidential elections in 2016 and 2020."

Interviewer: "What do you mean when you say these campaigns use the same mechanisms?"

Timberley: "State organisations in Russia, like the Internet Research Agency, the trolls from Olgino, and others, register thousands, if not hundreds of thousands of fake accounts, to manipulate public opinion. Many of these accounts pose to be American citizens. Hide their true proprietors. Some emulate political groups; even actually existing ones, mostly, but also made-up groups; easily mistaken for real, though. Some emulate actual profiles of office holders, create an evil twin if you like."

Interviewer: "What are these accounts created for?"

Timberley: "With this army of profiles, their controllers distribute manipulative content through Twitter, even more so, since they rebranded to X, Facebook, Instagram, YouTube and others. They create this content to foment outrage, fear, hostility, anxiety."

"These trolls have gotten much better than they were in 2016 and 2020 at impersonating legitimate individuals and organisations. Including more closely mimicking logos of official campaigns. They've expanded their use of seemingly nonpolitical content and commercial accounts; to obscure the intend of their propaganda."

Interviewer: "That sounds quite alarming, Professor."

Timberley: "They are amazingly efficient at targeting individuals with exactly the right message. Tailored to this person's character, disposition and situation in life."

Interviewer: "Tailored messaging? How does this work, Professor?"

Timberley: "The people behind these campaigns present a competitive person with different arguments and fear factors than someone classified as spontaneous, humanistic or methodical; to put this in marketing terms. With one you would reason. The other reacts best to appeals to empathy. Yet another is open for conspiracy theories. If you know which type of person you are sending a message to, you can tailor it for best impact. Imagine you wanted to convince your friends to stop smoking. You would probably use different arguments for each and every one of your friends, wouldn't you? Depending on temper. Use a different lead into the conversation? Wait for the right moment, which, again, might be different for each character."

Interviewer: "How do these trolls know what type of person I am?"

Timberley: "From firms specialising in creating profiles on people. They can tell you exactly how you need to approach your friends if you want your no-smoking pitch to be successful. It worked very well already in the elections."

Interviewer: "I get that for interfering in our elections. But what is the purpose in this case, in your opinion? What does Russia have to gain?"

Timberley: "The same reason, Jenna, as for meddling in the elections. I think Vladimir Putin's intention is to weaken our society by dividing us. The primary aim in influencing the elections was not to help a particular candidate into office he would benefit from in any particular way. In my view, the Kremlin simply wanted a president in the oval office who was bad for the country; would encourage hate and confrontation; strengthen the extremes instead of moderating to compromise. They achieved just that; I would argue."

Interviewer: "There are social media campaigns going on right now that continue Russia's efforts to divide our society and to weaken the United States? Is that what you are saying?"

Timberley: "Very much so. They have even multiplied their efforts on the campaign for the Big One. It is a perfect opportunity for them. Yet it is not limited to the US. It happens elsewhere as well. It is particularly effective here, though."

Interviewer: "That is very disturbing indeed. Yet, you state Russia is not the originator of the Big One?"

Timberley: "I have no evidence to suggest they are, Jenna. But they certainly take advantage of it. What I find equally disturbing, though, is another manipulation that happens in parallel. This time coordinated by the social media giants themselves."

Interviewer: "Tell us more about this. What is going on and why would that be a concern?"

Timberley: "The social media firms, of course, employ very different techniques. They do not create fake accounts on their own platforms. They do not create manipulative content. They don't have to. Because their users produce any sort of content one can imagine. But it is the platforms who determine which of the options they present to you."

Interviewer: "Social media platforms apply special selection criteria on the content you get to see?"

Timberley: "They always do. That is their business model. Usually, though, there are two goals: one is to show you content relevant to you; things they believe you want to consume. Because, should they get it right, you spend time on their platform. Which is the ultimate goal. To keep you engaged as long as possible. This attention they sell to marketeers."

Interviewer: "Which is a legitimate business goal."

Timberley: "It is. You could say they select in your interest. I will not get into the arguments about echo chambers right now. Important is another mechanism which contributes to this goal. The platforms discovered people engage more, spend more time when you create negative emotions like anxieties, fear, even hate. That engages people longer."

Interviewer: "You are saying negative news is better than positive news?"

Timberley: "We all knew that, didn't we, Jenna? Therefore, the selections presented to users usually have a strong bias not caused by a specific preference of the user but by the platform's general preference for confrontation."

Interviewer: "Would this not play into the hands of those who want to promote divide, fear, hate and negativity, like we just talked about, Professor?"

Timberley: "Absolutely. That is why the election campaigns run by Russia were so amazingly successful. Now, here is the point I'm trying to make: In this instance, the social networks have completely changed the way their algorithms work. They don't promote negativity, fear, hate and anxiety on their platforms anymore. Regarding the Big One, the social media giants focus their selection on making sure people get to be exposed to as many comforting messages as their specific situation allows. Should you not have any friends posting positive news in your tweets, X will struggle to show you such content. Yet this is rarely the case. In most cases, people will have a mix of friends with different opinions. The selection criteria for content presented to you with priority now gear towards conciliation, soothing messages, moderating tone. We are talking about a pretty strong bias for such content. That seems to be the case for all major social media platforms."

Interviewer: "Why do you think providers do that, Professor, if this reduces the time spend on the platform?"

Timberley: "In the current special circumstances, individuals spend much more time on social media platforms than usual, anyway. Because the entire society is currently soul searching for what to make of this threat. I think you do not need to incentivise usage at all right now. Yet, the main reason for trying to calm down the public is, they fear for the debate to get out of control. Which might eventually lead to a powerful push towards regulation. In the good case, the Big One doesn't actually happen at all, instead, gets uncovered as a hoax, people will soon forget all about it and go back to normal. That, I believe, is the hope."

Interviewer: "Seems there is a new type of cold war going on right now in the World Wide Web, Professor. Thank you for being here this morning, shedding some light for us on recent developments on the upcoming Big One. We will be right back after this..."

***

Shapes and Chalices

The art school building reminds Flake of a skills game he used to play as a kid, for which you had to put together a pyramid or a cube out of a set of odd parts that don't seem to fit to the task. Like a three-dimensional Tetris. In the case of this edifice two zigzagging shapes, one covered with historicist cement plaster and one with patinated zinc, giving it an industrial aesthetic, interlock with one another, connected by a transparent floating glass box.

Leeza and Flake follow a billboard that depicts a portrait of a beautiful young human of undeterminable gender to the first level open–air interior courtyard for the entrance of a photo exhibition called 'Shapes'.

Right behind the sliding door, a display blocks the visitors' path, showing a vintage style drawing of a Cary-Grant-type male and an Ann-Margret-type female. Fat, labelled block lines mark the male's pronounced brow ridge, angular shapes and square chin, while Ann Margret's archetypical face is labelled to be curved, with a smooth forehead and pointed chin.

Once they passed the 50s physiognomy lecture, the couple enters a first exhibition hall with portraits of celebrities; the wall on the left is reserved for photographs of males with labellings of their typically female facial features, like low cheekbone, forward set eyes or a small mouth, exemplified by the likes of Kiefer Sutherland, Johnny Depp or Liam Hemsworth; the wall on the right is covered with female celebrities, such as Angelina Jolie, Anne Hathaway or Julia Roberts, sporting rather angular shaped facial structures and high cheekbones.

Leeza scans the QR code on a signpost. "Bad news for men who have feminine-looking features," she reads from her handheld. "Their spouses will probably fantasise about masculine-looking men during week two of their cycle."

"Johnny Depp's divorce court records?" Flake asks.

"Nope. Journal of Evolution and Human Behaviour. High oestrogen during ovulation pushes girls to find a mate with a lot of testosterone. A strong jawline signals health and virility, it seems."

"I always thought girls are hopeless romantics," Flake grins. "Obviously just me being stereotypical again…"

Leeza continues to read from the exhibition app while they enter the next hall. "The portraits created by French-Canadian artist Ulric Collette in this section digitally composite photographs of two genetic relatives to make up one single face, using the left half from one and the right half from the other person's portrait."

"How cool is that?" Flake exclaims and walks straight over to a photograph of two very likeable meerkat-like visages. "Cousins Justine and Ulric," he reads from the caption below the frame.

"Bone structure seems perfectly identical to me. So much for male versus female features."

The two take a step back.

"Once you let it sink in," Leeza says, "it makes perfect sense as one face of a single individual, don't you think? A bit lopsided, maybe; then again, most people don't exactly have a symmetrical face."

"You could easily trim Justine's curved eyebrow from Ulric's bushy one," Flake says. "And with a bit of mascara, his eyes would look exactly like hers."

"Justine's lips are quite a bit fuller than her cousin's, though."

"Look at those stunning beauties," Leeza pulls her friend to the next frame.

"Siblings Genevieve and Jean-Michel share a nose," he says.

"It's even Jean-Michel has who has fuller lips than his sister. Both got beautiful, big eyes. To me, the left and right eye only differ as much as everybody's, don't you think?"

"Jean even got longer hair than his sister. You only have to take away the beard."

"Merged Jean-Genevieve would certainly turn many heads as a male or as a female!"

Flake grabs her hand and pulls Leeza towards a photograph at the very end of the room that caught his attention.

"Meet disarmingly cute Rastafarians Madineg and Renaud, mother and son," he says. "These two totally looked like one face from back there. Even once you get closer…"

The subtle differences between the left and the right side, between son and mother, seem just like a facial expression. The mother smiles ever so slightly, while the son looks very sincere, giving the combined face an ironic touch.

"It says here," Leeza reads from her display, "that scientist have tried to determine the perfect face. They have asked people about the features they like best in their preferred sex, created a mash-up of that and had the pictures rated. Look, this is the result." She hands Flake her phone.

"The girl looks like Emilia Clarke and the guy looks like a candy-ass version of Jay Courtney with Paul Rudd's haircut," Flake says.

"When asked about this," Leeza continues, "men and women could not agree on the perfect female features. Men prefer Shakira's blonde hair with full lips, Angelina Jolie's strong cheekbones, and a petite Miranda Kerr nose. While women's preferences for the perfect female are dark hair, Keira Knightley's cheekbones, Cara Delevingne's eyebrows, Blake Lively's nose and Natalie Portman's forehead."

"They're all wrong," Flake beams. "The perfect face, definitely, blends the tiniest of noses framed by porcelain cheeks, almond eyes with an amazingly cute inner lid fold, straight eyebrows and petite, heart-shaped lips."

Leeza growls at him briefly and continues to read. "The ancient Greeks thought it was all a matter of perfect measurements. They called it the 'Golden Ratio of Beauty Phi'."

"Golden Ratio? Like Da Vinci's Vitruvian man?"

"Pretty much, it seems. It was about the distance between your eyes, forehead, nose, lips, and all that. If you apply all twelve measures to mugshots of contemporary celebrities, guess who has the perfect face?"

"Please don't say Brad Pitt?"

"He's number three," Leeza smiles. "George Clooney is on one, followed by Bradley Cooper."

"Makes sense, I guess."

"For females, it's Amber Heard, Kim Kardashian and Kate Moss."

"But here comes the best part," Leeza continues, "when people pick their mate, it does not seem to be perfect proportions they are looking for."

"Instead…?"

141

"They look for someone that looks like them!"

"Like in that boyfriendtwin hashtag a few years ago? Thousands of gay couples sent in pictures of their mates who looked just like them."

"Not just same sex mates," Leeza swipes and zooms on her handheld.

"Here is a study on mixed couples. They created eight different versions of a picture of one partner and had the spouse rate the attractiveness of each. Each version they altered differently; by morphing the original with a second picture; a picture of the ideal face of the same sex, for example."

"To create a prettier version of that partner?"

"Exactly. Another one was a blend with the ideal of the opposite sex. They also blended the picture with average faces, same sex and opposite sex."

"The spouse had to rate which of these modifications they find most attractive?"

"Any of those and the original, unaltered photo, yes. However, the version that was rated highest by far was always the one morphed with the picture of the partner. Odd, isn't it?"

"People found their spouse most attractive when altered to resemble themselves more?"

"That's what it says, yes. Examples in hall three."

The walls in this next space are covered with tabloid-cut-out collages of celebrity couples, with a left and a right half of paparazzi face shots of both partners put next to each other.

"Gisele Bündchen and Tom Brady do look like identical twins," Flake says.

"The artist, Suzi Malin, is actually a portrait painter," Leeza reads out. "She created these collages to prove her suspicion that people feel attracted to mates that resemble them in many areas, not just looks."

"She's spot on. Mario Lopez and Courtney Mazza, Justin Timberlake and Jessica Biel, Ryan Reynolds and Blake Lively…they all could easily be identical twins."

Leeza swipes on her handheld. "In the next hall, we should finally find my friend Franky's photography."

The black and white portraits show people of all shapes and sizes, young and old, different tribes and colours; some correspond to the general ideal of beauty, others not so much. Leeza and Flake stop in the centre of the hall and take a long look around.

Each model is portrayed as two distinct personalities; one photograph shows the model with a male appeal; the second one shows the very same model with a female look. Yet, seeing them both at the same time, the observer can't tell what makes one call it either way. Long or short hair doesn't seem to tell you anything. Even a beard seems like a useless indicator for a male when the same person looks so convincingly female on the cleanly shaven picture right beside. None of the portraits shows the model particularly heavily made up. Both versions seem perfectly credible; for a lot of combinations, Leeza and Flake find it impossible to call which is the actual gender of the model. Even on the pairs that do seem possible to call, one could just as well be wrong.

"Franky had told me about some scientists," Leeza says, "who had interviewed young people in El Salvador. It turns out, young folks with no internet access, which seem to still exist down there, preferred more feminine men and more masculine women than those who used the web. Don't you think that's odd?"

Leeza finds Flake's complete lack of surprise and his obvious inner struggle to not engage in an argument right away about the manipulative powers of the internet quite amusing.

"Here comes Franky!" she suddenly bursts, bouncing at her friend.

"Leeza, darling. Glad you could make it!" Franky says, giving her a big hug. "This cutie must be the infamous Flake? He looks every bit as adorable as you described him!"

"I do not recall having ever said anything of that nature," Leeza smiles with faint indignation.

"Sorry if I ruined your bargaining position, darling!"

Flake is glad they keep talking about him rather than to him for now. For the life of him, he couldn't tell the sex of the mannequin doll beauty before his eyes, clad in a velvet blend of three-piece and track suit, with a long pompadour top haircut and an intimidating presence. Yet, he feels it should make some kind of difference to his own conduct. Even though, he couldn't say what difference and why.

"My bargaining position?" Leeza asks.

"Darling! In the first few weeks of any relationship, the hierarchy is determined. Your looks are one of the key assets in that equation. To be exact: your lover's perception of his sexiness score compared to yours."

"When ten mates with a five, the five will be the underdog for the rest of the relationship? Is that what you are saying?" Leeza asks.

"Sorry, if I boosted your guy's confidence level too much just there," Franky smiles gracefully, eying Flake top to bottom and bottom to top. "Your puppy speaks English, though, doesn't it? If it speaks at all…?"

"Congratulations on your work," Flake opens the ice cream shop while he still looks for clues in Franky's demeanour; the Marla Glen voice is certainly not helpful.

As if reading Flake's mind, Franky asks, "Are you aware of the platypus, a semiaquatic mammal, which has ten sex chromosomes? Not just two? I wanted this cute duck-billed, beaver-tailed, otter-footed guinea pig on the exhibition poster. But the curator rather put Ashi on the cover. Don't get me wrong. He is adorable. Ashi, I mean."

"Yet, people's binary way of thinking is so…limited…boring!"

The artist eyeballs Flake, sorting his thoughts on the equation with two unknowns and Leeza sinking herself into Ashi's portrait on the opposite wall.

"Let's get a drink!" Franky says.

The museum's roof top sky court offers a marvellous view over Stanford campus. "Let me ask you this," Franky says, toasting with a glass of red wine. "Once you've learned to love yourself, does this not make you gay, in a way?"

"Making love with your ego?" Flake grins.

"That's why you got Ziggy on the shirt, I get it," Franky smiles approvingly, giving Flake a flirtatious look. "White as snow he is," the artist adds, examining the counterpart top to bottom, "about the rest we'll speak in private, Leeza, if you know what I mean." She clearly doesn't. Franky raises a brow at Flake conspiratorially, smiles down on his zipper, and downs a huge gulp.

"Where are you on that, then?" Flake asks.

"Loving myself?" Franky replies, turns on a rather intimidating stare and adds in a very dark voice, "or being gay?"

"Isn't there a difference between love and physical attraction?" Leeza asks.

"Is there? Really?" Franky adds a touch of contempt to the stare. Leeza seems a bit off balance.

"Of course, there is, Darling," her friend bursts into a disarming smile. "I'm just messing with you. You know me."

"Yet," the artist continues, "isn't civilisation about overcoming animalistic instincts such as slaying your fellow man for no apparent reason, burping and farting at random and spreading your semen as widely as possible to preserve the species?"

"Being queer as a more advanced state of civilisation?" Flake says. "That's an interesting theory."

"What I'm saying is," Franky replies, "that we fall in love with a soul, not with a plum or a pole."

The artist assumes a stage pose. "Should it so happen that an unfortunate spirit should fall in love with another soul cut from the other tree, the misguided seeker shall not be condemned." After a few moments of holding the pose, Franky's sincere televangelist face cracks into a cheeky Fresh Prince smile. Or Fresh Princess, for that matter. Flake still couldn't tell.

"That was most unctuous," Flake says. "You'd make a great high priest of a queer church."

"Churches don't seem to have much love for my kind, do they?" the artist says, his smile freezing.

"Oddly so, I'd say," Flake replies. "Since Christ the saviour and his disciples started out as a boys-only club. And a major mistake, if you ask me. Queer people are a very lucrative target group."

"Statistically, gay men are better off than average," Leeza says.

"Which is fantastic for the Grand Sale of indulgence! Queer souls seek salvation just as much as any sinner walking the face of god's beautiful earth; yet, some lead a rather hedonistic lifestyle; that gives priests in confession all the good hooks to dwell on to make devotees buy more salvation credits. Plus, they rarely have kids, so they can bequeath their entire fortunes to their church when their time has come to meet their maker. If I'd ever found a religion, I'd make it as attractive for gay people as possible."

"Isn't Scientology already doing that?" Leeza smiles.

"Because of Tom?" Franky smirks. "I'm sure it's only a rumour that the Cruiser is a bottom rather than a Top Gun. Anyway, they are no fun. If you'd want to start a church that appeals to me, it needs to be a lot of fun. Wild weddings, hedonistic heavens, that sort of thing."

"For you," Leeza laughs, "it would be sparkles in the sacramental wine and Fahrenheit instead of incense in the burner."

"Maybe some techno gospel?" Franky says.

"Don't forget colourful velvet wear."

"Definitely bondage confessions!"

"Love that!" Leeza giggles.

"You need to be careful, though," Flake says, "not to make your congregation too hedonistic. You want folks to still feel bad about their earthly sins and buy salvation credits, right? Judgment Day shouldn't be Black Friday, throwing out blessings and all-inclusive trips to happy eternity at bargain pricing."

"Can we at least have an eternal party in paradise, please?" Franky cajoles. "A ball of the blessed? A rave for reincarnation."

"We shall see about that." Flake raises his glass for a toast. "Anyway," he adds, smirking at Leeza, "it's not called paradise anymore, I'm afraid, Franky. The garden of Eden, Heaven, Elysium, Arkadia…it's called Metaverse nowadays!" Flake's and Franky's broad smiles team up on their friend, who rolls her eyes.

"The best thing is," Flake continues, "Google and friends say they could market our new church straight at our target audience, even the closeted ones."

"How is that?" Leeza asks; her voice showing she's suspecting to be in trouble once again.

"Psychologist Michal Kosinski, the guy who they say has put Trump into the white house with his tailored behavioural targeting, claimed to have developed an AI to detect gay people just from photographs."

"No shit?" Franky gives Leeza a challenging look. She smiles apologetically.

"Yep!" Flake says. "He didn't know about your art, obviously. He said the artificial intelligence could show that gay men have smaller jaws and chins, slimmer eyebrows, longer noses and larger foreheads."

With her face contorted in pain, Leeza pulls a virtual arrow out of her chest. "You're right, this sounds odd," she says. "Yet, I've seen our big data folks come up with some pretty astonishing insights from people's data…"

"I'd call that artificial ignorance!" Franky snarls.

"Don't be such a heretic," Flake says, "questioning the wisdom of the Great Meta. Anyway, religion is exactly about believing in things that don't make any sense, isn't it?"

"I drink to that," Franky says.

"I've got Kosinski's app right here," Flake says. "I'll scan your face real quick…" he points his smartphone camera at the perplexed artist, "let's see…"

"What is it? What does it say?" Franky urges a little nervously.

"Still calculating…" Flake looks back and forth between the artist and his display several times.

"Oh!" he lets out.

"What does it say?"

"The AI identifies you with ninety-nine percent accuracy as…" he looks up from his display, first at Leeza's and then Franky's anxiously expecting face, "…a platypus!"

It takes about three seconds for the tension to disappear from Franky's face before the artist wipes for Flake and bursts out into earth-shattering laughter.

"Let's raise another toast," Flake says, "to the newly found congregation of the Church of All Shapes!"

***

VibeScore

Voice #1: "I know you folks are awfully precious about your little nuggets. But these are special times. Special times need special measures."

Voice #2: "We will not share all we have with all of you. No way!"

Voice #3 in a croaky falsetto: "My precious! One ring to rule them all, one ring to find them…"

Voice #2: "Idiot!"

Voice #3: "…one ring to bring them all and in the darkness bind them. In the land of Meta, where the shadows lie."

Voice #1: "Can we focus on the issue please, gentlemen? Not talking about sharing. I'm talking about using it. Your stuff, as well as our stuff and all the details every organisation in this room holds. To find those Siliconettes suckers! To stop them! You must want this as much as we do, right?"

Voice #2: "What makes you think we can identify these terrorists with all our stuff combined?"

Voice #3: "Don't play dumb, okay? They must have left some kind of trace. Somewhere in their online activities, their searches, their messages, their geo-data. Maybe we can narrow down suspects. These suckers have to be stopped before this gets out of hand. I guess we all agree on that?"

Voice #2: "Happy to look at your extracts and see if we find correlations when combining them with what we have. But our data will not leave the house."

Voice #3: "It already did. The Siliconettes have it."

Voice #2: "Impossible!"

Voice #1: "You are telling me you are not worried at all about what they will leak?"

The analyst with a teen face masked by a rather desperate attempt on a grown-up's beard stops the replay.

"The voice quality is astonishing," Special Agent Willis says.

"Was a pretty big conference room even," the analyst proudly explains. "Roughly thirty people. This is a mashup of a few separate recordings. From mics in the mobiles of four people, we knew would be in that gathering." He points at the screen. "This tool always uses the best sound bites and blends them on top of each other. Below you see the original tracks. We had activated a fifth device, but that was stuck in a bag or suitcase; hardly hear a thing."

"Any visuals?"

"Not really, mostly ceilings. The occasional glimpse of a face, when someone moved the phone."

"Let's roll the rest…"

"By the way, here's the list of people in that session. Some we knew, some we identified through voice matching."

"I guess I don't even want to know how you got the compare samples…?"

"No, you don't."

"Alphabet, Apple, Axiom…reads like a who's who. Platforms, brokers, media outfits."

Special Agent Willis hands the list to his partner. The analyst clicks play.

Voice #4: "You are asking us to give up our competitive edge?"

Voice #1: "We need to sort out the practicalities, of course. Maybe there is a neutral intermediate we can use. I don't know. First, we must agree there is an urgent need to act."

Voice #5: "Not sure I believe this is going to work. Even if we would all agree to join up all our insights. If you folks from Meta and you folks from Alphabet can't find anything useful in your buckets…"

Voice #1: "I'm absolutely sure our data scientists will figure it out once they really have a full picture to work with."

Voice #5: "What do you expect to find?"

Voice #6: "Maybe we can help?"

Voice #4: "You? How?"

Voice #6: "Happy to accept your apology for the arrogant tone. I don't have to be here. We are not the ones who have everything to lose in this."

Voice #1: "I invited them. We need to look at all options. What's your suggestion?"

Voice #6: "Mark is right, what you guys have is all pretty comparable. Maybe more of the same will help more. Yet we can provide something different. Maybe the missing link."

Voice #2: "You got my full attention."

Voice #6: "We call it VibeScore. It creates a 24/7 emotional profile; imagine it as a biorhythm; for any given moment in time, we can tell if a user is happy or sad, focused or distracted, two dozen categories; Not binary, but gradients; many such characteristics."

"Who is that guy?" Special Agent Willis inquires.

The analyst stops the replay again. "Voice analysis says this is Sebastian Coehn. He runs a startup called Tidwell. Just got funded by Peter Thiel and a few of his friends. Surely a unicorn in the making. I'll send you the intel from his phone and a full bio. Mostly a blank sheet, though. Sorry. Popped up out of nowhere only recently."

"Keep rolling."

Voice #2: "How does this work?"

Voice #6: "First, we have all those vital stats from your phone, your watch, your fitness tracker; heart rate, blood pressure, all that stuff. We amend that with lots of other indicators. For example, we measure the motions of the handheld. It's obvious, if your hand is shaking, when it usually isn't, that something must have happened. But you'd be surprised how many ways there are how you hold and move your device; depending on your condition. We can tell a lot from that. Motion sensor, proximity sensor, gyroscope, accelerometer. Every phone has that."

"We also analyse how you type. We all have a pattern. Kinds of typos you always make. How many. Kinds of typos you never make as well. How fast you usually type. That pattern changes with your emotional state. When you're nervous, you make more mistakes. When you're excited, you type faster. That kind of stuff."

Voice #3: "Seems voodoo to me?"

Voice #6: "We've done some tests with patients treated by psychologists for years. Not for mental issues. Self-reflection therapy for managers and new agers; that sort of treatment. We have shown the therapists psychological profiles we created with only three weeks of data. Let me put it this way: half of them were ready to return their diploma."

Voice #2: "When we match your mental state from your handheld scans with the content you engaged with…"

Voice #6: "It's not just handhelds. Typing-analysis we also do on big screen websites; plus, movements across the site. How long you take to click things and so on and so forth. Also here, deviations from your usual patterns are very telling."

Voice #2: "…plus we know where you were at the time…what you did…what you looked at…"

Voice #1: "We can see if reading a report on THS excites you, makes you nervous; we can detect if people with similar reactions to the same event were at the same location…"

Voice #2: "This could actually have legs."

Willis signals the analyst to stop the playback. "Let me get this straight. The kings of the Valley conspiratorially met in this hotel in Mountain View to work out how they can find the Siliconettes for us?"

"When we got wind on this," the analyst replies, "we thought it was a joke. Wasn't easy to get the judge to agree to the tap. But when we listened in, we knew this is serious."

"They plan to build an even bigger data base than they already have? Use some advanced new gimmicks on it they just invented?"

"I checked. None of those features are on file yet. Not sure if this can actually work. Wouldn't rule it out, though."

"Why do we get to see this only now? If that meeting already went down two days ago?"

"Didn't have authorisation to talk about it. To no one outside the bureau. Orders from the very top."

Willis looks like he's struggling to remind himself that killing the messenger won't propel the cause.

"We need to make sure," he says, "the neighbourhood watch doesn't conduct a private witch hunt for any suspects they identify. Incite the public. Before you know it, we have a lynch mob out there."

"Don't be such a wuss," Special Agent Friends says. "I'd love to know what these guys can tell us about our friend Flake Thomas. It could be the final nail to this phony's coffin."

"May well be," Willis replies. "Could just as well incriminate some innocent people. It's untested tech."

***

Aliens

"Hello. Is there anybody out there? Just nod if you can hear me.

"This is Awkward Andy. Welcome back to the number one channel for paranoid data-dystopians.

"Those of you who watched yesterday's episode already know my guest, Jacob Lysiky, a security expert who is here to talk to me about the Big One.

"Jacob, what do you say to the objection that storing all this information, the conspirators, THS, would need a colossal data centre, or even many massive data centres?"

"First: should the disclosure dump be mostly aggregates it would cut down the volume of storage needed significantly. With aggregate, I mean not all the searches of an individual, all the sites he visited. Only the conclusions drawn from this data. The users aggregated preferences."

"Like: Not all line items on his bank account, but the net value of inflow and outflow per month or per quarter?"

"Should that be the content of the Big One, the volume of storage needed could be extremely reduced. Still huge, though. The second point is: maybe this is not all dropped in giant data centres. Below the ground somewhere in North Korea, as the speculations go. Maybe they store the dump in a distributed manner on millions of computers. On your computer, your subs' computers. Maybe even my computer."

"Explain to us how that would work."

"Remember Napster? Those of you who are my age certainly will."

"That was like rack space for vinyls, wasn't it?"

"Close. Napster was a file sharing service. It used a new technology at the time called peer-2-peer networking. I don't want to go into too much technical detail, but what that meant was, in essence, they stored enormous amounts of files on millions of private computers. In Napster's case, music files and later movies as well."

"Napster itself only held a central directory, a list of content, so to speak, didn't they?"

"To locate the individual files, exactly. Users located the content via that central server and downloaded it in small batches from many sources. Shortly before pulling the plug, Napster had eighty million computers storing, uploading, and downloading data. Similar concepts could be employed here."

"That is ancient tech. There surely is more sophisticated stuff out there these days?"

"There certainly is. One example is grids of privately owned equipment working together to make enormous compute power available for non-profit purposes. Like the search for extraterrestrial life, the SINA project."

"Extraterrestrial life? You need to be careful with your spice consumption, I'd say, Jacob."

"We may not think this is a serious quest, yet it needs very serious storage and compute capacity. Millions of volunteers collaborate across a decentralised network to provide this capacity."

"Scientists also use such an approach for medical research, don't they?"

"Should you want to contribute to saving human rather than extraterrestrial life, the Folding@home project could be your thing. The project supports research on diseases such as Alzheimer's or HIV. For a long time, Folding@home competed for the title of the world's most powerful computer system, even though it was not a big central machine. It worked with tens of thousands of decentralised computers made available by volunteers in their homes. For the techies among your subs: It was the world's first exaflop computing system."

"The most powerful computer in the world is a grid of PCs in people's homes?"

"Quite advanced once, but yes, you could say that. There also is the so-called Interplanetary File System, IPFS."

"The Interplanetary File System?"

"Sounds like another joke, I know, but unlike SINA, this is not about aliens. It's a very serious attempt to move the entire internet away from big centrally hosted services that monopolists, authorities or, for example, authoritarian regimes could block. IPFS wants to move it to decentralised storage where basically everybody who takes part in the internet could offer to contribute storage space. And even get paid for it."

"That sounds great."

"It does. And it may be the future of the internet. One of the ways to get to Web3."

"In all these projects you just illustrated, Napster, medical research or the future infrastructure of the World Wide Web, even Web3, people take part voluntarily. Does this mean THS is a worldwide conspiracy of millions of people?"

"Not at all. The last example, which explains why not, is a so-called BOT network. In contrast to SINA and Folding, which serve noble purposes, and much more like Napster, these networks' predominant use is fraud."

"Such BOT networks are used to bring down websites, right?"

"BOT networks do not get set up to store data, generally. They get set up to send messages. Attack websites with millions if not billions of calls, pings. Send spam email. This kind of stuff. Such a BOT network is an extensive grid with a vast number of compromised computers. The user does not know his computer got infected."

"Participants of a BOT network have no clue their computer assists in a fraudulent attack in the background while they play GTA?"

"Correct. There is no technical reason such a BOT network could not also use a gigabyte or two or even 100 GB of storage, depending on the make of your computer and what the evil guys can reserve on your machine without being detected."

"Could you aggregate enough storage with this? Even for the Big One?"

"If you consider the biggest BOT networks we have seen so far, they often comprised millions of computers. '3ve,' for example, used up to 2 million hijacked computers plus numerous servers. ZeuS, one of the biggest ever, created already in 2007 and said to be still in existence, comprises 13 million computers. Mariposa had 12 million. ZeroAccess maybe 9 million. If you use 1 GB of storage per infected device, one million computers mean 1 petabyte of data. 10 million computers with 100 GB each is 1 exabyte of data."

"That would be a lot of account names and passwords. You think this could be how the Big One might be stored?"

"Should the data disclosed be aggregates, in my opinion, this approach could work. Don't get me wrong. That is still a lot of data. Yet, as we have just seen, there are ways to store it on millions of machines."

"Which would make it very hard to trace back to its originators, wouldn't it?"

"Another advantage of it, yes. From the perspective of THS that is, of course."

"This all sounds very scary, I must say!"

"Wanna hear the ironic highlight of my story?"

"Not sure I do...?"

"Are you aware that the security software on your computer, the software that is supposed to protect you from all of this, that this software might secretly be using your computer to mine crypto coins? At least if you are using certain anti-virus software."

"You are kidding me?"

"I'm not, I'm afraid! Some anti-virus software uses the combined power of the millions of computers that have the software installed to mine crypto currencies secretly in the background, while your machine would otherwise be idling."

"Probably with my consent hidden somewhere deep down in the fine print of their terms and conditions?"

"I bet!"

"Jacob, thanks a lot for joining me. It was truly a pleasure to talk to you, even though I have to up my Xanax now."

"You guys out there: As always, I leave you with the quote of the day, this time from Siggi Freud, the famous psychiatrist. He said: 'the paranoid is never entirely mistaken'."

"Thanks for wasting some of your precious time on my channel. Please consider subscribing or press the like button as your chance to vote for more supervision over the naughty boys who rule the world. I'm Awkward Andy, your friendly neighbourhood web-stinger."

Red Lever

Leeza seemed rather absent ever since she joined the team in the main cafeteria.

"What is it?" Tim asks. "Which planet are you on? We need to get this newsletter in today."

"Tell me, Tim, when we put up all the different choices for sexual orientation...what is it...? Twenty-odd different classifications all together...? Did we do that to give people the opportunity to express themselves more fully? Or did we just pretend to root for diversity, to insidiously...sneakily...introduce another means to learn more to sell people out?"

"Is that your fundamentalist boyfriend talking?" Tim retorts. Leeza's forlorn gaze begs him to focus on her question.

"Honestly? I think it is a blurred line. Same as when the 'like'-button came about. The guys didn't design it for the user to share his preferences with his friends. They invented it so the firm knows how to target folks better. In the end, it served both. A win-win."

"I read a lot about this during my studies," Mic says, "it's a classic. They had struggled for quite a while to figure out how they could best structure the newsfeed; users drowned in info-overload; stopped looking at it even, because it was too much; the team used all sorts of analytics to guess which of the posts folks would want to see first; from all his friends, his favourite media; easily hundreds per day. They tried to match interests, time spend, all of those things. Couldn't really work it out. Even considered asking a group of users to sort their entire feed manually to learn from that. If you look at it in hindsight, it's hard to understand why it took so long to have that simple idea: to ask if you particularly liked something."

"That is really very interesting, Micah," Tim says, "yet I don't think Leeza wanted a Facebook history tour."

"Today, this thing is iconic," Leeza mumbles. "A symbol for all of social media. An entire industry."

"What I wanted to say is," Mic insists, "for our services to improve, it needs a lot of experiments. Trial and error. Even after the thumb got conceived, they were not done. It makes a lot of difference, they discovered, whether you thumb it before or after you actually read the full post or even followed a link. Troops down in the engine room still constantly optimise."

"Is that why we need so much data?" Leeza asks. "Flake says we stalk folks through the entire web wherever they go. Are we?"

"For all the sites that link to our platform," Tim responds, "or allow to log in via our credentials. So yeah, you could say that."

"Not just us," Mic says. "Whenever you visit pretty much any site, they send all they get to know about you to thousands of other sites. All those sites enhance the profile they maintain of you with that fresh intel."

Leeza's eyes grow manga girl big and basset hound sad. "Is all that really helpful?"

"The problem with our algorithms is," Mic replies, "we need to train them with lots and lots of input."

"Train them? You collect my data to train an algorithm?"

"Well...yes...?"

"Elevator pitch on that, please?"

"It is not like everybody who subscribes to Miley Cyrus will appreciate a news article on flying saucer sightings in Napa Valley. The maths is not that simple. We feed our tools with lots of input. Then we tell the tool what the output was. And then we let the tool figure out which algorithm best predicts such an outcome from any other input."

"You went techie again!" Tim grouches. "Can you try plain English for once?"

"You see the red lever?" Mic snaps.

Tim's eyes throw an error 404.

"Did you not watch The Avengers? Never mind," Mic turns back to Leeza. "Remember how Zach assumed your family was from China? Let's say we wanted to train a little Zach-bot to tell where an Asian person descends from only by looking at his or her face. We could try to describe precisely what features to look for in a face to determine if it is from the Mekong delta in Vietnam or Guangdong province in China. Try to put that in code. That is hard to do. Impossible, actually. There are no clear rules, like: that type of nose is always from one particular region. This eye shape is always from that region. It is a mix and match and statistics and a variety of things..."

"I get that," Leeza nods.

"Therefore, we feed the Zach-bot a lot of mug shots. All the variations of Asian descent. As many as we can find, ideally."

"There is the first difference," Leeza smiles. "Zach, the annoyingly superficial one, not the artificially intelligent one, probably didn't meet many Asian people in his life."

"He wasn't trained with a lot of input, correct. However, input alone will not do. For all the Asian faces we feed the machine, we also need to tell it where this face is actually from. That is the second thing Zach's training failed on. He seldomly asks Asian folks where their families originally came from. We are all Americans, right?"

"Guilty," Leeza laughs. "I don't even know which part of Europe your family came from?"

"My family is from the beautiful city of Vilnius, which Napoleon called the Jerusalem of the North, and fDi magazine counts among the 25 Global Cities of the Future. But let's finish the AI-for-beginners tutorial here real quick. Only one more step. The important one, though. We let the machine figure out what the features are that tell us where a face on a mug shot might come from. It breaks the problem down into small patterns. It forms assumptions, tests them, forms new ones; it does this until most of the outcomes we feed it would have been predicted correctly. It's pretty much how your brain learned it as well."

"Seems pretty simple."

"Yes and no, I'd say. The idea is simple. Your brain is not. And so is our engine. It should be obvious you need to feed the tool a lot of mug shots to build such an algorithm. Thousands, better yet millions of faces; yet, the more data you feed it, the more complex the algorithm becomes."

"In the end, you have some sort of formula that represents how humans think?"

"We call them neuronal network even. The machine emulates how your brain works. In scenarios like the ones that were trained. You brain can do much more, of courses."

"In the scenario it was trained in, the machine becomes perfect?"

"The machine will keep getting better, as long as you feed it new data and also tell it when it got it wrong. Yet it is far from perfect. Algorithms get it wrong pretty often still. There was, for example, this case of a photo analysis software. It automatically sorted your pictures in folders with similar subjects. Like planes, buildings, various categories."

"Doesn't seem too hard to do."

"You'd think so, right? The thing exploded on them when the software created a folder it called 'Gorillas'. The user had never taken any pictures of gorillas. Very few animal pictures at all, but absolutely no gorillas."

"That was a problem because…?" Tim asks impatiently.

"That was a problem because the pictures filed by the software in that 'gorillas'-folder were photographs of a middle age couple. And this couple were people of colour. All hell and righteousness broke loose on the company."

Mic's excitement meets stony faces.

Uncomfortable from the subdued mood, he adds, "Luckily, we only show the user a banner he might not be interested in, or rank post highly he or she will ignore."

Tim gets up and roams around, while Leeza stares at the disintegrated foam at the bottom of her latte glass absentmindedly for quite a while, as if she's trying to read enlightenment from the coffee grounds.

"We form assumptions about people's political preference," she says eventually. "And on even more intimate matters. Don't we?"

"Sure. We can work out your sexual inclination or political affiliation just by looking at your clicks," Mic brags proudly, glad she broke the awkward hash.

Leeza looks at him with tender rebuke. "People may get hurt because we got it wrong."

"These models are everywhere, though," Mic mumbles, gazing down at his feet. "Banks decide on loans based on them. Insurance companies determine which rate to offer a prospect. More and more important decisions are made based on such models."

"Should we not let people know what algorithms we use? Would that not be fair?" Leeza asks.

"The point is," Mic says, "we can't."

"Because people would reject it?"

"That's not it. With sophisticated machine learning techniques, more and more, we will not understand it ourselves anymore."

"You lost me?"

"Such models become so complex it's not possible to tell what they do. What exactly the rules and steps are the machine has figured out to get to the best result."

The wrinkles on Leeza's forehead become ever deeper.

Ever since he had to listen to Flake's one-hour monologue the other day, on the beautiful patterns his friend sees in Leeza's little wrinkles, he can't help but find them rather hypnotic himself. He has a difficult time to focus on his point.

"Such neural networks can have a very high number of hidden layers, hundreds even, with many, many neurons…the weightings of the connections on all those levels can become so complex before the cost function gets close to zero…"

Mic gasps for tech terms like he'd be gasping for air after holding his breath for a couple of minutes. Leeza walks over to Tim, who grew paler by the second listening to Mic's tutorial.

"Are you alright?" she asks, stroking his back.

"We keep our users under surveillance 24/7," he says, more to himself, as if Leeza had activated a talking doll's play-button on the spine, "to feed a machine we do neither understand nor control, to create a benefit the user might hardly recognise…and why? Because we can? Or because someone actually believes this makes the world a better place?"

"Don't know anymore."

Leeza leaves her hand on his shoulder while her mind drifts off.

***

Big One Minus 3, Friday

Redmond

A particularly gleamy sun, following a hefty shower, beams from a brightening sky past patchy cotton candy clouds on millions of tiny amber blossoms sprinkled across the towering grass. A lupine-lined path leads past a panorama of lush green trees.

"This place is beautiful, alright. But why did we have to come all the way out here?"

"The days when you could have a conspiratorial meeting at Seattle Waterfront are gone. Evans Creek is my secure conference room whenever I do business in the area."

"The trench stomping through the meadows is with you, I assume?"

"Scanning for signals and drones. Gotta make sure."

"At least, you could have let me in on the dress code." The elegant man peers down at his buckskin brogues covered in mud. Then he looks at his companion's boots and Barbour jacket.

"I asked for a casual chat, didn't I?" his friend smiles.

"You said it is very urgent and very important. This is how I dress for very important. Last time you called me up with that special tone in your voice, we ended up buying LinkedIn. What did you want to talk about this time that is so top secret?"

He tries to wipe off the mud with his handkerchief.

"You could say it is something along those lines. Just bigger." The savvy pro protracts his point waiting for the moment of most impact. "Much bigger," he adds. As his friend realises he is merely spreading the dirt, rolls up his pants, slightly annoyed, and is about to stand up, the mystery-monger pushes the button: "I want to talk about wiping Meta!"

The punchline works as intended; the high-intensity task of processing this statement has the brain's automated background threads get out of step and his surprised friend stumbles on the rise. "What do you mean? Wipe Meta?" he stammers.

"You have been waiting for this opportunity for years. With the Big One, it can become a reality."

"What opportunity?"

"Saw what happened to Meta's stock yesterday? Down thirty percent. Again. Been up and down all week. When the Big One hits, the moment is there. The moment you have been waiting for."

"What moment?"

"To launch a new social network to replace Facebook."

"Push Facebook out? Even Google failed with that."

"And with balloons and many other wacky stuff. They actually failed in more things than they succeeded with. But that's not the point. The point is, until now, the compelling event wasn't there."

"What compelling event would that be?"

"When the data dump hits, Meta's stock will tank even further. Yet, they are too big to fail."

"Nonsense!" the dignified executive gets all worked up. "No one is too big to fail."

"Of course not. Usually. It's just an excuse for governments to channel money from middle-class taxpayers to corporate America, for which they didn't find any other devious ways yet. But that is not the point as well. The administration will save them! Unless…"

"Unless what?"

"Unless you present them with an alternative."

"What exactly are you suggesting?"

"I suggest Nadella stages a press conference Monday at noon and tells the world you will set up an ad free alternative to Facebook. Which doesn't collect any data. To make sure such a horrible event can never happen again and that the American people are protected from harm. You may also say '…from unscrupulous racketeers, hunting for your soul,' depending on temperament."

"With unscrupulous racketeers you mean Meta?"

"Don't worry, knowing Satya, he will find the kindest words ever. He's the guy you want to tell you on judgement day that you will need to go to hell. He'll make it sound like an upgrade on your all-inclusive."

"An ad free social media platform will have to be chargeable. People don't want to pay."

"Actually, that's not true. Users may not have been willing, in the past, to pay enough to make it profitable. But only a minority declines to pay at all. You should ask yourself how much that has changed with the Big One?"

"I don't know…"

"Look, Facebook sells ads for about fifteen bucks per month on each active user in the US and Canada. And they don't know how to shovel the money around quick enough for it not to start rotting in their deep, deep money pit. In case you sell it to folks for the charge of a Netflix subscription, you still make shitloads of money. I'm sure you'll come up with ways to boost profits. Maybe introduce ads again, just 'on request'." His fingers draw quotation in the air. "Plus, you get rid of those Meta bastards. Before they buy their way deeper into your turf."

"Okay, I get that. But why should it work? Even now?"

"THS's announcement shook Meta badly. Made investors think. They are ready to fall. Can't survive with those valuations. It'll kill *'em*. Congress can't let them fall off the cliff 'cause, come election day, none of these honourable gentlemen will want to explain to their voters that their favourite toy is broken and they have done nothing about it."

"I get that. But why support us?"

"While Zuckerberg has alienated many people in congress with his arrogance, you guys have been the Brady Bunch ever since the Netscape thing was settled twenty years ago."

"Maybe he will schmuse up to them in the hearing tonight?"

"Oh, sure. If he only knew how humans interact. Plus, he becomes more and more of a burden to them. Regulatory authorities in Norway and the UK already say companies like Meta are…" he draws quote marks in the air again, "'systematically non-compliant with EU regulation'. In plain English: illegal. Already today. Rules are just not properly enforced yet."

"That would be a major problem for many others as well."

"Uhhh yeah! Trust me, I've dumped a lot of stocks months ago. Once those privileges are gone, ad targeting by Facebook and others spying on users will be no better than that of any old school marketing firm."

"Eventually Congress will have to pick a fight, either with the EU or with some all-American tech giants?"

"Should another all-American tech giant offer them a way out of this dilemma…Congress could portray themselves as acting on privacy concerns; the protector of the American people; and still keep control of the Internet. Wouldn't even risk a lot of jobs. Meta only has fifty thousand staff around the globe."

"Imagine that, a company worth trillions gives a meagre fifty thousand people a job."

"And hardly pays their taxes. Less than half of the workforce sits in the US, even. You should suggest taking them all over."

"Why would Facebook not just offer their services ad-free in a charging model, if they get their arm twisted?"

"It would cut their business in half. Stock markets will abandon them. If the downturn is so drastic…it becomes a spiral; a self-propelling downward spiral of doom."

"Plus ego, of course. No founder can cut his baby in half. With an actual baby, I'm not so sure with this fellow, but with his brainchild…? Even though it was an immaculate conception."

"Nasty!"

"Didn't say he stole the baby…"

"He won't go down without a fight. Will not just hand over their users. And users will not want to leave Facebook because it means saying goodbye to your carefully curated timeline."

"You're right. People wouldn't accept that; would feel like a wildfire is burning down their house and all their life's memories with it. You will have to bring users' existing content to your new platform."

"Why should Meta allow that?"

"Congress will make them. It'll pass laws forcing platforms to provide interfaces. Technically, that's a piece of cake."

"Speaking of technology. This needs a complex platform. That's not built overnight."

"My friend…I'll ignore you said that. I know you guys have the complete thing in your drawers, ready to go. You have been wrestling with the temptation for years. The more Zuck poached in your neck of the woods, the more funding the project got. I know you're ready. Just switch off ads and switch on monthly charging. It's out there in no time. Making use of…no…healing the desperation in American homes and on the hill."

"The way you tell the story, it sounds like a no-brainer."

"It is! And you know what? You can snatch up WhatsApp and Instagram as you go as well, easily."

"Because they don't make any money? Just there to collect more data?"

"Exactly. Data that is of no use without the big pot. And when this evil empire makes its clearance sale, you can snatch a truck load of stormtrooper's Oculus remnants at a bargain price on top."

"Tell me again, why did we let a guy like you leave the firm?"

"Maybe it was because I said the Internet is not here to stay...? Na, that was the other guy...he's got to stay...Ah, I remember, because Balmer wanted to be the only Donkey Kong wildly jumping about the office."

"Yeah, right," his friend smiles reminiscently.

"Look, if I'd known lobbying in DC makes you so much cash, I'd have left way earlier. Anyway, will you take this to Nadella?"

"Sure will, first thing back in office." With a broad beam, he adds, "in our secure conference room."

"Good," his friend responds in an unexpectedly serious tone, "'cause I need your response today. Should you not want guaranteed domination in the Metaverse by getting rid of your biggest rival, I'll talk to Alphabet. Have a meeting with them tomorrow."

"You're meeting Alphabet?"

"For now, it is on another matter. But I'd hate to let this opportunity pass to create a big fuss. Someone will have to man up and confront these Meta bastards."

"Will get back to you today, promise. Can't promise the nature of the response, obviously."

"No worries," his friend winks. "I'm sure it will sound like a promotion. Where do you want me to drop you off?"

"Well, on your orders, I left my phone at home when you picked me up." He looks down at himself. "And I will obviously have to change."

Back in the car, while diligently trying to rub the dried mud from his shoes with his handkerchief, he asks as casually as possible: "Tell me, old friend, what can you tell me about this other idea you're talking to Google about? Without you having to shoot me, that is."

"No, no, it's fine. About how to wipe Tesla. Not gonna tell you how, though."

"You sure carry a lot of grudges against many people in tech, my friend."

"In Elon's case, it's not a grudge. I even like the guy. He's whack. Good whack. I like that. I would fight on his side in this battle, should he be prepared to make it worth my while. But not Zuck. He's mean whack."

"I certainly hope you will never carry a grudge against us."

"I'm over it. Besides, even I'm not crazy enough to pick a fight with HAL 2.0." He beams over at his friend.

"Tesla doesn't seem ready to fall, though? Didn't lose as much market cap in the recent turmoil as Meta or Google."

"Their problem isn't the data. For now. But they are probably even more overvalued than Meta. Facebook has an actual monopoly, as things stand; impregnable. Tesla has none of that. Markets evaluate them like a tech company, as if they were selling software or tech gadgets. They sell cars for the time being. Even if these cars get iconised, they are still just cars."

"Remember when you had to prove you made it by fronting a Beamer or a Porsche?"

"I remember when you borrowed my 911 to impress that girl."

"…who is now my wife for twenty years!"

"Yeah, right, it was Sue you wanted to impress so badly. Glad it worked."

The two men high-five.

"Back to the point. One cool gadget can't serve as grounds for a trillion-dollar market cap. Before the 911, there were Corvette, Mustang GT."

"Chevy Belle Air."

"Look, Tesla also employs less than fifty thousand people. Mercedes? Six times more. Mercedes makes five times the profit of Tesla. Three times the number of cars."

"Tesla is more efficient, at least."

"True. Electric vehicles are way easier to produce. Yet, I grant you, Mercedes is also behind in efficiency in their electric plants. My point is, none of this I can reconcile with a difference in stock market valuation of one to fifty."

"Tesla is fifty times more valuable than Mercedes?"

"Yes, Sir! That's the opening. Markets always tended to over-hype certain firms. But what's going on these days, with way too much money not knowing where to go, it gets bizarre sometimes. Which, once you find the right compelling event, occasionally allows you to burst one of these bubbles. Tesla will pop soon should Google be smart enough to follow my advice."

"Why Google? Why not help Mercedes wipe Tesla? They must want this badly, I guess?"

"Would I go to TikTok to put away Facebook? No. I came to you, my friend."

Essentials

Amy: "With only three days to go before the Big One, people are asking what we are going to do about it. We reported earlier, here on Good Morning America, many people already take measures into their own hands by deleting their social media accounts and dropboxes. Some even disconnect their computers from the internet. These are desperate attempts to limit the damage."

George: "Let me point out again, Amy, that we do not know which data the Big One will comprise. How big it is going to be? However, it's highly unlikely that deleting anything now will make any difference. I think we need to expect it is already too late for that."

Amy: "If that doesn't help, the question is: what does? What do we do now? Can we do something about it? How can people prepare? How can the nation prepare? With more and more people believing the Big One will have very severe consequences in general and also on them personally, some people are even asking: can we not simply shut down the internet?"

George: "The World Wide Web was actually designed to be particularly resilient to such interference. That was the whole point of creating it. Basically, packets of data, small subsets of any message or file, freely reroute to always find a way. The founding fathers designed it exactly to overcome attempts to block communication. Trying to cut all internet connections is like stopping all rivers in the entire world at the same time. That does not seem realistic. Yet, should you take the Meta family, Google, Amazon and a few others plus the major traffic hubs off the grid, for most of us, the internet would basically be gone. Not sure this would help much, but this could be one scenario."

Amy: "You think people should prepare themselves to live without a majority of internet services for a little while, George? Let us explore that thought for a moment. Would that be so bad? What would it mean to live without the web? I suppose my daughter would say it is impossible; maybe she thinks she would implode right away...but honestly, George? What does this mean?"

George: "Excellent point. Why is it so important all these services stay up all the time? Very few of them are existential, right? Think about it. At least, we should be good without Facebook and Instagram for a while. Amazon will hurt the economy big time. Yet, there are alternatives, right? Walmart will still be open for business. High street shops will gladly dress you up and equip you with whatever you desire. Do we need Google? When there is nothing to find, we don't need to search."

Amy: "At least we need Google Maps, George, since many of us seem to have forgotten how to get to a brick-and-mortar store, actually. And don't forget, supply chains for brick-and-mortar businesses heavily depend on the internet nowadays. Not all companies still own a fax machine. Another question is: What does this mean going forward, once this is all over? If we assume society survives this in peace? Do we all need to acquaint ourselves with the darknet where you can be completely anonymous, so that something like this cannot happen again? Or build a closed internet like they have it in China? Where the authorities regulate all services tightly?"

George: "We will speak with folks across the country about their views on the Big One and what they plan on doing about it, right after the break. Don't go away."

***

Metamorphosis

There had been no point staying in the office any longer, so Tim got to the café way early to meet with Leeza. Here, at least, nobody would eyeball him like they expect him to pull a gun and run rampage any second. Even Leeza had been evading him all morning. At least, she agreed to talk on neutral grounds about those messages.

After biting his nails for almost an hour, however, and downing four lattes, he can't tell anymore whether strangers peer over because the enemy caught up on him or because he nervously scans his surroundings all the time, suspecting anyone receiving a message on his phone of being in on the plot. When he sees Leeza levitating towards him in a lovely light-blue summer dress, swaying her delicate frame in slow motion, it feels like a Marian apparition; that fleeting emotional high is quickly thwarted, though, by Flake following closely behind her.

"What's the cockroach doing here?" Tim bitches, referring to the print on Flake's shirt showing Franz Kafka turn into monstrous vermin; as if avoiding his name, using disparaging terms instead, could make the rival disappear.

"Moral support," Leeza replies. When she sees Tim's eyes narrow to crenels ready to open fire, she adds: "For me."

"I am not dangerous, damn it!" Tim utters, more depressed than angry. "This day was a nightmare. I need to know what's going on. Please show me those messages. Seems quite a few people got those."

"I didn't even read most of them. All that crap about you." She hands him her phone.

Tim scrolls through messages, opens attachments, zooms photos; every click seems to up the voltage pulsing through his spine. His hands tremble.

"What is this? This is crazy," he utters.

"You tell us!" Flake says.

"It's none of your business," Tim retorts, then turns to Leeza. "Has he seen this?"

"No, of course not. Not without asking you first. Yet maybe Flake can help. As you said, quite a few people have seen this, anyway."

Hesitantly, Tim passes the phone, his sweaty, trembling fingers hardly able to operate the device, anyway.

"I just scanned the first few," Leeza says with the disgusted gaze of a spouse stumbling across her partner's Hustler collection. "The first one came with the subject 'what your hero doesn't want you to know'. Once I discovered it was about you, Tim, I stopped. Didn't want to see all that crap."

"Wow!" Flake says. "You're right. This is crazy! Like a Big One, just on one little guy."

Flake keeps scrolling through the evidence.

"Your top 10 list of porn…what did you need that for?"

"Not funny. Someone wants to zap me. I got a message saying: Only a selected few got a sneak peek. Next, we will put it all online. Should you want this to end, stop the campaign!"

"Chats between you and some Tinderettes…" Flake mumbles, "well, if two consenting adults like dirty talk…it's a free country…"

"…dumping your girlfriend via text…and another one…and another…

"…you subscribed to quite a number of OnlyFans profiles…from the names I suppose these ladies wear over-knees for drinks and stilettos in bed…?"

"…a list of Wi-Fi networks you logged into…just the ones with sleazy names…Carla's Cabaret? Empire Showgirls? Synn? Satin Seduction? Venus Trap? Let me guess: Strip Clubs…?"

"Oh. This is bad. An artfully crafted collage: some shots of you with various lovely Asian ladies, your boarding pass to Hanoi and a medical record of your herpes diagnosis; wicked! Not very subtle, though."

"...medical records of our father treated for drug abuse. Nasty!"

Flake looks up, straight at Tim. "You have been totally kardashianed, buddy!"

Flake keeps scrolling while Tim keeps slumping and Leeza keeps searching for words of encouragement.

"Look, Leeza," Flake turns the phone. "This is what I'm talking about. A list of keyword Tim searched for. A selection of the dubious ones only, naturally. Imagine you knew someone looks at all your online searches. All the time. You'd surely start censoring yourself. I guess there are totally acceptable reasons to search for almost anything. Even...let me see...even decapitation and dirty bomb, just to quote from the section with D..."

"I can explain," Tim says, "its..."

"...none of my business," Flake interrupts. "And nobody else's. That is exactly what I mean."

"This looks terrible, I know," Tim sighs. "All in one place. Every odd thing I have ever done. Like I only have a nasty side. This is not me; you know...?" Tim's turns away his watering eyes. Leeza puts her hand on his.

"Now I understand why Leeza stopped reading...statistics of you stalking her social media accounts. You seemed quite obsessed with her for a while. I don't blame you. This is extreme, though."

Leeza leans in on Tim. "Please tell me this is not why you started the campaign?"

"I swear, Leeza, honestly: I had no idea this is what I look like in my personal dump. When I look at that...I wouldn't hang out with that guy." Tim's voice cracks. "That's someone I'd try to avoid. I don't see me in this. I am not a bad person. I think. I'm not...I'm not like this."

Leeza strokes his shoulder, still pondering for something comforting to say.

Tim clears his throat and continues with a brittle voice. "The last message I got was: 'everyone you will ever meet in your life will see your dark side when they google you'. And it said there is even more." When Flake looks up from scanning the evidence with an inquisitive stare, he adds, "For the life of me, I wouldn't know what else they could dig up..."

"How can we help?"

Flake was afraid Leeza would ask this.

"This has helped already," Tim says. "You could be my eyes and ears in the office; keep me posted on what's going on? I'll work from home for a few days; until this cools over."

"Do you have an idea who would badger you like this?" Flake is quick to ask before Leeza can inquire about any more aid she could provide.

"Maybe these Siliconettes freaks don't like my face…"

"Not likely, if you ask me," Flake says.

"I didn't ask!" Tim snaps.

"It is, of course, well possible they don't like you," Flake retorts. "Yet, ten bucks say, it is not them."

"Why not?" Leeza asks. "What makes you think that?"

"In my view, THS don't aim to hurt individual people. They mean to show all of us how far we have allowed this to get. The monster we created."

"Does this not end up being the same?" Tim sighs.

"No, it doesn't!" Leeza gets all excited about the revelation she just had, glad she finally found a positive angle on this. "When everyone's secrets get exposed, we all feel what you just feel, Tim. People will see nobody is as good as they make themselves appear in their public profiles. And also, nobody is as bad as they seem when you just look at a pile of bad things."

Since the guys don't seem to share her excitement, she adds: "Being able to forget, to repress bad memories is arguably the most important feature of our brain. Yet the web never forgets, right?"

"Tim's dump is way nastier than your late fees for the public library, Leeza!" Flake says.

She gives him the wait-till-we-get-home look, while Tim is too confused and embarrassed to even react.

Flake's mind refuses to contemplate what makes him so certain his girl's lily-white dump would even make Jane the Virgin look like a naughty girl.

"Maybe we should stop the campaign?" Leeza suggests.

"How can you say that?" Tim replies. "This is too important."

"Whoever sent these might be dangerous. Who knows what they will do next?"

"I wouldn't even know what to do to stop the campaign. This is not in our control anymore."

"For one, you could stop sending calls to action three times a day. Maybe get off Twitter even. At least, send some tweets to cool things down. Drop your hall of shame collecting people's clues and pointers…"

"No way! Some gutless anonymous extortionists will not make me quit!" Tim bounces up as if to shake off the dirt. "I will go home and turn all this crap into something good." For a moment, he pauses, with a hollow glance, as if his brave words still need to persuade his doubting heart.

"Oh," Tim turns to Leeza again, "I didn't get a chance to tell you yet. The feds woke me up this morning. Found out my computer is still connected to Zach's messenger."

'Shit!' Leeza's face says. "What did they want?"

"Something about a USB drive with shitloads of intel on Zach's personal life; asked what I knew about it. Didn't quite get it."

"What did you say?"

"Don't worry. They know nothing about you guys."

"I'm worried about you!"

He leans down and gives her a lasting hug. "Thanks for everything, Leeza!"

Tim's cracking voice has her choking as she watches him leave.

"We should get going as well," Flake's concerned tone pulls her back into reality.

"What's wrong?" Leeza asks.

"Looks like my friend Miles, the muscled menace, will be here any minute."

"How do you know?"

"After you saved my butt on campus the other day, I created a really slutty profile the Greatest of all Time, the king of dick pics, couldn't possibly resist. Was a quick match; now I get notifications whenever the app senses a chance for me to meet the man of my dreads."

"I need some fresh air, anyway. Windy Hill?"

"No idea what that is, but it sounds like a lot of fresh air."

On their way out, a smile forces himself upon Flake as he realises that the collab between the goddess of shopping mall music and a zealous iTunes algorithm chose The Who's *I Can See for Miles* to accompany their exit. He starts singing along.

Duck and Cover

"Tim Rozen, the Silicon Valley product manager who started the #DontDoxxMyDudes campaign a few days ago, was fired by his employer today."

"When asked to comment, a spokesperson of the firm told MSNBC that the redundancy was advised because of repeated conduct by Rozen severely violating corporate policies and values. Rozen was not available for a live interview but told our reporter he was not informed about any details on these allegations, nor the particular instances of misconduct he was accused of."

"Rozen's campaign went viral immediately after its release on Tuesday and is the most referred to hashtag these last days."

"Not only Big Tech here in the US is getting increasingly nervous with the Big One coming close. In Hong Kong, police arrested dozens of members of the opposition, including several activist bloggers today. Political observers believe this latest development must be seen in the context of yesterday's arrests of over one hundred activists in China. Stuart in Beijing: what do we know about these arrests?"

"No charges were brought forward yet in any of these cases; neither regarding the arrests in China yesterday, nor in Hong Kong today. Speculations circulate, though, the authorities may suspect these individuals to be part of the conspiracy to drop the Big One next Monday."

"People could interpret this as evidence of the regime losing power, should such subversion happen under their watch, couldn't they?"

"Which is, of course, an impression China's political leadership wants to avoid at all costs. Another theory is these arrests were based on data from the Big One, which may reveal proof of anti-state activities of the arrested individuals."

"This could suggest connections of Chinese government officials to the Big One, couldn't it? Yet another diplomatic nightmare."

"This dilemma might explain why there are no reported charges; presumably we should not expect this to change anytime soon."

"Yesterday we reported on the arrest of three-star army general Qamar Aziz in Pakistan, who was brought before a military tribunal, sentenced to death and immediately executed, all within a few hours. What is your view, Stuart? Do we have to interpret incidents like this, since they take place at this particular time, as all being associated with the Big One?"

"It may well be the case some old scores get settled now, veiled by the data hack excuse. However, there is yet another dimension to this we need to bear in mind. The data could just as well disclose discrediting information about people in power."

"What kind of information are you referring to, Stuart?"

"Authoritarian regimes might fear corruption and nepotism could be exposed using information from the dump. Verifiably, even, with tangible evidence. Intrigues going on behind the curtains, in the ranks of power; vulnerabilities of people in office, which, once known, opposition could exploit; weaken the grip of the regime; fuel protest; instill doubts about the preparedness of a regime to suppress protest. It is difficult to say where this could end."

"Sounds like the Big One is not just putting lives of individuals, but entire regimes in jeopardy. Thank you, Stuart. Over to you, John, in Riyadh, Saudi Arabia, where we already have a casualty from the Big One. What can you tell us about this, John?"

"21-year-old Jamaal Samsar, a student at King Saud University here in Riyadh, burned himself today right in the middle of Deera Square. This is the biggest square in the city and also the arena used for public executions, something that still takes place regularly here in Saudi. Before Samsar put fire to himself, he was holding up a sign on which he appealed to the people behind the Big One not to release any information exposing queer or transgender people in societies like Saudi. The young student shouted: 'To expose is to kill' for about ten minutes before he set himself on fire."

"Bystanders had filmed this horrible scene and uploaded it to various platforms on the internet, haven't they, John?"

"Yes, that is correct. For a few hours, a video that shows the entire event was freely available on the internet. In those few hours, people clicked on it about one million times before it was taken off. It had reappeared a few times since then but always only for a few minutes before the platforms deleted it again."

"What do we know about this young man?"

"The young student descents from a village near Hafar Al Batin in the north, close to the borders of Iraq and Kuwait. He came to Riyadh for his studies about a year ago. We know very little about the young man's lifestyle. An LGBT community does not exist here in Saudi Arabia, like in many countries in the region. At least not openly. It is very difficult for people of diverse background to express themselves freely here."

"The social media presence of Jamaal Samsar shows the perfectly normal life of a young man from the middle class. Nothing in his content reveals particularities about his sexual orientation. Neither do we find any evidence of social activism. The most controversial activity in Semsa's feed is some likes he awarded to posts welcoming the release of Loujain al-Hathloul from prison. The young woman had been detained for three years following an act of protest: she had posted a video showing herself driving a car. Something that was strictly forbidden for women at the time here in Saudi."

"Jamaal Samsar's family did not want to speak to the press. Neighbours and friends describe the young man as an excellent student. Quiet, maybe even a little reclusive, yet always courteous and supportive. They all said this came as a shock to them."

"Thank you, John. I am joined now by Cassey Wheeler from H8NOMORE, a nationwide organisation to promote LGBTIQ rights. Cassey, welcome to our program. How would you comment on this horrible event?"

"Thanks for having me. Indeed, this is a horrible event. Way too many societies around the globe still neglect the basic rights of the LGBTIQ community. Forces in power in 70 countries still incriminate our community even today. In many others, there may not be legal repercussions, yet social marginalisation as a consequence of being queer. In China, for example, only fifteen percent of queer people ever come out to their parents. Jamaal must have felt the system even denied him the right to lead a decent life to take such a dramatic step."

"The young student obviously wanted to issue a statement to the people behind the Big One. How do you assess the threat of the data dump announcement for the LGBTIQ community?"

"The repercussions of such disclosure could, of course, be fatal for our people in countries which neglect our basic human rights. But it doesn't stop there. The issue is not just with those countries. We also see many people here at home very concerned about the Big One and what it might expose. People who haven't come out yet literally flooded our help lines and chats the last few days. Individuals who fear being exposed. They look for help in dealing with it. Some of these people are truly desperate."

"When we ask them what they fear might actually happen to them, we get to hear stories we should not have to hear any more in the US in the 21st century. Young people being afraid their parents or friends may reject them; they might be

subject to discrimination or even violence in their schools. People are even afraid to be cast out at work or in their local communities. Some tell us about precedents in their towns where victims of hostility felt the need to move to another state because of continued social or sometimes physical harassment. Some still even fear for their jobs, despite all legislation on diversity in recent years."

"What kind of support can your organisation offer to those individuals, Cassey?"

"Many people who call us say they do not want to be exposed by some anonymous data dump. They would much rather be the master of their own destiny, yet do not know how. We have kicked off a campaign to give these people moral and practical assistance. Under #MyOwnTerms we encourage people to write about the fears they had when coming out, their experiences and how they coped with it. Especially under difficult circumstances. We look for volunteers across the country prepared to lend people a hand when they face this tough choice. We hope we can offer such mentorship in every part of the country, every town, every village, so that nobody has to do this on his or her own. But only truly on their own terms."

"To that end, one consequence of the Big One could be the biggest coming out campaign ever. Thank you, Cassey, for being with us here today."

***

#DoDoxxThemDons

"X, formerly known as Twitter, Facebook, and a few other service providers have pulled the plug on the most used hashtag of recent days, #DontDoxxMyDudes. In an unprecedented move, the social media companies have announced today they will not show or forward messages anymore that contain this hashtag. Something like this has never happened before."

"You call it unprecedented. I would call it desperate. This morning, here on ABC, spokespeople of the platforms justified the move with the anxieties and irritations caused by this campaign. They referred to official statements from the NSA regarding the relevance of the Big One and the sharp contrast to conspiracy theories, that was the term they used, brought forward in the #DontDoxxMyDudes campaign. In their obviously aligned official press releases, the companies state they are concerned misleading information could be spread as part of this campaign. Such misinformation could effectuate public

fear and traumatisation. It could have, I quote, 'undesirable social consequences'."

"I agree, this is a desperate move. To me, it remains obscure why the companies saw it as their role to interfere in this debate at all."

"When asked why they banned the tag altogether instead of marking posts with comments like they have done on other occasions, the spokesperson of X said the sensitivity of the subject left the company no choice but to apply this precautionary measure in the interest of national security. Some political analysts interpreted this as a sign the tech firms might have experienced significant political pressure that led to this step."

"The former employer of Tim Rozen, the originator of the campaign, who was made redundant by the firm earlier today, also annotated that the firm had learned about personal problems of the young man and sought to protect him by taking him out of the line of fire."

"The move was widely criticised, wasn't it?"

"It was. And not just that. A few thousand people even organised flash rallies here in Santa Clara County and Washington DC against what they consider an assault on freedom of speech. In Santa Clara County, protesters marched to the headquarters of Big Tech firms while in Washington, demonstrators rallied on Capitol Hill."

"The ban also does not seem to have the desired effect, does it?"

"Unsurprisingly, users immediately circumvented the ban. Many users call out now to get revenge on Twitter and the others; to cancel their services altogether; a move which many of us may find difficult to do. Others call for coordinated efforts to take down the social media giants by flooding their websites. The famous hacker community Anonymous and other groups have launched Distributed Denial of Service attacks, in short DDoS, on various websites; these activists bombard the sites with millions and millions of connection requests to overload them. While giants like Facebook and Google seem to have managed the attack mostly well, only being down for an hour or two, some smaller service providers were unavailable for most of today. Even X was off the grid for six hours."

"In the web community, we also see widespread calls for a leaking campaign against Big Tech leaders. Tell us what this is about?"

"These activists appeal to the community to uncover information on senior executives of leading tech firms, banks, multinational corporations; basically,

any company, whose data might be specifically sensitive in the context of the Big One. As one activist put it in his widely shared post: 'make them feel what it means to be stripped naked for all the world to watch. Make them understand why it needs to be taken seriously'."

"This is sort of the evil twin of the #DontDoxxMyDudes campaign that was taken down today, isn't it? Don't stop the leak, instead create another one, in this case exposing the establishment which caused or at least did not stop the problem."

"The campaign is aptly labelled #DoDoxxThemDons, thus equating senior execs in the tech sector with mafia godfathers, often referred to as Dons. Posters often ironically combine the hashtag with others like #SavethemWhales or #FreethemBirds, probably to show this is as good a cause as protecting our environment. Interesting turn of events, I would say."

"I agree, indeed. Let us now look at what is happening in other parts of the world."

"Around the globe, the tension increases. After international media had published several isolated incidents over recent days, officials informed the public today that in total 1500 political opposition leaders from Hong Kong have requested political asylum in the United Kingdom since the announcement broke last Sunday. These leaders of the protest movement against mounting political pressure of China in the territory of Hong Kong fear for their lives and those of others, should information about them and their support networks be exposed."

"From Saudi Arabia, where no official opposition exists, yet many people are demanding individual freedom rights more and more openly, a few dozen men and women have requested political shelter in the US and various European countries."

"Clearly, pressure is rising. We will keep you updated with all the latest information."

"Watch this space!"

***

Spring Clean

"Hello! Is there anybody out there? Just nod if you can hear me!

"It's Awkward Andy. First, thank you guys out there for the exploding subscriber numbers on my feeds. Your number one channel for paranoid data-

dystopians could only grow any faster if we would play online games or give beauty tips. In a pitiful attempt to hop onto that train to fame, I'm wearing my space invaders tee today.

"Other than that, fear not. We're not in it for the money. On this channel, we will merely keep questioning the great imitation game happening online; spots, scars, and deformities will not be concealed.

"Let's get down to business, shall we? Here's another update on recent developments, since so much is happening these days and I want to make sure you guys have the full picture when you decide to kick your computer and smartphone. Which would be sad, since you couldn't watch my channel anymore. Maybe you should just kick your Insta and Facebook accounts. You wouldn't be the only one.

"Millions of users recently deleted their accounts for Meta's services. Investors are increasingly edgy about this. To cool things down, Facebook issued a press release today in which they explain much of the decline in user numbers with a clean-up exercise of the firm; deletion of fake profiles, accounts with made-up names and duplicates. The statement didn't work as planned; it just elevated concerns the company may have tampered with user figures in the past already. I suppose you could say, every move of the formerly all-powerful tech giant is eyed extremely critically these days.

"Another revelation brought to light today will certainly not help either. Leaked documents show middle management executives in major tech companies have set up an unofficial, you may as well call it clandestine, working group to explore the following disturbing plot: It seems this secret group wanted to bring together all major platforms that compile data on individuals; that means: you guys! These plotters wanted to inject all this data into one giant pool, including all the information these individual companies don't share with any third party so far. The aim was to support the investigations of the intelligence agencies and the police by identifying suspected members of THS. You could say the idea was to use a prefabricated Big One to track down the blokes behind the dangerous dump.

"Should that sound crazy and threatening to you, should you be thinking Minority Report right now? Welcome to the club!

"The employers of these Precrime wannabes, major tech firms in the Valley, have hastily issued aligned statements. The companies vehemently reject any involvement in this leaked initiative. Spokespeople of the firms unanimously

commented they consider these gatherings a strictly private matter of the involved executives. Cool, isn't it?

"Senator Cross of the lovely Grand Cuckoo state of Arizona offered a refreshingly different view, as usual. The senator welcomed the initiative. He said all tech corporations should endorse this idea under the supervision of the FBI, because it could only produce beneficial results. Should this work, the senator said, we will get those bastards, he actually used this term, and lock them away for the rest of their lousy lives. Should it not work, he added, this shows once and for all that America's tech industry is not at all as dangerous as the liberal east coast elite want Americans to believe. Dialectics at its best. You just have to love the man...

"As if this wasn't enough bad news for a day, chat protocols between senior executives at Facebook were also leaked, in which they discussed a potential change of the company headquarter's address. This address is 1 Hacker Way. The web community responded within hours with the launch of a poll for a new name. Tens of thousands of internet users have already taken part in these polls. Current leading proposals for the new street address for Meta/Facebook are 1 Spy Lane, 666 Road to Perdition and 1 Boulevard of Broken Dreams. Quite poetic for the geek squad, don't you think? Meta officially denies any consideration of a name change for the headquarter's address.

"I'll keep you guys posted on all the latest updates on the Big One. As always, I'll leave you with a quote, this time from Joseph Heller, later used in a song by Kurt Cobain: Just because you're paranoid doesn't mean they are not after you!

"Thanks for wasting some of your precious time on my channel. Please like and subscribe. As always, this is your chance to vote for more supervision over the masters of the Metaverse. I'm Awkward Andy, your favourite gloomy court jester."

***

Gate to Heaven

"Tim doesn't answer my calls." Leeza takes her eyes off of traffic to check her phone for the umpteenth time. "Or texts."

"The guy's gonna be alright. All just a bit much, I guess."

"He looked awful when he left us. And that was even before the firm dumped him."

Flake swallows his thoughts.

"Should we swing by his place before we meet Mic?" Leeza asks. "Check on him?"

"Maybe he just needs time to himself? Come to grips with all that's going on? Besides, we're already late."

Leeza's absent-minded stare dissolves into a timid smile. "You can't wait to meet Leo? Is that it?"

"Mic never even mentioned him."

"Maybe he wanted to be sure first? They only met a few times."

"He could have told me about that."

"You sound like you're his mum."

"Oh, no, trust me, that would be a very different sound," Flake smiles.

"You wouldn't bring a date to family dinner before you know it serious, would you?"

"You don't bring a gay date home to your die-hard conservative Jewish family ever! Especially a catholic Latino boy who may not be a virgin and, even worse, may not be circumcised. Mic's dad would fear lightning might strike upon them right away."

"If it's about the foreskin, they don't need to worry; from what I heard," Leeza smirks. "But you sure as hell don't tell your mum about the amazing sex with that bad, hot Latino."

"Gee! Way more information than I'd ever need. What else did Mic tell you?" Flake asks in pretend disgust. "Or maybe I should ask, what did he not tell you?"

"Jealous?"

The processing counter in Flake's eyes shows busy.

"You do recognise," Leeza leans over as they wait at a traffic light, "that Mic is as nervous introducing Leo to you tonight as he would be taking him home for family dinner, don't you?"

"Why would he?"

"Your opinion means the world to him. Try to be nice, okay?" She gives him a quick kiss.

The traffic light turns green and Flake's eyes turn blank.

Mic and Leo are so busy flirting they hardly realise their friends making their way through the bustling restaurant. Baba's Korean Kitchen had long been one of Leeza's favourites for the authentic food and chilled vibe. This hasn't gone unnoticed by the Insta hype cycle crowd lately, filling the place up to overflow with folks diligently arranging every dish served by K-pop-pretty staff for the inevitable food porn pic.

"So, Leo," Flake gets down to business right after the first round of drinks arrived, "you are dating my best friend, Mic?"

"Are we dating, Mic?" Leo beams over to his friend, batting his eyelashes seductively.

"Can you please be a little more subtle in your interrogation, Andy?" Mic smiles. "Give the guy a break, okay?"

"Just want to get to know the man who plucks my best buddy."

"It's fine, Mic," Leo says, answering to Flake's dissecting glance with a confident smile. "You know I enjoy being roughed up a little." He gives Mic a quick kiss.

"Don't worry," Flake smirks. "Don't want to know which pet names you gave each other. Yet. Just the basics first."

"Is this your version of nice?" Leeza nudges her friend, laughing.

Flake smiles at Leo in friendly expectation.

"Here's me in a nutshell," the rookie says. "25-year-old, superficial, self-centred prick with no ambitions in life. That's, at least, what my last girlfriend said when she dumped me."

"Your girlfriend?" Leeza asks.

"Took me a while to find out that sex with guys is just so much better. No offence."

"None taken." Leeza smiles.

"Leo just came back from a trip around the world," Mic attempts to get to less mined territory. "He's a very talented photographer."

"Wasting his gift on paparazzi jobs, mostly," Leo says. "One of my clients is a famous influencer. She took me along to document the trip for her channels."

"A famous influencer?" Flake asks.

"Leo may not talk about her in public," Mic says.

"Don't worry. Flake is not the groupie type," Leeza smirks. "What we can say, though: she has like millions of followers."

"You both know who that is?"

Mic and Leeza wink conspiratorially.

"And you're not going to tell me?"

"You see," Leo says, "it happened to me more than once that folks overheard me mentioning her name." He checks on the tables around them. "Last time, I spent the next hour being quizzed about her by total strangers, even though I didn't tell them anything. Folks just kept asking and asking. I had to leave the place."

"Leo is very trustworthy," Mic adds and gives his friend a quick kiss. "That's one reason celebs like to work with him."

Leeza's slightly paranoid look says she suspects their neighbours to be listening in already.

"Let's just call her C, shall we?" Leo smiles disarmingly.

"Tell us about the trip," Leeza says. "Where'd you go?"

"Can even show you. At most of the spots, I took a selfie for my profile."

He swipes the friends around the world: Leo supporting the Leaning Tower of Pisa, balancing the Giza pyramid on his palm, dangling the Eiffel tower from his fingers; Leo romancing the camera in the morning mist at the Taj Mahal, duck-facing in front of the Sydney Opera house, meditating in front of copper-glowing Ayers Rock in the sunset or shielding Big Ben with a Burberry-patterned umbrella against the English rain. Leo goofing around in front of beautiful whitewashed buildings clinging on to steep volcano rock at the coast of Santorini, Italy; a million hues of azure in the maze of winding streets lined with colourful pot plants in Morocco's Chefchaouen; the endless colonnade of thousands of vermilion Tori gates at mount Inari in Japan; and the mesmerising mega-mushrooms of light in Singapore's surreal Gardens by the Bay.

"You're a bit of a camera junkie, aren't you?" Leeza smiles.

"I'm a total show-off," Leo smirks. "Absolutely."

"Didn't even notice the sights in the backdrop." Mic smiles ever so sweetly and gives Leo yet another kiss.

"You are aware," Flake smiles, "that I can easily identify C by matching the Insta spots?"

Leo looks a bit confused while Mic rolls his eyes.

"Did you know, Leo," Mic changes the subject, "that a lot of the most instagrammable spots actually are in our home state, Arizona?"

"Absolutely," Flake confirms. "Grand Canyon, of course, Horseshoe Bend, Antelope Canyon."

"The Microsoft screensaver tour, I know," Leo replies. "In Antelope Canyon, we waited in line for two hours straight with about one hundred other folks in that narrow fissure to take the shot. And went back the next day again, because of better lighting."

"Sounds like a tough job," Leeza smirks.

"A very tough job indeed," Leo smiles back broadly. "We went on this crazy trip once; to take shots at Seven Magic Mountains close to Vegas, Slab City, in the Sonoran Desert, and some Joshua tree shots at sunset. All in one day. Really stupid idea."

"I've seen pictures of Slab City. It looks like it was just created as an Insta wallpaper."

"It possibly was. What else should get you out to the middle of nowhere in the desert halfway to Mexico? C packed dozens of dresses to be sure to bring something that would fit with the colourful sites. And a lot of black to go with the Joshua trees. The shots took forever."

"I feel you." Leeza smiles ironically.

"It gets worse," Leo moans in mock suffering. "When we stayed in San Diego that night, I have this horrible nightmare. I try uploading the pictures to the cloud, when a pop-up appears. Asking if I really want to store those shots. I confirm, but it asks again; and again. On the fifth attempt, it says: the exact same shots were uploaded two hundred million times to the cloud already! The app asks once more whether I really, really, really want to store them. I confirm again. Next, this stupid app shows me a few dozen photos just like mine. Even better. Clearest of skies, perfect shades, perfect cloud formations, most amazing colours. It has the audacity to ask if I am o.k. with just linking those to my timeline to save cloud space. Why the fuck would I want to save cloud space? I click on deny. The app says: Upload cancelled. I try over. Same pop-up. Whatever I do, the freaking app doesn't allow me to upload the shots. Then I woke up drowning in sweat."

"That sounds terrible." Leeza takes Leo's hand as if she is actually trying to comfort him. He smiles the cutest of smiles.

"It says here," Mic reads from his smartphone, "fifteen million people visit the pyramids in Egypt each year. Quite possible all of those guys and gals take pretty much the same snaps over and over. Ten million visit the Eiffel tower. Taj Mahal, Colosseum in Rome, Tower Bridge in London, Empire State…that's a huge data centre full of duplicates."

"At least," Leeza says to Leo in her most comforting voice, "you get paid for it. The other folks cueing with you in Antelope Canyon were just there for fun."

"Make no mistake," Flake smirks, "curating your social media profile is a very serious matter. And quite a popular career choice these days."

"Even with just a few thousand followers in the right niche," Leo says, "you can make a few grand a month. 100k followers can get you up to a grand per post even."

"Like the guy that does his call-in therapy sessions green-faced in a gecko suit?" Flake grins.

"He's got over two million fans even. On that level, we are talking fifty grand or more for one promo post."

"I read Kylie Jenner makes a million with just one post?" Leeza asks.

"She's the queen of Insta. Almost half a billion fans."

"Kylie isn't spelled with a C, is she?" Flake asks.

Leo smiles his Leo smile.

"That career choice could be just as doomed as Detroit," Flake says with a sinister look, "once they take down Insta altogether."

"Who takes down Insta?" Leo asks, looking alarmed.

"The government."

"Because of that Big One coming up? Is that how they plan to stop it?"

"Not because of those Siliconettes, no. Because of global warming."

Leeza and Mic smirk at each other behind his back while Leo fidgets at the edge of his seat. "I don't get it?" he asks. "What does Insta have to do with climate change?"

"Not just Insta. Snapchat, Tumblr, Flickr, Pinterest and all the rest of them; maybe even Facebook."

Leo looks like a kid just told of an ice cream ban for the rest of his life.

"More and more people travel to the Insta hotspots of this world," Flake continues in his seminar voice, "just to take a shot of their duckface blocking yet another famous view. No offence, Leo."

"None taken." The selfie junkie hangs on Flake's lips like a pre-school kid watching Punch and Judy.

"If you can't flex with it, what's the point, right? Folks may not bother to travel at all. Plan is to ban all vanity services until carbon emission is back in check."

"¿Qué chingados? Mic! Leeza!" Leo desperately looks for help. "Can they do this? Is this even legal?"

When he notices the friends struggling hard to keep their cool, he drops back, his head still spinning. Just in time before the friends would choke on their giggles, he bursts, slamming his hand flat on the table. "You're messing with me, aren't you?"

The four snort with laughter.

"You terrified me just there," Leo gasps in relief. "Pendejos!" He tries putting on a huffy face, yet the Leo smile takes over right away.

"I'd be fine without the hassle, jammed in a tin tube for twenty hours," Leo says, looking dark. "Got the Eiffel tower, the Venetian, even a pyramid and a castle, all right here in Vegas. Just a zero emission batterie load away. And much saver."

Mic glances over at Flake, worried what his raised eyebrow and twitching corner of his mouth should tell him. His best friend stares straight at his date for what feels to Mic like an eternity; as if everyone in the busy restaurant was holding their breath.

"Now you are messing with us, right?" Flake grins.

"Sure I am." Leo's smile embraces the friends and the entire world with them.

The duellists pull kisses off their seconds.

"It's a great idea, though," a relieved Mic says. "Could make us all rich."

"How could taking down Insta and Snapchat make us rich?" Leo asks.

"A friend of mine collects seed funding to create an app exactly for this: travelling the world without moving."

"How does that work?" Leeza asks.

"You take a selfie; anywhere; in your garden, in your living room, in the closet. Doesn't matter. The app crops you out from the background, anyway."

"Amazing technology," Flake grins.

"Next," Mic smiles back, "you choose where ever you want to go; every place on the planet; Paris, London, Lake Tahoe, Moscow; Slab City. Vegas, if you have to. The app searches the internet for photos of that place, which fit best to your selfie; angles, perspective, lighting and stuff. You pick one of those, the app cuts you in and adjusts resolution, brightness, luminosity, blur and all the rest of it; just like Insta filters. Tada: You got a selfie to send off to your homies that looks just like the real deal."

Leo seems alarmed again.

"Could be the next Snapchat, if you ask me," Leeza says. "Somewhat weird, but potential."

"Also works the other way round. You pick any location shot from the web and the app will direct you on how to hold the phone to take a matching selfie. The UI is really cool."

Leo looks like the only kid that did not get picked up after pre-school.

"Don't tell Zach about this, okay?" Leeza says, avoiding looking at Flake, whose smug smirk she sees in the corner of her eye.

"Maybe," Leo says absentmindedly, "maybe you're right. We shouldn't go."

"Whatchumean?" Flake asks.

"Look," he points at his smartphone. "This is the Gate to Heaven in Bali." The picture shows Leo in a goofy golden rooster kung fu pose, framed by two ornate, tiered, triangle-shaped gateposts before a perfectly symmetrical mount Fuji-style volcano under a clear blue sky. An upside-down reflection mirrors the tranquil scenery on a perfectly smooth surface.

"It is breathtaking!" Leeza says.

"In that tiny temple in the middle of nowhere, some forty people were already waiting for their turn on this shot when we arrived. The guy queuing in front of us said he'd already been waiting for over an hour. Completely crazy. The temple itself is not even that remarkable. The view on mount Agung is great, though."

"The app would really help here," Mic grins.

"It would," Leo replies. "Got lucky, though. A girl recognised C. When the word spread, they all wanted us to jump the queue. C declined, but they insisted."

"Let me guess," Leeza says. "They wanted their picture taken with a celebrity in return."

"Happens to her a lot. And I got fifty cameras in my back shooting me doing my job."

"There goes tranquillity," Leeza says.

"It was surreal. As surreal as watching folks imitate C's yoga poses for their pics. Plus, her signature jump."

"People!" Flake sighs. "You just gotta love *'em*."

"Wait till you hear the best part."

"Can it get even more awkward?"

"There is no pond at this temple; or a lake. Just sandstone."

"What do you mean, there is no pond?" Leeza asks.

"The area leading up to the gate is sandstone and clay. The tourists all bring a mirror."

"You're kidding?"

"It's true. A few years ago, some influencer had posted a shot with that perfectly symmetrical reflection; since then, everyone only wants the exact same thing."

"The Gate to Heaven is a fake?" Flake smirks at Leeza.

"Absolutely!" Leo says.

"I drink to that!" Flake laughs. They raise another toast. Mic gives Leo a winner's kiss.

"Having a good time, Mr Thomas?" Says a guy twice the age of his henchman. Both men wear tight dark chinos and long, black, blazer-style leather jackets over tees, looking desperately age-denying in a kind of antithetical way.

"NSA," the senior flashes a badge briefly while the boyish junior imitates a big, bad bouncer in the back.

Flake thinks he recognises the two runners who crossed their path at the Stanford Dish the other day.

"Wanted you to know we are watching," Daddy Agent says. He leans down to Flake. "Breathing down your neck Mr Thomas. Closer and closer. Till we finally get your crooked ass busted."

"Is your boyfriend over there not gonna get jealous when you bust up my ass?" Flake smirks.

"If you think this is funny, I'm happy to arrest you and your friends right here, right now." The agent dangles a pair of handcuffs in front of Flake's face.

"Sweet," Leo beams at Mic, claps his hands and bounces up and down in his seat. "You got us strippers for our date?" He eyeballs the agents from top to bottom. "Just hope the young guy is the one doing the stripping, though."

"You keep joking, Mr Hernandez," the agent replies, "and your next party is gonna be in a cell in Tijuana."

Leo's startled eyes seek help with Mic, who reaches for his hand.

"I'm shaking, officer," Flake chips in. "Not so sure about the CSI outfits, though. Always felt the good ol' motorcycle cop uniform was way more intimidating. And way sexier to drop, I guess. Isn't that right, Leo?"

"Don't test my patience, Mr Thomas? I'm not the forgiving type. Mr Hernandez' visa could be revoked in a snap." The agent actually snaps his fingers. "Not to mention his brother Ricardo, who entered this country illegally."

Leeza puts her hand on Flake's frantically stomping knee.

The agent turns to Mic. "Maybe your parents have some intel for us on the whereabout of your boy toy's little brother?"

"Enough!" Mic barks, putting his phone up. "I will record this."

"No, you won't, son," the agent says, his vicious stare conjuring Mic into dropping it.

"Assisting in trafficking is a pretty serious offence. I hope your mum and dad prove to be the law-abiding citizens our files have them down for; happy to cooperate with the authorities; tell us everything they know. Not that they seem to know that much about you."

Flake balls up his fists, biting his tongue. Leeza strokes his back, while Leo and Mic slump in their seats.

"It doesn't have to end with all your friends' lives in a total mess. There is still time for you to put it all right, Mr Thomas. I urge you to think about that."

Flake and the agent engage in a staring match, telepathically transmitting a whole raft of nasty insults.

"Just raise your hand whenever you are ready to talk. Literally! We will never be far. Good night, Mr Thomas."

***

Masters of the Universe

"The CEOs of the biggest social media and tech companies and the heads of NSA, CIA, FBI, and Homeland Security were summoned before congress today in a public hearing on the announcement to publicise vast volumes of personal information in three days from now.

"Congress demanded to hear from Big Tech and the intelligence community how they assess the implications of this threat to our nation and what they intend to do about it.

"Regardless of that common goal, policymakers were divided into two groups with members of both parties in both camps: Those who sought to limit heavy fire to queries on security of data and protection of privacy in Big Tech's IT systems. The other group of policymakers additionally intended to scrutinise how the online giants justify the collection of all the data in the first place, which

made such a threat possible. In the days before the hearing, this controversy had caused bitter fights on the agenda and proceeding rules of today's event.

"The controversy continued throughout the hearing. Often enough, the positions shining through in the particular questions from both camps were more telling than the expectedly and notoriously rather evasive answers we got from the tech leaders. The general line of defence was: no incidents were reported and that security and privacy are the most important concern of the companies. They all presented very impressive numbers on how many staff they employ in their IT security units and how much money each of them spends to make their infrastructure secure.

"When it got to the questions on the need for assembling all the data, the firms referred to the vibrant innovation in the sector. They put forward the argument, R&D to find new products to serve customers even better requires an extensive variety of such data.

"At this point, congresswoman Pointdexter asked Mark Zuckerberg, I quote, 'how come then, that the like button in 2009 seems to have been the last major new feature actually created by Facebook itself and all other noteworthy innovation was just acquired into the social media giant? Effectively buying out potential competition'.

"Zuckerberg replied by listing several modifications to the core site invented by Facebook's core team. The congresswoman retreated, many of these improvements benefitted Facebook or the parties buying targeted ad space from them much more than they benefitted the actual user; often even raised more privacy concerns, like graph search.

"The impression even neutral audiences were left with was that the congresswoman had a very valid point.

"Congressman Baker asked Google's Sundar Pichai the poisoned question how the founders of the search giant, Sergey Brin and Larry Page, might think about making the internet index and the search queries public; so that outside AI experts could take a close look and determine how this incredible treasure could be used best in the interest of the American people and people around the globe? He pointed out that the initial version of Google's search algorithm had been developed as part of a science project at Stanford University, thus benefitting tremendously from public funding.

"The congressman also inquired why a search engine would need to collect information about the movement of citizens through the entire internet, force over ninety percent of websites to pass extensive detail on user activity on to Google, and how it actually improved the search results. He wasn't thrilled with the long-winded and quite technical exposition, not only he saw as evasive.

"During the hearing it became exceedingly obvious that patience of lawmakers on Capitol Hill with Big Tech exploiting monopolistic market structures at the expense of user rights might soon be exhausted.

"I didn't do Mark Zuckerberg any good when he tried once again to picture his company as a target of fierce competition; he pointed at others that grow their user base faster, like TikTok, grow ad revenue faster, like Amazon, have more video users, like YouTube. He actually went as far as to say that only 10 cents per dollar spend on ads in the US go to Meta. Did he really think this made him look like an endangered species in need of help? It did not go down well with congress.

"Concerning the substance of the threat, we learned particularly little from the intelligence community. The directors of the agencies did what they do best: being secretive, respond to the inquiries of congress members with very few words saying even less; hiding behind national security being at risk should too much detail about their investigations be shared. Congresswoman Warren at one point exploded, denouncing that agencies do not even share relevant information with the Intelligence Oversight Committee, concluding that she was of the impression there is nothing to share because no progress was made. She went on to say she does not feel that the intelligence community takes the citizens' worries seriously and that they are up to the job of protecting the American people.

"Overall, a very tough day for the summoned masters of the tech universe. Maybe the best day of them all had Tim Cook, CEO of Apple, who said in this hearing, I quote: 'We've never believed that these detailed profiles of people, that have incredibly deep personal information that is patched together from several sources, should exist. They can be abused against our democracy'. He went on to say: 'I'm not a fan of regulation. But in this particular case, I think we've run the experiment. It hasn't worked!'

"Politicians from both sides of the aisle criticised Apple in the past for their treatment of workers in offshore factories and also for employing monopolistic behaviour in blocking out competition through their closed systems. However,

common sentiment was they are among the least to blame for privacy concerns
among the tech firms under scrutiny today.

"This was Lilian Waters for CNBC from Capitol Hill."

***

Big One Minus 2, Saturday

Confession

"In a dramatic turn of events, just one day after Twitter and other platforms had banned the #DontDoxxMyDudes hashtag, the initiator of this campaign, 32-year-old Tim Rozen, was found dead in his Cupertino apartment. This is ABC News."

"Rozen left a note in which he claims to be the originator of the data leak announcement issued last Sunday signed by The Horrible Siliconettes, tagged by the public meanwhile as the Big One. Clarissa, on the ground for us in Cupertino: tell us what we know about this tragic incident?"

"The cause of Rozen's death, according to a police spokesperson, was an overdose of Natrium-Pentobarbital. He was also heavily intoxicated with alcohol. Police classify the death as suicide."

"As you mentioned, Rozen, who worked as a senior product manager here in the Valley, has left a note, actually it was a social media post, in which he conceded to be solely responsible for the Big One. In this post, he indicated the announcement was unsubstantiated and that no data will actually be exposed. He declared he is sorry for issuing this threat and that he never expected it to have such dramatic effect. The content of the message suggests he felt overwhelmed by the consequences resulting from the announcement and from the subsequent campaign he had started, before it was, as we reported yesterday, eventually stopped by the major platforms. In the post, Rozen referred to the turbulences on the stock market, the international implications, people arrested for allegedly being connected to the Big One and the political and economic turmoil it has created. He explained he never intended and never expected this to happen and he sincerely regretted publishing the announcement."

"Do we have any information about why the young product manager had published it in the first place?"

"Yes, we do. In a second post, the police could uncover, yet that was never actually sent off, the young man explained his motives. This message reveals an unfulfilled love to a co-worker, which led him to issue the threat of the Big One;

the sole aim of this, though, was to initiate the #DontDoxxMyDudes campaign subsequently, with which he wanted to impress that co-worker."

"It seems the young man wanted to create a hero story for himself to get to that woman. I can only try to imagine what it must feel like, being the subject of a desire, maybe a desire she was not even aware of until today, that led to such tragic consequences. Thank you, Clarissa, for this update…"

***

Going Dark

When he hears Leeza knocking, Flake is only halfway done clearing the mess in his place. At best. Since she had called to say she was on her way over, there simply wasn't enough time, even though the faculty's guest apartment is tiny. Yet so tiny, there is just no space to move stuff out of sight.

It knocks again. Flake stashes another pile of clothes under the bed, then yanks it back out to fetch the 'Gattaca Corp.' polo and shoves back the rest. Half of his clean up time he was pondering on what to wear. The Gattaca shirt had been his first choice because he loved the odd muddy petrol colour and the movie. He also figured, amongst his selection, it would be the least contagious. Yes, it is another dystopian reference, yet the Gattaca Corporation had little to do with data at least. He didn't want to upset Leeza any further, with the Tim tragedy to cope with and all the rest of what's going on. Besides, most of his other gear was in the wash.

Then again, he wasn't sure if the subtlety would come across to his friend in her current state of mind, so he had changed into a plain white he kept for emergencies. Yet, that didn't feel good either. He scorned himself for the last fifteen minutes, for not bringing more choices and for not doing the laundry.

Flake changes on his way to the door, then hectically changes again when he realises the shirt was inside-out.

Without saying a word, his friend walks straight into his embrace, sallow and lost in thought.

"That Tim thing really got to you, didn't it?" he says.

"Can't stop thinking about it; should have checked on him last night…"

"There was nothing you could do." Flake squeezes her tight. "He may have even been…what good would it have done?"

"Maybe I could have talked him out of it?"

"Before or after he cut his wrists or shot himself in the face?"

Leeza breaks free and looks at him aghast. Yet, Flake much rather wants her to hate him right now than to watch her hate herself.

"Want some fresh air?" he asks.

The simple question has to cut its way through a spinney of muddled thoughts in Leeza's head first.

"Wandered around the neighbourhood for an hour already," she replies eventually. "Didn't help."

"I'm here for you. Let me help!"

Leeza pulls him close again.

"Anyway," Flake adds, "you shouldn't walk the streets around here at this time of day. First, it is un-American. When you are not in a vehicle, you are either shopping or jogging. We don't just walk around. And second, it is dangerous. This is not Kansas anymore, Dorothy. There are lots of bad guys out there."

The attempt to cheer her up a little failed completely.

"Actually, it wasn't the bad guys that made me feel uncomfortable," she says. "It was the good guys. What I used to think are the good guys."

"Whatchumean?"

"Have you ever noticed how many of these Waymos, Cruises, Titans and stuff are out there? It felt like every other minute one of those passed by. If it was not one of them, it was one of those street view cars. Maybe I'm getting paranoid, but I keep thinking these cameras are watching me. Following me, even. Let alone the CCTV cams on every crossing."

"Paranoid is good. I seem to have an excellent influence on you."

"I'm serious. It agitated me."

"That is exactly what you should be thinking!"

"Look. I'm shaking."

"Honestly, I don't think they are following you specifically. You might be a little too paranoid right now."

Leeza's adorable dimples signal Flake an attempted smile.

"So, you don't think I am of interest?" she says.

"To me you are. Very much so. Actually, the only person on the planet I have an interest in right now."

Leeza nestles against Flake's shoulder. Just as she is about to close her eyes, she spots a familiar face in the live stream on Flake's notebook. "Look! This is about Tim," she shouts. "Switch on sound."

"Great! I tell you I have only eyes for you and you only have eyes for this guy?" Flake complains only half-jokingly.

"The police released footage today from the scene of the suicide, showing the Rozen's apartment right after forensics had done their job and the coroner had carried out the body..."

"You think you know someone," Leeza says, "but you really don't. I would never have thought Tim could do something like this."

"Kill himself or drop the Big One?"

"He seemed a nice guy. Got along with everybody. Not a political person, really. As far as I could tell. Never heard him engage in debates about politics. Until the Big One, that is. To focus on our project was quite difficult lately."

"Well, there was more to him than the pretty facade, that's for sure. I don't wish to be judgmental, but some of what they leaked was pretty weird, don't you think?"

"...Rozen was obviously a troubled character. His mother died early and his father had serious issues with excessive use of alcohol and other drugs. With this package on his shoulders, he never seemed to settle into a steady relationship. He was a workaholic; compensated for the emptiness in his life with laser focus on his career. The investigations will have to show what alienated him with his firm, the business conduct of his employer, even the entire tech industry, that he would fall on the idea of the Big One..."

"That is odd," Flake says, "how come they don't mention the blackmail...?"

"...an idea that would ultimately cost him the job he had worked so tirelessly for and ruin his existence. An idea that got him into a state of despair, he only saw one way out of: to end his life..."

Since there is no second chair, Leeza sits on Flake's lap.

"...Rozen had spent a lot of time in dark net forums, presumably to find accomplices and ingredients for the leak of enormous volumes of private data. What exactly he bought in forums like the dark market further investigations will have to reveal. The search history investigators could already recover was, I quote one detective on the case, 'not overly concerning'."

"It would seem the young man initially intended to create a data dump, as described in the announcement, yet failed to accomplish that goal. He subsequently must have decided to go ahead with publishing the threat regardless of his inability to back it up..."

"They still play the whole thing down," Flake says.

"...his activities in the darknet included, however, seeking opportunities to acquire firearms and drugs."

"No way!" Leeza jumps up. "I would have noticed if he had been on drugs, surely. We pulled many overnighters in the project..."

"Maybe he needed the dust to manage just that."

"I know what dudes on cocaine behave like. Trust me. Tim was not on drugs."

"Maybe he sold the stuff? Maybe he was after money to buy passwords on the dark net."

"Maybe...as I said: you think you know someone..."

"I definitely know too little about you. Why would you know about dudes on dust?"

"You always claim we all should have something to hide, don't you?" For a second Leeza beams like Mummy's little darling eager to trade her older brother's secret for tickets to *Frozen*, before her face turns gloomy again.

"All this dark net stuff, the cocaine, none of this was in the blackmail messages the other day. Don't you think that's odd?" Flake asks.

"They wanted him to end the campaign. Maybe they saved the best for last?"

"Yeah, maybe. Yet Tim said he couldn't think of anything else. And who are 'they'? If Tim is THS, who was badgering him to end his campaign? Someone who didn't know he was the guy behind the Big One? An accomplice that didn't agree with #DontDoxxMyDudes? But why? Who? This does not add up."

i"…yet the explanation for all of this may not be one of a young man radicalising himself in dark net chat groups. According to the police, Rozen might have done all of this for a very personal reason: unfulfilled love. After he had sent off his confession to be the initiator of the Big One, in which he apologises for it and called it a major mistake, he wrote a second message. In this second message, Rozen explains, he fabricated the threat to expose millions of people's personal information to impress a girl; that he had planned to portray himself as an activist who fights for people's rights; he had plotted for the campaign spread under the hashtag #DontDoxxMyDudes to be his means to become a hero in the eyes of this girl, a co-worker of his. To get the admiration of a girl who so far seemed to have neglected his advances…"

"You think this is me?" Leeza gazes absently at the news feed. "Ever since they reported this, I keep thinking…"

"No way this is you!" Flake shoots.

Leeza turns to him, looking confused.

"I mean, he could have been secretly in love with you… Who could blame him…? If you ask me, how can anyone not be in love with you…? That does not mean Tim was in love with you, I mean, I don't think this girl is you…"

Leeza stares at her feet. "I thought so."

"Even if it was you… Don't you dare blame yourself for this. None of this is your fault."

"How can you say that? Should he have done it to impress me, it cost him his job. It cost him…how can I not blame myself?"

"You didn't ask Tim to do any of this; you did nothing to encourage him. It was Tim's choice. The guy obviously made a lot more very wrong choices."

"Still, I should have been there for him."

"Are you crazy? The guy stalked you. Don't make this your problem…"

Leeza hectically waves her hand to shut him up and leans in on the screen.

"…the second message, however, was never sent off. Here in his study, on his tidy desk, we see Tim Rozen's notebook exactly the way he left it to take the pills and wait in his bathtub for his death. You can see the message on the screen, signed and ready to send. The only thing missing is the addressee of the message…"

"That doesn't make any sense," Leeza says. "Tim never used his notebook for messages. He only ever used his handheld. He was even faster typing with two thumbs than using a keyboard."

"...investigators are, of course, keen to find out who he has written this message for. We can only speculate why he wrote such a message, a very personal message, and then decided not to send it. Maybe he didn't want the woman to feel there was anything she could have done..."

"You sure?" Flake asks.

"Positive. Tim would have done PowerPoint on his handheld if that was practically workable."

"Let me scan the messages again, please. Maybe we missed something."

"Sorry, gone; deleted them and the box cleared."

"There must be a way to get them back."

"Maybe Micah knows?"

"Excellent thinking, Watson. Hey computer, call Mic."

Leeza looks at him as if he just ordered Scotty to beam them to their friend. "Didn't you call those things wiretaps?"

The Dolby surround voice of Scarlett Johansson fills the room. "Do you want me to stop spying on you?"

"No, it's fine, Samantha," Flake smirks. "Just don't tell anybody about what you hear, okay?"

"You hurt my feelings!" Samantha says.

"Alexa has feelings?" Leeza looks as if she actually had been beamed.

"Don't compare me with that..." A beep masks the rest of Samantha's insult.

"Now we hurt Sam's feelings again," Flake smiles. "I had Mic build me my very own version. Sam doesn't report anything I say or do back into Bozo or the evil empire. The cool voice tech is a beta from a bunch of Mic's friends in a startup. Wicked, isn't it?"

Leeza rolls her eyes.

"Sam," Flake commands, "stop bitching and call Mic. Please."

"Okay, fine," responds a miffed Samantha, "but only because you said please...calling Micah..." She selects Welcome to the Machine as caller tune.

"Ahoy Andy!"

"Are you guys alright?" Leeza asks.

"Leo was up all night. Cried his eyes out. Freaked out completely when he learned about Tim's suicide."

"That's why we need your help, Mic. Leeza binned all that compromising stuff she received on Tim; and the delete cache cleared. How do we get it back?"

"Why would you want it back? The guy is dead. Leave him his peace."

"Mic, please!" Leeza says, "we feel something is wrong here. We just saw a news report. They picture him as a desperate workaholic on drugs, madly in love with the wrong girl…"

"You shouldn't condemn yourself for this, Leeza. It was Tim's choice."

"You are saying…?"

Cancelled noise fills the line for eternal seconds.

"Oops…sorry…everybody knew Tim was going full Titanic on you…"

"Mic," Flake intervenes, "you are not helping. The news report did not even mention Tim's extortion. They don't seem to know; or care. Instead, they report a ton of stuff about Tim that wasn't in the messages we saw; need to check that. Need to get them back!"

"There is a backup on a central server; overwritten only once a week. Likely, your messages are still there."

"Can we access it?"

"Yep, from the campus LAN."

"Once we are in your offices, can we also find out which PC Tim's last message was sent from? The one where he claims to be THS?"

"What are you up to?" Leeza asks.

"Later. Can we, Mic? Can you?"

"Even if I would know how to do it…This kind of stuff gets you fired. Or arrested. Don't you think we are in enough trouble already?"

"Great. Can you meet us there in twenty minutes?"

"Ahem…"

"Mic?"

"Okay, give me thirty."

***

Straight Talk

"Welcome to 'Straight Talk' here on Fox. I am your host, Barnabas Straight.

"This congressional hearing yesterday was a joke. Just the same old bullshit. For years now, the democrats are annoying us with their whining about Big Tech stealing the 2016 elections, manipulating voters. The beauty about democracy is: voters are so much smarter than politicians. They often get it right. Politicians lied to them for decades and did nothing to improve people's lives. Those politicians got elected and stuck in power without the help of Big Tech. Relying simply on old-fashioned propaganda. Finally, people found them out, found out it is all just words but no action. They wanted the government to focus again on making their lives better. I suppose most people would agree today that with The Donald, they had not chosen the right guy to go fix it. He let them down as well. Big time. As big time, as only The Donald probably can.

"Yet, they didn't vote for him because of Big Tech and manipulation. They voted for him because they were, for the first time, not manipulate anymore by the old elites who just played the system to stay in power and favour their friends.

"Hillary is a classic example, a poster child of this arrogant elite. And she ran a lousy campaign. Yet, she still won the popular vote. Don't let them fool you with these stories about micro-targeted advertising that convinced exactly those five thousand voters in Michigan to tip it for The Donald; or the ten thousand in Wisconsin; twenty-five thousand in Pennsylvania. It was pure luck, for Christ's sake, not some advance mathematics. If you ask me, The Donald was just as surprised as the rest of us. Actually, I don't even think he wanted to become president. He used the campaign to build his brand; he wanted to use that attention to make a ton of money. Because he was actually broke at the time! He never really showed any interest in progressing the country, did he? All he ever did in office was also to build on his brand. It wasn't politics for four years, it was marketing. He totally failed the people that had sent him into that oval office.

"So, in 2020, voters told him: you're fired! With a big majority. Despite Big Tech's interest. Actually: despite voter fraud, by the way. Wanna know what I think regarding the fraud allegations?

"Picture this: The Donald knows he lost the popular vote in 2016. He knows it was pure luck that got him into office. So, he orders his people: we can't take that risk again. This time I have to win the popular vote. His gang says: Hilary got 66 million votes. Just like Obama in 2012. We would have to get you 67 or

68. But that's gonna be tough, coming from only 63. The Donald, being The Donald, says: not enough! He challenges his people: what was the highest number of votes any candidate ever got? They say that was Obama in 2008. Almost 70 million. But that was exceptional. It will never happen again. The Donald, being The Donald, will have none of that. I want 75 then! he says. End of discussion. Go get me 75 million votes. It is going to be a triumphant victory. The greatest victory ever.

"His people were desperate; had no idea how to do this fair and square. Luckily, this guy and his camp are not particularly hooked on fair and square. So, they find a way. And The Donald starts whining about the potential to manipulate the vote in the weeks leading up to the big day. How does he know? Make a guess! Why would he talk about it publicly, you ask? Well, who suspects the guy that shouts: Fart?

"Why did he never stop talking about it, even after it was clear he lost? Well...Nero burned Rome, didn't he? When it was clear, he lost it...In any sense of the word.

"The Donald eventually gets 74 million votes. Just to find out on election night that it wasn't enough. The other guy, Sleepy Joe, got 80.

"Think about it. Go back to the footage of election night when The Donald declared he must have won it. That there is no way he could have lost it. He was absolutely sure because he knew they had secured him more votes than ever.

"If you ask me: when he first talked about manipulated votes, I think he knew what he was talking about. It was the wolf crying wolf! Just look at the footage again. You can see it in his face. He can't believe they beat him at his own game. That was the only explanation he could come up with, and it shocked him. You see it in his eyes in that press conference. The confused way he stutters around...it's obvious!

"Yet, they didn't beat him at his own game. It was simple: many more people than ever before decided that change is needed. They only had the choice for the lesser evil, if you ask me, but they went out to vote. And I believe social media had a lot to do with it. Not in that manipulative sense the liberals want to make you believe. But in a very positive sense. It made people aware. The democrats should thank Big Tech and not beat it up all the time.

"I say: stop whining! Get on with it! Go make people's lives better. Big Tech can help with that. Google, Amazon, they are heroes. They created hundreds of thousands of jobs. They have created the cloud, making IT so much more *efficient. Those two and the rest of the bunch, Twitter, Facebook, WhatsApp, they all provide brilliant, useful services. Big Tech is not the problem. It is, often enough, the solution.*

"Now that we know that this Big One was just a big prank on all of us, a doomsday scare story dreamed up by some whining lunatic to impress a girl, certainly a member of the sissy-ass liberal elites ignorant of their privileges and always lamenting, we can get on with our lives and go back to enjoying the amazing opportunities brought to us by the relentless innovators of the tech industry."

***

Orange Is the New Black

The spacious office is flooded with the moonless gloom of a star-sparkling wallpaper sky behind the two-story glass facade; dim emergency exit lights along the walls create a sense for the dimensions of the huge warehouse-style building. The open space is loosely patched with tiny conference fish tanks and kitchenettes. Despite it being Saturday night, quite a number of people still work away on illuminated islands scattered across the different zones.

A sensor switch turns on one of the floor lamps every time Leeza and Flake come close, lighting their way desk by desk. "I don't like coming to the office at night," Leeza says. "The way the shadows dance on the roughcast concrete. The dark spots between the pipes and ducts under the ceiling...looks like something is hiding there. It freaks me out." She stops and signals Flake to listen to the silence.

"I'm a major wuss. Every few seconds something scares me," she says, still not moving even a finger. "When people many desks down just type away...after a while, in the corner of my eye, I suddenly see their desk light go out and I wince." The floor lamp next to the couple switches off with a clicking sound. Leeza shrugs a bit, even though she waited for this to happen.

"Every once in a while, someone stretches himself out and I get spooked again, because that switches the lamp back on." She pulls Flake into a cone of light that only flashes up because of that very motion; *like life and demise of Schrödinger's cat,* Flake thinks.

"Tonight, it feels particularly creepy."

"I see," Flake says. "But why are you whispering?"

"I don't know," Leeza whispers.

"You work at this place. It is perfectly normal for you to be here. Even at this late hour; even on a weekend! I guess?"

"You're right," Leeza still whispers. "It just feels like trespassing, anyway."

From floor light number five onwards, Leeza stops wincing.

"Look, Mic is already there," she says with a deliberately firm voice as they approach his illuminated island in a rather secluded section of the floor.

Mic extends a Vulcan greeting without looking up from the keyboard. "Got your backup restored. The messages should all be there." Leeza checks her phone.

"I noticed something strange," Mic adds with the conspiratorial voice of the sesame street sales guy who offers to buy a letter off of you. "Something suspicious."

Flake prods his friend on the shoulder. "Just spill it."

"Someone messes with Tim's data. Big time. Remember, Leeza, we had used your profiles to create the initial ROSE beta? To find commonalities between the two of you? Identify viable chat subjects?"

"You did, eh?" Flake turns to Leeza. "What kind of matches did you find?"

"Andy!" Leeza gives Flake a grim look.

Mic smirks like a kid sneaking up on his parents making out. "She calls you Andy when she is angry. How cute is that?"

"Spill it!" Flake urges.

"I kept this copy of Tim's profile. When I compare it to what is up today, it's different."

"How different?"

"Beatles versus Stones? Ossi versus Elvis? Someone significantly changed a lot of the scores. Political preferences, purchasing habits, affiliations, entertainment preferences. It's all over the place. Someone inserted events, pictures and likes in his timeline; changed his browsing history; added visits to websites we keep on the special watch list, if you know what I mean."

"Figures," Leeza looks up from the phone. "We were right, Flake. A lot of the stuff they talked about on the news was not in the messages I got. None of the darknet visits, extremist YouTube channels, the dirty stuff."

"The porn is legit," Mic smirks. "Was already there when I pulled the dump. Didn't show you. Didn't provide too much for ROSE to hook a conversation on."

"Good to know," Flake gives Leeza an inquisitive look.

She caresses his shoulder.

"Wasn't talking about porn," she says. "Searches for drugs, guns, explosives."

"It's like someone is manufacturing a virtual Tim to fit their confession story," Mic says, looking cowed.

"Who?" Flake asks. "Did you find out which machine Tim's farewell message was sent from?"

"Got the ID. Wasn't Tim's, for sure. Still need to figure out who it belongs to, though. But first I gotta puke."

"What's wrong?" Leeza asks.

"Don't know. Either the burrito I had earlier or the fact that my employer messes with people's lives."

He rushes off towards the restrooms. While Mic turns the corner, Flake wraps his arms around a staggered Leeza. "I'm sorry," he says.

"What are you sorry for now?"

"For being right about these kinds of companies."

"You're an idiot."

"Let's not fight now."

"Later? Promise?"

"Check…"

Protected in Flake's embrace, Leeza closes her eyes. She feels a heartbeat, yet couldn't tell if it is hers or his; or both in unison. For an endless moment in her lover's arms, it feels like it all will come alright again.

A clicking sound pulls her back. The endless moment of salvation only lasted the sixty-second until the sensor automatically turns off the light. The couple keeps holding tight in the dark, stalling the return to sobering reality.

As Leeza's eyes slowly adapt to the gloom, a weird feeling of imminence overcomes her, causing her to break away from the embrace. When the lamp gets triggered, Leeza lets out a suppressed scream.

"What is it?" Flake spots her spooked eyes and turns around to follow her gaze.

"Do you mind telling me what you are doing here?" asks a tall, scarcely visible silhouette two desks down. As the shadow advances towards them, the next floor lamp unhides a pony-tailed middle age tech geek in a black trench.

"Why are you sneaking up on us, Drax?" Flake confronts the lurker.

"Oh, hi Colin!" Leeza trills and puts on a forced smile. "Wow, you scare me just there."

She turns to Flake. "This is Colin Neill. He is our Chief IT Security officer."

"Working late, Colin," she turns back to the stalker, trying to sound as casual as possible. "You know how it is?"

"Yes, Leeza, I know how it is. People rarely tailgate strangers into the building for the extended business hours, though."

"I was scared coming here this late all by myself. I know I shouldn't have brought Andy along. I'm sorry. Can we not forget this ever happened?"

"Mr Thomas is just here to give you a hug once in a while? Is that it? Well, who can blame you? He's a good-looking fella."

"What do you want?" Flake chips in.

"No, Mr Thomas. The question is: what do you want here?"

"Okay. I admit it," Leeza says, "we are not here to work on a project. Maybe you can help us, Colin. We saw a report on Tim on the news. And it seemed odd. All the stuff they said about him. It made no sense."

"Don't understand?"

"I received messages before he died. Someone pressured him to stop his campaign; exposed many nasty things about him. But in that coverage, they talked about much worse stuff, even. We hope to find out what is true or not. Can you help us?"

"It is perfectly normal to have doubts when you find out someone you felt you knew does something terrible. Like Tim did. You doubt yourself. That won't heal by doubting everyone else, Leeza."

"I don't think Drax here wants to help us," Flake turns his back on Colin. "He knew who I am. Seems to me he was bushwhacking us."

Leeza is as perplexed about Flake's suspicion as she is about missing out on the clues. "Why are you here, Colin?" she asks. "Is the firm spying on us, too?"

"You should be careful with such accusations, Leeza. There's a straightforward explanation for why I am here. You know how this company works. When Tim died, HR wanted a list of all staff who might need mental support; that were close to Tim; might find it tough to handle this tragedy. We ranked all of our staff according to the level of affiliation to Tim. Common friend's, common interests, posts, likes, you know the drill...the whole shebang." The security officer comes closer and closer, growing taller on the way.

"You, Leeza, were quite high on the list, of course. Your joint projects, Tim stalking your profile…I had my staff implement an alarm. Should any of the top twenty on this list do anything out of the ordinary, posts which show distress, any abnormal behaviour, it prompts an alert."

The shadow man puts on a concerned face. "You coming into the office at this hour, on a weekend, triggered such an alert. When the CCTV system notified me of your tailgating, I thought I had to come in and see for myself."

In Colin's back, down the hall, Leeza spots Mic on his way back. She drops herself on the desk, noisily pushing stuff to the side, and exclaims in a theatrical voice: "You see, Andy? Colin is here to protect us. Now that's settled, will you help us, Colin?"

Mic turns on his heels.

"You have access to all systems, don't you, Colin?" Leeza asks.

"I have a certain clearance, yes. Care to tell me what exactly you are looking for? The logs will tell me, anyway."

Leeza spins her handheld on the tabletop. "We need to know who sent these messages to blackmail Tim. Is it not possible to identify who collected all this nasty stuff? Who could have access to all of it?"

"I will ask one of my team to look into that first thing on Monday."

"What we actually want to understand, Drax, is…" Flake starts, but gets interrupted by Leeza.

"Why do you keep calling him Drax?" she asks.

"Your friend calls me Drax," Colin replies, "because back there I mastered the ability to stand so incredibly still that I was invisible to the eye. It's a Guardians joke. Isn't that correct, Mr Thomas? Andy?"

While the shadow man tries to stare Flake down, Leeza discreetly opens a chat with Mic and rests her finger on the voice recording button.

"How do you know Andy's name?" she asks.

Colin pulls out his phone and starts a dial. "Agent Willis. Its Colin Neill. Sorry for the late call. I thought you might like this. Guess who I just caught breaking into our offices? What did you call him the other day: the ivory tower anarchist…yep, he's right in front of me. Do you want me to pass on a message? Talk tomorrow. Bye now." Colin turns to Flake. "The NSA wants you to come by their offices tomorrow. You know where that is, I understand?"

Flake stands up to Colin's stare. The interrogator eventually turns to Leeza. "You honestly want to inquire Tim's death?"

"Actually," Flake says, "what we really want to know is why this company would kill one of their own."

"We didn't kill Tim. Why would we?"

"Because his campaign became a threat to you? Because you suspected him to be behind the Big One? That's what the police try to make people think, at least."

"Colin," Leeza intervenes, "you said: Tim died. You didn't say: he killed himself."

"You should let it go," Colin says. "You step on the wrong toes here. I know who you father is, Leeza, but even he cannot protect you, should you not stop this nuisance."

"Tim was a friend. I can't just get on with it if I got the feeling something's wrong."

"Was he, Leeza? I checked the data. In your friends list, you have more than a hundred contacts that rank higher in engagement level with you than Tim does. Did. That one-night stand doesn't make you friends. You'll get over it."

Flake tries focusing the upcoming rage on the bearer of the news.

"By the way," Colin adds, "our tools don't deliver promising projections for your relationship with the nosy wannabe intellectual here either. He means trouble as well."

"That's none of your business," Flake hisses.

"You're right. Just as none of this is your business." Colin picks up his phone again. "Carl, can you come over to area D, please? We have an intruder."

When the security guard arrives, Colin points at Flake. "Escort this young gentleman from our premises. He illegally entered our property and our systems. No need to call the cops, though. Should he comply! The NSA will deal with him, anyway."

"Let's go buster," urges the huge, cowing man, reinforcing the request with a sturdy clamp on Flake's arm.

Colin turns to Leeza. "Could we have a word?"

"You should come with me," Flake objects.

"Take this man out, now!" Colin commands, "and come back afterwards."

The guard pushes Flake towards the exit.

"I will not leave without her!"

"Leeza can make her own choices!" Colin gazes deeply into his colleague's eyes. "There's something I want to tell you."

"I don't trust that guy," Flake urges from half way to the exit. "Please, come with me."

"Colin won't hurt me," Leeza says. "I meet you at your place later."

"I really think you should come!" Flake insists.

The guard twists his arm. "Let's go. I don't want to get rude." He shoves Flake down the hall. Click after click, cones of light show them out. Colin seems hypnotised by that spectacle while Leeza eyeballs him, trying to make sense of this all. She slides down onto the chair and pushes the voice recording button for the fifth time. The security officer drops at the opposite desk.

"I'll level with you, Leeza. I don't think Tim killed himself. But it was not this company or any of its management who wanted him dead. I admit we wanted him to stop his campaign. But no one here is so scrupulous to kill for that."

"I wish I could believe you."

"Tim should have just stopped when we nudged him with a truck. He might still be alive today. We wanted so save him, not kill him."

Leeza tries to read Colin's mind from his stare but can't figure him out. "Who is scrupulous enough to kill him, then?" she asks. "It seems you have a theory on that, Colin?"

Colin, in turn, seeks to conjure Leeza into letting go. "Trust me, you should not want to know that. Let me say this much: a very influential authority made it crystal clear to the highest levels of management in this firm that we need to solve the Tim issue."

"The Tim issue?" Leeza spits aghast.

"We said we can handle it. These powers have a vested interest we come back to stability in this whole situation. We knew this was serious. We open our drawers and checked what we could use on Tim. He was an easy target, as you have seen. So, we nudged him with some vigour."

"It didn't do the trick, did it?" Leeza asks.

"Tim should have better left it at that. When we couldn't show the expected results quickly enough, they lost patience and took it from there."

"It wasn't you guys who faked the incriminating evidence? And who is 'they'?"

"You know we don't make the fake. We just play it up."

"To turn Tim into the UNA-bomber was their idea then?"

"You ask way too many questions."

"But to kill an innocent man?"

"They killed the Kennedys, didn't they?"

"Who killed the Kennedys? And what does this have to do with anything?" Leeza looks at him as if Colin suggested the Big One was an alien conspiracy.

"Powers exist that have the capacity and the willingness to kill people for some cause. And get away with it. Even if it is the president. So why not some random Valley workaholic with a relationship issue and a drug problem?"

Leeza feels like in those dreams where she falls, tail spinning, into a dark, infinite hole in the ground.

"Next, you'll tell me we never went to the moon, right?" She tries to pinch herself.

The glimpse of sarcastic cheerfulness pushing up Colin's eyebrow irritates her big time.

"I will not allow them, whoever that is, to plant this on an innocent friend," she says.

"This is not the time to be sentimental, Leeza. Important interests are at stake. Interests that will be preserved at any cost."

"It is wrong. Very wrong."

Colin's raised eyebrow makes a last pitying attempt to hypnotise her into letting it go.

"You honestly think this lame pawn plot will do?" Leeza pushes back.

"The way I see it, there are two options," Colin replies. "In case the Big One never actually takes place, the story of the infatuated, rebuffed workaholic who sets up a hero story for himself to get the girl could work just fine. Audiences have bought into way dodgier storylines."

"What if it does take place?"

"It depends on the damage done. Should it be really bad, the writers might have to add a few more twists to the script. They may add a connection to the Russian mafia or Russian intelligence; using the dark net plot, maybe."

The dark, bottomless hole sucks up Leeza's fighting spirit. "That's the end of it?" she sighs. "It's that easy?"

"In option one," Colin proudly continues his brief lecture on high treason and subversion, "lawmakers will introduce some toothless regulation. It will soon blow over. In option two, congress will approve budget and authority for increased surveillance; so that, going forward, we can detect dangerous activities of individuals like Tim earlier...so, yes: I think this will do."

"What if people see through the scam?"

"Not likely at all. But that, Leeza, is where you come in."

"Me?"

"If it needs more than the Tim story, your friend Andy presented himself as the ideal conspirator. The infamous influencer, the anarchist activist and blogger, has recruited poor Tim for the fight against big monopolies. Your friend has been quite vocal for years now. Very credible radicalisation story. The NSA has gathered a bunch of cool stuff they can work with already."

"Fake more evidence?"

"I don't know, and I do not want to know."

A minute ago, Leeza hoped to wake from her fall dream. Now it feels more like the urge to switch off a movie whose plot just turned too bizarre.

"How do I fit in there?" she asks while Colin types on his handheld.

"They asked me for my assessment," he says. "I give it to you, Leeza, you are not easily intimidated. In normal times, this is a good thing. Now this is a problem."

"What's that supposed to mean, Colin?"

"Carl will take you down to the car park. They will take over from here."

"To do what, exactly?" Leeza realises there is no remote to switch off the angst. Nor a pinch to wake her up.

"As I said, Leeza, I don't know, and I don't want to know."

"That's crazy, Colin!" she bursts. "This is not what we are."

"What 'we' are, Leeza, is the most successful business ever. You don't get to beat all others by just playing nice."

Colin hits redial. "Where is Carl, damn it? What the fuck takes him so long?" He checks his phone.

"I'll take you myself. Let's go."

"Carl had to pick up a new key card," Flake hollers from a distance while he waves the guard's badge. "He will be back." A cautious smile imposes itself on him as he realises the incidental movie quote.

"Come on, let's go, Leeza," Flake reaches for her hand.

"I can't allow you to leave," Colin retorts.

"What are you going to do about it?"

The security officer pulls his hand from the pocket of his coat, holding a gun. He points at Flake.

"While we have our nice little chat," Flake says unfazed, "a pop-up appears on the screens of everyone in this building, inviting for pizza and cake at Leeza's desk." Colin notices an incoming message on the monitor in front of him. A status bar in his eyes reports slow progress in processing the options.

"There must be a few dozen of your colleagues still working away on humanity's bright future," Flake says. "They'll surely flock in, any second."

He gives Leeza a quick kiss. "I'll meet you at your car. But first it's my turn for a word in private with Colin."

"You sure?" Leeza asks.

Colin aims at her.

"I need to know what you said about me," Flake smiles as he steps in Colin's aim. "See you in a minute. Try to avoid that Carlinator, okay?"

Leeza hurries down the hall.

"What's with the gun? You said you guys are no killers." Flake seeks to prove his leap of faith in Colin's anxious eyes. "Especially not," he adds, "before I have spelled out to you how I will disclose this company's treasure trove on dump day."

Colin drops first his jaw and then the gun, gawking at Flake as if he had just announced the advent of Elvis in the building.

"Will show you at your computer."

"My computer?" Colin pockets the gun.

"Everyone in security knows tech is not the problem," Flake says. "The human factor, right? More often than not, it is the IT security geeks who think they are so clever, but make the dumbest mistakes."

Colin stumbles through the office like a drunk all the way to his secluded desk. As if he was held at gunpoint, the unsettled security officer follows Flake's orders and unlocks his machine. Just as a wallpaper of an orange Tesla appears, a tin trashcan hits him on the back of his head. His face drops flat on the keyboard.

"What a shot, Mic!" Flake applauds. "Hope you didn't cause lasting damage there. That was wicked."

"Needed to work on first attempt, didn't it?" Mic smiles proudly and a little surprised about his own determination.

"You sure the cams are not taping this?" Flake asks.

"Colin likes to control everyone else, but his desk, actually the entire section, is off limits. Only he can watch what the cameras see, but they don't record."

"Good. I don't want you connected to any of this. Interesting, he would get away with the blind cameras."

"Colin babysits the big boss since the early days. Single digit employee ID. They first met at a crypto conference during the boss' geek-peak days. Rumour has it, Colin knows who Satoshi Nakamoto really is. They even say he was there when the Bitcoin White Paper was written."

"So, he might even be fairytale rich twice, eh?" Flake fetches the gun from Colin's pocket and drops it in a drawer three desks down.

"Is Leeza safe?" Mic asks.

"Went off to her car. I will go check on her now. Your job is to delete tonight's logs and all traces. Should you choose to accept it?" Flake winks.

"Whatever you say, Ethan," Mic nods conspiratorially.

"Should you be caught," Flake replies, "we will disavow any knowledge of your actions. This message will self-destruct in five seconds!"

The boys perform their unique version of a country-kid-mocking-ghetto-gangs handshake.

"Not sure how much I can do," Mic mumbles, already on the job.

"Will send you the video I just made of Colin entering his password. Shouldn't be too hard to read it out in slow motion."

Mic looks at him as if Flake had announced to perform Viva Las Vegas in a sparkling Elvis outfit. "What made that neurotic so rash he didn't notice you record him?"

"I'll explain some other time. Need to get Leeza to a safe place."

"Oh...once you're done, I suggest you change Colin's password. Carthaginem_esse_delendam would be a good one, don't you think?"

"Copy. Take this way to avoid the cameras." Without looking up, Mic points at an exit right behind him.

Half way to the basement car park, Flake receives a message. 'b careful. Shady characters down here'.

Leeza awaits him at the bottom of the stairs. Through the glass door to the parkade, they see two suits weaselling about her car.

"What takes them so fucking long? Damn it!" the younger guy's rants.

His partner produces a phone. "I'll call that Neill guy."

"What do we do now?" Leeza whispers.

"Do you know where Colin might have parked his Tesla?"

"How do you know he has a Tesla?"

"Call it intuition," Flake grins.

"How does that help?"

Flake holds up a buzzing phone in a polished orange hard-shell, the display announcing an anonymous incoming call.

The couple hurries up the stairs and down again at the opposite end of the building.

Like any well-behaved intelligent device, once it recognises its owner's phone approaching, the Tesla invites the couple in.

"Buckle up, Dorothy," Flake quips as he boots the car. "Kansas is going bye-bye."

One thousand utterly noiseless electric horses glide as unobtrusively down the car park as one can, boxed in a flashy orange chassis.

As they reach the section where the hunters lie in wait, Flake stops in the staircase's shadow and lowers the window. Insults echo through the open space.

"This side is the only exit," Leeza says.

"Those Brooks Brothers can't hear us coming, right? Plus, they don't expect us in a Tesla. With the black windows, they don't see us. This monster gets from zero to 60 in like two seconds. Before they even know what happened, we are out."

"Okay, Baby Driver," Leeza kisses him good luck, "let's try that!"

Flake shuts the window, slowly advances to the edge of the shielded space and adjusts his position.

On three, as he hits the electrons full throttle, the Tesla jackrabbits off, pressing the couple in their seats; short of breaking the sonic barrier, no roaring cylinders, no squealing tyres, no sound at all announces their run, so the speeding fugitives make it quite far before the suits even take notice.

"What the fuck! Stop the car!" hollers Brooks junior.

"Need to check if it's the girl," commands his partner.

Junior suit charges after the vehicle, waves a badge and yells, "U.S. Marshal Service. Stop the car right now!"

The display flashes a speeding alert when the Tesla arrives at 30 miles an hour. Flake's eyes hectically flip between the dashboard and the dashing officer.

"What do you think?" Leeza closes her eyes. "Are we gonna make it?"

The electronic horses gallop ever faster, yet so does the hunter who seems to speculate on cutting them off after an upcoming turn.

"Doing good!" Flake exclaims, clenching the wheel, his heart hammering away at the speed of the engine. "This thing is damn fast."

He barely reduces speed sliding into the curve, anxiously watching their hunter going strong. "Yes, yes, yes!" he cheers the thousand horses as they come out of the turn; his blood pressure approaches dangerous levels; he accelerates even more, short of breath, as if he was running. In one corner of his eye, he sees Leeza sending off hurried prayers to whatever deity she may think can help right now; in the other he watches the relentless runner zeroing in on them; yet yard for yard rapid mental curve approximation lets Flake's confidence grow that the charging officer will miss them by a tight margin.

The Tesla's risk assessment of the incoming human object, however, arrives at a very different conclusion; flashing warning messages and alarms announce that the car's artificial intelligence decided to hide behind Asimov's rule number one. "No, no, no...!" Flake yells, vigorously kicking down the accelerator. Underwhelmed, the AI sticks with its cowardly verdict and initiates an emergency brake routine.

Squeaking echoes fill the abandoned garage with infernal noise as the Tesla skids for about 20 yards and comes to a stop right as the officer arrives at the driveway.

"Fuck!" Flake shouts, smashing away on the steering wheel.

"What happened?" Leeza asks.

"Fuck that tech shit! We would have made it, if it wasn't for this dipshit chicken chip-set!" Flake frantically kicks the pedal. The Tesla only reacts with a faster flashing frequency of the full screen collision danger warning sign. "You can't even run over bad guys anymore."

"We can't hit a federal officer! Don't want anyone to get hurt!"

"Don't want you to get hurt! I'm sure the bugger would have jumped."

The deranged suit produces a gun, steps in front of the car and puffs. "U.S. Marshal Service. Get out of the vehicle right now. Slowly. Make sure I can see your hands at all times!"

"Now what?" Leeza asks.

"You stay put," Flake replies. "I will get out and lure him away from the car. Once he is out of the way, you move over and hit the metal."

"Get out of the vehicle now or I will have to apply force," the officer commands.

"I won't leave you," Leeza says.

"Don't worry about me. I have a date with the NSA tomorrow, remember?"

Flake gets out and slams the door.

"Put your hands up!" commands the officer.

"Easy, okay?" Flake strides away from the car. "Didn't want to steal the stupid thing. Just borrowed it for a joyride. Would have returned it later...in some rough neighbourhood."

"Where is the girl?"

"Wish I knew." Flake moves towards the staircase. "A rather unfriendly guard escorted me out of the building. So, I figured I'll get some sweet revenge on this Colin jerk; have some fun with his Tesla. The plan was..."

"Get over here!" the officer commands.

Flake keeps creeping sideways.

"Step over here, I said! If you don't stop this, I will have to shoot."

"There are cameras all over the place!" warns his partner on his way over for backup.

Flake slows down a little. He doesn't dare to check on the car even from the corner of his eye, yet should have diverted the Marshals far enough for Leeza to get in the driver's seat.

"I ask you one more time: where is the girl?" the junior officer barks.

"Take care of this guy. I will check the car," the senior instructs and turns towards the Tesla.

Leeza jams in reverse and pulls up to Flake; he jumps in the back and she hits it. As the fugitives speed off, the senior officer pushes his partner's gun down. "They won't get far," he says.

"It is a dead end. Let's go."

"Any more ideas?" Leeza frets.

"Still calibrating."

"What if they shoot?"

"Have they dropped down a wormhole?" the senior officer wonders as they reach the end of the garage with no trace of the flashy vehicle.

"I will get that sucker!" the driver hisses and circles the staircase at full speed.

"Stop!" the senior shouts as they pass a separator wall between fire zones. "Go back!"

The driver pulls the brake, jerks the wheel around and reverses in a squeaking power slide. Just as he speeds up, the Tesla turns the corner and glides through the dust cloud past him. Frenziedly, the officer turns his ride once more and takes up the pursuit.

While the getaway car heads towards the exit ramp, the narrow one-way lane and dozens of columns across the lot frustrate every attempt to overtake. "Fuck! Fuck! Fuck!" a furious officer repeats like a Tourette patient as he jams away on the wheel.

"It must be the chick driving!" he rants as the Tesla exits the premises to enter the circle road. "Only my grandma waits at a fucking stop sign in the middle of the fucking night. I'll pull them over now." He sets out to overtake.

"Let's not rush things," his partner says.

"What the fuck…?"

The orange sedan turns onto the expressway feeder road. "Have to stop him right here, right now!" the junior officer urges. "We stand no chance against a Tesla in a speed race on the highway."

"I'll check with headquarters to get new instructions, now that she's got company. They're not even speeding. Our anarchist doesn't want to add traffic law violations to his record, it seems."

"I will bump that bastard off the expressway."

"No, you won't! No unnecessary attention. We don't want highway patrol on our case. As long as they just roll, we will tail them and get new orders."

"What are they up to?"

"The girl lives in Los Gatos. Maybe that is where they are headed."

"Maybe Mexico?"

"Doubt that. Probably still considering their options."

***

"Great," Leeza sighs, "now we've got the feds on our tails. Or whoever these guys are. Maybe we should have left it alone."

"We can't leave it alone. This is obviously way bigger than we thought."

"That's what I'm saying. That's exactly why we should leave it alone!"

Flake folds his hand into hers.

His eyes meet hers in their windshield reflection.

"Do you think Colin is right?" Leeza asks. "About people just going back to normal. No matter what happens? They just can't be bothered to act?"

"You know when they did all these prequels?" Flake says. "Star Wars, X-Men, Alien…how Vader became dark, Magneto malicious and Xavier bald…"

"Yeah?" Leeza takes her eyes off the traffic to check on him quickly, curious where this may go, relieved that Flake's mind seems to be as odd as ever; because her own is utterly confused.

"I sometimes wonder," Flake says, "what a prequel to 1984 would be like? How the world got into accepting Big Brother in the first place…"

Leeza gazes at some place far beyond the taillights of the busy traffic.

"Speaking of Star Wars," Flake says after a while, "what was that Darth Vader thing all about Colin delivered back there?"

"No idea what are you talking about?"

Flake imitates a dark tinny voice: "I know who your father is…"

"Oh. Yeah. My dad works at the Korean consulate in San Francisco."

"Okay, suppose that also settles where you will spend the night."

***

"I'm sure K-girl is driving," speculates the junior officer while nervously rotating his hands on the wheel. "We should force them to stop. I'll barely touch the car. It'll only need a tiny fender bender to make her surrender. You'll see."

"What if she loses control and crashes? Bumps into other cars? A pile-up, at worst? We can't risk that. The job is to bring her in. Not to make a fuss."

"What is she wanted for, anyway?"

"We shall bring her in. That's all we need to know."

Delighted with his incidental rhyme, the driver chants, "A fender bender to make her surre-hender…"

"Can you please stop that?" his partner grumbles.

"Fender be-hender…"

"I said stop!"

"…surre-hender…"

The Tesla changes from Highway 101 onto interstate 237.

"That's not the way to Los Gatos. Maybe they try to get across the border to Nevada?"

"Won't help them."

"Maybe they don't know that. Could speed up any time. With a good chance of losing us. No idea what they think they are doing."

"The girl's family lives in San Francisco. Maybe they take the long route there? To confuse us."

"It works. I am confused."

With Cisco city in the distance and traffic getting busier, the convoy changes to Interstate 880.

"You really want to wait this out?" the driver asks. "What if they head to a popular place with lots of spectators? What do we do then?"

"Leave me alone and drive. I need to think!"

"Well, think faster, damnit!"

***

Leeza checks on Flake every once in a while. Sometimes he gives her an iffy smile. Most of the time, however, he gazes emptily at nothing, the activity indicator in his eyes in an infinite loop signalling a buffer overflow error. *He will come up with an idea of what to do next,* she thinks. He has to.

"You will not go to the NSA tomorrow, will you?" she eventually wakes him from his overclocking coma.

"Course I will!"

"Can we not hide somewhere until this is all over?"

"They'll find us."

"I know! We need to take the batteries off our phones. This way, they can't track us. Saw that in the Snowden documentary."

"You can't take your battery off your phone anymore. Guess why?"

"We will throw them away!"

"They'll find you. Trust me."

"But you do not have to make it too easy on them. I say you shouldn't go."

"I can't let them put on a witch hunt for me for hiding from the authorities. I have to find out how this all fits. These buggers on our tail, my friends in the agency, that Colin guy…"

"Maybe we should call the cops? FBI?"

"For all we know, the blokes hunting us could be the cops or the FBI. We don't know who is in on this and who is not."

"You seem to trust these NSA guys, though…?"

Flake reaches for Leeza's hand and kisses it.

"I'm scared, Andy!"

"I know."

"I don't want to be on the run."

"I know!"

***

Unusually light traffic on the interstate triggers the antsy officer again. "This is not good," he mumbles. "They could try to lose the tail any time now."

"We will stop them as soon as they leave the highway," his partner says.

"This is the result of all that thinking for the last half hour?"

"Don't worry. Can't lose Blackpink. Got an extra pair of eyes on them now," he points up.

Five miles down, on open track just outside of Fremont, the Tesla slows and comes to a halt on the shoulder.

"Seems like they came to their senses at last," jubilates the junior officer. "Maybe detected the drone and know they can't hide?"

"The guy might be dangerous," his partner says. "We don't know if he's armed. Let's put on the vests."

The two officers approach the car with guns on point.

"Step out of the vehicle!" the junior officer shouts. "Slowly. I want to see your hands at all times."

"You'd better do as you are told," his partner hollers from the back. "Don't make this any worse."

"Last warning. I will not repeat: step out of the vehicle now."

"Go ahead, open the door," the senior instructs. "I have you covered."

"How do you even open this stupid thing? There is no handle."

"There is a handle. Just press it."

"I'm not stupid. It doesn't work."

"Step back. Let me try. Cover me. But easy, o.k.!"

"Shit, you're right, it doesn't work. The battery must have died. That's why they stopped."

"There must be a fucking way to open this fucking door."

"Not sure there is."

"So, now what? We call in AAA?"

"Get out of the car! Or we will have to break in!" shouts the senior officer and steps back. His partner runs up and smashes the handle of his gun against the back door window full force. To no effect. "I'll shoot it!" he hisses.

"We do not want to leave any traces, do we?" his partner replies. "Pick a stone or something."

The officer searches the area for a suitable object, yet drawing a blank. "This is ridiculous! Once this fucking door is open, I will kick some fucking teeth." His colleague hands him the lug wrench from their trunk. He smashes the rear door window. "What the fuck!"

"What is it?"

"There is no one in the fucking car!"

"Bullshit!"

The officer smashes the front door window. "Nobody! Is in! The fucking! Car!" He reaches inside and opens the door. A golf bag is buckled up in the driver's seat.

"Wonderful!" moans the senior officer. "Let's get out of here before anyone sees this."

***

"You should stay at my family's place as well tonight," Leeza says. "Consulate staff can take you to the NSA in the morning. Should be safe."

"If I am not bothering anyone."

"My parents will be delighted to get to know you. Trust me, you'll bother no one. You'll have a separate room in the east wing." Leeza glances over with a governess look, then pulls the red Tucson into a wide driveway leading up to a Victorian mansion, which could easily have such a thing as an east wing. "And here we are," she says.

"When you said your father works at the consulate, you meant…"

"…he is the consul, yes."

"Why didn't you tell me?"

"You didn't seem the groupie type!" The hint of a smile flits across her face.

***

Big One Minus 1, Sunday

Me and My Monkey

A tall, scrawny police apprentice practices his bad cop stare in a daft kind of way as he shows Flake to what looks like a proper interrogation room. The space is equipped with just a lightweight table, two foldable chairs and a mirror covering a major part of one wall.

This time Flake also receives the full waiting game treatment.

"Wow. This is so cliché," Flake addresses the observers he suspects behind the mirror. "Even flickering neon…"

"At least, I am not handcuffed to a hook in the ground…"

Flake roams around the space.

"…with a bag over my head…"

"…tiled floor, drain…is this where you do the waterboarding?"

Flake folds one of the chairs, raises it, as if to smash it against the mirror, then puts it back down and rearranges the furniture neatly in its original position.

"Where are all the file folders from last time? Still at the scanners? I brought the floppy disk."

The delinquent sits himself on a chair. He starts improvising a drum set on the tabletop, using the fingertips for snare, flat hand for toms and the elbow for bass drum. The scarcely furnished room creates quite a bit of reverb.

Flake starts mumbling the second verse of King Crimson's *21st Century Schizoid Man*, spitting the 'p's in politicians, pyre and napalm at the mirror wall. He then accompanies his drum set by imitating guitar and sax in turn.

After he finishes the one-man-band performance, he gets up and roams around again.

"You guys could have at least put some tabloids in here…Weekly World News, National Examiner, Enquirer, Daily Bugle…the stuff you use for your daily briefs…"

The agents stage their entrance after twenty minutes, extending no form of greeting.

"Now we have you down for a chargeable offence, buddy," Special Agent Friends opens the chat. "Breaking and entering. Identity theft. Intellectual property violations. I hope this means you will show a more cooperative attitude this time."

"Willis & Friends," Flake says. "Glad to see you didn't break up." He strips off his sweater, revealing a polo showing pictures of the four Beatles and a caption of their song title 'Everybody has something to hide but me and my monkey'.

"Let me see. Where did we leave it off last time?" Special Agent Friends drops and urges Flake to sit opposite him.

"On the news, they said you got your man," Flake says. "That Rozen fellow?"

"Tim Rozen is just a puppet. You, Mr Thomas, are the puppet master."

"Take away the armour, what remains? Blogger, Prankster, Snowflake, Puppet master? Okay!"

"Did Rozen not deliver? Is that why you broke into the office in Menlo Park? To hack the firm's databases yourself?"

"You believe the Big One is not ready yet?" Flake swivels the chair and leans on the backrest. "That the activists…I prefer to speak of activists instead of terrorists…you are confident that the activists are not yet in possession of the files they claim to expose?"

"You tell me!" The agent and Flake engage in a staring match.

"Many major corporations have been hacked in recent years. Many of which you would have thought would have quite sophisticated security systems in place. I suppose it is safe to assume that any firm can be hacked."

"You think, or you know?"

"It is a race the good guys can't win. There is way too much money in it for the bad guys. Why would the really clever guys, the coding elite, the exceptional talents, spend their lives working in a bank's IT…"

"You certainly see yourself as part of this exceptional elite, don't you?"

"…let alone work in public service, as white hackers, to help you guys in the agency to defend society against malicious code? When there are millions, if not billions, to be earned with black hacks. Public service can't keep up with that, I suppose? At least not in academia, it can't. How about the spy trade?" He beams at the agents, one after the other.

"Despite your annoying messiah act, you and your THS conspirators are just ordinary crooks, after all, in it for the cash, isn't that right?"

"For now, my Uber fare will do. Thank you."

"This plus two billion dollars?" Special Agent Friends shouts.

"What the hell are you talking about?"

"We are talking about the ransom request you issued an hour ago," Special Agent Willis says from the back while his colleague's stare attempts to stab Flake's eyes out. "Two billion dollars payable to a specified coin wallet to stop the dump from happening." Willis approaches the table. "Payable by governments, should they want to avoid the fallout, or by, I quote, the greedy data-monsters to keep their exclusivity on exploiting the people; or by individuals afraid of what might be exposed about them. Signed by The Horrible Siliconettes."

"Don't feigned that's news to you!" Friends shouts even louder.

Flake rises absentmindedly, gazes blankly past the agents and starts wondering about like a sleepwalker.

"Sit back down and start talking!" Friends shouts a little toned down yet just as aggressively.

"This doesn't make any sense," Flake utters to himself.

"Oh, I think it does," Willis says. "You waited until the public was nervous enough; induced the chaos needed so that people would be desperate enough to pay up; with the clock ticking; only hours before god-knows-what might happen; making your claim way more powerful. Very clever."

"Sit the fuck down!" Friends jumps up, obviously ready to enforce his command.

"You're in way over your head, son!" Willis says. "Intrusion to corporate databases, terrorist threats to national security and blackmail will get you booked for the rest of your lousy life with no chance for early release ever."

Flake sleepwalks back to the table as if his overclocked brain can only provide minimal resources to control his movement. He sits down and puts his sweater back on in even slower, trembling motions.

"Start spilling some intel!" Friends hisses. The agents watch Flake's dilated pupils wander about wildly, quite like in a RAM sleep, but with his eyes wide open.

As his computations get completed, a window pops up on Flake's blank screen. "No, it doesn't!" he announces the result.

"What, for fuck's sake, is that supposed to mean?" Friends looks back and forth between Flake and his partner.

"Tragedy of the commons!" Flake says.

Agent Friends' stare demands a more detailed elaboration to avoid advanced interrogation techniques.

"The Nash equilibrium?" Flake adds. "Game Theory? Neumann and Morgenstern?" The agent is clearly about to lose it any second now. "People will only pay into that pot if others do so as well," Flake explains. "They can't tolerate others to benefit for free from their contribution. Such a game can work, but you have to give the process time. Allow people to witness others pay their share. If that was THS's plan, they would have issued the claim earlier."

"You will not wisecrack your way out of this, punk!"

"Should you want governments and corporations to pay up, you wouldn't issue a public statement. Doesn't make any sense, either."

"You may not have planned for this to be an extortion?" Willis intervenes. "You may have rather wanted this to become a revolution. But you failed to get the data; people are not marching in protest. Tragedy of the common dreamy anarchist, I call it! So, you reconsidered. Figured, you may just as well use the opportunity to become rich? Like you said, billions to be made in black hacks. A last, desperate attempt to get something out of it. Wouldn't be the first self-proclaimed idealist to sell out!"

"Two billion dollars is pocket money for what is at stake here," Flake replies. "Google's profit in a week. Not even a dollar from every Facebook user. If you ask me, whoever issued this claim are freeloaders."

"Is that why you were so shaken when you learned about the ransom request?" Special Agent Friends probes. "Because you're pissed someone is piggy-backing off of your grand score?"

Flake closes his eyes, waiting for his heart rate to drop below one hundred.

"Tell me!" Friend shouts.

"Guys," Flake says, "you are confusing me. Are you charging THS with being extortionists? Or do you agree the ransom claim is a bad joke? Which would mean you are charging THS with being idealists?"

"There is nothing idealistic in that terrorist threat," Willis says, "regardless of whether the ransom claim is legit."

"Why is it so hard for you boys to accept those THS activists may have very honourable motives? Maybe they just want the authorities to do their job?"

"What job would that be," Friends works himself up again, "if not to put terrorists like you away for good?"

"The job to protect the basic rights of the American people! Bottom line is not that such data can be hacked and exposed. That's unavoidable given the balance of power. The issue is that such data exists. That comprehensive databases exist containing every personal detail and every online activity of every human being on this planet. Data gathered without individuals being aware. American citizens not recognising they were surrendering their lives to some megalomanic corporations. And no US authority has protected them and stopped these firms from tricking, bribing or forcing American citizens into this worst deal ever..."

"Are you done with that grand speech?" Agent Friends barks, "because I am done listening to your crap. You better tell us what we need to know to stop this attack or you will rot in jail. We will not tolerate you threatening national security because of some weird, romantic socialist vision of a united society."

"You are not listening at all," Flake barks back, his voice shaking. "I am telling you exactly what you have to do to stop the actual threat to national security. The actual threat to national security, and to democracy, by the way, is universal surveillance conducted by private sector companies."

Friends and Flake eyeball each other fumingly.

"Okay. Let's all calm down," Special Agent Willis intervenes. "Tell me, what world is it you want to go back to, Mr Thomas? The internet is the most revolutionary invention of the last hundred years and it has changed the world in so many positive ways. And the US lead this space. Is that it? Is it hate against the system?"

"The Europeans actually invented the internet," Flake replies. "The US were just better than the rest, to find devious ways to use this great tool to exploit ordinary people and make a few people rich. Immensely rich. Like Carnegie plus Rockefeller plus Vanderbilt rich. Obscenely rich."

"It's the classic, right? Your aim is to create a more egalitarian society? Keep great innovators from commercially benefitting from their creations?"

"The geniuses who conceived the internet have not become obscenely rich. Actually, the man they commonly label the father of the internet, Sir Timothy Berners Lee, has acknowledged something went very wrong with his invention. He called it 'dysfunctional' and said it had stopped being a force for good. And you know why he thinks so? He said the way we use it today is designed with 'perverse' incentives. He said he worries that pursuit of short-term profits could go at the expense of human rights, democracy, scientific fact or public safety. This is the actual threat to national security. This is what you boys should concern yourselves with."

"Is that the goal?" Friends hollers. "To show the world how wrong things are going? You know what? I think my colleague is right: you do not have any data. You and your conspirator friends are all talk. You cannot stand that the world, in fact, doesn't want to be saved. That it doesn't even need saving. That people don't feel tricked or forced. That they love the amazing ways in which they can interact now. You are blind to that!"

The agent leans in ever closer. "You dreamed up some crazy vision that issuing this threat will make people awaken in shock and march in protest with you to Capitol Hill? You thought you will not even have to deliver? Even when there is no dump, there will still be a revolution? You know what? You are wrong!

"On Tuesday, people will wake up, turn on their computers, nothing will have changed and it will all be back to normal. Like the millennium bug. Your bluff will be evident. You will have failed! Miserably!"

Flake and Friends meet in another staring contest. The abysmal contempt in the agent's eyes unsettles him, though. A worrying inclination creeps up on him; this time, he may be pushing it; it's not one of his prank videos; this might not end well. He concludes it wouldn't be smart to crack jokes about the agent's quite ignorant millennium bug comment at this stage, even though he would have about a million things to say to that.

"Look, son," Special Agent Willis eventually breaks the silence while the opponents keep staring, "we can hold you here for as long as we want. And we will. Until you cooperate. I can only encourage you to help us stop this before any more damage is done. Would count in your favour. For now, you will enjoy a cell of your own with no distractions; allow you to focus on making the right decision."

These buggers are prepared to throw away the key after all, Flake thinks; he rubs his cold, sweaty hands on his pants; when the squeaking door is thrown open with a loud bang, his heart drops to his boots; he stares spellbound at the entrance.

The gawky police officer enters the frame; this time, though, he looks to Flake like the grim reaper, posturing and puffing himself up as if to proclaim the damning verdict in people versus Flake.

Before the scowling officer can announce the assassination squad, however, a grey-haired gentleman in a glen check suit squeezes past him and takes the stage. "What exactly are the charges against my client, Mr Thomas?" the uptight man with a headmaster's aura demands to know.

"And who are you?" Willis confronts the intruder.

"The name is Maximilian Shield. I am here to represent Mr Thomas."

"Which neck of the woods did you crawl out of?" Special Agent Friends jumps up.

"Do we want to get into the subject of why my client was denied proper reading of his rights and legal representation in this investigation against him until now? Or shall we focus on the charges you intend to bring forward?"

Willis prudently places himself between the counsellor and his partner. "For one, your client broke into a corporate office yesterday," he says.

"Do you have proof of that?"

"We sure do!" Special Agent Friends interjects from the back.

"What kind of proof is this?"

"Surveillance cameras that show him trespassing."

"You mean tailgating?" corrects the counsellor, "accompanied by an employee of the firm. Is that something NSA deals with these days?"

"I learned," Flake chips in, his heart rate almost back in check, "some stupid mistake has wiped out the security tapes from last night, actually."

"Is that the case, agents?" Shields inquires. "Or can we see the footage?"

"Your client," Special Agent Friends towers over Flake, "helped by some conspirators, also broke into the firm's systems to gain access to company data. And he just admitted tampering with the security camera recordings."

"Mr Thomas did not admit to anything of that nature. He provided the NSA with valuable intelligence your own investigations should have brought to light."

"We also have a ton of evidence connecting your client to the terrorists planning the Big One," Willis says.

"What evidence would that be, precisely? Evidence that could convince my old friend Lawrence Burke, the District Attorney of the beautiful County of Santa Clara, to issue an arrest warrant for Mr Thomas? That evidence better be air tight. Larry is not a very patient person should you try to misuse him to bend the law."

"You just stated there was no hack, no Big One," Flake intervenes, "that it's all a hoax. Should that be your working hypothesis what do you want to keep me here for?"

"Your announcement caused widespread fear in the public," Willis replies. "Manipulated the stock markets and incited others to leak corporate information for you. With the help of this Rozen fellow. It's a long list. More than enough to put you away for a mighty long time."

"Can you provide any evidence for a connection between my client and Mr Rozen?" Shield asks. "These are all very serious allegations. Should you not be able to produce any similarly serious evidence right now, though, that credibly connects my client to any of these charges, to Mr Rozen and especially to the release of the announcement itself, I suggest you continue your investigations until you have obtained such evidence. Until then, we will make ourselves available, should you have further questions. Come on, Andrew, let's go."

Special Agent Friends steps in Flake's way as he gets up. "You are not going anywhere, buddy!"

The counsellor starts a speed dial. "I suppose I have to bother Larry, after all. I just hope for you Larry junior's softball match is going well, and he is in a good mood..."

Willis puts his hand on his partner's shoulder.

"You are free to leave."

Special Agent Friends looks at Flake like he engages in quite an explicit daydream involving attack dogs as he watches them exit.

"Thanks a lot for saving my butt, Sir." Flake says to Shields back out on the street. "These boys seemed determined to put me on a plane to Gitmo. The agents had one viable question, though. How on earth did you get here?"

"Well, my old friend Benjamin said you might talk yourself into trouble. He seems to think you have authority issues."

"Does he?" A restrained smile flits across Flake's tense face.

"You may want to lay low for a while," Shields says. "They are not done with you yet. Here is my card, in case you need further assistance."

Back in the interrogation room, Friends is furious. "Why did you let the sucker walk? This guy has an agenda. And he is obviously lying. I have totalled at least a dozen occasions of him showing deceptive behaviour."

"Come on!" his partner says. "Your famous five second rule again?"

"Deceptive behaviour within the first five seconds after a question is asked is a proven sign of a lie! That's science."

"You actually believe in that bull, don't you? Besides: Wouldn't you think a gifted people manipulator, and I grant you that's what Thomas is, such a guy who aims to bring about a revolution, may have read that book as well?"

"Fuck you!"

"You're welcome."

"You bought into his dramatic stage act when we told him about the ransom?"

Since his partner doesn't give him an answer, he adds: "What do you suggest we do now?"

"Trust me. I know DA Burke. He eats investigators for breakfast. We have to give him more than some kitchen psychology from an interrogation for beginner's seminar."

"Fuck!" Friends slams his fist against the wall. "I say we put this douche under maximum pressure. Extended interrogation protocol. I'm sure that snowflake will melt in no time."

"We don't do that anymore."

"That is the next fucking mistake. Damn liberals!" He notices his partner's disapproving look and adds, "you know damn well there are no nice guys. We just don't know enough about them!"

"In case you are right, letting him run free may help us after all. He may lead us on to something, now that we have rattled his cage. We'll put him on watch 24/7."

***

Doubts

"…Mr Neill is a prominent figure in the industry, one of the first employees of the social media giant and responsible for the firm's IT security. He is also a major shareholder. Highway patrol found his Tesla two miles outside of Fremont this morning. The vehicle was violently tampered with, which led to speculations about an abduction of Mr Neill. The report coincides with rumours about a major security breach at the firm.

"After a ransom request for the enormous sum of two billion dollars payable to a coin wallet in order to stop the Big One was published this morning, the *disappearance of Mr Neill is yet another incident nurturing speculations, especially after the death of Tim Rozen, a senior product manager at Neill's firm and allegedly the originator of the threat to expose millions and millions of personal data sets. Even though it is unclear at this point if Colin Neill's disappearance is in any way connected to the Big One, it makes people even more sceptical about the official version still upheld by the authorities of an unsubstantiated act of a single perpetrator.*

"While right after the death of Tim Rozen and his self-indictment, public concerns about the Big One seemed to subside yesterday, in a quick survey conducted today a vast majority of people stated to have doubts or even severe doubts whether the authorities are telling them the full truth on this matter. That shouldn't be a surprise to anyone, given that neither the Office of the Attorney General nor the intelligence agencies have issued clear statements whether they believe this ransom request to originate from The Horrible Siliconettes indeed or whether they consider this the act of freeloaders trying to exploit the public unrest."

***

Smoke Curls

"Please allow me to show you to the study, Sir. Mr Kendrick will be with you momentarily."

Timberley follows the white-gloved assistant past an open staircase dominating the palatial foyer of the English style country house. Through a massive double-winged door, they enter the wood-panelled library with top-to-bottom bookshelves and vast windows overlooking a park-like scenery.

"May I offer you a drink, Sir?"

"No, thank you," Timberley replies while he hands the man his hat, "it is a bit early for me."

"Very well, Sir."

Just as the assistant turns the corner, the host rushes towards Timberley with wide open arms, beaming with joy. "How long has it been, Benjamin? Three years?" The stocky silver beard, wearing jackboots and breeches, pulls his visitor into a firm, lasting hug.

"I'd say since you retired as a senator and retreated yourself here on the west coast."

"How nice of you to put it like that. You know I didn't retire. I was doghoused by my own people." Kendrick pours two single malts and hands one to his guest.

"I heard you were doing well ever since you left the hill," the professor muses. "Even without a seat in the house, not a lot happens there without you having a hand in it, somehow. That's what they tell me."

"That's what folks say?" The old friends toast.

"Well, you know me. Can't just cultivate orchids or whatever it is they expected you to do when you retire. But whom am I telling this? You churning out widely recognised papers hasn't slowed down either."

"Some smart people write most of that stuff for me. I'm just the pretty face on the cover."

"As usual, Benjamin: way too modest. That's why you are an academic and I'm the politician."

On Kendrick's cue, both men drop into heavy chesterfield chairs.

"Actually," Timberley hums and haws, "one of these clever people working for me is the reason I urgently needed to see you."

"I thought you wanted to reminisce."

"Since I'll be over in Stanford all summer, would have paid you a visit soon, anyway. If it was only for your wine cellar."

"That I understand."

"Today, I came here to ask you for a favour. For one of my staff. He seems to be on the radar of the intelligence agencies."

Kendrick indulges in a sip of single malt and in the fact that for once in their long friendship, he is the one with the answers. "Mr Thomas has exhibited profound reluctance to cooperate and to explain some of his more suspicious spare time activities. That's what I heard."

"So, you have heard? I assure you he is a good kid. He is like us when we were young."

"Like you, you mean?"

"You know what I'm talking about. The young man is headstrong? Yes. Presumptuous? Certainly. Provocative? Absolutely. And quite confrontational in that. A wiseass? At times. But he is also well-intentioned. An evangelist for what he thinks is right. An agent provocateur. But not a foreign agent. And certainly not a terrorist."

"Even though my friends at the NSA have not used these exact terms, the profiling sounds familiar."

"I was hoping you could talk to your friends and make sure this assessment translates into a discontinuation of the prosecution against Mr Thomas?"

"I'd love to help you!" Kendrick looks at the tumbler he rotates clockwise on his armrest. "Waited a long time for you to ever need my help. Yet, I am afraid, can't do anything in this particular matter."

"Did the agencies find anything tangible that incriminates him?"

"No. It's not that."

"What is it then, Randall? You must want the true culprits to be caught just as much as I do. Can't allow anyone to pin this on some starry-eyed idealist just to show quick progress."

Kendrick halts the rotation and looks up from the tumbler, his friend straight in the eye. "You have to understand, Benjamin," he leans forward in his chair, "you have put yourself in a very dangerous place. This is way bigger than you think."

"That means what, exactly?"

The question hangs in the air like cigar smoke welling up.

"You're indeed not seeing it, are you?" Kendrick leans back again.

"Seeing what, Randall?"

"You have spent too much time in that Massachusetts Ivory Tower, Jim." Kendrick enjoys his word play for a moment before his face darkens again.

"Please help me understand," Timberley says.

This friend rushes down another sip. "We didn't fail to regulate Big Tech. Wasn't an accident they grew so big…built those monopolies."

"What are you saying?"

"Why do you think it turned out that way? Because politicians are all short-sighted bean counters? Dealing with the insignificant problems of their constituents in some small district in heartland America?" Kendrick downs his whiskey. "We made them, Benjamin. We made them."

Timberley finishes his drink as well. "Can't follow, I'm afraid," he says.

Kendrick gets up, collects the professor's glass and walks back to the bar.

"Why do you think we gave some up and coming online book store a massive price advantage over Barnes & Noble for so long, suspending sales tax?" He pours doubles. "Why, do you think, did we allow Bezos to change prices depending on the buyer's urge? The corner shop can't do that. They can't say, oh, you are wearing an Apple watch? In your case, the attaché case you want is fifty dollars more. Oh, you are dressed in a polyester suit. Let's make that shirt a little cheaper, so you don't shy away from buying it. We allowed Bezos to do that. Which meant extra profit; become wealthier and thus bigger; get more customers, more data, more power."

He hands Timberley the drink and wanders back to his chair. "Why do you think we let that happen? If we were mostly concerned with our constituents, many of which own shops in their neighbourhoods; are employed by retailers on high street or low street."

Kendrick drops, leans back and crosses his legs. "You never bought into the official story of lower prices through online competition, did you?"

Timberley takes a sip and watches the rhetorical question dissolve in the thickening air like curls of cigar smoke. Into the final vapours he says: "You make them seem like our very own all-American oligarchs, Randall."

Kendrick won't allow his train of thought to be derailed. "Why do you think," he asks, "we let Facebook put spy cookies on every website? Suck up every potential competitor? Why did we allow Google to track your every move on the web? Allowed the most used browser in the same hands as the operating system on the spy device everyone carries in his pocket? Because it creates better service?"

"I think I have an idea where this is going," Timberley frowns. He can't tell if his friend is prepping the punchline or trying to filibuster out of a disturbing confession.

"Why do you think did we not even intervene when those companies put wires into everybody's homes?" Kendrick raises his glass to take another sip, but changes his mind and puts it back down.

"Why do you think that is? Because we trust these companies to only use it for the common good?"

"Let me make a guess," Timberley replies. "NSA, FBI, CIA, all would love to get their hands on natural language recognition, which actually works. Under all real-world conditions. This is the way to get there. Maybe the only way, certainly the fastest."

"Don't forget," Kendrick adds with a boyish smile, "once people are used to talk freely with wire taps around…"

"This is diabolic!" Timberley says, stretching his neck like the rabbit with the snake already coiled around it.

"Don't get me wrong," Kendrick says, "not everyone in DC got all geeky suddenly, at the turn of the century. We all know Hillary can hardly handle email. And if it didn't have slots, you could fit your dick into, Bill was also not very interested. If Walmart could have gotten the people in the shops to tell them their lives' stories and take home a device that keeps track of their every move...well, there would have been no need for the online giants. We may have given them some proper rules to play to. Sam Walton and his friends surely donated a lot of cash to change minds in the administration. Yet, it was just too tempting."

"Instead, Washington tilted the rules on this new playground in favour of some selected few?"

"We didn't allow them to become all-powerful...we wanted them to. At least, that was what we wished for."

"Because only when they are unavoidable," Timberley completes his friends train of thought, "only if there is no way around using online shopping, to use social media, to communicate with your grandchildren via messaging, only if everyone needed to subscribe to the all-dominant service providers, individuals couldn't object to the surveillance?"

Timberley's probing look doesn't warrant an answer to his rhetorical question, but to the ethical elephant in the room: how could you ever agree to this?

Kendrick seems lost in thought, somewhat relieved, somewhat uneasy still.

"Do you even hear what you are saying?" Timberley urges. "Should the government have asked people for even fractions of this, it would be called a surveillance state. Most dictatorships in history couldn't ever even dare impose that on their population."

Kendrick swallows a big gulp. "It seemed a brilliant idea at the time to let them collect it for us. We didn't expect it to grow this big. A machine kicked in. A self-propelling system."

Timberley looks like his brain is busy recalibrating a significant share of its synapses. "You created octopuses that reach into every corner of people's lives to spy on them for you? This sounds more like China to me than like the United States of America."

"I'd put forward we did it a fair bit more subtly, wouldn't you agree?"

Kendrick recalls sarcasm doesn't go down all that well with his friend. He finishes his drink and gets up to fix himself another one. "Even clever people like you didn't see this."

Timberley seems lost for words; better yet, lost for words he wouldn't discard straight away as unhelpful or uncivilised.

"Can you see now, Ben, why we cannot allow some activists, who are still hooked on this 'don't be evil'-bullshit, to put this all at risk?"

"Your great plot against the American people...?"

"Oh, don't be so self-righteous, Benjamin. After 9/11, everybody agreed, should we want this country to be safe, we would need to make use of all options at our disposal. That gave it the crucial push. Before that, it was more experimental. The giants were still midgets."

Kendrick downs the drink he just poured and fixes himself a new one. "It still is just a coincidence," he smirks on his way back, "that Crystal City is only a ten-minute drive to Langley."

"You mean from Amazon's HQ2 in Arlington to the CIA headquarter...?"

"Passing by the Pentagon on the way even; and another ten minutes to the bureau in downtown DC."

"A coincidence or god's version of irony," Timberley sighs.

"I like that." Kendrick smiles a bitter smile. He hands his friend a drink, who parks it on the side table, since he didn't finish his last one yet.

"You don't seem comfortable with all of this, Randall. Did this go too far, even for you?"

"The point is," Kendrick clumsily falls into his chair, "even if we wanted, we couldn't stop it now." He stares at a drop he spilled on his armrest. "No one," he says while he wipes it off with his bare hand, "not even your activist friends can have an interest in destroying this industry altogether."

Timberley downs the rest of his drink, looks at the empty glass for a while, exchanges it with the one he had parked, leans back and peers at the crystal some more. "Power is not a means; it's an end," he mumbles to himself. "No one ever seizes power with the intention of relinquishing it...I see..." He looks back at Kendrick. "Do you honestly think the business models of Big Tech are so fragile?"

"It's not just the dependency of Meta and Google on the data they assemble," Kendrick says with a black look in slightly glazed eyes. "Just the data brokers turn over two times the budget of all our intelligence agencies combined. 200 billion dollars. All of that depends on the ability to collect information on individuals to sell them stuff."

Kendrick downs a mouthful as if the size of the gulp should match the gravity of his point. "It's bad enough that Europe put in these laws to regulate all this. Potentially wrecking it. We work very hard to convince folks on the hill not to make the same mistake."

"DC and Big Tech's lobby squad have thrown carrots and sticks at your friends in the old world for years on this," Timberley says.

"With some success, I would add," Kendrick says. "The Big One puts it all at risk. I'm sure you see this is a serious problem!"

Now Timberley takes a sip appropriate to the size of the matter.

"Here's to the Irish!" Kendrick toasts with a jolly melancholia in his gaze.

"It wasn't hard to convince them," he breaks his friend's shock freeze. "Few people will reject a billion-dollar pay check."

"On top of unregulated monopoly status," Timberley mumbles, "allowing these guys to ditch taxes of hundreds of billions, you mean? Get even bigger, even faster."

"At first," Kendrick says, "Sergey and Larry wrestled with this quite a bit. But when they saw how much money they would get to build all their toys, their balloons, all of that, they stepped aside, handed the firm to the adults and went on to play in the backyard.

"Jeff wasn't that precious about it from the start. He probably already saw himself in his spaceship, to baldly go, where no man has gone before." Kendrick chuckles.

"So, they signed a pact with the devil to hand all their data to the agencies," Timberley says.

"Are you calling the Clinton administration the devil?" Kendrick seems in quite a jolly mood.

"She-devil, I suppose." Timberley's mind drifts off in many directions at once in an attempt to connect all the dots. "Quite ironic that Putin used your toys to keep Hillary out of the oval office in 2016."

The jolly mood vanishes from Kendrick's face. "There is more to this, even," he says in a dark tone.

"It can hardly get any worse, can it?"

"We don't know yet, to be honest."

"What do you not know yet?"

"First: we don't know if the Big One actually exists. And if it does, where it comes from."

"Sure it is not homemade?"

"Honestly? No, we are not."

"What are you saying, Randall?"

"Could be an internal leak. Someone from inside the agency who wants to, I don't know, send a signal, follow the path of Snowden, expose the deep state, make people aware, whatever. Cannot rule this out."

"That sounds terrible."

"Could even be worse. It could be…"

"What could be worse than that?"

"…could be Russia."

Timberley regrets his Putin remark, as if not mentioning it would have changed anything.

"The NSA got hacked by Russia?"

"We're pretty sure it's not that. Could be, though, and there is some evidence to suggest, that people from within the agencies have sold data to the Russians. For years already."

Timberley downs the rest of his drink.

On his way over to the bar, Kendrick explains. "During the Trump years, as the new administration took office, they fired tons of people; many positions vacated for a long time; herds of new folks coming in, people from the outside with no experience or roots in intelligence, no background. We knew all along this turbulent period may come back to haunt us." Kendrick hands his friend another single malt.

"Why would Russia publish that data? Isn't it more valuable to them if no one knows about it?"

"They might have gotten wind we are on to them. That the leak will be closed soon. May want to use this for one last blow. An attempt to destabilise us." Kendrick turns the caramel-coloured crystal in front of his glazing eyes as if he actually expects it to offer a glimpse into the future. "They use the new propaganda tools quite skilfully already to divide our society, stir up conflict, deepen the trenches. You described it very well on NBC. They might believe such a leak is what it takes to start an unrest. A revolution. The next storm on Capitol Hill. Whatever."

Timberley sits on the edge of his chair. "Randall, why are you telling me this?"

"To warn you, Ben. You're my friend. I don't want you to get in trouble."

"You know damn well I can't just lay back and watch."

"People get hurt, or worse, if they interfere in such important matters of national security."

"Are you threatening me?"

"Not me. I'm not…" Kendrick avoids his friend's concerned gaze.

It's Timberley's turn to look for enlightenment in the crystal lowball.

"What do you know about the death of that guy who allegedly confessed to being the Siliconettes?" he asks. "Tim Rozen?"

Kendrick swallows the answer with another big sip of single malt. "One of two things can happen. Either there is going to be a drop. I can only hope we do not find leads into Russia."

"What if you do? Is the administration prepared to go to war on this?"

"No idea."

"Who else can it be? Did the agency or the bureau come up with any leads? Who benefits from this?"

Kendrick gets up and walks across the swaying ground to the vast window overlooking the well-groomed estate. "That brings me to the second option, which we believe is much more credible. The Big One does not happen. Never was real in the first place. Just a hoax, a test, a warning. I don't know."

"By whom? Who is testing us?" Timberley joins his friend gazing at the gently swaying trees in the park and a daunting pile of clouds over the bay.

"People like your assistant? Activists who want to prove to the world we're on the wrong path?" The two friends collude in staring at nothing for a while.

"What's next? How do you see this pan out, Randall? A lot has changed in this last week. There is no way back to the old normal, is there?"

"Asking me?" Kendrick turns to his friend. "You're the smart one in this room."

"You know I will not keep quiet on this? I can't. Suppose you do not expect me to?" Timberley puts down his empty tumbler.

"I trust nobody's judgment more than yours, Benjamin. You understand the consequences."

"Good bye, Randall."

"Fare well, old friend."

Doomsday Dome

"The public doesn't seem to buy into the official version on the Big One. That it was a single individual, blinded by unfulfilled love, who issued the threat to expose people's data to become a hero in the eyes of an adored colleague. That the threat is unsubstantiated. Especially since more and more rumours on security incidents at major corporations are coming up by the hour.

"All over the country, and in fact all over the world, people are preparing for the Big One to go ahead. By deleting their Facebook and Instagram accounts; their dropboxes and clouds; wiping apps off their smartphones.

"In several cities, we have even witnessed incidents of panic buying already. Citizens stockpiling food and goods for everyday use. These people seem to believe supply chains might collapse in the aftermath of the data dump; just as if the Big One was an actual earthquake.

"The manager of this Wal-Mart outlet in Austin, Texas, yesterday tried to restrict the quantity of items shoppers could lift out of the store to distribute stock more evenly among patrons. Outraged customers got into a fight, first amongst each other and eventually with staff trying to appease enraged shoppers. Shop windows burst, fixtures got damaged and a lot of inventory got destroyed. As more and more shoppers swarming in from neighbouring stores got involved, police had to step in and separate the crowd before the ever-growing riot would get completely out of hand. Such incidents were reported across the country.

"Other people approach the situation completely differently: on all five continents, activist organise so called Doomsday Domes. The most extreme of those have already started, set up as multi-day rave events lasting until Tuesday noon.

"We are connected to Jennifer Connelly, who reports for us live from one of these events. Jennifer, tell us what's going on."

"Sure, Tom. Here, on the outskirts of St Louis, it feels a bit like Mardi Gras meets Woodstock meets Burning Man. The festival is huge. Estimates go all the way up to five hundred thousand party people gathered here in no-man's-land near the little town of Waterloo. The organisers have built an entire city for the event on this usually very peaceful ranch surrounded by golf courses."

"Acts scheduled to perform on five different stages spread across the vast ranch include the hottest DJs like David Guetta, Skrillex, Marshmellow, Zedd or Hardwell, but also the likes of Drake, Beyoncé, Rihanna, Imagine Dragons and Coldplay. And BTS, of course!"

"That sounds a bit like Live Aid. I understand there is also a charitable cause behind these events?"

"The proceeds of all official Doomsday Dome events will go to a foundation. Users across the globe can take part in a poll online to determine what this foundation will spend the money on. Participants can vote on projects to fund causes like legal counsel for whistleblowers, research in encryption technology, Web3 protocols or open-source data privacy solutions."

"We were told some A-listers got banned from participating in these events by its organisers?"

"That is correct. Acts like Madonna, Shakira or Justin Timberlake did not get an invite to any of these Doomsday Domes because of their involvement with tax evasion practices uncovered by the so-called paradise papers leaked a few years ago. Organisers seem to be worried what the Big One could reveal about these artists. For the same reason, the session just outside of London will go down without Irish uber-band U2, since their front man Bono was one of the most prominent cases when the paradise paper story first broke."

"How is the mood with the party crowd? You mentioned Mardi Gras and Burning Man. Is it a celebration or a funeral?"

"I would say it's an interesting blend. While many of the ravers stream parts of this event live on their social media channels or upload short captures every few minutes, others gather every night at midnight for a ritual Burning of Bookmarks, as they call it. They conjure around enormous bookmark bonfires and toss symbolic blue origami paper birds, which look a bit like the Twitter logo, into the flames as a symbol for deleting one or more of their social media accounts permanently."

"Burning of Bookmarks? That sounds interesting."

"This doomsday festival is a celebration of social media while it's still fun and at the same time a staunch farewell to it. The overall atmosphere here is very peaceful, I must say."

"Thank you, Jennifer. Not so peaceful are the protester groups rallying again, for the third day in a row, in front of the headquarters of many Big Tech firms charged to be potential sources of a lot of the information to be leaked tomorrow. Similar rallies are taking place in front of branch offices of NSA, CIA, FBI, and Homeland Security. People here are waving banners accusing the agencies and the bureau of failing to protect them. Others protest against the intelligence community for spying on the American people. It is a diverse

conglomerate of attitudes and reasons prompting folks to take part in these rallies. The overall sentiment in this crowd, though, we can only describe as explosive."

"As the crowds grew bigger and bigger yesterday, local authorities called in the national guard to protect the properties. I wouldn't be surprised if, eventually, the heated atmosphere would lead to direct confrontation between the protesters and the police and national guard. Rallies are scheduled to continue tomorrow."

"Latest polls show 60 percent of Americans believe the Big One will actually take place. Tutorials on how to delete online data, profiles, entire accounts and also chat and browsing histories are by far the most clicked content on YouTube for days now."

"It seems like, in a way, the Big One has already taken effect. The foundations of the digital world as we know it seem shaken quite a bit. Yet, maybe, this was just the foreshock..."

***

Carousel

Seen from Fishermen's Wharf, Coit Tower on top of Telegraph Hill, made to glow by the low sun, outshines the Transamerica Pyramid and even the Salesforce Tower down in SoMa on this beautiful afternoon. Proud parents record their kids on the historic carousel on Pier 39. The queue for Bubba Gump Shrimp on upper level reaches all the way down the stairs to ground floor. Sea lions lolling on swim floats in front of the promenade cheer on the tourists taking their picture in golden sunlight.

"Why the pier, Professor?" Leeza announces their arrival as she and Flake make their way towards the waterfront through hordes of couples and families mingling in front of souvenir shops and food stalls, enjoying the last hours of sunshine over San Francisco Bay before the announced storm. "Want us to do the full sightseeing tour?" She smiles.

"I figured it would be the safest place we could choose," Timberley replies. "With all the visitors around, no one will want to create a big fuss."

"Should they book us on the spot," Flake snuggles up to Leeza, "the boat to Alcatraz departs right over there, doesn't it?"

The professor looks up at a flock of seagulls. "Did you notice the birds?" he asks. "How they get carried away by the gusty wind?"

"Like this one, greedily eyeing that tourist's clam chowder?" Leeza points at a gull right over their heads that holds steady in midair, ready to take advantage of an inattentive second to snatch the bread straight out of the man's hands. "Whoops, there you go, lurker lifted a few feet by a squall."

"That makes it hard for the little spy drones. Too big a risk for the expensive equipment to collide with a gull. There's one above every tourist's head."

"Gulls?" Flake asks.

"You think they are watching us?" Leeza asks.

"Oh, I'm sure."

"Let's play some I spy with my little eye," Flake quips. "Whoever detects an agent first, wins."

Flake scans the crowd. "What about the guy with the headphones? Pink linen shirt. Messenger bag. Doesn't he look suspicious? Who comes to this place all by himself?"

"Oops, no," Leeza laughs, "boyfriend approaches."

"The one on the phone. Striped dress shirt, raised collar. Turns back and forth, looking for something?"

"Wrong again. Now he is waving."

"Don't be fooled," the professor says. "The agents will not look like agents. They will mingle; tourists; couples. I'm sure there are cameras, directional microphones, all of that. However, we will only discuss how to avoid being persecuted for something we didn't do, won't we?"

"I see, Professor," Leeza says. "Yet, in Tim's case, someone messed with the evidence. Manipulated it."

"Leeza is right," Flake says. "It's easy to deep fake voice recordings. With enough footage, you can manufacture a file of us saying anything you want. Not even your wife could tell it is not you saying whatever they put into the voice bot's mouth."

"Flake has Scarlett Johansson read him bedtime stories," Leeza sighs, rolling her eyes. "How do you know what's real and what isn't? Toss a coin?"

"My muse strikes again!" Flake cheers. "Leeza, you are brilliant."

"I am?"

"Bitcoin!"

"Bitcoin?" the professor wonders.

"Okay, smart boy," Leeza says, "don't you think we should concern ourselves with our physical safety first, before we consider safe havens for our finances?"

"Bitcoin is a blockchain." Flake beams like he just discovered the best life hack ever. "Blockchains determine a valid transaction through a community who verifies it. Once enough users have verified a transaction, it becomes unforgeable. Whoever wanted to counterfeit it would have to create a ton of verification certificates as well."

"That is very interesting," Leeza sighs, "but what does this have to do with our situation?"

"Should several correct records of a conversation exist," the professor explains with an appreciative smile while Flake is already off scanning the crowd, "a forged version would need to prove it is more credible."

"Excuse me? Could you do us a favour?" he addresses an Asian couple dressed in matching colours.

"Want me to take picture?" the husband smiles delightedly.

"Where are you guys from?"

"Japan. Is our silver wedding."

"Congratulations. Well done. My girl, the lovely Leeza over there, is from Korea."

"Beautiful lady. You very luck man."

"I sure am. What line of work are you in, if you don't mind me asking?"

"I work for accounting firm; my wife work in sales; retail fashion."

"No technology companies. Perfect. Look, guys, this may seem odd to you, but it is really important. I'd like you to record us with your own phone. We will do nothing spectacular. Just talk. And you keep taping. Okay?"

"Is this sort of candid camera thing?"

"Well, I suppose you could say so. I would really appreciate if you could play along."

"Crazy Americans. Is okay my wife record me? While I record you?"

"Sure! Brilliant idea!"

"Apologies," another tourist intervenes. "I couldn't help overhearing your conversation. Sounded odd. I like odd. Want me to record you as well?"

"Oh, that'd be great!"

"Love the tee, by the way!" The guy winks conspiratorially and points at the print on Flake's polo: Archibald Tuttle Repair Shop. "Brazil!" he adds. "Best movie ever! Told you I like odd."

After he recruited two more camera crews, Flake hurries back to his friends. Quite a number of bystanders noticing the odd proceedings prepare their phones as well, not to miss out on whatever might happen next.

"Feels weird to be taped," Leeza says.

Just as Flake is about to get started, Leeza's scowl tells him this is not the right time for a lecture on ubiquitous use of smart city surveillance devices.

"Have you had word from Micah yet?" the professor asks.

"Nothing," Flake replies. "Off the radar completely."

"Doesn't have to mean anything bad. Maybe he just dug a hole for himself until this has all cleared over. Would actually be a good idea. What about you, Leeza? Your father's position certainly provides some protection…"

"Dad has arranged for me to fly out to Seoul tonight. He believes I am safest there."

"You think the airport might be a problem, Professor?" Flake asks.

"Dad has friends at Samsung," Leeza says. "They operate like a shuttle service to Seoul for their senior execs with a corporate jet. They will take me along, Dad said. I'll travel on diplomatic passport."

"The revolution flies first class these days…cool!" Flake grins. "Anyhow, a conspiracy plot conceived in a private jet is called a corporate strategy, not an act of terror."

Leeza gives her friend a censuring look.

"That's good," Timberley mumbles, a little less disquieted.

"What about you, professor?" Flake asks. "Will they not come after you as well? Especially after your gig on national TV tomorrow?"

"I am too much of a public figure," he replies. "And a British citizen. Plus, too much well documented history to fake, I guess. I am more concerned about you."

"You know I'd love for you to come with me to Seoul," Leeza says.

"I am not bailing!"

"Don't pick the wrong fight," the professor says. "Let the dust settle."

"Hide under a rock? Allow them to hang it on to me? No way! Don't want to be on the run for the rest of my life."

"We gain nothing with you ending up in Leavenworth either," the professor replies. "Not even Maximilian may get you off the hook next time."

"Couldn't we go public?" Leeza asks. "Win people's hearts and minds for Andy's case? Persuade them he did nothing wrong? Wouldn't that protect him from being their fall guy?"

"How do you suggest doing this?" the professor inquires.

"Leeza wants to wad me in her cosy community cocoon," Flake waves off.

"Your girlfriend has a point, though. The system will hardly act against one hundred million Americans wanting an innocent man to walk free."

"I'm not the ideal candidate for everybody's darling, I'm afraid."

"You don't have to be Ferris Bueller, exactly," Leeza says, "but folks will quickly see you are not Tyler Durden either!"

Flake puts on a huffy face.

"You are way more boring than that," Leeza rips.

"Oh, thank you!"

"I mean…what I'm saying is…you are the clever guy with deep reflections on life, who just wants to have a little fun," she grins. "Not the guy that blows up the city."

"Thanks again!"

"Don't be upset. Even I do not want to fight right now."

"No, I mean it. You are perfectly right. We need to weave a cosy cocoon of mediocrity around me."

"You lost me."

"We must show how dull and unthreatening I am. Make sure they can't fake evidence against me. My grand boringness must be on file…"

"Still don't get it."

"Could you shoot a brief clip, please?"

"Becoming a camera addict, aren't you?"

"Not sure if I'm saving or surrendering my soul with this," Flake sighs.

"Pardon?"

"Never mind. Ready?"

"Take one. Rolling."

Flake straightens himself out, harrumphs and puts on his rendition of Steven Colbert. "Hello! Is there anybody out there? Just nod if you can hear me.

"This is a special version of my usual feed, so I'm gonna do proper introductions. This is Awkward Andy. Andrew Thomas. ParanoidDroit on my other channel. Most folks call me Flake. Address and social security number are below to avoid any mix-up for what I am about to ask of you. Don't forget to like and subscribe but moreover: please spread the word. Via all channels available to you.

"I'm in a bit of trouble with the authorities. They want to lock me up for this announcement of the data dump. The Big One. THS. I have been called horrible before; many times, actually; yet that doesn't make me a Siliconette. I need your help. Help to make my entire life completely transparent.

"I ask everyone out there to leak anything you can find on me. Hashtag FlakeQuake. Should your company operate CCTV cameras anywhere, in a mall, in the street, should you have access to footage of cameras on traffic lights, in public spaces, in private facilities, please find every picture or clip that shows me and upload it to my vault on WikiLeaks. See link below. Should your company deal with any sort of communication, messaging, file transfers, anything of that nature? You have my explicit consent to publish it all.

"You work for Google, Apple, Samsung or a weather app or anybody I'm not even aware of, that has location data on me and can plot my life's journey: please post this as well.

"You work for a retailer? See if I bought something off your outfit. You work for a streaming service, and yes, also the juicy ones please, let it be known what I watched, looked for, showed an interest in, clicked away; all the activities that are tracked: publish it. If I ever Tinder'd, Blendr'd or 3funned you or messaged you in any other app, feel free to tell the world.

"Let's see how close we can get to the Truman Show, folks. Metaverse edition."

"Should you work for a file storage company…I will not tell you which storage I use, you shall not rely on me being truthful here…want you all to check if you can find any data of me and upload it.

"I will also not tell you which banks I use, which phone companies, cable, insurance…you will quickly find this anyway in what others upload. I ask you all to see if you can find me in whatever information your company has. And publish it, please. You have my explicit consent.

"Also, should your company have this kind of data and you cannot find me in it? Publish that as well. I want it to be known what I did, but also what I didn't do."

"I ask all you AI wizzes out there to do your magic on everything that gets uploaded. Look for any correlations you can find. Any bit of intel you can squeeze out of every byte of my history. Deep-learn like crazy, please.

"My friends from the NSA, should you be listening, and also the other security agencies: please scan your printouts and load those up as well. I'm sure you will have some consultant from Booz who sits in the next cubical and can show you how it's done."

Flake adjusts his stance and clears his throat to keep his voice from cracking.

"I shouldn't have to do this. To object to 24/7 surveillance, to tracking of your every move, is not a sign of bad intentions or evil conduct. It is your 4th amendment right."

Flake coughs and looks around aimlessly like a groom in a churchyard having second thoughts.

Then he looks straight back into the camera. "As always, I leave you with a quote, yet this time the quote is not some ironic aphorism. It's from Moxie Marlinspike, the founder of Signal, a secure messaging app. He said: we all should have something to hide!"

Leeza puts down the phone. "You just asked folks to create a big one on you! You sure you really want to do this?" she asks.

"No, I'm not. I just can't think of any better option."

"Any suggestions on how to spread this fast enough to even make any sense?"

"Maybe…" Flake gets on his tiptoes.

Leeza follows his gaze towards some commotion in the distance but can't quite figure out what's going on.

"Looks like help is on its way…" Flake almost smiles in his sacrificial death wish mood.

"Hey Asshole!" A bellowing force rampages through the throng on the pier, "I told you; you can't hide from me forever! You are so dead!"

"Bully fails get a lot of clicks on YouTube, don't they?" Flake winks at Leeza. "Especially with a celebrity like the quarterback of the Cardinals in a leading role."

"You want to get your ass kicked to boost click rates?" she asks.

"Kicks for clicks. Why not? Whatever works, right? A call for action clip will certainly spread a lot faster with a fun intro of a big bully making a fool of himself."

"Shall I get a medic or a shrink?" Leeza turns to the professor for help.

"I will kill you right here, right now!" The cardinal king and two of his teammates emerge from the throng.

"What was that thing about manly pain?" Flake escorts Leeza to the sideline of the arena formed by the parting spectator crowd. "The joy of getting hit on the jaw? Boy's stuff, remember?"

His friend rains single serving question marks on him.

"I guess I'll find out!" He grins.

"Professor, could you please take care of Leeza for me? Wouldn't want her to get in the middle of this."

"Hey, Kong!" Flake turns and confronts the rioter.

"This is going to hurt!" the king hisses. "I will enjoy this so much!"

"All I did was try teach you some manners," Flake recaps events in the previous episode for the audience behind a wall of cameras aimed at them. "To treat ladies with respect. Manners maketh men, you know?"

"You shouldn't stick your nose into other people's business! Now I have to break that puny little nose of yours, so you don't forget again. Ever!"

"That nose smells fear," Flake feast on the king's lame tough talk. "Is that why you brought some backup?"

"It is one on one: your face, my fist. My boys will just make sure you can't run this time."

The duellists circle each other like sniffing dogs.

"Which of you boys is Marvin?" Flake smirks at the humongous roadblocks. The king's eyes turn to arrow slits, his carotid swells alarmingly; he looks ready to hulk out of his tight designer dress shirt.

Flake swanks into a martial-art pose, one foot forward, legs wide apart, knees bend, fists rotating randomly. "Huuuuoooooohhhh," he utters as he stares down his opponent, beckoning him Bruce Lee style to bring it on.

The vengeful quarterback is happy to oblige, lunges at his opponent, tackles him forcefully into the pier's wooden rails, follows up with two hard hooks to the midsection, knocking the wind out of his victim, and steps back to inspect the effects of his attack. Flake sinks to his knees.

"Are you alright, Andy?" Leeza is held back by the professor.

"I think this is going great," Flake groans, short-winded. "Don't worry!"

"Yeah!" the towering tormentor spits. "I think so, too! I will beat the shit out of you so bad, your pretty girl will have to take your sissy-ass home in pieces."

"You better watch your language, Kong," Flake pants as he rises to his feet, "when talking about your cravings for my ass." He points at dozens of recording smartphones. "There might be kids watching at home."

The triumphant quarterback turns to the filming phalanx, flexes a muscle and roars like a boasting animal. As he turns his attention back to Flake, he is hit with a roundhouse swing to the abdominals, delivered with all the force the keen hoop shooter can put into it. The punch doesn't impress the powerhouse even a puny bit. He smiles and launches his rival off into the ropes even more ferociously. "I'll mop up this pier with your sorry excuse for a body, you piece of shit!"

"Glad you are not camera shy, Kong!" Flake puffs in pain. "Wasn't sure about uploading the cool footage of our first gig."

The comment pushes the expected buttons; the cardinal closelines Flake into the banister for a third time, followed by two mean jabs to his abs. He grabs him by his neck and slings him around, straight into the front line of spectators. The merciless camera crew pushes Flake back into the squared circle.

"Got him right where I want him," Flake tries to calm Leeza as she is about to jump to his rescue. "Trust me!"

"Are you out of your mind? You expect me to watch you get beat up like that and do nothing?"

"Just tell me," Flake asks, his smile slightly distorted with pain, "do you think I look sexy when suffering?"

"Idiot!" Leeza grumbles and gives him a quick kiss of encouragement.

"I am Flake's tormented abs," he grins. "I am Flake's confused sense of reality. I am Flake's complete lack of respect for authorities…"

"Not funny. Please make sure you don't end up like Jared Leto, okay?"

"Ready to die?" growls the king and hits a few more muscle poses, while his peer among the sea lions enviously engages in a grunting match with the roid-raged aggressor trying to win back the tourist's attention.

The athlete grabs his massively outsized opponent by his collar and pulls him up head-to-head. "Let's give the audience some closeups!" He smirks.

In a rapid surprise move, Flake grabs the enemy's thumb, jerks it down and clenches it against his forearm. The king squalls and winces in pain.

"It's called junkyard Aikido," Flake clamps ever more tightly on the overstretched limb. "Really painful, isn't it?"

Locking this move was quite a bit harder than in the drills with his thousand-year-old Korean Mr Miyagi type sensei and his class of big city wannabe warriors back in Boston, so Flake is pretty proud of making it work. He applies some more pressure, stretching the chords even further, making Kong scream like a cat kicked on its tail.

"Like vegan violence, you know? No blood must be spilled for this…"

A high knee knocks Flake off balance and allows the big man to jerk his hurting hand from the agonising hold. The king's follow up round-kick misses the target only by an inch.

The perplexed powerhouse shakes his numbed wrist while chasing his opponent through the ring, trying to instantly avenge the insolence of resistance. When he eventually corners his bait, the king launches a straight kick to the chest, right on target. As he bounces back from the rodding, Flake is met with a cross cut he manages to blocks with his shoulder. Seriously shaken, though, he can just about duck the follow up punch, delivered with such dedication that the momentum gets the king off balance for a second. Flake uses the opening, grabs hold of the king's wrist, wrings the brawny arm with a few rapid body turns, folding it into another lock hold, the wrist and elbow joints bent inside and twisted.

The king screams and squirms in pain as Flake, cheered by the ecstatic ringside audience, tightens the screw bit by bit stopping just short of inflicting permanent damage. The fuming athlete breaks free with a roundhouse backhand haymaker that sends an outcry through the crowd and knocks Flake off his feet.

Korean Mr Miyagi had advertised his Aikido class as a street proven self-defence tutorial, yet wax on, wax off dry runs in class didn't quite prepare Flake to the impact of a two-hundred-pound professional muscle monster. The punchball picks himself up and shakes off the daze, while the stricken king conducts a check on the integrity of his hinges. Once that's validated, he promptly turns it into another muscle show-off.

Despite the undeniable physical supremacy of the quarterback, the roaring crowd clearly scores round one for the underdog, while both men prepare for round two.

"You should actually thank me, not chase me," Flake calls through the ring. "Didn't even tell your two girlfriends how many other Tinderettes you sent those dick pics to."

"Every chick on the planet wants a piece of this!" The model athlete hits another pose for the crowd. "Even your pretty little lotus over there will want to leave this arena with a true champion when I am done here!"

"I'm sure she will!" Flake smiles ironically, doing the Ali shuffle. "Float like a butterfly, sting like a bee!" He gives Leeza a wink.

"Die like a man!" the heavyweight menaces, setting the massive muscles in motion to reinstate pecking order. On arrival, he throws a series of jabs and hooks. Flake slips the first, absorbs the second, ducks the third and blocks the fourth punch with his other shoulder. He ignores the numbing impact of the hits and makes a grab at the king's exposed fist; he clenches the tip to the ball of the king's thumb, causing a stabbing pain that brings tears to his rival's eyes. Flake holds his grip and squeezes tightly. The athlete's agonising pain and disbelief of the unexpected hassle with such an unworthy opponent erupt into the fierce roar of a wounded grizzly. The big man rotates like he is about to launch his victim off in a hammer throw. Just before the flywheel forces would lift the Flake-hammer off the ground, the lightweight let's go.

The combatants knead their palms and shoulders while sizing each other up from a safe distance.

"Cry like a baby?" Flake comments on the king's still pain watered eyes, trying to provoke the next unguarded attack right away. Yet his adversary's unpleasant experience with the impact of tempering with even the smallest of joints cautioned him.

As the uneven bullfight continues, the swordless matador time and again seeks to jump on the nape of the Minotaur to rip off his horns while evading being knocked out on the way in. Over and over the predator's fists land devastating blows, yet almost as often, Flake causes the creature fierce pain as he twists and turns chords and joints before the bull bucks him off.

Soon enough, to hit Flake hurts the king's tortured limbs almost as much as it hurts Flake's bruised body.

Even though the fan favourite certainly suffers more hard hits, the excited crowd also scores round two and three unanimously for the underdog.

The king opens round four with a jump kick that sends Flake stumbling straight into Leeza's arms.

"Can we end this now, please?" she begs. "Tell me you have an idea?"

"Still warming up," Flake wheezes.

The king hits some more poses for the cameras, not quite as energetic as before, yet still effective in building up his ego.

"Stop kidding around!" Leeza urges. "What was your plan when you started this?"

"To figure it out when I need it?"

"Let me put it this way," Leeza sighs in disbelief, "that guy put some mighty dents in your spacecraft. He seems determined to rip you out of your spacesuit. Don't you think it is about time to come up with a plan?"

"Good point, Houston!" Flake turns to Timberley. "Professor, could I borrow your vaporizer for a second?"

Someone in the audience streams *Eye of the Tiger* to a jambox. Flake slips the inhaler into his pocket and swaggers back in the ring, where the king is busy trying to win over the booing crowd.

"Yo, Drago!" Flake calls the attention of his opponent. "Look! I don't want to snap your wrist, okay? Or your elbow joint. Or your shoulder." Flake twists and turns his folded hands left and right, inside and out. "Yet, eventually, this is exactly what will happen." He cracks his fingers.

"I will break every bone in your scrawny little body!" retorts the red ruffian.

"One wrong move; a jerk, a twist, an inch too far. This could do permanent damage." Flake randomly rotates his wrists. "You may not play ball for quite a while. I'm sure you don't want that, do you?"

Before any doubts can poise his mind, the raging bull stampedes about and launches his size 13 LeBrons, as soon as he arrives in striking distance for a round-kick to the head. Flake ducks the telegraphed move as if it was delivered in slow motion. *This must be,* the surprised Aikido academic thinks, *what Korean Miyagi meant when he taught them about the flow; the moment when body and mind act as one; when the next move just follows like crash follows fall.* In perfect timing, his high knee, delivered in mid-air to the bull's private parts, hits its mark right on target.

The king's outcry of pain fades into the groaning crescendo of spectator's half pitiful, half sardonic 'Ohs' and 'Ahs,' as the big guy drops to his knees.

"I am Flake's smirking revenge!" he quips. "Suppose you won't be playing with those balls for a while, either…"

The king's team mates storm to their captain's aid. They check on him quickly, worried for their leader, yet excited to get to play offence, finally.

Flake skips and shuffles about Bruce Lee style. "Okay. Which one of you wants to go first?" he brags, randomly alternating floating tiger claws and rotating willow leaf palms. "Don't be shy. There is enough for everyone."

David's audaciousness baffles the Goliaths as much as the ringside crowd. At least a hundred smartphones tape this epic battle by now.

The attackers exchange looks to align on the next play, then prepare to go for a concerted tackle.

Flake backs up a few steps. "Look, guys, I don't do threesomes, okay? Besides: triangular relationships of your captain got us into this mess in the first place."

As the huge linebackers seem ready to make their move, Flake pulls out the inhaler. "This was all great fun alright," he says, aiming at the attackers, "but we'll leave you to it now; suggest you don't try to stop us. A solid shot of pepper spray will work just as well as trashing your testicles."

Lost for leadership, the stalled offence regroups and lifts their groggy captain to his feet. Before the squad leader can issue any instructions, the fugitives weave their way through the wall of cameras zeroing in on the plucked rooster.

The sea lions down on the floats grunt, clapping their flippers as if to cheer the king's limping exit, propped up by his buddies.

"You could have told me I'm dating Shang-Chi!" Leeza says as they board a BART coach at Embarcadero.

"Wait till you see me kick ass in a rap battle," a still adrenalin inundated Flake replies and starts beatboxing.

After a few beats, his overclocked synapses start unloading in rhymes:

"The wharf is a war zone, it's time to deploy

Battling this bully, my rhymes a decoy

Eminem's essence, in every verse

Vaporizing hate, it's a lyrical curse

His ego inflated, like overused laxatives

My words hit hard, like explosive adjectives

Still don't give a fuck, just like shady Slim, in this lyrical battle, I'm bound to win.

He's a giant in stature, but a midget in heart

My rhymes hit hard, tearing his script apart

He thought he was a king, ruling with crown

My Aikido is seismic, tearing the clown

A Kong in stature, but a puppet on strings

I'm an epical force that freedom brings."

All eyes in the car are on Flake. He ponders whether golden teeth to his left, who seems not to appreciate the endorphin induced performance at all, doesn't follow up on his really mean stare because of a twisted sense of honour amongst bad dudes with an attitude not to go off on a guy that looks like he had been knocked up badly today already; or whether he is just being stereotypical again, and the fellow is a hard-working family man with bad dental coverage and a pointed taste in music, not looking for trouble at all.

The plain vanilla Japanese tourist across, in a Ninja Turtles shirt, looks at Flake like he's gonna drop 50 cents any second. Then again, the awed gaze may indicate he's thinking of ways to chat up Leeza.

The chilled dude to Flake's right with a skinny Snoop Dogg frame drowned in Biggie's wardrobe squints with glazed eyes like he would offer Flake some of his organically grown Kush, should he just be able to muster up the energy to move a muscle. Flake would truly appreciate a smoke to fade the pain, now that the adrenalin starts dropping.

***

Day of the Big One, Monday

Quicksand

"Today is the day of the Big One. The big data dump. In case anything actually happens. Some seventy percent of the American population are convinced it will. And over sixty percent believe it will directly affect them in one way or the other.

"Wall Street opened for business about two hours ago. With virtually just minutes to go until noon, until we will find out if the Big One is just a hoax or what it is exactly, Jim Wheeler over on Wall Street, what do the stock markets believe? Is the Big One priced in already?"

"Good morning, Tom, good morning, America, on this very special day. The stock markets started extremely nervously. Tech stocks are down twenty percent and more already. Some of them by over fifty percent compared to valuations two weeks ago, before the Big One was announced. Trade is very volatile, with some investors, who obviously bet on it being a hoax, hoping to buy at bargain prices. Others are taking to their heels. Automatic stop loss algorithms have also kicked in already, reacting to the volatility. The first few minutes of this anxiously awaited day have been quite chaotic, I would say."

"Specifically, tech stocks are under pressure, aren't they, Jim?"

"That is exactly right, Tom. It is almost ironic. When seeking investors' money in recent years, you had to have the over-hyped buzzwords big data and analytics written all over your stock, all over you IPO prospectus. Today it feels like everybody is afraid to go anywhere near any stock that has to do with this. Like it is a contagious disease."

"Microsoft announced a press conference at noon today. Do we know what this is all about?"

"It is not just a press conference, Tom. Microsoft stages the event in the Meydenbauer Events Centre, a huge venue in Bellevue, nearby their headquarter in Redmond. It is more like a full-fledged fair than just a press gathering. Yet, nobody really knows what the firm will be presenting to 3000 hand-picked guests."

"We heard a lot of rumours the last few days about the announcements to be expected, though, didn't we, Jim?"

"That's right, Tom. Many analysts expect the software powerhouse, after successfully attacking Google's turf with the OpenAI technology, for example the ChatGPT based Bing, to go after Meta next, offering a platform similar to Facebook or Instagram. Or they might even go after Amazon and expand large-scale into consumer retail. The timing of such a platform launch might be well chosen, with many of these formerly unconquerable giants left exposed right now and maybe even worse off after whatever happens at noon."

"Is it fair to say, Jim, our economy is built on some very fragile concepts? If something like the Big One can instantaneously devaluate so many business models in the eyes of investors, have we been sitting on a time bomb for the last few years? Was our entire economy, or large parts of it, built on quicksand? What is your view on that, Jim?"

"As you know, stock markets don't just trade stocks, Tom, they trade expectations. To form expectations about the future requires some form of consensus on the fundamental mechanisms determining this future. Stock markets are not very good, in fact they are terrible, whenever the consensus about such fundamentals is in question. Here, the basis of some of the fastest growing and most profitable corporations is under attack. If you will, the basis of our future. The nation is debating if we even want to tolerate these business models going forward. It is difficult for markets to adjust to that."

"We saw similar patterns of rapid stock decline, almost fifty percent, with 9/11, with the financial crisis in 2008 and with the pandemic. And we see it today. You don't seem to believe markets will be very good at making the necessary adjustments in this particular case?"

"Markets need guidance. There are too many open questions at this stage. As long as the jury is out on such fundamentals, markets tend to fail. Insecurity has the potential to lead to a downward spiral, a self-fulfilling prophecy of doom. A one-in-a-century depression could be the result."

"Are you suggesting we might witness the start of that?"

"A lot of negative momentum is building up. Many stocks are dropping by the minute. I certainly hope markets will come to their senses; act rationally; ultimately, the SEC may even suspend trading until the economic fundamentals are well understood, Tom."

"It may not be the end of the world, Jim, yet it seems like we may see the end of an era today. This beautiful Monday definitely is the day when our system is put to a test, the outcome of which may depend on whether the Big One actually takes place..."

***

Quagmire

Timberley watches half a dozen choppers circling the Transamerica Pyramid in the distance while the crew around him completes last checks before the live broadcast from the improvised roof top studio will continue. He notices some staff fall into hectic activity peering at the tower and listening to updates on their headphones.

On his wish, NBC had handled the interview secretively and only announced the location on short notice to avoid any outside interference. On his way over, the professor had crisscrossed the city in multiple metro lines, cabs and even cable cars to lose any tails. He detects three oddly misplaced characters on the sidelines, whose executive attire just won't fit the TV studio setting. Either NBC saw the need for compliance counselling to make sure he wouldn't say anything that would get the broadcaster into trouble, the professor wonders, or the agencies were impressively quick to come on location after the interview had started only ten minutes ago.

"Back online in thirty," an assistant producer hurries the team.

"Ready, Professor?" the interviewer, sorting her notes in the foldable chair next to him, breaks Timberley's brooding.

"I'm fine, Jenna, thanks."

The assistant counts them down from ten with his fingers.

"We are back with Professor Timberley, institute professor at MIT and advisor to several administrations. Professor, before the break, you talked about an analogy to the Eisenhower times. Tell us where you see the commonalities."

"In his farewell address to the nation, President Eisenhower coined the term of the military-industrial complex. He warned that the potential for a disastrous rise of misplaced power exists. And will persist...Only an alert and knowledgeable citizenry, he said, can compel the proper meshing of the huge industrial and military machinery with our peaceful methods and goals, so that security and liberty may prosper together. Should Eisenhower give that speech today, he may well refer to an internet-intelligence complex."

"Eisenhower was afraid the US military and the industry supplying it, who both had become extremely powerful during World War II and the block confrontation succeeding it, the cold war, that these two mighty powers could collude to influence politics in negative ways. In your analogy, Professor, who are the players you are thinking of today?"

"After 9/11, congress gave card blanche to the intelligence community, putting practically no boundaries anymore on what they could do. In a rather hysterical atmosphere of mistrust and suspicion, we installed immense new structures, like Homeland Security, the massive built out of the National Security Agency, and much more."

The three suited sideliners' reaction tells the professor the gentlemen feel addressed.

"When these newly empowered organisations were seeking ways to obtain as much information on as many individuals as possible, fate gave them a tool so all-encompassing as their ambition: the World Wide Web."

"The intelligence community realised that this medium presents yet unknown opportunities. With more and more activities performed in the online realm, it allowed the providers of dominant platforms to amass unprecedented levels of breadth and depth of knowledge on all of us. Forces in power also understood people could be coerced into providing ever more personal information the more these platforms became something users would not want to live without; the deeper it would reach into every aspect of people's lives. Thus, governments, lawmakers and regulators allowed monopolies to be established so that individuals would feel the needed to opt in should they not want to miss out."

"What makes you think Eisenhower would have seen it this way?"

"It was Eisenhower who eventually stopped McCarthy."

The sideliners' reaction to his McCarthy comment strongly suggests FBI, the professor muses. He feels tempted for a second to add some remarks on Hoover's contributions to the plot, just for confirmation.

"Where do you see the analogy to McCarthy, Professor?"

"Think about it, Jenna. When people say they are critical concerning the collection of all this data, the argument commonly made is: who has nothing to hide has nothing to fear. A classical McCarthy argument. A point, by the way, that your friends in Great Britain, where I come from, put forward for decades already to justify the almost universal use of CCTV cameras in public spaces."

"You believe this argument doesn't hold water?"

"Edward Snowden put it like this: 'To argue that you don't need privacy because you have nothing to hide is like saying you don't need freedom of speech because you have nothing to say'. The painful experience with McCarthy showed where this argument may lead."

The professor notices the sideliners engaging in a hefty debate amongst themselves. "Jacob Appelbaum," he continues, "the journalist who surfaced that US intelligence even hacked the phone of the Chancellor of Germany, one of our closest allies, explained the effect of that argument like this: When society goes bad, it's going to take you with it, even if you are the blandest person on earth."

"What exactly is your concern, Professor?"

"We are speaking about universal mass surveillance, Jenna. Performed by private companies and shared with US intelligence agencies, with extremely little oversight from anyone. Even the presidential advisory committee under the Obama administration concluded current rules may allow the government to obtain data from the private sector that it could not legally collect itself. And to outsource to the private sector analysis, it could not itself legally perform. In other words: government organisations instrumentalise private monopolies to circumvent laws aimed at restricting government powers."

"You argue authorities, regulators and lawmakers did not just turn the other way, but in fact have actively created market conditions to foster it?"

"Yes, I do!"

The interviewer notices the professor's interest in the sideliners as Timberley peers at one of them having a seemingly very unpleasant conversation on the phone.

"Big Tech spends excessive amounts of money on lobbying on the hill," she asks. "Besides some forty million dollars spend on direct lobby activities, those firms generously fund think tanks and research institutes to support their case. Do you see this as proof the sector is battling hard to fend off attempts to regulate them?"

"Definitely not."

"You see me puzzled, Professor. You will have to explain, please."

"Regulation to dismantle these monopolies and introduce truly competitive conditions limiting the leverage monopolists have over individuals and thus their ability to dictate the terms is an existential threat to these corporations. These firms make a combined profit of over 200 billion dollars. Profit, not revenue. Every year. Over 200 billion. That equals the combined federal budgets of Argentina, Chile and Uruguay. And growing. If these guys are worried, they will certainly spend much more than a few million on solving this problem."

"What do you make of that, Professor?"

"Isn't that obvious? They are either not worried; or the influence takes other routes."

Two of the sideliners are meanwhile engaged in a quarrel with the producer of the show while their colleague is still roasted via phone.

"You referred to 9/11 earlier, Professor," the interviewer asks, glimpsing over to the commotion. "What do you say to people who put forward we need these measures to prevent terrorist attacks on US citizens and that some compromise on data privacy is well justified to protect our nation?"

"Well, quite simply," the professor says, directing his words at the agents listening in the back, "that this is not what they designed it for. Organised crime and terrorist organisations know very well how to circumvent all of this. When the New America Foundation, an independent policy research institute, looked at over 250 terrorist incidents, they concluded that all knowledge obtained was via classical police work. It had nothing to gain from the unjustified mass surveillance we are talking about."

The professor has the full attention of the agents and the producer now. His interviewer just seems to receive some information via her earpiece. "Do you feel," she asks carefully, "we live in a surveillance state? A suppression state, even?"

"Well, Jenna, let me give you an example. The Ministry of State Security in Eastern Germany, the so-called Stasi, despite all their enormous efforts and resources, by far did not have the level of insights into people's lives as our intelligence community has today. And here I am only talking about the individuals Stasi had ruthlessly stalked for any arbitrary reason."

The interviewer glimpses over to the outraged agents and a producer looking extremely concerned.

"The same is true," the professor continues, "for other authoritarian regimes distrusting their own people. Some private companies and agencies like the NSA have access to one hundred times the detail on every single one of us. Including those who have not even made it into their focus just yet."

One agent sets off to take the stage yet is ordered back by the guy with the phone glued to his ear. The producer fiddles with her headset nervously.

"What would you say, Professor," the interviewer asks, "why administrations, at least five different administrations since the late 90s and early 2000s, have pressed ahead with this?"

"You are asking why they collect all this stuff on us? There are two plausible explanations. The good one is simply because they can. We allowed them. Should that be the case," the professor makes eye contact with the agents, "I suggest we tell them: look, we changed our minds. Let's not have that anymore."

"And the not so good explanation?"

"The not so good version is," he turns back to the interviewer, "someone plans on using the information to control and manipulate us."

"Should this be true, what would be the consequence? In your view?"

"Why do you think people in Eastern Germany were afraid of Stasi listening in? The vast majority of citizens did not engage in any counterrevolution. They just wanted to get on with their lives. Did nothing wrong. A key reason they were afraid of Stasi was that it was completely arbitrary what they might consider wrongdoing tomorrow. What actions, choice of words, thoughts even, could get you in trouble."

The professor turns straight at the camera. "What makes us certain, things we do today, we would be fine with should everyone know about them, will not be a reason for stigmatisation or even prosecution tomorrow?"

"The US is a country where one hundred million people have a gun at home and defend their right to do so, because they do not trust the government, the system, whatever you call it…. Why would we trust the rules we live by to today will not get changed to something very different tomorrow? This is absurd. Who says we will not have a social scoring system tomorrow, just like the one China is already enforcing? Insurances are already proposing to punish smokers, obese people et cetera…your car insurance is cheaper when you allow surveillance of your driving style…all first steps. Baby steps, I grant you, yet testing the waters."

"You seem very alert, Professor."

"I am indeed! So should be all your viewers!"

"Do you think this is what the people behind the Big One set out to do? Sound an alarm on us?"

"It would be an awfully hard way to learn this lesson."

"Is there anything good you could see emerge from this?"

"The American people should recognise the level of information private corporations and your own government amass on every one of us is utterly out of proportion and has to change."

"Even the father of the Patriot Act, Jim Sensenbrenner, concluded the intelligence community misused the powers that were given to them after 9/11, didn't he?" The interviewer firmly faces her producer standing next to the camera, signalling her to keep going. "That the activities of surveillance had gone far beyond the original intent; that the agencies had overstepped their authority."

"Yes, he did!" the professor replies. "However, even that epiphany of quite influential people in Washington wasn't enough to pass a strong bill to put an end to it. Yet it shows some people on the hill are having second thoughts. I would argue that even people believing mass surveillance somehow improves our ability to fight off evil must realise that since the data can get hacked, it poses an even greater threat to national security. Imagine what China, North Korea, Iran or Russia could do with an undetected leak. Such a database of doom is a digital death wish and should just never exist. That's the only way it cannot get misused. By anyone, local or foreign powers."

"With the Big One only an hour away, Professor, what is your prediction? Do you expect a big dump of data to take place indeed, that discloses very personal information on millions, if not billions, of individuals? And if so, what do you reckon will happen next?"

"My guess is as good as your, Jenna, as to the likelihood of any information actually being exposed. My hope would be, though, it should be largely irrelevant; that this last week has created an awareness, we need to push for fundamental change. That we are on a wrong path."

"Even if no data should get exposed today, there will still be consequences?"

"I encourage everyone to go pay a visit to the #FlakeQuake-vault on WikiLeaks to see firsthand the excessive level of personal information, of intimate detail that is available on all of us. The optimist in me wants to believe this should convince everyone it is time to step in."

"Thank you, Professor Timberley, for being with us on this truly exceptional morning. At noon, we will all know more."

***

Peak Post

"This is Fox News Live."

"Welcome to this very special Monday edition. The day of the Big One."

"Do you remember the milk crates challenge?"

"People stacking milk crates to staircases and climbing them?"

"Yes, exactly. Many folks took that as a welcome break from always the same old boring make-up or dance challenges on TikTok."

"I remember very well. The towers got higher and higher; folks ever more daring. Most of the fragile constructs eventually collapsed during the climb."

"Ultimately, TikTok banned the challenge as people started getting themselves seriously injured."

"Last week, a new challenge got kicked off, trending on top of the list of TikTok, Instagram, YouTube shorts and other apps, with thousands of pictures and videos uploaded and millions and millions of views."

"Yet this time with a serious background. The originators of this challenge seem to hope you can reason with the group calling themselves The Horrible Siliconettes."

"Rather than paying ransom money to some coin wallet, you mean? An ultimatum allegedly issued yesterday by the extortionists threatening to publish people's most intimate secrets."

"The originators of this challenge dare folks to post video or photo shots in life-threatening situations while issuing their protest against the announced massive data dump commonly referred to as the Big One."

"We have some examples for you to what extremes folks will go pleading to stop this threat. Trust me, climbing even the highest crate towers was a walk in the park compared to what is coming your way. Here are our top picks."

"These activists recorded their protest lying on rail tracks outside of Kyoto with a bullet train approaching, holding a sign saying #StopTheDrop."

"These two took selfies hanging off a cliff in the Grand Canyon waving the same sign."

"And swimming with sharks got this old school surfing veteran, who didn't even bother putting on diving gear, to a million clicks only yesterday."

"At least, the sign seems waterproof and reads #DontDoxxMyDudes."

"In this selfie, which went viral as well yesterday, the young man presents his protest note saying 'No More SiliconeHeads' on the boom of a fifty-yards crane fixed on the twenties' floor of a high-rise construction site."

"I have no idea how this girl will ever manage to get back off her boyfriend's shoulders while standing on top of a radio mast mounted to the roof of a thirty-story building in Malaysia."

"Agree. Totally scary. There seems to be good teamwork at play, though. She holds up the selfie stick and the protest sign while he holds the remote control and the responsibility for a secure footing."

"Given that a lot of what we just saw is extremely dangerous, it is a miracle we do not have to report any casualties so far."

"Just as remarkable as the fact that, so far, none of the social media platforms has dared to take this challenge off the web. It seems Big Tech welcome every attempt to stop the Big One even if it violates their community rules big time."

"The protesters' messages seem to vary, though, and with that possibly also the target of the protest. Most of the signs the activists present read #StopTheDrop."

"Yet we also saw different content. No More SiliconHeads, for example, could be considered a protest against the social media giants of the Silicon Valley rather than the extortionists. Many people blame Big Tech for the fact that a large-scale dump of personal secrets of millions, if not billions of people would even be possible."

"A special version of this protest challenge, the endgame, if you will, is going on as we speak, just minutes before the Big One will go down."

"Or not. Which is the big mystery of the day."

"This is live footage from one of our broadcast choppers over Hudson Yards in midtown Manhattan. The young lady has chosen the top of one of New York's highest skyscrapers to take part in the challenge."

"She stands on a tiny grate platform at thirteen-hundred feet, with no form of balustrade or glass wall to keep her from falling down one hundred and ten stories. The girl has been up there for almost an hour. Police are on location trying to get her down."

"Similar protests are happening all around the globe at this very moment. Our correspondents report high-rise highjackings by activists in all major cities from Rio to Rome, from Bangkok to Berlin, Cape Town to Tokyo…"

"…Stockholm, Singapore, Sydney, Seattle, all over the world."

"You can see some of the events unfold in these live broadcasts from international TV stations."

"Pretty much at the other end of the world, in Tokyo, where it is the middle of the night right now, these three climbed all the way up to the peak of an enormous advertising screen on top of a high-rise's roof."

"The protest sign, therefore, is an LED ticker running #StopTheDrop in turn with 'No More SiliconeHeads'."

"Look at their feet reaching over the area they stand on. The video wall is barely eight inches deep."

"Horrifying indeed."

"This lady decided that the appropriate attire for the occasion, standing on an antenna mast on top of a skyscraper in the early evening in London, is a black dress and a pearl chain."

"Her sign is just as cultivated. It says 'Please No Doxxing'."

"The upper-class activist can probably wave over to her neighbour, this gentlemen on London's Tower Bridge. He picked what looks like an Elton John stage costume from the seventies for the occasion."

"This girl balancing on top of the arch of Sydney's Harbour Bridge, overlooking the beautifully illuminated famous opera house and the city skyline, can soon be watching the sun go up down under."

"Personally, I get a severe case of vertigo just from looking at the footage."

"Same here."

"Activist have also conquered the tallest buildings across the United States. Look at this guy goofing around while actually hanging over the balustrade of a Chicago high-rise."

"Carrying his entire weight with just one hand while the other handles the selfie stick."

"Holding the sign with his teeth, for Christ's sake."

"Completely insane."

"Agree. I wonder how this guy made it to the very top of Gateway Arch in St Louis, the world's tallest freestanding arch structure?"

"While this young woman seems all relaxed at the top of the railing of Golden Gate Bridge."

"Here you have a couple on Space Needle in Seattle. Not on the observation deck in five hundred feet; not on the roof of the observation deck; no, at the very top of the antenna at six hundred feet."

"And finally, this guy, sitting on the sloping surface of the Transamerica Pyramid's glass roof."

"You didn't know the iconic San Francisco landmark had a glass roof? Look at the amazing cathedral-style crystal top the young man is sliding down. It's called the crown jewel."

"Unsurprisingly, so close to the Valley, he is holding a sign reading 'No More SiliconeHeads'."

"The activist in all these different cities in countries all over the world…"

"…it must be thousands from what we hear…"

"…seem to act in somewhat of a concerted way, all climbing up these landmarks shortly before the Big One is expected to be dropped."

"I wonder what the protesters are up to?"

"Something is definitely going on as we speak. There is activity at all those sites right now, you see?"

"It seems a few of them are nestling with backpacks they brought along."

"Looks like it, yes. Some are fondling with their jackets, hoodies…"

"Right now, most of the activists are carefully groping their way to the very edge of the rooftop, mast, bridge, crane or platform, or whatever it is they picked as the spot for their act…"

"The young protesters all hold up their signs again…"

"…taking another selfie and then facing towards one of the many TV choppers circling their exposed lookouts…"

"Do you see that? It looks like each and every one of them is wearing a plain shirt now with the same slogan printed on it."

"Yes, you're right. Seems to be a coordinated protest indeed. Thousands of activists have conquered landmark sights around the globe to post the same message to the world. A true endgame, as you called it."

"Can you read what it says? Can we get the camera to zoom in closer?"

"Our colleagues on location confirmed the imprint on those shirts reads, **#JumpIfTheyDump**."

***

Don't Be Scared...

"Okay, Ferris, can we just let it go, please?" Cameron begs.

"Ferris, please," Slone earnestly endorses her boyfriend, "you've gone too far...you'll get busted!"

Ferris turns to the second screen: "A: you can never go too far. B: If I'm gonna get busted, it is not gonna be by a guy like that."

The TV screen goes dark abruptly.

Leeza looks at the alarm clock next to her bed. Twenty minutes to go until the Big One...

A cursor appears on the black screen. Character by character, it spells out,

'DON'T BE SCARED...ITS ME'

Few seconds later,

'FLAKE!' appears.

A blinking cursor waits for input.

Leeza reaches for the remote on the nightstand and starts typing.

'YRU ON MY TV?'

'U DUMPD UR PHONE...COULDN'T REACH U...'

'DADS RULE: NO TRACES. HOWD U FIND ME?'

'WWW+CAM ON UR TV.'

'???'

'WAN2C?'

Flake appears on the TV screen next to Leeza's own video image. His voice sounds from the TV speakers.

"I miss you."

"Miss you too. My dad insisted. Can be very persuasive."

"Good man."

"Not dressed for the occasion?"

Flake looks down at his daring flower print shirt. "I thought I was? These are Chrysanthemums. Your favourites." The fleeting smile on her sad face pains him.

"Didn't know you can do sophisticated stuff like this," she says.

"Like what?"

"Like hacking a TV halfway around the world. Turning it into a telescreen."

"That's simple. I collect your signal bouncing off the moon…"

Leeza looks like her mind is a moon away.

"Why do you know how to do something like this?" she asks.

"I don't. But I know people."

"You know people?" Leeza had been poring over this whole mess non-stop ever since they had parted ways at the airport yesterday. Even in the few hours of sleep she managed to get, her wrought up mind hurls Flake, Tim and Mic with droves of baroque zombies into a red-hot molten cast iron inferno; professor Timberley towering broodingly on top of it all. Weird stuff. Then she would fall into that deep, dark hole opening up behind the gate…none of it made any sense. The more she had been pondering, the less she was clear about anything.

"What people?" she asks.

"What do you mean? All kinds of people. Many people who can do cool things with tech."

"Like hacking into databases?"

"Leeza, what is it?"

"Like exposing people's secrets to the world?"

"Leeza! I'm not a SiliconHead."

"I didn't ask you that."

"Okay."

"Should I ask you, though, would you tell me honestly?"

"Yes. I would tell you."

"You sure? Honestly?"

"I am sure."

"You swear?"

"I swear I would tell you honestly."

"Are you the Siliconettes?"

"I already told you."

"Say it."

"I am not a Siliconhead."

"You have nothing to do with the dump? You said you'd tell me, didn't you?

"No! I mean yes, I'm sure I'm not a SiliconHead."

"Leeza?"

"Leeza, what's wrong? Don't you trust me?"

Leeza crouches and wraps her arms around her legs. "Have you heard of Micah?" she asks.

"Can't reach him. Disappeared from the face of the earth. No ping from Leo, either."

"Just like Colin. You said Colin was knocked out when you left him with Mic?"

"Mic was supposed to clear us and get out of there as fast as possible."

"Using Colin's login credentials?"

"What are you saying, Leeza?"

"Don't you think it is odd there is a major security incident the very next day? An incident the firm is so secretive about, it has to be extremely serious?"

"Are you suggesting Mic had any part in that? What if Colin subdued Mic? Made him disappear? Or his friends did, like they wanted to do with you?"

"Mic is my best friend since pre-school."

"That's what scares me."

"What do you mean? That Mic and I…wow. This is paranoid."

"You said paranoid is good…" Leeza says with no trace of irony.

"Besides, this is exactly what you'd say if you were the bad guys, wouldn't you?"

"I suppose.

"Leeza?"

"The Samsung guys prepared a dossier for Dad…" she says with a faint voice.

"Dossier?"

"Mic went to the same seminars in Cambridge as this data analyst. Elijah Miller. Who blackmailed Zach."

"The guy who got shot?"

"The dossier said Mic and this Miller guy were even in the same study group…"

"Leeza, what is it?"

"It said you met him as well…"

"That guy was really awkward!"

"Awkward?"

"Different kind of awkward. Totally convinced he would be rich and famous one day. Left in senior year, founding his own start up with a friend. Didn't work out, as far as I know."

"Leeza?"

"Leeza, you know I like to argue. A lot. But this is not the right time. It's anyway more fun if we can make out at the end."

"How is FlakeQuake coming? Are people uploading a lot? A lot of people liked the video."

"Wicked, isn't it? Expecting a collab-call from MrBeast any day now."

"The plan works?"

"My vault on WikiLeaks will soon be the biggest on the site, bigger than Manning even. Just way more boring."

"That's good."

"It's good I'm boring?" As much as her combative tone earlier had disheartened him, it was still way better than the anaemic fatigue in her voice just now.

"Are you aware it took Apollo 11 exactly eight days to the moon and back?" he asks. "Yet the world they returned to had completely changed by what they had done up there."

He's almost sure he saw Leeza glimpse back up at the screen for a split second.

"May take a while until we can be together again," Flake shoots once more for a more encouraging response.

"Still want that, don't you?" he asks.

Leeza's watery eyes gaze at some far distant horizon; maybe the place where her mind is.

"Almost noon," Flake says.

"It is, I suppose…" Leeza replies, her fragile voice barely audible. "Need to get some rest…"

"It was a bright cold Monday in April and the clocks were striking 13: 1 6…"

THE END

You're still online?

It's over!

Go analogue.

Go!

References

In the chapter VibeScore, voice #3 quotes a line taken from J.R.R. Tolkien's *Lord of the Rings.*

In the chapter Smoke Curls Professor Timberley quotes a line from *1984* by George Orwell. The last line of the chapter Don't be scared also quotes the famous first line of Orwell's book.

The epilogue text pays homage to the very first post-credit scene in a movie, 'Ferris Bueller's day off'.

Printed by BoD™in Norderstedt, Germany